Praise for Evelyn D

MURDER OFF THE BOOKS

"A fast-paced mystery with a lively and indomitable heroine, a tough-guy hero, and a lovable dog." –JoAnna Carl, author of *The Chocolate Bridal Bash* and other *Chocoholic Mysteries*.

"Evelyn David's quirky sense of humor sparkles on every page. *Murder Off The Books* is a clever, witty romp with plenty of twists and surprises. A laudable debut." –Kathryn R. Wall, author, *Bishop's Reach* and the *Bay Tanner Mysteries*

"*Murder off the Books* is a fast-paced, engaging read with memorable characters and a plot that never quits. Readers are sure to hang on and enjoy the invigorating, unpredictable ride." –Judith Kelman, author, *The Session* and *Backward in High Heels*

"…suspenseful, fast moving, and funny. Before the mystery is solved, Rachel is up to her ears in conflicts…and needs all of her wit and grit to survive. Readers should enjoy this entertaining tale." –Philip Craig, author, *Dead in Vineyard Sand* and other *Martha's Vineyard Mysteries*

"*Murder Off the Books* should definitely win the award for 'Best Performance by a Wolfhound since The Hound of the Baskervilles.' In this quirky mystery, comic relief is provided by the heroine's unusual job and hero's constantly rotating fleet of undercover vehicles (most notably a pest control van)." –Lynne Murray, author of *A Ton of Trouble* and other *Josephine Fuller mysteries*.

A Sullivan Investigations Mystery

Murder with a Whiskey Chaser

Murder Off the Books

By

Evelyn David

MURDER OFF THE BOOKS

A Sullivan Investigations Mystery

Book One

An Echelon Press Book

First Echelon Press paperback printing / March 2007

Echelon Press

9735 Country Meadows Lane 1-D

Laurel, MD 20723

www.echelonpress.com

ISBN 978-1-59080-522-0

PRINTED IN THE UNITED STATES OF AMERICA

10 9 8 7 6 5 4 3 2 1

To John, with much love and heartfelt gratitude.
–Marian–

To my parents and brother, who didn't laugh when I said I was writing a book! Thanks for your unconditional love and support.
–Rhonda–

Murder Off the Books was a collaborative effort, and we don't just mean by the two authors. If it were not for the encouragement, support, and generosity of family and friends, this book would still be an unfulfilled dream.

First, we are eternally grateful to Karen Syed, owner of Echelon Press, who believed in us (even when we doubted ourselves), pushed us (when we were drifting), celebrated with us (as we arrived at each step of the process), and always shared her wonderful humor and outlook on this crazy thing called "the writing life."

Thanks too to Kat Thompson, editor extraordinaire, who carefully and with incredible insight, kindness, and judgment, reviewed our manuscript. Her suggestions were always helpful and made our book stronger.

Merci beaucoup to Robert Diforio, an exceptional agent. Bob gave us hope at a time when we had very little. He believed in our book and us, and suggested the creation of Evelyn David, the name.

Thank you to the John J. Fox Funeral Home in Larchmont, New York, and Hart Funeral Homes in Tahlequah, Oklahoma. The care they provide grieving families was evident from the moment we entered their premises.

We must give special mention to Pam and Rick Weltman for their fantastic creative contributions and wonderful support.

Special thanks go to Kate Kelly, Linda Loew, Linda Dawson, Cathy Frank, Carole Johnson, Linda Landon, Stacy Barnett, Katrina McDonnell, and Mary Ann Pritchard for their unwavering support as we moved from concept to execution of this book.

And finally to our families: The Dossetts, David, Betty, and Terry; and The Bordens, John, Charles, Rebecca, Sam, Jessica, Dan, and Maggie, you made the path to this book that much easier to navigate and the satisfaction that much greater to enjoy. With love and thanks.

Prologue

Friday Night

The pop of a human head cracking against rock sounded surprisingly loud. As the man fell against the wall of the clock tower, the killer unscrewed the silencer from the gun, musing about the number of details involved in planning and executing a perfect murder. And this was certainly not a perfect murder. Several loose ends were going to need tying. Next time a list might come in handy.

Sunday Night

Murder victims shouldn't have to wait. Discount store shoppers, people with broken dental crowns, drivers in the middle of rush hour. Those people deserved to wait. Expected to wait. But not…

She was tired of being last on everyone's 'to do' list.

Ten minutes. Way too long to be hiding in a closet. Way too long to be in the dark.

She really couldn't stand cowering in the dark. If she had to cower, she'd do it in the light–just like always.

She clicked on the flashlight she'd grabbed in her frantic dash from the bed to the walk-in closet.

Much better.

The light was comforting. The light was… The light was… risky.

She hastily clicked off the beam and disappeared back into the shadows.

She left the closet door ajar. Like everything else in her life–slightly warped. Once fully closed, it couldn't be opened from the inside. She'd be stuck in there until…until what? Who'd rescue her?

She wished again that she hadn't left her cordless phone downstairs.

Run. She wasn't going to be able to run.

Her right foot tingled–numb.

Rachel Brenner shifted, stretching out one bare leg, quietly trying to move her foot, thinking that at some point she might need to slip down into the living room and search for her second cordless phone, the one that fit into the charger on the kitchen wall and had been missing for a couple of days. She'd probably find it under the sofa or between the cushions. That's where she'd look first–if she had time.

"Enough," she whispered. "Concentrate on something besides the damn phones."

Dust. The closet floor was cramped–and dusty. Stifling a sneeze, she decided she had some serious cleaning to do if she survived. If she didn't, well it would be someone else's problem.

She wiggled her toes until the feeling returned and then rose to her feet intending to open the closet door and listen.

Two steps. Her heart pounded so loud that she couldn't think, much less hear.

Looking around, she grabbed a twenty-year-old trench coat that had belonged to her ex-husband and rolled it into a ball. She pressed the material against her chest to muffle the sound.

Stupid. No one else could hear her heart. No one else could hear her. The coat's owner hadn't.

Thoughts of Charlie cleared the noise from her head.

She peeked through the crack in the door. And listened.

Nothing but the furnace and the sound of her own ragged breathing.

She held her breath and opened the door a little wider.

Nothing. She didn't hear…

No. She heard it again. Something…just…there. A shuffling sound–still downstairs.

Rachel carefully closed the closet door again and returned to her spot on the floor, this time sitting on the bunched trench coat, instead of hiding behind it.

She hugged her knees to her chest and stared at the bits and pieces surrounding her and wondered what would happen to all of her things when she was gone.

Sam would be the one to have to deal with selling or giving away her lifetime accumulation of clothes, costume jewelry, and mis-matched china and silverware. Oh, he'd probably keep a few things. He might want some of the old family photographs she'd organized into albums. Thank goodness she'd gotten them labeled last year during one long, miserable night right after her divorce was final. At least Sam would be able to tell his children about her side of the family and put the correct name to the face.

Her brother wouldn't be of much help. Dan had his own problems. He was settling into a new job and a new life. She sighed and stretched out her legs. Rachel nudged a shadow in the corner with her toe. A well-used hockey stick–another remnant of her ex-husband, something from his glory days.

She flicked on the flashlight again and played the wavering beam over the clothes, empty suitcases, and shoes. God, she had too many shoes. She glanced at the row upon row of neatly labeled shoeboxes lining the shelf above the clothes rod, and the additional stacks on the carpeted floor beneath. Setting down the flashlight, she picked up a nearby box and peeked inside.

Beautiful black leather pumps, $89 on sale. Never worn. She glanced in another box. All purchased within the last two years and she'd never worn any of them. Her well-worn favorites were in a heap by her bed: Nikes, Reeboks, high-topped, brightly colored basketball shoes. The pumps, well, they were mostly just…

Rachel set down the box. They were a mistake. They were her way of trying to be more like the women Charlie Brenner had been screwing the last three years of their marriage. She frowned and put the lid back on the box. Like the woman Charlie currently lived with now. Tina of perky breasts and four-inch heels.

Tina would love all those shoes. Charlie would probably give them to her too, Rachel realized. Help Sam by taking them off his hands. Her shoes on Tina's feet. No way.

The spurt of anger and the loud sound of a closing door gave her the courage to act.

Rachel got up and grabbed a pair of sweat pants off a hanger and pulled them on. Picking up the hockey stick, she stalked out of the closet.

Tina could buy her own damn shoes.

One

"Why does my ice cream truck smell like ham?" Jeff O'Herlihy asked as he finished tightening the lug nuts on the new tire.

A tall, well-toned man in his mid-fifties, with salt and pepper hair, replied. "About 3:00 a.m. Whiskey got tired of banana popsicles. Why does a funeral home director have an ice cream truck anyway?"

Jeff used the tire iron to lever himself up from his crouched position on the pavement. "I'm branching out."

Mackenzie 'Mac' Sullivan looked at his old friend in amusement. "Right." He'd known Jeff since high school. They had been in the Army together, had been together in the Iranian desert trying to pull pilots from burning rescue helicopters, and had, by some miracle, both returned in one piece, more or less. Through it all, Jeff had some wild moneymaking scheme running, even in the middle of a firefight. Need a pair of canine flea collars to strap on your boots to keep the sand fleas at bay? Jeff could help you out for a reasonable fee. After college Jeff had stepped into his father's shoes at O'Herlihy's Funeral Home, doubling their gross in the first year, and Mac had joined the police force, working his way up to a gold shield. Twenty years later, Jeff remained happy at O'Herlihy's, but Mac had started over in a new career.

"Believe it, old man. My youngest has informed me that he's not coming into the family business. Sean claims it's too depressing. So I'm adding a few branches to the O'Herlihy corporate tree. Even hired some extra help so I'd have more time out of the funeral home."

"Right! Like you're not going to supervise every burial. And I just can't see Sean doling out ice cream to kids. Last I heard he was planning on being a professional fisherman. Tell me the truth. Someone couldn't pay their funeral bill?"

Jeff grinned, his graying red hair still giving him an impish charm. "I took it and two freezers full of Eskimo Pies in payment. My new office manager will have to figure out how to record that transaction in the funeral home ledgers and keep me legal with Uncle Sam. I'm thinking it's a good test of her abilities. You should come by and meet her. I inherited her and a part-time cosmetologist in the

Franklin buyout. I made a killing on that deal."

"You're all heart."

"Hey, I'm not embalming bodies just for my health, you know." Jeff wiped the grease from his hands on a rag. "Got to make a profit somehow. Besides, getting back to Sean.... He's never going to make it as a fisherman. He gets out on the water and twenty minutes later he's the same color as a lobster."

Mac stared at the new tire, a rueful expression on his face. "It would have been nice if a spare tire for the truck had come with your latest trade. Last night was the first time Whiskey and I ever had to catch a bus to get home from a stakeout. She's not comfortable on those little seats."

"Beggars can't be choosers. Buy your own car if you don't like borrowing from my fleet."

"Fleet is it now?"

"Six hearses and some miscellaneous vehicles–sounds like a fleet to me. Say, I didn't know buses let dogs on board," Jeff commented, giving the large Irish wolfhound a pat behind the ears. "She didn't scare the hookers and drug dealers?"

"You're a snob, Mr. O'Herlihy. Other people ride the bus at that hour. I sat next to a perfectly nice gang member and his protégé." Mac put on a pair of dark glasses and pulled a leash from his pocket. "Hey, Whiskey pretends to lead me around. No one seems to have any problems with her."

"Right. Since she's the size of a small bear, I imagine they keep their opinions to themselves."

Mac grinned. "Want to let a blind man and his bear drive your ice cream truck back to your place?"

Jeff tossed him a set of keys. "Nah. Take the hearse. I'm gonna drive this clunker home and unload what's left of the ice cream before it melts. Plus, like I mentioned before–my new office manager starts today, I need to show her where the bodies are buried, so to speak."

"Keep it up. I'm sure she'll be charmed with your mortuary humor. And I wasn't kidding about the banana popsicles. Whiskey went through quite a few. Put them on my account."

"Your account's too big as it is. I'll send you a bill," Jeff grumbled, hopping up into the ice cream truck and starting the engine. "I need the hearse back by 2:00 p.m. sharp. Got a gig."

Mac nodded his agreement. He and Whiskey watched the truck drive off, then walked over to the nearby hearse, a flicker of a curtain in a nearby house his clue that they had an audience. "Come on girl. We've given the neighbors plenty to talk about."

The dog gave a quick bark in agreement.

"And since Jeff just told us where the sister of our number one suspect is going to be today, we've got time for breakfast."

"Are you writing this down?" Rachel inquired as the pudgy, baby-faced patrol officer asked her the same question again. "I'm forty-two. I've told you that three times. Don't you believe me? I told the first cops who came what happened. Not that they were much help. Who are you?"

The young policeman ignored her, instead shaking his cheap ballpoint pen, hoping to get the ink flowing. His large fingers couldn't seem to hold the pen tight enough to keep the print inside the form's small boxes. "The first officers on the scene answered the 9-1-1 call and checked that the perps were gone. I'm investigating the case. How long have you lived at this address?"

"Ten years–no eleven. Sam was almost eight when we moved in. It used to belong to my Great Aunt Rose. I got to keep it in the divorce settlement. It was..." Rachel stopped as she realized she'd given the man more information than he wanted to hear.

"Height and weight?"

"I didn't see anyone. I told you, I stayed upstairs until I heard the kitchen door shut and then I ran to my neighbor's house."

His face expressionless, the cop just stared at her, his pen poised over the wrinkled form. Rachel's face reddened as she realized his meaning. "You want to know my... You've got to be kidding!"

The rookie cop's face suddenly became animated as he grinned, showing two rows of dazzling white teeth. "Yes, Ma'am."

Rachel sighed, the anger that had been building to an explosion, rushing out with her breath. She brushed her curly brown hair back from her face, holding it in a ponytail for a few seconds, wishing she had a clip handy. Spying one on the windowsill, she reached past the policeman and snatched it up. She caught a whiff of the young man's aftershave. She knew it instinctively. The tangy, crisp smell of Old Spice; her grandfather's favorite, now enjoying resurgence in popularity among young men. But it still reminded her of barbershops and burr haircuts. Suddenly she realized that the cop had said something to her.

"What did you say?"

"I asked how long you thought the intruder had been in your house."

"I'm not sure. Maybe ten or fifteen minutes. I don't know." Rachel took a moment and looked at the young cop more closely.

"But I know you, don't I?"

He nodded. "Yeah. Joe Bryant. My kid brother was in Sam's class in elementary school. Sam made varsity my senior year. I remember you coming to all the basketball games."

"You played on the basketball team?" Rachel narrowed her eyes in concentration. "I don't…"

"I've put on a few pounds since then." He gave her a rueful look. "But I'm gonna get back into shape. I've started running. How's Sam?"

"Fine. In college." Distracted, Rachel glanced around the mess in her once immaculate kitchen. "Are you going to be able to find out who broke in here?"

The cop shrugged and then answered truthfully. "Probably not. But since nothing much was taken, I don't think you need to be too worried. I'm guessing it was just some kids. Some initiation thing maybe."

"I heard that there had been several break-ins in this neighborhood over the past six months," Rachel said. "What club are these kids joining?"

"This is D.C., Mrs. Brenner. Robbery is the most common crime in the District."

"They broke the glass in my door," she pointed out unnecessarily, since glass shards lay scattered over the tile floor.

The young cop didn't even look up. "Smash and grab. The most common mode of entry."

"They also went through my desk in the den. Papers and bills are all mixed up."

"And stole half a ham," the cop added with a slight smile. "I'm sorry they scared you. I did write it all down, Mrs. Brenner, and I'll file the report. But unless you know who might have done this, I don't think I'll get too far putting out an APB on half of a hickory smoked–"

"Fine," she interrupted, walking over to a closet and pulling out a broom and dustpan. "You've made your point. I need to get this mess cleaned up, get Foley's to put in a new windowpane, and then I still have to show up for my first day of a new job, a job I probably won't keep since I'm late. Do you want me to sign something or do you want to grill me some more about my age?"

Two

"Stay here and take a nap. And don't take anything apart that you can't put back together by yourself," Mac warned the Irish wolfhound as he parked a white panel truck, with Big Sal's Appliance Repair painted in red block lettering on the sides. He'd driven the hearse for less than an hour before exchanging it for something a little less conspicuous and a lot easier to park. The panel truck was the best Jeff had to offer.

After gassing up the truck, the private investigator returned to the funeral home and parked in the side lot under the shade of a large oak tree. He rolled down the windows partway and checked the back for anything laying around that the dog could eat. They'd just had a late breakfast, but he wasn't sure the French toast and scrambled eggs had satisfied her.

The truck came fully equipped. It had enough tools, wires, and broken appliances piled in boxes to look authentic. Hell, Mac thought, it *was* authentic. Salvatore Marini, Senior, had made a decent living with the truck until his infamous last job. Mac had read about it in the newspapers. His eyesight failing, the old man had crossed two wires that he shouldn't have on a swimming pool pump. When he tested it, half of Arlington went dark. Jeff O'Herlihy had given him a nice send-off, deluxe hand-rubbed walnut casket and a violin player at the viewing, but Little Sal was a little short on cash until the estate settled. Jeff had taken possession of the truck only hours before.

"I'd let you wait for me under the tree, but you know what happened last night," Mac muttered glancing over at the dog sitting in the passenger seat, looking out the side window and pretending to ignore him.

"You never should have gone into that house. You know that."

The dog turned her head in his direction and whined.

"I don't care about that cat. That cat belonged there. You didn't. We were just going to watch the house. See who came and went.

Make some notes. That's all."

The dog gave a sharp bark as if in disagreement.

"Okay. So maybe when that guy broke in I considered doing something, but–"

The dog barked again, interrupting him.

"Well, we'll never know now, will we? Before I could get through to the cops on my damn cell phone, you scared him off and then chased into the house after that cat. I could have been arrested going in after you."

Whiskey whined and then made a series of noises as though presenting justification for her actions.

Mac rolled his eyes. "Right. Now explain the ham."

The dog ducked her head and turned away.

"That's what I thought. You consider that while I'm inside pretending to shop for caskets."

* * *

"That'll be $27.95. Make out the check to Foley Hardware," the repairman with the six-pack-a-day paunch grunted.

Rachel glanced at the new pane of glass in her kitchen door window and sighed. She quickly completed the check and handed it off with a curt thanks. She was already more than two hours late for work, but obviously couldn't leave her house until he finished fixing the door. Although, how likely was it that a ham-stealing thief would be back? On the other hand, he did forget the mustard.

Something brushed against her leg. "Thanks for all the protection," she muttered. "You'd sell me out to Jack the Ripper for a stick of gum."

The butterscotch fur ball looked up from her empty food dish in disbelief.

"I've been kind of busy," Rachel said, getting out the kitty kibble and pouring it in the dish. "You might have bared those claws a little last night."

The furry fraidy cat snorted at the dry food, waiting patiently for something good to appear in her bowl.

"Only part of you I saw last night was a tail ducking under my bed. I don't know when you followed me downstairs." Rachel opened a can of expensive feline morsels and plopped a sizeable dollop on top of the dry food. "While I was hiding in the closet I have to admit to wishing you were a Doberman, but I guess you came through for me at the end, didn't you?"

Snickers meowed and Rachel flashed back to the long, slow seconds as she'd crept down the dark staircase, a hockey stick clutched in one sweaty hand, the polished banister in the other. Eleven steps to the bottom. Eleven steps without air.

Lightheaded, she'd taken a deep breath when her fingers had finally wrapped around the end of the banister. The house had been as silent as a tomb. She'd thought for a second that maybe the intruders were gone. She'd thought about looking for the phone. A sudden noise coming from the den at the back of the house had banished those thoughts.

Rachel looked at the can of cat food in her hand and the scene from the previous evening replayed in slow motion…

The hockey stick hitting the floor with a clatter… Her fingers fumbling with the stubborn lock on the front door… The cat yowling… The sound of a chair toppling over in the kitchen… The cold fear of someone rushing up behind her as she'd worked the deadbolt from the warped doorframe… The relief when she'd remembered to kick the base of the door and the lock slid open….

Snickers meowed again and Rachel's thoughts returned to the present.

"Yeah, I know, it's over. But I'm going to have nightmares for years about trying to get that door open." Rachel added another spoonful of cat food to the dish. "Wonder what you saw in the kitchen last night?"

He sat in the waiting room, watching for her. Yesterday, he'd discovered that she'd been unemployed for the last two weeks, laid off from her job at Franklin's funeral home. Apparently, she wasn't so much laid off as traded. For once, Jeff's constant chitchat had actually yielded some useful information. He glanced at his watch and the open door of the empty office that a pinch-faced Myrna, Jeff's ancient secretary, had directed him to.

Rachel Brenner had yet to show up for work and Myrna continued well into her standard rant about the irresponsible work habits of people under sixty. But he'd expected Thayer's sister to be late. Filling out police reports always took more time than the crime.

After an hour, Mac walked back to the panel truck and let Whiskey out to stretch her legs and patrol the wooded area behind the building. The dog was bored and so was he. It didn't seem likely that Dan Thayer would show up on his sister's first day at work, but he hadn't worked out a Plan B yet for finding the man and his employer's missing money. He only hoped one of the O'Herlihys didn't show up and blow his cover as a client.

"Can I help you find something or someone?"

He dropped his newspaper. Damn, he was getting sloppy. He could just as easily be facing the subject of his surveillance instead of a teenager with rainbow hair.

"I've noticed you wandering around. You didn't seem to be with the Coughlin funeral party. Are you shopping for yourself or a loved one?"

Mac forced his face into a semblance of bumbling incompetence, thinking he didn't have to stretch his acting skills to achieve that expression. He should have made sure he mixed with the mourners gathering in the chapel. He made a show of looking at her nametag, trying to buy some time. The lack of a preplanned cover story showcased his second error, counting the flat tire. His third if he counted Whiskey's grand theft ham. Which he didn't. He couldn't control everything, he reasoned. The cop voice in his head said that was a load of… Okay, he took Whiskey with him on the stakeout so maybe that was his fault.

"Carrie, I'm-I'm," he stumbled along blindly, "I'm trying to plan ahead. I'd like to see something in oak with a good seal."

"Okay. I'm new and I'm mostly here to do hair and makeup, but I can show you the display models. When would you need to take delivery?"

"After I'm dead?" Mac hadn't meant to make it sound like a question. "I have a small house and a large dog. Do you have anything for dogs? Maybe a sidecar type thing?"

Mac watched the rings in the girl's eyebrows rise

Okay, so maybe next time he'd work on a better plan B.

Finally able to leave for work, Rachel contemplated taking her car rather than walking. The Blue Dog, as her son called the 1995 Dodge Caravan wreck she drove, had been in a bitchy mood for the last week, starting when it wanted, sputtering indignantly when pressed over forty miles an hour, and emitting heat only on odd numbered days. Today, she didn't feel like coaxing it. She walked the twelve blocks to the O'Herlihy Funeral Home.

Pushing open the front door, Rachel took a deep breath as she walked across the lush carpet. Arthur Franklin had kept his word, making sure that both she and Carrie had jobs, when he sold out to O'Herlihy's. She was grateful for his intervention but a little nervous about working at O'Herlihy's. The owner had a wild reputation–or at least wild for a funeral home director. Last year one of his funerals made the front page of a national newspaper. A graveside service that had ended in a family brawl when the client climbed out of the casket and declared the whole thing an April fool's joke. The only ones who found the stunt funny were the client and the funeral home director. Oh, well, at least the pay was better than what she'd been making. She'd just have to learn how to lighten up a little bit or maybe keep her office door locked.

Three

"Mrs. Brenner, are you okay? Do you have any idea of who broke into your house? Did they have guns?" asked her mile-a-minute interrogator, Carrie Taylor, teenaged friend of her son, part-time college student, and a part-time cosmetologist.

Rachel smiled. Carrie had more earrings than common sense and changed her hair color as often as her underwear, although the purple streaked bangs were generally a constant. Carrie had earned her cosmetology license the year before and it helped her pay for college.

Carrie had shown up before Rachel had even settled into her new chair. The teen had brought in sub sandwiches and sodas from the nearby deli, to celebrate their new jobs and to find out the scoop on Rachel's break-in.

"Yes, no, and I doubt it," Rachel answered before she took a large bite. The lack of breakfast had caught up with her.

"And…I meant to say earlier…" Carrie mumbled the rest of her sentence, her mouth full of tuna on wheat.

"What?"

The teen swallowed. "There are two cops–detectives–outside talking to some woman who has to be a hundred if she's a day. The legendary Myrna Bird? She was gone the day I met Mr. O'Herlihy. Anyway they were asking about you, the cops, not Ms. Bird."

Rachel set down her sandwich and repeated her previous question, "What?"

"There are two cops out there," Carrie nodded at the closed door. "The young one's kind of hot. But the old one reminds me of my Dad on a bad day. Think they cracked the case already or are you in some kind of trouble?"

"I have no idea," Rachel admitted, getting to her feet. "But I better find out. And you'd better get back to work."

"Hey, I already handled a client–a living one." Carrie giggled. "Can O'Herlihy's arrange a funeral for a pet? Wonder if I need a separate license to do dog shampoos?"

"Good morning. I'm Rachel Brenner. Can I help you?"

"I'm Tom Atwood." The young African-American detective flashed his badge. "And this is my partner, Eddie Gorden." The older, white officer nodded in acknowledgment.

"Is this about the break-in last night? Did you find out who did it?" Rachel crossed the room and stood behind her new desk.

"What break-in?" Atwood asked.

"My house. Someone broke into my house last night. If you're not here about that…" Rachel's voice drifted off. "There was glass every–"

"Do you know Daniel Thayer?" the older cop interrupted, his obvious lack of interest in her break-in confusing.

"Know him?" Rachel's voice rose. "Of course I know him. He's my brother." She looked frantically from one policeman to the other. "Did something happen to Dan?"

"We want to ask Mr. Thayer some questions," the older cop said, his tone a warning that trouble lay ahead.

"About what?" Rachel's brain began trying to make sense of the situation. The cops weren't here about the burglary. Something else had happened, something involving her brother.

"There's been an incident at Concordia College," Atwood said.

"That's…that's where Dan works," Rachel said softly, sinking into her seat. "What kind of incident?"

"What does your brother do at the college?" Gorden asked, ignoring Rachel's question.

"He's assistant comptroller. He started working there about four months ago. But why ask me? Why don't you ask Dan?" Rachel faced the younger cop, looking for answers.

"Have you heard from your brother recently?" Atwood asked.

"No, we haven't talked in several weeks. Why don't you talk to Dan?"

"Seems your brother hasn't been seen since Friday night," Gorden said. "We've checked his apartment and he's not answering his telephone or cell phone. I repeat, have you seen or heard from your brother?"

"No. But maybe he's away on..." Rachel faltered. She took a deep breath, squared her shoulders, and faced the detectives. "Tell me what the hell is going on or I'm not answering another question."

"Late Saturday afternoon, Vince Malwick was found dead in the clock tower of Concordia College. Some alumni got quite a shock when they climbed up for a view of the campus," Atwood said.

"Malwick? He's Dan's boss. Was it a heart attack or..." Rachel left open the question, not really wanting to hear the answer. She knew the police wouldn't be in her office if Malwick had died of natural causes.

"Murder," Gorden said.

"I'm sorry. But what does this have to do with Dan?"

"We're investigating everyone who worked with Malwick. Seems that co-workers heard your brother and Malwick arguing on Friday afternoon. They believe that Malwick fired your brother. One more time, Mrs. Brenner. Where's your brother?" Atwood asked.

"I don't know. I haven't spoken to Dan in weeks. But there's no way..."

The older cop took out a business card and pushed it across the desk. "If you hear from your brother, call us."

Rachel waited until the door closed behind them before reaching for the telephone and dialing her brother's number. The answering machine picked up after four rings.

"This is Dan. I'm not here. Leave a message at the beep."

"Dan, it's Rachel. Call me at the O'Herlihy's Funeral Home as soon as you get this message. It's important."

She hung up frustrated. Swiveling her chair around to face her computer, she called up her home e-mail account. She paused for a moment, then typed, "Where the hell are you?" Then immediately re-thought her first instinct and went for the obvious. "Call me immediately."

Whiskey sniffed the bag and then raised her eyes to Mac in disbelief.

"They're tamales."

The dog growled and took two steps back.

"Sorry. I thought it was worth a try." Mac chuckled and tossed the takeout bag toward the dumpster located in the parking lot near the repair truck. "No, Golden Arches nearby. The deli was too crowded."

They both watched as the brown, grease-stained bag hit the metal and bounced onto the pavement.

Whiskey barked, letting him, and anyone in the general vicinity, know that his hook shot needed work.

Mac glanced around, noticing that several women, dressed in black, with small children, were watching him.

Whiskey barked again.

"Hey, I don't need any attitude from you too." Mac sighed and walked toward the dumpster. "It's not as though I've been having a wonderful time either. This detective business is harder than it looks. We're both going to have to adjust."

The wolfhound dashed in front of him and picked up the bag, begging him to play.

"Unlike you, I got almost no sleep last night. I am not going to chase you." He got close and reached out his hand. "Give me the bag."

Whiskey backed up a dozen feet, the bag hanging from her mouth.

He narrowed his eyes. "I don't have time for this; I should be inside making sure the police don't haul off my best lead. Put it down."

Whiskey dropped the bag and immediately started to squat.

"Don't you dare," he warned, noticing out of the corner of his eye that their audience was getting bigger. The Coughlin service must have finished. "Don't you dare, not if you ever want to see another hamburger."

The dog hesitated, then sat down, squashing the sack.

"You're not funny," he whispered as he leaned against the 125-pound canine, trying to shift her, so he could retrieve the bag. "This is a serious place. Do you see anyone acting amused? Do you see me smiling?"

Whiskey whined and licked his face from chin to ear.

Mac heard their audience burst into laughter and couldn't help but grin at the pleased expression on the large dog's face.

Rachel was halfway through the casket invoices when the phone rang. She grabbed for the receiver.

"I'm fine," she said as soon as she heard the fear in her son's voice. "Did Carrie call you?"

"I'm coming home," the college freshman declared.

"Don't be silly." Rachel smiled as she looked at the photo she'd just unpacked and placed on the corner of her desk. It was one of her favorites. A candid shot showing a mop-topped, gangly young man with gold-rimmed glasses, and a crooked grin, flanked on either side by his best friends, Ray Kozlowski and Carrie Taylor. "That watch cat of yours, however, was a total bust."

"Hid under the bed?"

"Faster than a New York minute."

"You really okay? Ray said–"

"Carrie called Ray too? Look, Sam, I mean it. I'm fine. Don't worry. The police are calling it a prank. Maybe some kind of initiation. I can't believe they took my ham." She tried to get the whine out of her voice, but didn't quite succeed.

The chuckle on the other end was worth it, she decided.

"You know who's working the case? That guy on your basketball team, a couple years ahead of you, I can't remember his name. The younger brother was in your class." Rachel searched her pockets unsuccessfully for the cop's card.

"I know. I heard Joe Bryant joined the police force," Sam supplied. "His uncle was a cop."

Remembering her latest encounter with cops, she asked, "Have you heard from your uncle?"

"I got an e-mail from Uncle Dan about a week ago, asking me some questions about our fantasy baseball team. Why?"

"I can't seem to locate him. Don't worry about it. I've left a couple of messages asking him to call me, so he'll probably be in touch soon."

"Well if I hear from him, I'll tell him that you're looking for him. Look, I just wanted to make sure that you were okay. I gotta run or I'll be late for chemistry."

"I wouldn't want that." She laughed. "I'll talk to you later."

"Okay, love you. Good luck with the new job."

"Love you too." She held the phone a few moments, smiling softly, then turned her attention back to the numbers in front of her. She'd gotten through the last month's account receivables, when she heard a ding from her computer.

"Roy Rogers" appeared in the subject line of the waiting e-mail. Rachel looked around her empty office, irrationally fearful that someone might see the message; a message as short as it was cryptic.

"I swear it's not what you think. Keep checking your mail. I'll be in touch. Tell Sam not to trade Clemens. Love ya."

"Shit," Rachel swore under her breath, quickly deleting the e-mail. "What the hell have you done now?"

After his tug-of-war game with Whiskey, he drove back to her house to wait. Thanks to his dog, he'd become a minor celebrity among the funeral crowd. He left before he attracted the attention of the funeral home employees. Since she was on foot, he figured Rachel would come straight home from work.

He knew a lot about her from the records a friend at the DMV had let him view in exchange for some football tickets. Rachel Elisabeth Thayer Brenner. 2587 Rittenhouse Street, Northwest, Washington D.C. Forty-two-years old. Brown hair. Blue Eyes. Height five-seven. Weight 125. No wants. No warrants. One ticket in the last year for faulty brake lights.

Turning a page of a wrinkled newspaper, Mac surreptitiously observed the house.

"What do you think, Whiskey? Do we wait a little while longer or maybe leave and come back after five?"

He glanced at his stakeout partner. The dog seemed to be grinning at him.

"Oh shut up. It's not funny, and despite the rave reviews of the parking lot crowd, neither are you," Mac grumbled. "We wasted half the day. Dan Thayer never showed and I don't think Jeff's new makeup girl believes I'm in the market for a dog casket."

A sharp bark barely preceded a fierce rapping on the driver's window.

"This is my wife, Kathleen," Jeff said, adding "And I think you met Sean the other day. They've come to steal me away for dinner."

Rachel shook hands with her boss's wife and nodded at the teen lounging on the sofa in O'Herlihy's office.

Kathleen smiled. "How was your first day?"

Unlike her husband's fading red hair, Kathleen's shone a deep auburn. Rachel pegged it as Autumn Ginger #5. Rachel grinned. Professional hazard. She'd done too many years of hair and makeup work before concentrating on accounting. At Franklin's she had kept the books and done the monthly billing. Jeff wanted her to be available to do both accounting and cosmetology at O'Herlihy's. She didn't really mind. She had done both when she'd worked for her grandfather a lifetime ago.

"I'm afraid it was more like a half day. Your husband was very understanding about some police business I had to deal with."

Kathleen shook her head. "Jeff mentioned the break-in at your home. Is there anything we can do to help? Jeff's best friend could advise you on some security precautions. He's got his own business."

"Thanks, but I've got it under control," Rachel answered, wondering if the other woman could sense the lie.

She didn't have anything under control.

Four

Edgar Freed was punctual, even if he looked like death on wheels. Mac had to hand it to him; the old man stood waiting on the sidewalk outside his house at 3:00 a.m., scooter chair and all. The black felt fedora and faded suit jacket worn over his flannel pajamas must have been the old guy's idea of a disguise.

"I see you got my note," Edgar wheezed.

"Whiskey doesn't usually sport a bandana. I couldn't miss it." Mac resisted tilting his head to match the old guy's permanent sideways list. The meeting with Edgar was a direct result of an earlier encounter with the old man's wife, Elinor.

"I'm almost sure I read in the newspaper that you were dead," Elinor Freed had exclaimed, adjusting her bifocals and peering into the open driver's side window of the appliance truck.

He'd been so focused on the Brenner house that he'd failed to notice the old woman creeping up on him.

"You need to do some advertising. You can't run a successful business just going door to door. Especially if you're too embarrassed to actually knock on doors."

The old lady had offered him a glass of water, a long list of small repair jobs she wanted done, and advice. Lots of advice.

After a tricky beer cap removal operation from her garbage disposal–a beer cap that her ailing husband had to explain–Mac had escaped the Freed home, relatively unscathed. Whiskey had left sporting a new bandana and a note from the old man.

"Well, let's get a move on. We don't want to be seen. Can you get this contraption in your truck?"

Mac considered his options. Apparently the old man was serious. Mac hadn't been sure when he'd read the scribbled note wrapped in the cloth that had been tied to Whiskey's collar. Edgar had claimed to have vital information for him about the 'goings-on' in the Brenner house. Afraid the guy was going to blow his cover, Mac had maintained his surveillance of the Brenner house, while also keeping one eye on the Freed house. At a quarter of three, he had gone back to his truck, gave Whiskey a bladder break, and drove around the block, timing his arrival in front of the Freed house to match the old man's instructions.

"Can you walk?" Mac asked, instead of asking the real question in his mind. Was the old man gonna keel over dead in the immediate future–like in the next few minutes?

"Not far. But a big guy like you ought to be able to lift this scooter."

"Why don't you just tell me whatever–"

"Not here. Besides..." The old man waved him closer.

Mac leaned over, holding his breath as the odor of Ben Gay and peppermint assaulted his nose.

Edgar Freed chuckled. "I'm gonna have to show you where to dig."

Mac straightened. He motioned for the old man to get up.

As he hefted the red scooter chair into the back of the truck, Mac sighed. Why did he ever think the private detective business was going to involve red Ferraris and beautiful bikini-clad women throwing themselves at him?

The novel wasn't holding her attention. Rachel took off her reading glasses and pinched the bridge of her nose, the steady thrum of Snickers breathing on the pillow next to her reassuring. "Glad one of us can sleep," she whispered.

She adjusted the pillows behind her back and wished she could stop worrying about Dan. Tossing the book on the bedside table, she checked her alarm clock. Less than four hours before she had to get up for work. Once again, Dan was the cause of a sleepless night. Just like he'd done all those years to their mother and grandparents.

The light from her bedside lamp flickered, diverting her attention from her brother to the break-in. She wondered if she should have left the lights on downstairs. Sam's best friend, Ray, had appeared on her doorstep minutes after she'd arrived home from work. The young man had methodically checked her locks and replaced a few that didn't pass his scrutiny. Carrie had joined them for pizza afterwards and both teens had worked hard at distracting her from her worries. But now the house was empty except for Snickers. And it was dark.

"Okay, just stop it. You've got to get some sleep and you don't really believe that having the lights on is going to stop someone who is determined to get in." She reached to turn out the bedside lamp, double-checking that the portable phone was in its cradle next to her alarm clock. Her fingers around the switch, she paused and instead, leaned over the side of the bed and peered underneath. A hockey stick and a baseball bat lay just under the edge.

Satisfied with her security precautions, Rachel shut off the light and rolled onto her side. If her intruders came back, she wasn't going to be doing any more hiding.

"So are you Fed or a private dick?"

Edgar Freed sat in his scooter chair right behind the driver's seat. Mac had engaged the brakes on the scooter but he still had visions of having to stop the panel truck too quickly and the old man ending up in his lap.

Mac glanced in his rear view mirror. "Private Investigator. Just for future reference, why didn't you believe I was a repairman?"

"I saw you the night before driving that ice cream truck. Figured you were staking out that divorcée's house. Besides, you didn't make Elinor pay you on the spot. No repairman I know just sends a bill."

"You seem to see a lot for someone in your condition. How's that work? Your wife park you out on the roof with a pair of binoculars and some bird feed?"

The old man cackled. "Elinor doesn't know what I do after 8:30. She goes to bed with the chickens."

"So what's your story?"

"You were right about the binoculars. My great nephew got me a pair of those night vision goggles like the ones the military uses. He's a Navy Seal. Done real well for himself." The old man shifted in his chair. "Anyway, mighty interesting stuff goes on in this neighborhood at night. I just drive myself out onto our second floor deck and take a gander at who's doing what."

"And that's how you saw someone digging in Mrs. Brenner's flower bed on Saturday night?"

"10-4," Edgar responded. "And not just someone. It was the woman's brother. Elinor pointed him out to me before. My wife keeps track of who's who around here. Me, I'm more interested in what they're doing."

The old man laughed again, which brought on a coughing fit.

Whiskey, who'd watched the proceedings without comment to this point, barked an alarm.

"I hear him, girl," Mac responded, hoping he wasn't going to have to do CPR on the man before the night ended. He hated the taste of peppermint.

The touch of a damp, sandpapery tongue licking at her cheek woke her. Rachel jerked and almost knocked her feline companion off the bed.

"Damn it, Snickers. You know I hate it when you do that." She scrubbed at the side of her face, trying to erase the crawling sensation.

In the dark, the cat's unblinking green eyes seemed to glow as she stared into Rachel's face.

"What is it? I'm not feeding you anything else this late, so forget it."

The cat arched her back and hissed.

Rachel reached out a hand and stroked the cat's fur. "Is this some kind of delayed reaction to last night's events? I know we're both a little twitchy but we really need to try to get some sleep. I have to work tomorrow and you have to…well, do whatever you do all day while I'm at work."

The radiator in her bedroom clanged as the furnace switched on.

Snickers hissed again and jumped to the floor. She stalked over to an armchair and used it to climb onto the windowsill.

"It's too cold to open the window."

The cat stared out into the night, and then turned back toward her.

"If you are trying to tell me the Wilson's light is out, I know that. The police told me the bulb was broken."

The cat's eyes narrowed to glittery green slits.

"Oh, for heaven's sake." Rachel tossed back the covers and hurriedly crossed the chilly room. She scooped up the fluffy sentry and quickly returned them both to the warmth of her bed.

Tucking the cat under the covers next to her side, Rachel slowly stroked the cat's fur, whispering, "Go to sleep. I'll make sure nothing sneaks up on us."

"The gun should be right about there." Edgar pointed to a spot under a rose bush about a foot from where Mac was kneeling.

"Gun!" Mac's voice was a little louder than he'd intended, but the old man had failed to mention a gun before.

"What did you think we were digging for? Bulbs?" Edgar cackled and then coughed.

"Shush. We don't want to wake her up," Mac warned, glancing at the dark house, glad he'd left Whiskey in the truck.

The old man nodded, lowering his voice to a whisper. "It was late, just past 11:00 p.m. on Saturday night. The brother drove up and instead of going to the front door; he came around to the side of the house and started digging by that bush. I saw him pull a gun out of his jacket, wrap it in one of those knitted caps, and stick it in the hole. He covered it up real nice with some of that cedar mulch you see there."

"How did you see all that? The goggles?"

"Nah. Didn't need them. The Wilsons'," Edgar pointed to his right, "have one of those motion detector lights. When the brother walked across the yard, it lit up."

Mac looked toward the house the man had indicated. He didn't remember any light when Whiskey was busy stealing a ham on Sunday night. "It must not be working now."

The old man shrugged his bony shoulders. "Hasn't worked since the burglary. Think the thieves did that?"

"I don't believe in coincidences. What happened after you saw Thayer bury the gun?" Mac continued sifting through the loose soil and mulch around the bush, trying to avoid catching his coat on the thorns.

"He left. Just got in his car and drove away."

Mac leaned back on his heels. "Okay, I've found the hole but nothing is here now. How come you didn't call the police?"

"Did call–twice. They put me on hold–twice. I don't have

enough time left in this world to be spending any of it on hold."

Mac dusted off his hands on his jeans. "You didn't see anyone around later that night? Or how about the burglary on Sunday night?"

Before the old man could answer, the lights in the house began coming on.

"Let's go," Mac whispered, scrambling to his feet.

The sound of the back door opening panicked both men.

"Save yourself," Edgar gasped, waving Mac toward the nearby oak tree. "Get up there. I'll divert her."

Feeling as foolish as he probably looked, Mac climbed the tree, hoping there were enough leaves left on the branches to hide him.

Rachel Brenner came around the house, flashlight in one hand, baseball bat in the other. "Mr. Freed? What in the world are you doing out here?"

The old man jerked upright in his scooter chair as though her voice had awakened him. "Who's that?"

"Rachel Brenner," she answered, shining the flashlight at him and then drawing close to the elderly neighbor she'd known casually for years. "What are you doing here?"

Edgar rubbed one hand across his wrinkled face and then blinked several times. "Is that you, Miz Brenner?"

Rachel lowered the light so it wasn't shining in the old man's face.

Edgar groaned, and then reached out a shaking hand to the woman. "Miz Brenner?"

Personally, Mac thought he was overdoing it a bit, but since he was the one sitting in a tree like a squirrel, he didn't appear to be in any position to criticize the old guy.

Rachel dropped the bat and took Edgar's hand. "Yes, it's Rachel Brenner. Why are you in my yard, Mr. Freed? Where's Elinor?"

"I-I." Edgar paused. "I must have been sleepwalking. Can you take me home?"

Rachel frowned, glancing pointedly at his scooter chair. "Sleepwalking?"

The old man nodded. "I guess you'd actually call it sleep rolling." He turned on the scooter chair and it began moving slowly over the grass. Calling over his shoulder, he added, "I'll go home now–if I can find my house. It's a terrible thing to get old, Rachel. Don't ever do it."

She hurried forward. "I'll just walk with you. Everything is going to be fine."

"Let's keep this our little secret," the cagey Edgar added as he maneuvered the scooter chair up on the sidewalk. "Elinor gets wind of this, she'll stick me in a nursing home. Course if she did, she'd have more time for her neighbors."

Even from his tree branch, Mac could tell from the way Rachel's back stiffened that she didn't think more time with Elinor Freed was a good thing.

"My lips are sealed," she told the old man.

Mac swung down from the tree, landing more heavily than he would have liked. "Yeah, Rachel," he sarcastically mumbled. "Getting old is the pits."

Five

"I can't tell you and you've got a hell of a nerve asking." Lieutenant James Greeley glared at his former lead detective. It was barely ten in the morning and the dapper head of detectives moved to light up his third cheap cigar.

"I didn't say a word," Mac said with a smile, and dropped down onto the chair opposite his old boss. "Just stopped by because Roseanne said she had some homemade lasagna for Whiskey."

"Yeah right," snorted the forty-five-year-old lieutenant who loved designer suits and snow-white shirts. "The only thing Roseanne makes that's homemade is trouble." He spat the tail end of his cigar into the gunmetal waste can.

"Got that right." Mac laughed. "Nothing on that body is homemade."

"Keep your hands off my clerk if you don't want to catch something nasty." Greeley frowned at him, adding a second warning, "And I don't need you poking your nose into the Malwick case."

"Because you've got your star detective working on it?" Mac drawled.

"My star detective retired. But if you're referring to Eddie, don't worry. I've got Tom dogging him."

"He's got game," Mac grudgingly conceded, crossing his arms. The right one was a little sore from his tree-climbing stunt. "But he's just a kid."

"Not for long on this job." Greeley leaned back in his chair and kicked his snakeskin booted feet up on top of his desk. "So who's paying the bills this month?"

"Ganseco Insurance. They cover Concordia College against loss. Vince Malwick was the comptroller and supervised the accounts that are short more than a half million dollars. Unfortunately Vince is also very dead."

"Yeah, no contest between the .38 caliber bullet and the guy's brain," Greeley agreed.

"Well, Ganseco sends their condolences to his widow, Gina Malwick, and the college, but they really want the money back." Mac leaned back in his chair. "So if the guy who offed Malwick happens to be the same one who stole the money, we have a common interest."

"Who tipped off the college about the shortfall?" Greeley asked.

Mac pulled out a notebook and checked the entry. "An anonymous e-mail to a board member–Jack Starling–last Wednesday with specifics about which accounts didn't reconcile."

"And Malwick's role?"

"So far, he's clean, but that's just on the first pass. If he didn't take the money, maybe he found out who did, and they decided to keep him quiet," Mac suggested.

"Yeah, that's my favorite theory," Greeley said. "Maybe the killer is a new employee at the college, someone who has a checkered history and didn't get along with Malwick."

"Daniel Thayer?"

"So you've already been digging." Greeley raised an eyebrow. "What do you know about Thayer?"

"Quite a bit." Mac pulled out his notebook and flipped to the correct page. "I checked with neighbors from Vermont where he lived a couple of years ago. Lots of booze, a couple of busts for disorderly conduct, a little gambling, but no grand theft."

"Until now." Greeley smiled around his cigar. "Maybe he just never had the opportunity before. He made a big jump with this last job."

Mac nodded. "He's got a Yale degree but never held a job longer than a ski season. He moved around a lot, until three years ago. Then all of a sudden he changed his lifestyle. Moved to D.C., got a decent job, and began attending AA meetings two or three times a week."

"Have you figured out how he got the job at the college in the first place?"

"Before the job at the college he was the volunteer bookkeeper and resident counselor for United We Care, a nonprofit group in the district that ran a couple of shelters, until they were absorbed by the Salvation Army," Mac explained. "When UWC closed its doors, Jack Starling, who sat on the board and is also a trustee of Concordia, recommended Thayer for the opening in the comptroller's office."

"The same Starling who got the tip-off about the money?" Greeley asked.

"One and the same. I'm not sure how–or even if–he fits into all this."

Greeley scribbled a note. "I'll have Joanne Giles check into it. She's running down the backgrounds on the university staff."

"You'll let me know if..."

"Yeah, sure. But getting back to Thayer–I don't think it's a coincidence that money began disappearing right after he started work." The lieutenant made his point by tossing the soggy cigar at the waste can, and missing.

"What's your theory on the clock tower?" Mac asked, ignoring the discarded tobacco. "Why would Malwick meet someone there?"

Greeley shrugged. "Good question. I'm assuming he wanted privacy. It was homecoming weekend and the place was crawling with people."

"And you think they met to..."

"Talk about the missing money. Maybe Malwick thought he could get Thayer to make restitution. It didn't look particularly good to have this money stolen on his watch, so maybe Malwick was hoping to keep it all quiet."

"But he was seen arguing with Thayer on Friday, right?" Mac pushed. He flipped through his notebook, double-checking the date.

"Yes, my guys picked up reports that Malwick had been edgy all day, then blew up at Thayer over some software. Seems Malwick's new laptop didn't work. Thayer had been responsible for overseeing the contract for the new computers so Malwick blamed him."

"Over a computer glitch?" Mac sounded doubtful.

Greeley laughed. "I've been known to heave a chair across the room when my damn computer freezes."

"So you think Thayer pulled a gun because of the argument? I guess that would be one way to have the last word."

"No, Thayer blew his boss' brains out because he stole more than a half million cool ones and needed time to get out of town before Malwick could turn him in. Getting the last word in was just a bonus."

"So your investigation is a done deal except for actually catching the guy," Mac offered as he stood.

"Yep. And it is just a matter of time before we find him."

Mac had barely exited the lieutenant's office when he found himself face-to-face with Roseanne Colucci, the department clerk. The peroxide blonde, on the far side of forty, hustled across the squad room and appeared to time her arrival to accidentally bump into Mac, her red talons grabbing hold of the well-muscled arm for balance. His sore arm.

"Mackenzie Sullivan, you handsome devil, how are you?"

"Fine. Good to see you, Rosie." Mac smiled, gently prying off each finger. "What's happening?"

"I was hoping that you and Whiskey could come by tonight to eat that lasagna. I'm also making *frittata di zucchine.* You know what that is?" the clerk whispered, tapping one of her two-inch nails on Mac's lapel.

"No," Mac answered slowly, his eyes twinkling.

"It's an Italian egg dish that can be made the night before and heated up for breakfast."

"Does it have zucchini in it?" Mac asked.

"*Certamente*," Roseanne said breathily, pressing close enough that Mac knew he was going to smell like her favorite perfume all day long. "Obsession," she'd told him once with a sly smile.

"That's a shame. Whiskey's allergic to zucchini. Thanks for thinking of us though." Mac walked quickly out of the squad room, with the dog close at his heels.

"Here's where the bulk of the cosmetics are stored. Mr. O'Herlihy said to make a list of anything special we need and he'd order it." Rachel fitted a key into the lock on the cabinet located in a small but functional room adjacent to one of the three prep rooms in the basement. "We'll be using this room and Mr. O'Herlihy and the other part-time cosmetologist will use the room down the hall. You can keep your kit locked up in here. No one will bother it."

"Good. Over at Franklins, the receptionist was always getting into my stash of fingernail polish. And she never screwed the caps back on tight." Carrie picked up a jar of pigment powder. "There are at least ten more skin tones that should be in here. I see Chinese but no Japanese. And I like using Cinnamon, not a mix of Dark Brown and Flesh."

"Make a list." Rachel moved to another cabinet. "The restoration materials are over here. Eyecaps, mouth formers, Super Glue, clay, wax, plaster, splints etc. There's a case of dowels sitting in my office."

"I'd like to get some experience doing restorations; will you have time to show me?" Carrie replaced the jar and picked up a tube of Super Glue, examining the expiration date.

Rachel nodded. "Mr. O'Herlihy will still do most of the major restoration work, but he wanted me to take on some of the minor procedures. I'll teach you what I know–most of which came from working summers for my grandfather. Some of my techniques might be a little dated."

Carrie grinned. "It's the results that matter. As long as the client looks good and nothing falls off during the viewing–who cares if you're using a cow bone or plastic prosthesis. If the shoe fits…."

"I can assure you that I've never resorted to using animal bones, bovine or otherwise." Rachel laughed and ushered the teen out of the room in front of her. "I'm not sure what Mr. O'Herlihy uses. Whatever you do, don't open up the coolers down here. I figure at some point in working for O'Herlihy's, plausible deniability is going to be important."

"I think it's time we went to college," Mac said as he and Whiskey walked to their newest mode of transportation. The private detective and wolfhound clambered into a yellow panel truck decorated with a large black cockroach painted on the side. The giant bug was turned over on its back, legs up in the air, and lying next to a tombstone marked RIP. Jeff O'Herlihy had recently buried Malachy Flynn, the elderly patriarch of a dynasty of exterminators. The family motto, "Dead–as in Forever," ran along the bottom of the truck, which had been offered in exchange for the polished oak casket with cream satin lining that had sent the ninety-two-year-old great grandfather to his reward.

Colleen Flynn McCourt had gladly traded the ancient truck for a fitting sendoff for her grandfather, but Frank Flynn, the old man's grandson and Colleen's brother had other ideas. According to Jeff, Frank planned to continue the old man's business and demanded the truck be returned.

"Frankie's been sniffing more than pesticide," Jeff muttered as he handed Mac the key. "He threatened to unexterminate the funeral parlor."

"What the hell does that mean?" Mac asked.

"He threatened me with cockroaches," Jeff whispered.

"Bugs at forty paces?" Mac chuckled.

"Just be sure and lock the van when you park it. You never know with a loony tune like Frank Flynn. I'm going to sell it as soon as I can. Meanwhile be careful and keep an eye out for him."

"What's he look like?"

"Oh you'll know him when you see him," Jeff grumbled. "Short, balding, with a gut the size of New Jersey. The lunatic wears a hat in the shape of a cockroach, says it's advertising for the business."

"You want to come with me or guard the bug truck?" Mac asked, as he pulled into a parking spot.

The dog put a paw on his arm, then sneezed, shaking her head in annoyance.

"Yeah, I know. Roseanne marked me good with that stuff. I'll have to have this jacket dry cleaned."

Whiskey gave a short bark in agreement.

"Okay. You stay here. Watch out for big cockroaches."

Mac leaned past the dog and rolled down the passenger window part way.

Whiskey sneezed again.

"Damn stuff is worse than that skunk spray you picked up last year."

Mac thought he saw a spark of understanding and sympathy in the big dog's dark eyes. And something else.

"It's not funny."

The dog barked happily.

"Just for that you can forget about any homemade lasagna!"

Mac locked the doors and stalked off, thinking he needed a partner that didn't talk so much.

"Good morning, Mr. Sullivan. I'm Audrey Fieldstone, Vice-President for Finance, and Treasurer of Concordia College." The fifty-something woman with the short silver hair and sparkling blue eyes held out her hand. "Jack Starling gave me a call and said you might be dropping by. He didn't mention that it would be this morning. I'm sorry you had to wait."

"No problem, I used the time to tour the campus. Thank you for seeing me without an appointment." Mac shook her hand. Before sitting in the chair she indicated, he took the opportunity to glance quickly around her well-appointed office. The room seemed spacious despite the fireplace, dark ornate bookcases, navy blue sofa and armchairs, and the massive walnut desk. One wall in the office was covered with framed diplomas and photographs.

He stepped closer so he could view the documents. "Very impressive." He meant it. Her degrees were stellar. B.A. in Math from the University of Vermont. MBA from Columbia. PhD from Yale. He focused in on the photographs: Audrey Fieldstone with the mayor; Audrey Fieldstone with the D.C. Representative; and Audrey Fieldstone with the head of the local Red Cross chapter. Ms. Fieldstone seemed to be a very busy woman.

"Thank you. Now, what can I do for you? Or rather for Ganseco?" She smiled at the detective, but Mac noticed that her smile didn't quite reach her eyes. Without waiting for him to answer she added, "We're going to need Ganseco to pay our claim sooner rather than later or I'll have a choice between laying off professors and paying the electric bill."

"I understand." He had his own bills to pay. He needed to solve this case quickly and get his check from the insurance company nearly as much as Ms. Fieldstone did. "What can you tell me about Vince Malwick?"

"He was a terror of a man but seemed to be an excellent comptroller," the woman calmly answered. "I've been at Concordia for three years. Vince had been here forever. I learned very quickly that he was as much a part of this institution as the bricks and mortar.

You didn't cross him if you wanted something done quickly."

"Who would have wanted to kill him?" Mac asked, watching her body language, looking for signs of deception.

Audrey Fieldstone relaxed back in her chair and stared him straight in the eyes. "It would be easier to tell you who didn't. I think he might have gotten along with his secretary, Angela Lopez, and maybe Lenore Adams, head of the computer department." She sighed. "Mr. Sullivan, I'm afraid if disliking the man is reason enough to kill him, then everyone on campus is a suspect."

Mac nodded, writing down the two names in his notebook. "What about Daniel Thayer?"

"I'm sorry," the woman said. "I was at a conference in San Diego when Vince hired him and I just haven't had a chance to meet Mr. Thayer. If he's the one who killed Vince and stole the money, then I have to share part of the responsibility. I signed off on his employment based on Jack Starling's written recommendation and...and because it was always easier to just give Vince what he wanted."

"Why do you suppose he would have agreed to meet someone in the clock tower?"

"God only knows. It probably appealed to his sense of the dramatic. Vince always had an over-blown sense of his importance to the college."

Six

Mac took the stairs to the second floor, checking the numbers on the doors until he arrived at 206, the Comptroller's Office. Underneath was a small, brass plate inscribed *Vincent Malwick.* Pushing open the door, he walked into a large room furnished with three standard issue metal desks and a row of matching filing cabinets.

"I'm looking for Angela Lopez," Mac said to the student sitting at the first desk. Glancing up briefly from her game of Minesweeper, the co-ed, with very long, straight black hair, cocked her head toward the corner, indicating the other occupant of the room, an unpleasant looking woman with a phone growing out of her shoulder.

Angela Lopez was talking in a low voice on the phone to someone whose replies were loud enough for him to hear across the room.

Looking up, she gestured for him to come over and take a seat in front of her desk, while she continued her conversation.

"I understand that you have bills, but until outside auditors have finished…" Lopez finally lost patience, cutting off the caller in mid-rant. The secretary to the recently deceased Vince Malwick put the receiver back in the handset and glowered at her visitor. "What do you want?"

Before Mac could answer, the woman held up her hand in admonishment. "I'm warning you–you won't get paid any faster by harassing me in person. In fact your bill will go to the bottom of the pile." She swept her hand over the tall stack of paper in a large wire basket taking up a quarter of her desk. "A pile that's getting bigger every hour. So tell me," she asked, giving him a tight smile, her beady eyes flashing, "do you want your bill at the bottom of this pile?"

Never breaking eye contact, Mac slowly got to his feet. He placed his hands on the edge of her desk, and leaned forward, looming over her and her paper hostages. "The question is does

Concordia want their bill at the bottom of Ganseco Insurance Company's claim pile? I got the impression from Ms. Fieldstone that the college might need the money in order to avoid a layoff of non-essential personnel. Wonder if Vince Malwick really needs a secretary anymore?" He waited for the wheels to turn.

She rolled her chair back from her desk a few inches, regaining her personal space. "What company did you say you represent?"

"Ganseco Insurance," Mac answered.

"I see." She nervously licked her lips, "Insurance payments are due quarterly and..."

Mac shook his head. "I'm investigating the recent embezzlement of college funds." He produced his private detective ID, as well as a letter from the insurance company. "I understood that the President had sent an e-mail asking for cooperation. Cooperation that I don't seem to be getting."

Lopez sighed. "I've told the police everything I know."

"In your interview with Detective Atwood, you said that the accounts in question had always reconciled and that you had the paperwork to justify all payments to vendors, is that correct?"

"Yes," the secretary answered, "at least those payments that I was involved with. I didn't have the authority to issue a check of over $200 without Mr. Malwick's approval." She raised her eyes to meet his. "I've been with the college for almost twenty years and never had my work questioned."

"I'm not doubting you, Mrs. Lopez," Mac said, putting up his hands in defense. He was telling her the truth–he didn't doubt her. She was a bully but not a thief. "Then can I assume that you were surprised when the computer account discrepancies were revealed?"

"Yes."

"What did Mr. Malwick say?"

"He was upset, of course," she sniffed. "Asked me to produce all the invoices related to the college computers–hardware, software, and maintenance–which I did."

"How many vendors are involved?"

"DMG has the contract for new hardware purchases. Computer Doctors has the contract for on-site computer maintenance. There are several vendors that provide software."

"There's more than $500,000 missing. Who got overpaid?"

"Dan Thayer said Computer Doctors and DMG did."

"Your tone indicates that you don't agree."

"All I know is that I log in all invoices. Someone may have authorized extra payments to those two vendors but I didn't see any extra invoices."

"You didn't issue the extra checks yourself?"

"Absolutely not. Regular vendor checks are cut by another department; it's all computerized."

"They may print and mail them, but this department authorizes the payments?"

"Yes."

"So who authorized the extra payments to DMG and Computer Doctors?"

"I don't know." Lopez sighed. "But Mr. Malwick thought Dan was involved."

"Why?"

"Because all the extra payments were made after Dan started work here."

"Who can authorize payments besides you?"

"Legitimately only Mr. Malwick of course and...and Dan Thayer."

"How did Malwick and Thayer get along?"

Her eyes narrowed. "Fine."

"Mrs. Lopez, if you're not honest with me, this investigation is going to get bigger, last longer, and involve more paperwork." Mac glared at her. "Do you have a good lawyer?"

"I've got nothing to hide," the secretary retorted, her hands gripping the edge of her desk.

The PI took a step closer and pointedly laid his hand on the stack of invoices in her in-basket. He remembered that the problem with using the physical dominance technique was that it only worked on some people for a short period of time–then you had to give them a reminder. "Then you better start cooperating with this investigation. What happened last Friday?"

Mac walked down the stairs to the main exit of the

Administration building. Apparently the anonymous e-mail tip to the President, revealing that funds were missing, had been the spark that had resulted in an explosion between Vince Malwick and Dan Thayer. Mrs. Lopez had overhead most of it–shouts about computer accounts, passwords, set-ups. Mrs. Lopez had seen Dan Thayer storming out of Malwick's office. Thayer hadn't spoken to her, just grabbed a few personal items off his desk. Later, Malwick told her Dan wouldn't be returning and to clean out his desk and bring him any papers she found.

"What did you find when you went through Dan's desk?"

"Not a lot. Letters to various vendors, some D.C. maps, blank bidding forms and envelopes, copies of recent reports, and…"

"And what?"

"Two receipts. One from Arlington Chrysler Dealers. It was a down payment on a Jeep Cherokee. The second receipt was for a cruise to Antigua, set to sail next month. He'd already asked for the time off, but told us he needed the time to deal with some family business. He lied to us."

Mac took a step back. "Lying may have been the least of it."

The concrete and glass computer center at Concordia College was the jewel in the small campus' crown. It had been opened amid much fanfare two years earlier, and still attracted visitors.

Mac scanned the building directory and headed for the stairs. Lenore Adams, director of the computer center, had her office on the second floor. According to Ms. Fieldstone, Adams had worked closely with Malwick developing the specs for the computer systems and upgrades that the college put out to bid each year.

The glass-fronted door of the director's office was covered with a rumpled piece of paper which read, "As a computer, I find your faith in technology amusing."

Mac pushed open the door.

"Can I help you?" A young woman in her late teens reluctantly looked up from her computer screen, then stood and stretched. Her short spiked black hair was shaved over her left ear, which sported a silver hoop earring the size of a tennis ball. A red plaid flannel shirt, cargo pants, black studded leather belt, and heavy work boots completed the receptionist's attire.

"I'm looking for Lenore Adams."

"She's on the phone," the young woman glanced over to the console. "Is she expecting you?"

"My name is Mac Sullivan, representing Ganseco Insurance. Ms. Fieldstone said she'd tell her that I'd be stopping by today." He handed her a card and smiled as her eyes widened when she read "private investigator" under his name.

"She's been out most of the morning. She's just now gotten on with Microsoft tech support so it could be a while. You want to wait?"

Mac nodded and sat down in a molded plastic chair. A quick glance at the end table revealed a half dozen computer magazines and a copy of the Concordia Clarion, the student newspaper. The headline, "Death on Campus," caught his eye.

"Everyone talking about the murder?" Mac asked picking up the newspaper. The photograph under the headline was of the clock tower–sort of. The photographer had deliberately skewed the perspective so that the top of the tower seemed to be falling toward the camera. His stomach roiled just looking at it.

"Yeah. The newspaper put out a special edition. Great picture, isn't it? Beats all those prissy homecoming queen photos," the young woman said, suddenly appearing next to his chair.

Mac wondered how she could move so quietly in those boots.

One long blue fingernail tapped on the newspaper. "I heard the shooter took it lying on his back and pointing upwards."

"Shooter?"

"Yeah. The cameraman…oh. You thought I meant… No." Lenore Adams' secretary went back to her desk, crossed her arms over her chest, and stared at him. "Are you investigating the murder?"

"Not exactly." He tried the famous Sullivan smile on her. "I'm sorry I didn't get your name earlier."

The girl's green eyes narrowed in suspicion. "Julianna Jarrett. Everyone calls me JJ."

"Mac Sullivan."

"Yeah, you said." She gave him a tight smile. "You know–

earlier."

"Right." Damn smile wasn't worth the dental bills. The girl was looking at him like he was about to offer her candy to sit on his lap.

"Did you know Vince Malwick?"

"No." JJ picked up a ballpoint pen, clicking the button in and out.

"No?"

She clicked the pen. "Not really."

"Mr. Malwick never came here to see Miss Adams? Never called?"

Click. "He never came here, while I was working." *Click. Click.* "Uh, his secretary and that new guy called a lot. I spoke to them, but Malwick never came on the line until Lenore was on hold."

"You call your boss Lenore?"

Click. "What else?" She stared at him.

He didn't know what else. He was wasting time. "Miss Adams still on the phone?"

JJ looked at the lights on her desk phone. "Yeah." *Click. Click.*

Mac got to his feet and walked over to the lone outside window in the office. He was surprised to see the clock tower only a few hundred feet away. The winding halls on the second floor had turned him around, rendered him directionless.

"Mr. Sullivan?"

Mac turned to see a woman in her late thirties standing by JJ's now empty desk. He hadn't heard the girl leave.

"I'm Lenore Adams." The woman's ash blonde hair brushed the lapels of her tight red designer suit. Her wide blue eyes sparkled with pleasure as she held out her hand to him.

Mac gave her his 'all business' smile, while trying to avoid looking at the long legs revealed by the very short narrow skirt. This woman was trouble. Big trouble.

* * *

Lenore Adams sat down at her desk and looked directly into his eyes. "How can I help you, Mr. Sullivan?"

"I'm working for Ganseco Insurance. Can you describe your involvement with the purchases for the college's computer systems?"

"Certainly. It's part of my job to write the specs for the

hardware and software that the college orders."

"Specs?"

"For some departments, like the science programs, they know exactly what they need and I merely review their proposals and pass them along to be put out to bid. But for most of the humanities and the administration, I review what each office has and upgrade or replace as needed."

"And Malwick's office was responsible for the bidding process?"

"Yes, my job was to make sure that the companies understood what they were bidding on and then to check that what we received met the contract specs."

"And you worked directly with Malwick on this project?"

Adams nodded. "For the first couple of years I did, but recently…"

"Recently, what?"

"Vince assigned one of his assistants to work with me."

"Who was that?" Mac asked.

"Daniel Thayer."

"Did Thayer understand computers enough?"

"Absolutely. He was very techno-literate."

"What was Thayer like?" Mac probed.

"What do you mean?" Adams asked, her eyes shifting to the gold watch on her left wrist.

"Easy going? Intense? Smart?"

"All of the above."

Mac made a note in his book, giving himself time to consider his next question. "Did you spend much time with him?"

"The bidding process is fairly lengthy."

Mac pushed. "I meant outside of the office?"

Her eyes widened. "What are you implying?"

"Nothing." Mac had the impression she knew exactly what he was asking. She just didn't want to answer him. "I'm just asking if you and he ate a meal together, took in a movie or something. I was hoping for some insight into the guy's personal life."

"We had coffee a few times, but we talked mostly about work."

Mac nodded encouragingly. "Was he friendly with anyone else? Someone special?"

Adams frowned and sat up a little straighter in her chair. "I have no idea."

Mac waited a moment to see if she'd add anything.

She didn't.

Mac flipped to a clean page in his notebook. "Do you know if he got along with Vince Malwick?"

"I think you can say that he didn't have much respect for Vince," Adams said, settling back in her chair.

"What makes you think that?"

"He said Vince Malwick was more concerned about the tops of his skis than the bottoms."

"Let's pretend I don't know anything about skiing." Mac smiled. "What does that mean?"

Adams shrugged. "Dan was saying that Vince was more concerned about how things looked than with how well things worked."

"When did he say that?"

"About two months ago–when we were working on the current round of bid proposals."

"Did you agree with his assessment of Vince Malwick?" Mac asked. He held up his hand, "And no ski analogies, please."

"Vince was getting the job done–barely. But his methods were fast becoming obsolete."

"His accounting methods?" Mac asked with a grin.

"That too," Adams answered. She immediately held up a hand and smiled, "Just a joke. Vince wasn't my type."

He chuckled, wondering what her type was. Maybe dinner might be a good way to… Hold on. Think with your head, a whiny little voice that sounded a lot like his Junior High principal, reminded him. He had a job to do and he remembered Whiskey waiting in the truck for him.

"Did Vince have a type?"

"He's married or was." Adams smiled. "But you know that. Are you asking me about the rumors?"

He wasn't, but he would have if he'd known about any rumors. "You're very perceptive."

"The college grapevine had it that he was shopping around for someone to replace wife number two."

"Did you hear a name?"

"Nope, but you can bet he was in the market for someone more my secretary's age than mine."

"Do you think the current Mrs. Malwick knew?"

Adams laughed. "I think the current or–is it former now–Mrs. Malwick was doing her own shopping."

Mac made a note to pursue that angle, even though a little voice in his head questioned Lenore Adams' motives in telling him about Gina Malwick's indiscretions. Was Lenore trying to redirect his investigation away from her? "Again, did you happen to hear a name?"

"No." Adams paused, but then added with a smile, "But the talk is she attached herself to one of the trustees during the homecoming reception on Saturday."

Mac decided to get Lenore Adams back to the line of questioning that he'd planned to pursue. He could always track down Gina's alleged affair through another source, a source that wasn't also a suspect. "I heard that last Friday, Malwick and Thayer had a loud argument. Do you know anything about that? Something about the new computers not working?"

Adams looked surprised. "Not working? What do you mean?"

Before he could answer, Adams yelled, "JJ!"

The girl instantly appeared in the office doorway. Mac wondered if she'd been listening to the conversation.

"Have you heard any complaints about the new computer systems?"

JJ shrugged her shoulders. "Yeah, a few. Did you know the Computer Doctors lost their maintenance contract?"

"They didn't lose it," Adams snapped. "It's frozen until the bookkeeping problem is fixed. Never mind that now. Who has computer complaints?"

"The English, History, and Sociology departments lost data. Luckily their files were backed up by the university-wide system, so I walked them through recovery."

"How come I hadn't heard any of this?" Adams said angrily.

"Excuse me, there was a murder? And with all the homecoming

stuff I haven't seen you since–"

"Give me the details of the complaints right now," Adams demanded, reaching for a file on her desk. "Mr. Sullivan, is there anything else you need from me? Apparently I have some problems of my own to troubleshoot."

Mac noticed immediately that either Whiskey had learned to unlock truck doors and let herself out, or someone had broken into the truck and let her out. Now he was willing to consider that his dog was smarter than he'd been giving her credit for, but the wild look in her eyes and the scrap of fabric hanging from her mouth, a scrap that looked suspiciously like the khaki back pocket of a pair of coveralls, tipped the scales in his mind toward the break-in option.

"Hey, girl," he whispered, slowly approaching the back of the truck where she stood.

Whiskey spit out the soggy fabric scrap as though tossing it on the ground in front of him was explanation enough.

He knelt down in front of her and gently ran his hands over her head and down her quivering sides, checking for injuries. She didn't flinch from his touch so he gathered that her agitated state was due to anger not pain.

"Looks like you did a good job guarding the truck, girl." He stroked her head and smiled when she visibly relaxed. "Let's take a look at the damage."

Mac straightened up and walked around the truck to the open driver's door. The glass had been knocked out, the safety glass doing what it was designed to do; shattering into thousands of tiny cubes. No other damage was apparent. The ignition remained intact. The wires still connected. A man's leather wallet lay on the floorboard. It wasn't his.

He opened it. Forty-seven dollars, a gas card, a Visa, and a driver's license, all in the name of Frank Flynn. "Hey, girl. That was the bugman. According to the info on the license, you're taller than Frankie-boy. Hope you didn't hurt him too bad. Course at one-seventy-five he's got more than fifty pounds on you."

Whiskey leaned against his leg.

He looked down and rested his hand on her head, his fingers

scratching behind her ears. "Jeff's gonna buy you a big steak–with Frank Flynn's money–for saving his truck."

Seven

"Where do you want this desk, Mr. Sullivan?" A sweating Ray Kozlowski, dressed from head to toe in black, his long hair tucked behind his ears, asked as he and sixteen-year-old Sean O'Herlihy struggled to maneuver the battered junk store treasure through the office doorway.

"In the back room," Mac grumbled from his seat on the orange shag carpet that covered the floors of the two-room office. He was busy trying to figure out why the perfectly good office chair he'd purchased, along with several other World War II-era government surplus chairs and tables, tilted dramatically to one side.

"This place is a dump," Sean, ever his father's son, exclaimed upon seeing the two-room office.

"Yeah, but what it lacks in ambiance, it more than makes up for in affordability." Mac gave up on the chair. He'd save it as an interrogation tool. Keep his suspects off-balance.

"Huh?" Sean used the edge of his faded Bass Pro Shop T-shirt to wipe his sweaty forehead.

Ray sighed. "He means it's cheap."

"Are you gonna paint it at least?" Sean asked, staring at the dingy walls. "I don't think your customers are going to think you're any good if you don't fix it up."

"I thought you wanted to be a fisherman not an interior decorator," Mac joked, getting to his feet, surprised the young man would even notice the office's condition.

Sean blushed, his fair skin hiding nothing. "I'm just saying that unless your clients are bums, they're not going to be impressed."

"Well guys, I don't have time to impress anyone right now. I'm going to have to get back to work on an insurance case that I'm investigating. Thanks for hauling this stuff for me." Mac handed each a twenty-dollar bill.

"No problem," Sean said. "If you happen to see my dad anytime soon, it would be cool if you'd mention I did some work for you. He's on my case about getting a job after school."

Ray handed the younger man the keys to his truck. "I need a minute to talk with Mr. Sullivan. Mind waiting for me in the truck? When I get through, I'll take you home."

"Fine. Can I drive?" Sean grinned, knowing the answer.

"No way." Ray quickly grabbed the keys back before Sean could react. "Wait outside for me or catch the bus. Nobody drives my truck but me."

"Sure, I'll wait. No problem." Sean grinned again and left.

"What's up?" Mac asked. He had met Ray a year earlier at Fletcher's Kennels, the place he boarded Whiskey sometimes. The shy young man had been working two part-time jobs: weekends at the kennel and a few hours after school at the garage where Jeff, with his growing fleet of used vehicles, was a preferred customer.

Ray glanced at the carpet, scuffing his black boots across the deep shag. "I'm not sure I've ever seen carpet like this before."

"Okay. I admit the carpet may be older than you are. Is that all you wanted to tell me? 'Cause I don't think that's anything Sean doesn't suspect." Mac smiled.

At the mention of the other boy's name, Ray backed up enough to see out the dirty front window and down to the street below. "The kid better not mess with my truck."

"Ray? I'm getting older by the minute. What do you need?"

"How much do you charge to find someone? Like by the hour or what?"

"So this is business?" Mac asked, dragging up a chair for Ray at the metal conference table. He then grabbed another chair for himself, along with a notebook and pen. "I need some details before I can give you a quote."

Ray had taken the chair that Mac had indicated, his eyes widening at Mac's reaction. His normally slumped posture straightened. "Okay."

The teen's chair listed to one side and the young man automatically compensated by leaning in the opposite direction.

Mac waited. He waited for a complaint about the chair or for Ray to tell him what he wanted. But when neither came, the detective realized that the young man expected him to take charge of the conversation.

Mac started with, "Name?"

"Raymond Edward Kozlowski. That's K-O-Z-L-O-W-S-K-I"

"Thanks. But I was actually asking who you wanted me to find." Mac waited pen in hand and then a thought struck him. He remembered seeing the teen carrying a pizza box into the Brenner house. He realized what was coming before Ray said the words.

"Daniel Thayer. Mrs. Brenner's–the mother of my best friend–it's her brother. I want you to find him. Or rather Sam Brenner and I want you to find him. I told him you were the best PI in town. We're going to split the cost."

Mac wrote the name down in his book, buying some time so he could think this complication through. His case had just gotten a whole lot easier or a whole lot harder–depending on how you looked at it. He sighed. With his luck the latter option was more likely.

Two hours and a dozen problems later, Rachel walked home. Her feet stopped and she realized she was there. She also realized that her porch light was off and her front door was ajar. The light she'd deliberately left on so she wouldn't come home to a dark house and the door she'd locked and doubled-checked before going to work.

Rachel looked at the useless key in her hand and considered her options. The cell phone that she'd forgotten to recharge was in her purse along with her billfold and a paperback book. She didn't think the $20 in her billfold along with her maxed out Visa was enough to convince any uninvited visitors to leave.

She backed off the porch and hurried down the sidewalk, hoping Tuesday night wasn't Althea Martin's church bingo night. She planned to wait with her neighbor until the police came and threw the persistent thieves into prison, preferably for the rest of their miserable lives. She was passing the Wilson house when she became vaguely aware of the sound of a truck motor, but it didn't really register until she heard, "Hey, Mrs. Brenner. Where are you going? Need a ride?"

Rachel stopped in her tracks and turned around, recognizing Ray's voice. "Someone's in my house. I need to call the police."

A strange expression flitted across the young man's face. Rachel didn't have time to identify it before he parked his truck and jumped out, pulling something from behind the seat. "Don't worry," he said, slamming the truck door shut. "I'm going to make sure they think twice before bothering you again."

She glanced at his filled hand, then paled as she realized what the tire iron and his words meant. "Oh, no you don't. You're not…"

Her words fell on empty space. He ran across the Wilson yard and onto her porch before she could finish her order. "Ray! Stop!"

He never slowed down, just jerked open the front door and disappeared inside.

"Shit!" Rachel looked up and down the deserted street. Sighing, she looped her purse over her shoulder, then bent down and picked up a football-sized concrete garden gnome from the flowerbed edging the Wilsons' front yard. Armed with the gnome, she reluctantly followed the young man into her house.

From his spot on the Freeds' upstairs deck, Mac leaned back in the lawn chair and handed back the night vision goggles to the old man in the scooter chair parked next to him.

"Did she just steal Dewey Wilson's yard doo-hickey?" Edgar asked, before taking a whiff of oxygen from the tank hooked to the back of his chair.

"Yeah." Mac shook his head. "Strange woman."

"Speaking of strange women, Elinor will be home from that bingo thing soon so she can see her game show. You'd better take off."

"Thanks for the seat and the beer," Mac responded. He got to his feet and folded up the battered aluminum chair the old man had provided. "I'll stick this back in your shed."

The old man sucked down some more air, then said, "Take the beer bottles too. Elinor is checking the trash now for evidence, thanks to you."

Rachel crept into the dark house, hugging the living room wall and listening for sounds of confrontation. The silence confused.

"Ray?" she whispered, inching toward the portable phone she was sure she'd left on the coffee table. Patting the mahogany surface, she came up empty, except for a candy bar wrapper that hadn't been there before. "What the hell?"

A dim light from the den barely illuminated a path through the dining room. As she tiptoed around the table, past the buffet, Rachel debated two possible courses of action: whether to back up Ray in the den, since she was now convinced he was being held at gunpoint; or crawl to the kitchen, call the police, grab the butcher knife, and then challenge the intruders. Her decision was made for her as she tripped over a dead body or...a garbage bag of dirty laundry which she smelled, more than felt, as she went sprawling across the floor.

"Lady, are you crazy or just hopped up on drugs?"

Mac chuckled. The radio host certainly knew how to enflame his listeners–all two of them. He put the cab in gear and accelerated down Rittenhouse. He needed groceries, dog food, and a haircut. The haircut could wait but he definitely had to swing by a store for the rest before he picked up Whiskey. She hated shopping. She also hated talk radio.

A female caller's voice filled the air. "Crazy? I'm not the one who's advocating doing away with the Juvenile Justice System. You can't treat a fourteen-year-old like an adult. I don't care what crime they committed."

Mac turned up the volume. Normally, he kept the radio set on a country music station, but since Whiskey wasn't with him, he was free to please himself. The wolfhound had unambiguous ideas about what constituted music and what was just annoying noise. Most talk show hosts had her howling within two seconds, the only exception being a morning radio personality on NPR. The woman's slow, low-pitched voice put Whiskey to sleep every time.

The host of tonight's show was apparently doing a call-in segment on D.C. crime and Mac quickly realized that the topic and the man's harsh rhetoric weren't going to lull anyone to sleep.

"Marsha from Georgetown, wake up! It doesn't matter how old the robbers and murderers are. Society has a right to protect itself. You'll change your mind when it's your front door that gets kicked in. Next caller."

Mac noticed a Safeway store on the corner. He turned in, promptly finding the only pothole in the parking lot. Peeling his bruised forehead off the cab's tattered headliner, he found an empty spot near the entrance.

"Kevin from Capitol Hill, you're on."

"D.C. needs more cops. That would cut the crime rate."

"Kevin, how would you suggest we pay for them? The ones we have aren't making a living wage."

Turning off the radio, Mac got out of the cab. He didn't need to hear the caller's answer. The city's budget was like his–in the red. The city needed a bigger tax base. He needed to find Concordia's missing money and get paid.

"Don't be mad. Aren't you glad to see your favorite son?" Sam Brenner gave his angry mother another unsolicited hug.

"No, I'm not glad to see you. You should be in Philadelphia in your dorm room studying. When you graduate from college and get accepted to medical school, then I'll be glad to see you." She frowned at him and then turned her glare on the skinny young man sitting at her kitchen table. "And you–I can't believe you'd scare me like that–letting me think you were rushing in to attack the intruders in my house."

Ray blushed, but couldn't resist a grin at the memory. "Sorry, but it was too good an opportunity to pass up. Sam had called earlier and asked me to come over, so I knew he was the one in your house. I kind of liked being a hero."

Sam grinned. "Yeah, but you weren't the one in danger of getting hit with a leprechaun."

"Gnome," Rachel and Ray said in unison.

"Whatever." Sam picked up the T-shirt he'd dropped when Ray had come screaming into the house waving the tire iron like a lunatic, and again when his mother had followed in his friend's wake, a hunk of concrete precariously balanced in her hand.

"Why did you turn off the porch light?" Rachel asked, walking over to the refrigerator and checking to see if a miracle had occurred within. Nope, still empty.

"It was daylight when I got here. I just thought you had forgotten to turn it off."

"I left it on because I knew it would be dark before I got home."

"Sorry." Sam grinned and pulled the T-shirt over his head. "I guess I should have called you at work and let you know I was here. How's things in the funeral business anyway?"

"Dead," she gave the automatic response, then caught herself. "Don't change the subject." She glanced over to the kitchen table and saw the empty, dripping carton of ice cream and the damp towel. "Sam!"

"I was hungry," he said with a shrug. "I took a quick shower–"

"How long have you been here and how many classes did you blow off?"

"About an hour and only one chem lab. I'll make it up later in the week," Sam said quickly, looking to forestall any more maternal explosions.

"Sit down, Samuel, and start talking," she said, crossing her arms across her chest. "Why are you here?"

A brief exchange of glances between the two teens convinced Rachel that the unexpected visit home was more than the need to catch up with old friends.

"Would you believe I had a lot of laundry and no quarters?"

Rachel shook her head. "Yes, but you also have enough underwear to last at least two more weeks, so try again."

"Uncle Dan's in trouble," Sam said hesitantly.

"What do you know about it?"

"He emailed me. He's being set up for murder…" Sam lifted his chin, adding, "And he didn't do it."

"Even if that's true, he had no right involving you two." She ignored their protests and walked back into the hallway. She took hold of the garbage bag she'd tripped over earlier, dragging it into the den.

"Mom," Sam protested, jumping back as she dumped the dirty clothes onto the carpet next to his bare feet. "We're his family. We have to help; that's one of those laws of nature or something."

"A social contract," Ray suggested, looking over the mound of clothes.

Sam gave his friend a surprised look, then turned back to his mother. "Yeah, it's what Ray said–a social contract. We have to help him."

"Fine. If he shows up, I'll help him: I'll feed him a meal; I'll give him a bed; and I'll even do his laundry." Rachel held out her son's once white T-shirt. The front was now covered with a dark red stain. "Is this blood?"

"Barbeque sauce. There was a party at a fraternity house and–"

"Stop. That's enough information." Rachel tossed the shirt in the pile that would need soaking. "About the other thing–I don't want you involved. Your uncle needs to go to the police and tell them what he knows."

"He can't go to the cops. They've got all kinds of evidence that makes him look guilty of stealing and murder."

Rachel calmly finished her sorting and picked up a pile of dirty jeans.

Trying to help, Ray scooped up the pile of whites, wrinkled his nose, and hurriedly shoved the clothes in Sam's direction.

Rachel headed for the laundry room, calling over her shoulder, "Ray, how are you involved in all this?"

"Sam called me from school after he heard from Uncle Dan."

Rachel nodded. "And?"

Ray shrugged. "Sam told me to call Carrie and that we should meet him here around 7:00 p.m. After dinner we're going to break into the college computer system and get some hidden files that Uncle Dan needs to prove his innocence."

Rachel whipped her head around and stared at the pair in disbelief. "What?"

Sam gave her a weak smile. "If you don't feel like cooking we can order take-out."

Eight

Whiskey barked, getting to her feet as Mac approached down the tiled corridor of the funeral home basement.

"Hey, girl. Did Jeff put you to work guarding the new arrivals?" Mac patted the dog's head, laughing as she tilted her head so he'd scratch behind her ears.

"Like most ladies, she was enjoying the pleasure of my company." Jeff O'Herlihy stepped out of the cooler, shutting the door before Mac got a look at the contents. "Something wrong with the cab I loaned you?"

"No. It's fine. Well, the upholstery could use some work. And the suspension's shot. Got anything better?"

Jeff smirked. "Not at the moment. What's the problem? Customers complaining?"

"Not mine." Mac grinned. "How about yours?" He sidestepped the aging redheaded imp and opened the walk-in cooler door. "What are you hiding in here? Or who are you hiding in here? Did you knock off the cockroach king?"

"Hardly." Jeff flipped on the cooler light. Instead of bodies, the shelves were stacked with about fifty cartons labeled "USDA Grade A Prime Rib" and a few cases of beer.

Mac grimaced. "That's disgusting."

Jeff smiled and grabbed two beers. "See, that's why I didn't want to show you. I knew you would freak out over the details instead of looking at the big picture."

"You've got meat stored in your mortuary cooler. That's freaky by any normal person's standards. I'm almost positive that it's against some law." Mac took a closer look. "Where did you get all this?"

"Don't worry it won't be here long. A semi broke down over near the National Mall. Company needed to unload it fast before the Park police impounded it–and their truck. The driver had one of my cards, they called, and I came to their rescue. Got all this for less than half of fair market value."

"Your cards? The driver had a card for O'Herlihy Funeral Homes and thought calling you was a good idea?" Mac declined the beer Jeff held out.

"No, not those cards. I told you I was branching out." Jeff set down the beers and dug a business card out of his wallet, tossing the detective an embossed, burgundy-colored square. "These cards. The color was Sean's idea. Easy to find if you're carrying a lot of business cards."

Mac squinted at the fine print. "O'Herlihy Solutions–call us if you've got a transportation problem."

"Catchy, isn't it!" Jeff snagged one of the beers and ushered his friend out of the cooler. "If I can't handle the problem, I've got a string of subcontractors to help. My business is about to double. I may even catch something I can pass on to you. Generate some income so you can decorate that dump of an office you moved into. Maybe you could even hire someone to answer your phones."

"I see you've been talking to Sean." Mac chuckled. "I'm supposed to tell you that he was gainfully employed for a couple of hours earlier today hauling furniture into my dumpy office."

"Good. I keep hoping he's going to get interested in something besides fishing. He wants a new truck instead of the car I got him. But this time I'm gonna make him pay for half. He can work for me or flip hamburgers, I don't care."

"He's just young." Mac smiled. "Give him a few years. Maybe he'll go into decorating. He seems to have an interest in that area."

Jeff popped the top on the beer and took a swallow. "A few years ago that thought might have scared me to death. Now not so much. I'm enlightened. Besides…." He grinned. "Decorators make good money."

Mac laughed. "Speaking of making money, I've got to get going. Thanks again for the use of the cab."

"So you're going back to work?"

"Yeah. I just stopped by to pick up Whiskey. Thanks for watching her by the way."

"No problem. Drop by tomorrow and I'll introduce you to my new office manager."

Mac smiled. "I just might do that."

Rachel nibbled at the orphaned heel of garlic bread that had been lying in the breadbasket. She wiped it through the puddle of clam sauce in the bottom of the pasta bowl, the remnants of the hastily thrown together dinner. She swallowed the morsel as she stacked the dirty dishes into the sink. It was too quiet in the house now that the kids had left to go to the movies. Thank God, she'd talked them out of getting involved in Dan's mess.

The phone rang, breaking the silence.

"Hello." She cradled the phone against her shoulder while rinsing the silverware.

"Is this Rachel Brenner?" The voice was low, muffled, like the caller was using a cell phone inside a building.

"Yes, who is this?"

"Who I am doesn't matter. Is your brother Dan Thayer?"

"Yes. Can you talk louder?" Rachel reached for the pen and pad of paper she kept by the phone. She decided that the caller was a woman, but she didn't recognize the voice. "What-what do you want?"

"I have something…" The voice trailed off and there was silence.

Rachel strained to hear. She picked up the faint sounds of two voices–a conversation, then nothing.

"Hello?" Rachel yelled into the phone, frightened that she'd lost the connection. "Are you still there?"

"I have something that Dan needs. Where is he?"

"I don't know. I haven't heard from him," Rachel said, deciding not to tell the anonymous caller about Dan's e-mail. "What do you want to give my brother?"

"Never mind. I need to give it to Dan. He'll know what to do with it. I'll try his apartment again."

"Listen, you can trust me. I'll give it to him," Rachel pleaded

"Dan talked about you a lot." There was a pause and then the caller softly added, "We didn't always get along, but he showed me a photo he kept on his desk. He loves that kid of yours."

Rachel was surprised, not by the emotions Dan felt for Sam, but that he'd talk about her at all. With tears threatening to overflow, she ground the heel of one hand against her eyes. "Then tell me where you are," Rachel whispered. "I'll come to you…please. I'm so scared for Dan."

The silence again unnerved her.

Finally, the caller said, "I have to get it from my office. Meet me in the far corner of the parking lot next to Concordia's gym. Do you know where that is?"

"I'll find it. Wait for me, please. It'll take me about twenty minutes to get there."

Again, silence, and then, "I'll be waiting. But if you bring anyone…"

"I won't. I promise." Rachel listened for a response but the woman disconnected the call.

"Wow, so much for having to sneak in," Sam said, looking at the throngs of people going in and out of the computer lab.

"Hey, Carrie."

Carrie turned and saw a young woman with long dark hair approaching them on the sidewalk, her arms filled with a computer.

"Hi, Tia. What's happening?"

The young woman awkwardly shifted the computer equipment. "There's some kind of problem with all the new computers–something to do with the networking cards and memory. There was a major crash just before 3:00 p.m. You should have heard the screaming. The rumor is that Ms. Fieldstone threatened to fire Ms. Adams. So Ms. Adams told all the department heads that she'd have them fixed tonight, if they'd send their units over. So the department heads–notice you don't see any of them hanging around here–packed the student aides off with the computers, totally ignoring that we might have a life and important plans for this evening."

Carrie gave the girl a commiserating smile at the same time she gave Sam a nudge with her elbow. "You still working in the Accounting Office? Things must be weird over there with Mr. Malwick getting murdered."

Sam took the hint and held out his hands. "Tia, let me hold that for you."

"Thanks." Tia gave him the hard drive and turned back to

Carrie. "Weird doesn't even come close to covering it. I don't mind Malwick being gone. That guy gave me the creeps. But Mrs. Lopez has been worse than usual. She never has understood that being on work/study means that sometimes I work and sometimes I have to study or do other things."

"Why don't you ask to be reassigned?" Carrie questioned.

"I did, but I think old lady Lopez did something with the paperwork. It's been weeks since I filled out the request. I'm filling out another one and this time I'm gonna walk it over to the V.P.'s office myself. I tell you, my social life has definitely tanked since I got assigned to work there. It's amazing that I was chosen–"

"Is the computer fixed?" Ray asked, trying to move the conversation along.

Tia nodded. "Yeah, finally. I'm going to miss a party the football jocks are having. That new quarterback can't run but he is really–"

Carrie interrupted, asking, "We're not busy. Do you want us to take the computer back to the Accounting office for you?"

Tia grinned and quickly handed over a set of keys.

"Whoa. Just a second. I need to see some ID," demanded the aging, bald security guard in the Administration building.

Carrie snuck a quick glance at Sam and Ray. Sam was carrying the computer hard drive.

"We're just bringing back the computer for the Accounting Department," Carrie said quickly. "It's for–"

"I don't care who it's for. I need to see some ID and you have to sign in. It's after 6:00 p.m. and ever since the..." The guard waved his hand to finish the thought.

"Of course. The security must be so tight since..." Carrie said, stalling for time.

"Damn right. It's tighter than a fat lady's girdle. Every time I turn around there's another bigwig poking his nose into who has access to what and where everyone is. They don't seem to understand that I'm not like those lightweights guarding the other buildings," he patted his holstered gun. "Millie and I have this place locked down tight."

"Millie?" Carrie asked, wondering if there was a second guard to worry about.

"My gun. The prettiest .38 caliber you'd ever want to know," he said. "Millie and I've been together for more than twenty years. She never leaves my side."

"Cool." Carrie forced a smile, hoping the man wasn't actually issued bullets for his, uh…Millie. "But the thing is…I left my ID in the car and we're just doing a favor for Tia. Do you know Tia Hu? Works in Accounting?"

"The one old Vince Malwick was chasing? Asian girl with skirts shorter than the hair on top of Kojak's head?" The guard laughed hard at his own joke.

Carrie joined in even though she didn't have a clue who that guy, Kojak, was. "That's the girl."

"Look, just sign in and don't go anywhere but to the Accounting office."

"No problem." Carrie picked up the pen by the book. "I'll sign us all in."

"It's a regular damn convention here tonight," the guard grumbled. "Half the administration is in. I've already gotten chewed out by the Vice President, the Dean, that bitch from Computers, even some guy who claimed he's on the Board of Trustees. What's his name?" The guard looked down the open page. "Starling. Hell, I don't know why everyone is so concerned about that idiot Malwick. Whoever offed him did the world a favor; the guy tried to force me to retire twice."

"What's happening tonight?" Carrie asked as she turned the book away from the guard and signed in Jim Carrey, Adam Sandler, and Gwyneth Paltrow.

"Emergency meeting because of the–"

"Of course," Carrie said quickly, putting down the pen, and deliberately smudging the signatures as she brushed her hand across the ink. "Thanks."

The three teens hustled over to the nearest staircase.

"Since when does Gwyneth Paltrow have purple hair?" Sam whispered.

Carrie smiled. "She would if she had any sense of style."

"Please, please, please start," Rachel prayed as she turned the key in the ignition of the Blue Dog. A brief whirring noise was followed by silence.

"Shit." She slammed her hand against the steering wheel. Taking a deep breath, she tried the key again, but this time, there wasn't even a sound. "Shit, shit, shit."

She thought for a moment, then hastily unlocked the door. Feeling the bite of cold raindrops against her face, she grabbed an umbrella she kept in the vehicle, and headed to the front of the house and the long walk up to Connecticut Avenue where she hoped to find a cab. To her surprise, a yellow taxi sat parked in front of the Wilsons. She broke into a run, yanked open the back door of the cab, and hopped in without a moment's hesitation.

Nine

"My mother will kill me if we get arrested," Carrie muttered. Nervously, she connected the monitor and the keyboard to the hard drive that the repair form had indicated was assigned to A. Lopez. "We need her password. All the Accounting computers are networked."

Ray scratched his head. "How do we come up with her password? It could be anything."

"Not really. Think about it. What's the most important thing about a password?"

He shrugged. "That it's secret?"

"No. That you can remember it. People pick something easy. Something they can remember. Their birthdays, their kids' names, their pets' names."

"Oh. Well, no problem then," Ray snapped. "We just need to find out all that personal stuff about a complete stranger and we've probably got about a half-hour max to do it before the security guard runs us out of here."

Carrie raised her right eyebrow–the one with the silver ring adorning it. "Look at the photos on her desk."

"So? She's got a kid. Or a grandkid, more likely."

"Hand me that appointment book. I bet she's got emergency numbers in there."

Ray tossed her the black spiral date book. "I'm going to go watch for the guard." He hurried out into the hallway.

Carrie began thumbing through the pages. "Alexander. Her grandson's name is Alexander." Carrie keyed in the name and then smiled as a menu screen appeared. "We're in."

Sam handed her a wrinkled piece of paper. "This is the file we need. Just copy the whole folder."

Carrie popped a disk into the drive. "Athletic Department Laundry Costs?"

Sam shrugged. "As good a place as any to hide the dirt on

someone."

They watched the screen as the folder downloaded.

Ray cracked open the office door and informed them that the security guard was talking to some Hispanic woman down at the entrance and it looked like they were both headed upstairs.

"We've got to get out of here," Carrie said, turning off the computer.

With the disk tucked securely in Sam's pocket, they left, using the opposite staircase from the one Ray had seen the guard about to use.

A flash of lightning crossed the sky and a crack of thunder followed.

"I hate driving in the rain. You can't see what's right in front of you," Carrie said, unlocking her car door.

Ray climbed in the front passenger seat, and Sam slid into the back.

The person watching from the shadows pulled on a pair of leather gloves before walking into the Administration building.

The rain pounding down on the cab's windshield, along with the dim streetlights, obscured his vision so badly that he could barely make out the sidewalk much less the small brick house. Mac slumped down a little further in the driver's seat, thinking he was getting too old for stakeouts. He used a rag to wipe the condensation from the side window. Even Whiskey was getting nervous.

Mac glanced at the Irish wolfhound, who was riding shotgun in the battered yellow cab. The large dog whined her displeasure.

"I know, girl. Five more minutes, then we'll go home and watch the game."

He had barely gotten the word 'game' out when the back door to the vehicle was suddenly jerked open.

Seconds too late, Mac ducked and pulled a handgun from under the seat.

Whiskey growled at the intruder, then whined as a spray of rainwater landed on her face.

He took aim but could only see a waving purple umbrella.

"Concordia College and there's five bucks extra if you can get there in less than fifteen minutes."

"I'm off duty," Mac growled, hastily sliding the gun back under the front seat.

"I don't give a damn," his passenger snapped. "This is an emergency." Her voice rose as she slammed the door and closed the umbrella. "I'll report you to the–"

"But, I'll be glad to take you there on my way home," Mac interrupted, recognizing his passenger as Rachel Brenner. He wasted a half-second, wondering how he'd missed seeing her come out of the house, then started the cab and executed a quick U-turn, heading toward Connecticut Avenue.

Whiskey put her front paws on the back of the seat and stared at the woman with friendly interest. Giving a welcoming whine, the dog leaned forward, stretching her body toward the backseat in order to give the woman a chance to stroke her head.

"Your dog is drooling on me," Rachel snapped, ignoring the dog's invitation. "Can't you keep him back?"

"It's a her. Whiskey. That's her name." Mac gave the dog a commiserating look. "Sit down, girl. The lady doesn't like dogs."

Whiskey whined and leaned her six-foot frame even further over the seat, giving the woman her most pitiful look.

Rachel sighed and patted the dog's nose. "I like dogs just fine. I just don't–"

"You just don't like Whiskey. That's okay. She's sensitive but she'll get over it." Mac hid a smile as the woman glanced guiltily at the dog and gave her a quick scratch behind the ears.

Satisfied with her conquest, Whiskey settled back down in the front seat.

"I was about to say that I don't have time…Look, I don't want to be rude but could you and your dog just take me where I'm going. I'm not up for a conversation."

"Okay."

Mac negotiated the cab through the half-flooded residential streets, wondering if Rachel Brenner was finally about to lead him to her brother. He couldn't imagine what else might have precipitated this late night trip to the college.

The rain eased a little and Mac was able to pick up some speed, driving swiftly through the streets of the district.

"Any building you want me to–"

"Do you know where the gym is?"

"Sure. It's clean across campus."

Rachel nodded. "That's where I'm headed."

"Basketball season starting early?"

"Huh?" Rachel answered, looking frantically around the dark, wet campus.

"I asked if you were going to a basketball game or something."

"No, no…I'm just…just meeting someone." Rachel moved closer to the door, preparing to exit the cab as soon as it stopped.

He glanced back at her pale face as he eased the cab to a stop in front of the deserted gymnasium. "You want me to wait for you?"

"No." Rachel thrust a $20 bill into his hand and flung open the door. "Keep the change."

Mac watched Rachel walk quickly through the pouring rain around the side of the building. Once she was out of sight, he switched off the headlights and edged the taxi around the opposite side of the building to the far parking lot. He turned off the engine and coasted the last few feet, hidden in the shadows of some large dumpsters. He scanned the lot, finally spotting her moving across the pavement.

He watched her run through the rain to the corner of the parking lot, the umbrella banging off the side of her coat. She paused and pivoted around, apparently looking for something…or someone.

Mac surveyed the area but… He tensed, noticing the car at the same time she did.

Rachel slowly walked toward a dark sedan parked at the edge of the poorly lit lot.

Squinting, Mac could barely see the outline of a person in the driver's seat, leaning against the window. He watched Rachel knock on the window, and after a moment, open the car door.

The body falling from the car had him switching on the ignition and speeding forward, even before his brain registered Rachel's scream.

The cab's tires splashed water over both Rachel and the body as he pulled up alongside. "Get in!" He leaned across Whiskey and tried to open the stubborn passenger door.

"What?" Rachel backed away from him, her foot brushing the arm of the woman lying on the ground. Shocked, she glanced down again. "Oh, God."

The right side of the woman's face was missing.

Whiskey barked a warning, just before the back glass of the cab shattered.

"Lady, get in before we all end up dead." He yanked on the passenger door handle and it fell off in his hand.

Rachel hesitated and looked uncertainly at Mac. "She needs help."

"She's dead. You know what dead looks like. Get in the back! I can't get this damn door open." He turned as the sound of squealing tires caught his attention, just managing to catch a glimpse of a dark car rapidly backing up the driveway of the gym.

"Now," he ordered, tossing the useless handle over his shoulder.

Rachel took one more horrified look, before getting in the back of the cab. She had barely pulled the car door closed before Mac pressed his foot on the accelerator, executing a 180-degree turn.

"Keep your head down and buckle up."

Ten

"The stupid belt doesn't have a catch on it and there's glass all over the seat." Rachel's voice was getting higher as panic set in.

Whiskey stood up and leaned over the back of the front seat, whining at the woman, as though offering encouragement.

"That woman's head was... Oh, God, this is a nightmare. Stop the cab. We have to call the police!"

Whiskey barked in agreement.

Mac commanded Whiskey to lie down and be quiet, hoping the woman would follow suit. The dog complied.

He pulled out into the street, tires squealing, the rapid forward movement tossing his passenger sideways against the door like a rag doll.

"Stop this cab and let me out of here! Chasing a murderer is crazy."

He glanced over at her deciding that she was safer with him than alone on the street. "Sorry, Lady. You're along for the ride now. Did you see which way the black car turned?"

"Right," she answered, gritting her teeth in frustration. "And don't call me Lady."

"West?"

Exasperated, she exclaimed, "Whatever direction 'right' is, that's the direction the car went."

"Thanks." He made a sharp right turn.

Rachel was thrown cross-wise on the worn seat by the abrupt motion. Struggling to get up, she yelled, "You're a terrible cab driver. You're going to kill us both."

Mac pressed the gas pedal almost flat to the floor, trying to keep up with the speeding car ahead of him. The sedan's tires squealed as it rounded narrow corners, barely missing the sides of cars in its path. He knew if he didn't catch his prey quickly, he'd have to drop the chase. There was no way the battered yellow cab, with lousy suspension, was any match for the getaway car, which was just far enough ahead to make the license plate unreadable.

"Stop, stop, stop."

He ignored the indignant voice behind him, sensing an opportunity as the sedan pulled within a few blocks of Truxton Circle.

"I'm calling the police, you lunatic," she warned. "Stupid cell phone."

Mac felt something hard bounce off the back of his head, as he made a sharp right turn onto Florida Avenue, still in pursuit, but with a widening distance between the two cars. He heard a thud as the body in the back seat collided with the right passenger door and slid to the floorboard. Luckily, he'd engaged the locks before hitting the gas, mostly to protect Whiskey. The Irish wolfhound picked up the cell phone that had landed on the front seat, hoping for some tasty morsel, but quickly spit it out in disgust.

"Be quiet and stay down," Mac yelled over the mutterings of the enraged woman behind him.

"Don't you ever clean the carpet in this wreck? It's filthy. There's gum down here!"

"It's not really my cab, Lady!"

"I'm in a stolen cab? Oh my God! What the hell did I ever do to deserve–"

"Shut up, Rachel, so I can concentrate. I'm just gonna get a tag number–"

She crawled up on the seat just in time to be pitched back to the floor as he hit the brakes.

"You're crazy…absolutely, stark raving… How did you know my name was Rachel?"

"Damn, damn, damn." The cab screeched to a halt, narrowly missing a semi blocking the crosswalk. He could see the black sedan shoot up Florida Avenue and out of sight. He smacked his hand against the steering wheel.

Whiskey's growl was his only warning before he felt thin fingers grab his right ear and yank, effectively turning his face toward his passenger. Attached, his body naturally followed.

Mac was looking at a demon from Hell, judging from the vision in front of him. Rachel Brenner was now sporting a complexion closer to the color of her purple umbrella than her normal pale tones.

With her heaving chest and rage-filled eyes, he half expected to see fire shoot from her fingertips. He feared the woman had reached her limits.

Whiskey sat up, her growls becoming more menacing as she sensed an explosion coming.

Finally, the creature pinching his ear gained enough breath to express her ire. "Who the *hell* are you? Where are we going? And how did you know my name?"

He ignored the pain in his ear and considered his limited options.

With no answer immediately forthcoming, Rachel sighed, releasing him from her grasp. She put the strap of her purse over one shoulder and grabbed her umbrella while simultaneously reaching for the door handle with her right hand.

"Whiskey, watch her," he ordered, pressing down on the accelerator.

The hound jumped over the seat back, putting both paws on the woman's lap, before baring her teeth and growling.

"Oh shut up," said Rachel, daring the dog and its master to contradict her. She futilely searched for a way to unlock the door.

Whiskey let out a series of threatening barks.

"I want out of this cab, now. I've got mace and I'm not afraid to use it."

Mac took one hand off the wheel and dug for his wallet, tossing it to her over his shoulder. "Police business," he shouted, cursing as a delivery truck pulled in front of him. "Spray anything in this cab and I'm licensed to shoot you."

"Right," Rachel responded, pushing at the dog who'd now settled on her lap. "I just hope your deputy doesn't have fleas."

Mac rubbed his abused ear, then pulled a cell phone from his pocket. "No fleas, and I think we've about got that ringworm cleared up. Don't we, girl?"

Whiskey barked once as though in agreement.

Rachel cringed and redoubled her efforts to move the hound off her.

Mac kept one eye on her while he reported the murder to the police, hiding a smile as Whiskey gave the woman's face a lick.

Rachel sipped the lukewarm coffee the patrolman had given her from his own thermos, and hoped her hands would stop shaking. She sat sideways in the police cruiser, the passenger door open, and her feet planted firmly on the wet pavement of the gym parking lot.

She looked up and recognized the two detectives closing in on her. They were the same ones who'd waylaid her in the funeral home after the break-in at her house. Atwood and... She couldn't remember the older one's name.

"So we meet again, Mrs. Brenner," the older cop drawled. "You seem to be right in the middle of a lot criminal activity in this town. I'm thinking everyone would be safer if we locked you up."

"Detective..." She paused, glaring up at him. "I don't remember your name."

"Gorden," the younger cop offered. "I'm Detective Atwood and he's–"

"She's got it now, Tom," Detective Gorden sneered. "It's enough that she knows we're the ones who are going to arrest her as an accessory to murder. Unless she spills what she knows about this whole mess, we can continue this conversation down at the jail."

"Eddie, there's no need for that tone," Detective Atwood asserted, crouching down near Rachel's knees. "I'm sure Mrs. Brenner wants to help us catch the killer. After all, she was almost killed tonight too."

Rachel took another sip of coffee and wondered if the two D.C. cops had trained by watching old episodes of NYPD Blue. Their good cop/bad cop routine was pretty lame. In fact, the whole evening felt like a bad made-for-TV movie. The phone call, the rain, the body, the gunshot, the cab driver who wasn't a cab driver–it was all too much for her to process.

The cab driver–Mackenzie Sullivan–that's what he'd told her his name was–stood nearby talking to a tall black detective who was chewing on an unlit cigar. Every once-in-awhile he'd look over at her, checking, she supposed, to see if she was still where he'd left her. Their little talk on the way back to the gym had been full of surprises...

As he drove them back to the murder scene, Rachel studied the photo on the ID card she'd found in the wallet and compared it to the profile of the tall, rather thin, man sitting in front of her, impatiently holding a cell phone to his ear. The photo must be new. He looked the same in both; salt and pepper hair in need of a trim, square jaw with a small scar near the chin, and tired blue eyes with squint marks fanning the corners.

"You're not a cop, you're a private detective."

He waved a hand to silence her as he gave the murder location details to the police. "We'll be there in ten minutes…yeah, a dark-colored Nissan. I couldn't make the plates…yeah, I know it's one of the most popular cars in the city…I have her with me."

Rachel supposed she was the 'her' in question.

He snapped shut his cell phone and turned to face her. "I was a cop for twenty years. I retired about eight months ago."

"How did you know my name?"

He hesitated for a moment.

Glaring at him, she wondered if he would try to dodge the question or defer answering her.

He gave her a long look and apparently decided it wasn't worth the effort.

Clearing his throat, he said, "Your name came up as part of an investigation I'm handling."

He was going to have to do better than that. She countered with, "Why?"

"What do you mean?"

Rachel took a breath. The man was being deliberately obtuse. "I mean, why would *my* name come up in any investigation you're involved in. What's the case? Who hired you?"

"That's privileged information."

"Sell that line to someone else! You were sitting outside my house and you're not a cabdriver, so I can only assume that you were there to watch me. I want to know why. Who the hell are you?" She looked down at the ID card and read the name aloud, "Who are you, Mackenzie Sullivan?"

"Like I said, I'm a private investigator and I'm…" He paused.

It appeared to her that he was trying to guess how much she knew and then figure out how little he could get away with saying.

"I'm working on an embezzlement case."

Embezzlement? Dan? A fresh infusion of fear coursed through her. "You think my brother–you're–you're…"

"I'm just considering all possibilities," he offered.

"Well, dammit, you can start considering someone else! My brother is being framed and if you were any kind of detective, you'd already know that…although judging from your driving skills…." Rachel slid toward the door.

"Just calm down, I told the police I'd bring you back to the crime scene."

"I'd rather walk." She glanced around the unfamiliar neighborhood. Hell, after tonight, what was out there didn't scare her as much as what waited for her back at the campus. She straightened her back, and pulled on the door handle. "Unlock the damn doors!"

"Don't be stupid. I'll drive you back," he insisted.

"Are you calling me stupid?" The man was impossible.

"No, Ma'am! I just meant that you don't know where you are, the police need to talk to you at the scene, and I'd be more than happy to drive you." He used the same tone Dan always adopted with their mother when trying to reason with her hysterics.

Rachel sighed, the anger draining away. She wasn't her mother; she wasn't the hysterical type.

She looked out at the dark street again and reason prevailed. "Okay, but just to be clear, I'm not helping you find my brother and if I see you outside my house again, I'm calling the cops or a lawyer."

Mac nodded and put the cab into drive. He glanced in the rear-view mirror at his reluctant passenger. "Mind telling me why you were meeting Angela Lopez?"

"I do." She crossed her arms and stared out the window as they traveled back toward the college. "Who's Angela Lopez?"

"The woman leaking blood all over the pavement."

"Oh." Her posture remained defiant, but she was sure the shakiness of her voice betrayed her fears.

"Shame about her grandson." He sighed. "No telling what will become of him now."

She knew what he was doing; trying to manipulate her into talking. It wasn't going to work. Rachel reached up and pushed a stray lock of dark curly hair behind her ear, continuing to stare out the side window.

He didn't say anything else; just continued to drive.

The dog rested her large head on the edge of the seat back and stared at her.

Oh, what the hell. "Who is Angela Lopez? How is she a part of all this?"

"She was Vince Malwick's secretary. Why did you want to meet her?" He glanced at her in the mirror again.

This time she met his gaze. "I got a phone call. From a woman. She didn't give her name. Said she had something to give Dan. Something he needed to prove his innocence."

"What?" He slowed the cab as a traffic light ahead turned red.

"I don't know. Now, it's your turn to share."

Mac shrugged. "I interviewed her as part of my investigation. She worked in the same office with your brother–the same office as the guy who got his brains splattered all over the inside of the campus clock tower."

"Dan didn't do it. He didn't kill anyone. He didn't steal anything."

"How can you be sure?" he asked, turning into the campus drive. "He's running like a guilty man."

"He's running because he's scared," Rachel whispered, biting her lip as she saw the flashing lights of the patrol cars encircling the gym entrance. "Danny always runs when he's scared."

Eleven

"She looks more stunned than scared," Greeley observed, casually turning his head to observe the woman sitting in the patrol car. "She in it with her brother?"

"Nah. I doubt it… Maybe." Mac rubbed the back of his neck, trying to ease the muscle that had knotted up sometime between hearing Rachel's scream upon discovering the body and the instant the back window of Jeff O'Herlihy's junker cab had shattered. "I'm not sure about Thayer yet, but I doubt Rachel's involved."

"Rachel, is it now?" Greeley chuckled. "Watch it that you don't lose your perspective. You of all people should know better than to underestimate the female sex."

Mac glared at him. "I didn't–"

Greeley frowned and waved his cigar at the other man. "Forget I said that. Hawkins made his own choices. It's history. Just be careful that history doesn't repeat itself. "

The private investigator nodded, his anger fading as quickly as it had come. He had no intention of reliving the past. He'd paid enough for that mistake. His partner had paid more.

Mac's cell phone rang. He gave Greeley an apologetic look as he pulled it out of his jacket pocket. "Sullivan."

Greeley chewed on his cigar and blatantly listened to Mac's side of the conversation.

"No. I haven't found him yet, although there have been some developments." Mac glanced toward the police car and then back at Greeley. He lowered his voice. "Ray, everything is fine. But I am going to have to talk to you about something. I've got another client and your interests may conflict."

Mac listened for a second. "I don't have time to get into it now. We'll talk about it tomorrow."

Greeley narrowed his eyes, continuing to listen.

Mac shrugged, speaking briskly into the phone. "Okay. I'll talk to him too. Later. Right now, I've got to go."

Mac flipped the phone closed and slid it into his pocket.

Greeley raised his brows but didn't ask about the call. "Back to Mrs. Brenner–why did she come here? To meet her brother?"

Mac shrugged. "Rachel–uh Mrs. Brenner–told me she was meeting some woman who called her and claimed to have information that would clear her brother."

Greeley paused a moment, then said, "You know Thayer could have killed Lopez, then shot out your back window for show–thinking we wouldn't believe he'd take a shot at his sister."

"I considered that. But my gut tells me Rachel isn't lying about Lopez's call. And if it was Thayer doing the shooting, his sister doesn't know it."

At Greeley's skeptical look, Mac added, "You can check Rachel's phone records; verify that Lopez made the call to her."

"Speaking of phone records, Lopez was talking on her cell phone to her daughter when she was shot."

"So you know the time of death." Mac glanced over at Rachel who calmly tried to ignore Eddie Gorden's attempts to rile her.

"Just minutes before you called us." Greeley shifted his feet, his trademark cowboy boots offering him little cushion from the hard pavement. "Did you get a look at the plates?"

Mac shook his head.

Greeley looked him up and down. "Losing your touch, old man? Guess civilian life has slowed you down."

"I had a little trouble with my passenger and the junker I was driving," Mac grumbled. "Don't count me out yet. I haven't lost anything but maybe my sense of humor."

"Yeah, well your sense of humor was kinda twisted. Nobody's gonna miss that." Greeley stuck his cigar back in his mouth and gave the other man a tight smile. "Why don't you take *Rachel* home now? See if she'll tell you where Thayer is hiding and then give us a call."

"I don't think she knows where he is," Mac mused, walking away. "But he'll be in touch sooner or later."

"Sooner would be better," Greeley shouted after him. "Too many people near Thayer are getting killed."

Mac watched Rachel's face blanch as the lieutenant's words reached her.

She found it oddly soothing, running her fingers through the long hair of the hound stretched out across the front seat, hindquarters on Rachel's lap, majestic head on her owner's thigh. "I should have taken a cab," Rachel muttered.

"This is a cab," Mac said with a small smile hovering at his lips. He pulled out of the campus gates and headed for Rittenhouse Street.

"No. A real cab with a rear window that isn't in shards, driven by a real cabbie who isn't trying to convict my brother of murder," she said indignantly.

"I'm not trying to pin a murder rap on anyone. I don't even care who killed Malwick and Lopez," Mac interjected.

Then in response to her disapproving expression, he added, "Well, I care but solving the murders isn't my responsibility. My job is to find out who embezzled a half million dollars from Concordia."

"Dan didn't do that either!"

Mac gave her a sideways glance as he slowed for a traffic light. "Look, maybe your brother didn't kill anybody. Maybe he just took the money. If that's the case, he better turn himself in now, before he gets stuck with a couple of first-degree murder charges. With a good lawyer, he could be out in under five if he makes restitution on the money."

"Dan didn't steal the money."

"How do you know that?" Mac pushed. "He's been spending money like a kid with a free pass in the video arcade."

"That's not Dan," Rachel insisted. "He lives in a crummy apartment in a crappy neighborhood. He buys his clothes at the Salvation Army, salvages furniture from the dump. He's like the last living hippie."

"So why did he just buy a brand new Jeep?"

"What? He'd never buy a new car. He'd never buy a 'new' anything."

"I saw the receipt. $35,000 and change. He's supposed to pick it up next week."

"That just doesn't make sense. Maybe whoever is setting up Dan…" Her hand went to her left wrist, her fingers tracing the gold bangle that Dan had sent her a month ago for her birthday. She knew it was expensive and had tried to refuse it, but he'd had her name engraved on the inside.

Mac's eyes followed her hand's movements. "I showed his photo to the manager of the car dealership. It was definitely your brother who purchased the car."

"I-I don't know what it means," Rachel stammered, pulling her sleeve down over her bracelet.

"He also bought two tickets for a week long Caribbean cruise."

"Dan? Don't be ridiculous."

"The travel agent confirmed the purchase," Mac said softly. "Maybe you don't know your brother as well as you think."

"It just doesn't make sense," Rachel whispered to herself.

"Does your brother know how strapped you are for cash?"

"I beg your pardon," Rachel snapped.

"I don't mean to be rude, but did your brother know that you lost your job. That you were draining your retirement fund to pay for your son's tuition and that your house is mortgaged to the limit?"

"How dare you," she sputtered. "I have a job and the rest is none of your business."

Mac turned onto Rittenhouse Street and stopped the cab in front of the small brick house.

"Look, I confess that I ran a quick background check on you to see if you were part of the embezzlement scheme. Clearly you're not. You applied to refinance your second mortgage a week ago."

"I can't believe you have access to my finances. Is there nothing private?"

"Not much," Mac answered. "But the question is, did your brother know?"

"Absolutely not."

Mac pushed. "If your brother knew that you needed money to put your son through college, don't you think he'd do whatever he had to do to help?"

"He'd never kill anyone," Rachel whispered, her fists in a tight knot, her fair complexion suddenly stark white.

"But would he steal to help?" Mac asked. "Maybe things just got out of hand. He didn't set out to hurt anyone. Maybe he thought that the college would never miss the money. Maybe he planned to pay it back."

"No! Dan would never do that…besides he didn't know…" Her voice softened. "He thought that Charlie–that's my ex-husband–that Charlie was paying Sam's tuition. He's–he's supposed to–I mean it was in the divorce agreement, but…"

"Look, the evidence is piling up fast against Dan Thayer. A half million dollars is missing. Two people are dead. Your brother had access and motive, plus he didn't stick around to defend himself."

Rachel sighed and looked down at the dog who had once again settled comfortably on her lap. "I'd run too if someone was trying to blame all that on me. Have you even considered that my brother is being framed? That he didn't do any of it?"

Mac calmly leaned back against the headrest. "My investigation has told me one story about Dan Thayer, and it doesn't have a happy ending. Why don't you tell me another story–the one about the Dan Thayer that you know? I'm ready to listen. You've heard from him, haven't you?"

Rachel hesitated a moment, then nodded. "He e-mailed me on Monday afternoon. Told me that I shouldn't believe what I heard about him. It was from an e-mail account I'd never seen before."

"How can you be sure it was really from your brother?"

"He made a reference to his favorite Roy Rogers boots," she said with a small smile. "Dan wore them for a whole year when he was five–even after they got too small. Grandpa finally threw them away to keep Dan from crippling himself. I don't think anyone else alive knows about them."

"Did he ever talk to you about his work at Concordia?"

Rachel shook her head no. "I mean he told me his title and a general idea of his responsibilities when he took the job, but we never really talked about it."

Mac thought for a moment before asking. "What did he think of his co-workers?"

"I think he mentioned someone named Jack once. When we'd talk, it was about other stuff." Rachel paused, then added, "I'd–I'd gone through a divorce, so mostly we'd talk about Sam. Dan wanted to help with him."

"If you hear from your brother again, have him contact me," he said, turning off the ignition. "Here's my card."

She reluctantly took it, then reached for the door handle, her hand finding the empty space where the handle used to be. She turned her head and glared at him.

"Got to get that fixed." Mac chuckled and opened his door, stepping outside. He motioned for her to get out on his side.

Rachel struggled to slide out from under Whiskey.

Mac extended his hand as she slid across the well-worn upholstery, her shoulder brushed against him as she got out of the cab and walked past him.

He remained standing near the open cab door, watching to make sure she got inside her house safely, narrowing his eyes as her pace slowed and then stopped.

She turned around and faced him, her posture ramrod straight. "I can't explain the new car or the cruise, but I would bet this house that my brother never stole a penny from anyone. And I would swear on my son's life that Dan Thayer didn't kill anyone."

Mac nodded. "There's only been two people in my life that I've trusted that much and only one of them deserved it. I just hope your faith isn't misplaced."

Rachel looked out at the dark street and the cab with the shattered window. "You're not going to sit out there and watch my house all night are you?"

"No," he chuckled, then added, "You going to be okay?"

"What?" Surprised, she stared at him.

"When things quiet down, you're going to remember Angela Lopez's face. You're going to remember that someone took a shot at you. Right now you're still running on adrenaline, another hour from now you might get a little shaky."

"Remember where I work; I've seen dead bodies before."

"It's different when someone is killed in front of you."

"Is that experience talking again?"

"Yeah." He sighed. "And it never really gets any easier."

Twelve

"Here's the keys." Mac tossed them onto Lieutenant Greeley's desk. "Thanks for the wake up call this morning. I wouldn't have wanted to get more than three hours sleep in a row."

Greeley smiled around his unlit cigar. "I've got two murders to solve, you can sleep later."

Mac sat down in the visitor's chair and glared across the desk at his former boss. "Yeah, well try not to destroy the interior of the cab or Jeff's gonna have my head."

"That bullet last night almost got your head." Greeley leaned back in his chair. "Thanks for bringing the cab in. The crime scene guys didn't find the bullet that shattered your back glass. Last night they figured it for going through the glass at an angle and then passing through your open driver's window into that prefab building next to the gym. But no luck. Fitz wants to check out the cab's interior."

Greeley set his soggy cigar in an ashtray and picked up a coffee cup. "Are you going to the funeral?"

The change in subject was abrupt, even for Greeley. It took Mac a beat or two to catch up. "Funeral? Malwick's?"

"Yeah."

"Last I heard the widow was still too upset to finalize the arrangements. Did the coroner release the body?"

"Yeah, and Mrs. Malwick has decided that sooner is better than later. The funeral is set for tomorrow afternoon."

"Where?"

Greeley grinned.

"O'Herlihy's," Mac guessed.

"Bingo. Your buddy Jeff has probably got one of his people giving the guy a makeover as we speak. Not sure he can do much with the guy missing about half his face. Our killer seems to prefer headshots. Something I should tell you." Greeley took a sip of coffee, then added, "Malwick took two to the head. The coroner said the first one took off the guy's right ear."

"Torture?"

Greeley nodded. "That or our killer is a really bad shot."

"What's your plan?"

"I've got Eddie over at Judge Stockton's getting authorization for a wire tap."

"A wire tap? For a funeral?"

Greeley chuckled. "In a manner of speaking. We're going to wire the casket for sound. Anyone decides to confess their guilt while sobbing over the body, we're going to see that they do penance."

"Jeff know about this?"

"Figured you could tell him when you let him know what happened to his cab. By the way, you're going to be needing another ride. If we find the bullet in the cab, we'll probably keep it until after the case is closed and the trial is finished. Tell Jeff if he plays nice, I'll get his window fixed before we give it back."

"He'll be thrilled." Mac rubbed the back of his neck. "Have you gotten any leads on the Lopez murder?"

"About a half hour before the shooting, a security guard overheard an argument between Lopez and a woman named..." Greeley picked up a jumbled file folder and rifled through it. "Lenore Adams. She works over–"

"I know who she is," Mac interrupted. "What kind of car does she drive?"

"Late model, black Nissan." Greeley waited. His expression conveying his hope that Mac could confirm or eliminate the car as being the one he'd chased the night before.

Mac shook his head. "Sorry. It's a 'possible'. I didn't get a good enough look. She got an alibi?"

"Not a great one. Tom is trying to confirm it. Reportedly, she was buying something to eat in the Student Union when Lopez was shot."

Mac scribbled a note in his little black book. "What did they argue about?"

"Some kind of computer problem. The guard said there have been a lot of those lately."

"Arguments or computer problems?"

"Both." Greeley's telephone rang and he wearily glanced at it and then back at Mac. "Probably Judge Stockton calling to complain about Eddie's attitude. I swear I'm gonna have to send the guy to some kind of charm school. For some reason women can't stand him."

"Yeah, well he doesn't do too well with men either." Mac got to his feet. "Take your call. I better go give Jeff the good news."

"Mac?" Greeley had his hand over the speaker part of the phone. "That guard also mentioned some college kids being in the Accounting Office late last night. Two boys and a girl with purple bangs. Ring any bells?"

"Nope." Mac gave the lieutenant a tight smile along with the lie. As he walked out of the police station, he decided it was past time to schedule a meeting with his junior clients.

"My Dad's gone to see what's holding up his last order of caskets. He said with the murderer at the college running loose, he's expecting to need more." Sean O'Herlihy bit into a slice of pepperoni pizza. "Want some pizza?"

Mac glanced at the half-dozen remaining slices scattered in the grease-stained cardboard box. "How old is that pizza?"

Sean smiled, tomato sauce decorating the corner of his mouth. "It's this week's."

"I'll pass." Mac sat down on the sofa across from the elegant oak desk Sean had littered with food, soda cans, and a stack of unopened textbooks. "Looks like you've taken over your father's desk. You sit there long enough, he's gonna get ideas again about bringing you into the family business."

Mac wasn't sure whether the greenish tinge that crept over Sean's face was caused by the thought of becoming a mortician or the spoiled pepperoni kicking in.

When Sean didn't respond, Mac shut his eyes and rubbed the kink in the back of his neck. He tried not to think how comfortable the sofa felt, tried not to think how much he'd like to stretch out and take a nap. His earlier meeting with Ray and Sam had not gone well. Ray was hurt that he hadn't mentioned the Ganseco job but Sam Brenner was enraged. He sighed. It was the first time he'd met Sam, but he'd bet good money that 'enraged' was the kid's default position. And neither teen would discuss what they were doing at the college the night before. He hadn't had the energy to press.

He'd hoped to talk with Rachel or Carrie, but according to Sean, both were hard at work on Vince Malwick. There was probably something wrong with Rachel doing Vince's makeup but he was too tired to figure out the ethics.

"What do you think?"

Rachel had to smile at Carrie's enthusiasm; although she was a little surprised the teen had started without her. Jeff O'Herlihy had embalmed the body and taken care of holes left by the bullet, but he'd left the makeup and missing ear for them to deal with.

Rachel looked from one side of the head to the other, then looked back to the reconstructed right side again. "It looks like a perfectly good ear. But don't you think it should match his left ear?"

Carrie grinned. "He had ugly ears. I thought I'd improve him. After all this is his last chance to look his best. And you know no one will see the left side anyway, what with the casket swinging open for a right side viewing."

"I was going to show you how to make a clay one, but I got tied up on the phone." Leaning closer to Mr. Malwick's new ear, Rachel studied the wax replica. "How did you make this? A mold? I almost think I see piercings for ear rings."

Standing behind her, Carrie blushed and surreptitiously pulled some dried plaster of Paris from her purple hair.

* * *

Apparently he'd been quiet too long for Sean's comfort. "I don't know when Dad will get back. It's cool if you want to wait though."

"How come you're not in school? Some kind of teacher holiday?"

"No," the teen mumbled. "They gave me a holiday all my own."

The detective chuckled. "Suspended? Again?"

Sean's face turned the color of his hair. "It wasn't my fault."

"Never is; least that's what your father tells me."

"You try having a father that embalms people for a living. There's only so much harassment a guy can take without giving some back."

"I don't see any bruises on you."

Sean flexed his right fist, then rubbed at a scraped knuckle. He gave his father's long-time friend a smug smile. "They hurt my feelings. I just shared my pain."

"Yeah, well, I'd feel sorry for you, but I've got my own problems–like making a living, finding a murderer, and figuring out how to explain to your father that his cab is impounded until further notice."

"Can't help you with the first two, but I think maybe the cops already told him about the cab."

Surprised, since he thought Greeley was going to let him tell Jeff, Mac asked, "Lieutenant Greeley called him?"

"Nah. I think it was the one that Dad calls Fat Eddie. Dad did a lot of cussing."

Mac winched. "Cussing at me or at the police?"

"Both," Jeff O'Herlihy announced walking into the office. He crossed the room and set a briefcase down next to the pizza box, frowning at the crumbs scattered across his desk. "But I've had time to calm down now." He gave Mac a sideways glance and added a deep Irish brogue to his speech. Pacing back and forth, he exclaimed, "I'm ready to accept the burdens that the good Lord has seen fit to lay upon my shoulders. Missing caskets. Suppliers stealing me blind. The police interfering in my funeral services. My ungrateful son fighting at school, risking his education. My good friend destroying my profits right and left. My sainted wife–"

Mac sighed. "Is this going to be a long sermon? Cause I only got about three hours sleep tops last–"

Jeff held up his hand for quiet and resumed pacing the room.

Mac sighed again and crossed his arms, settling into the sofa cushions for a protracted stay.

"Where was I?" Jeff asked, pausing and looking up toward the ceiling as if asking for divine assistance.

Instead, Sean chimed in, "You were about to bitch about Mom trading stocks with her club."

Jeff slapped the top of the desk, bouncing a piece of cold pizza over onto his nearby briefcase. "Watch your language!"

Mac chuckled, watching Jeff pick cheese off the leather. "How's Kathleen's stock portfolio doing? I might be needing some stock tips myself."

"I'll give you a tip," Jeff growled, walking over and standing in front of his friend. He leaned over and pointed a cheesy finger at the other man's chest. "Buy yourself a car!"

Thirteen

"Hello," Rachel said with minimal civility. She had a headache and a strong feeling things were spinning out of control.

"Rach?"

"Dan, where the hell are you? Don't answer that! I know I asked you to call but the police might have a trace on my phones. Somebody else has been killed." The words came tumbling out so fast she could barely breathe.

"Rach, calm down. Are you okay? Is Sam okay?"

She took a deep breath, but her heart was beating so loud and so fast that she wondered if she were having an attack. She sank down in her desk chair.

"Dan, listen to me," she tried to sound parental and authoritative. "Somebody killed Angela Lopez last night."

"Angela's dead? What happened to her?"

"Dan, stop. Listen... Someone murdered her. Half of her face...oh God, they blew off half of her face. It was horrible. Worse than anything I've ever had to deal with when working at Grandpa's. Then whoever killed her shot out the rear window of the cab and we tried to follow and get a license plate, but the car was too far ahead and..."

"What cab? You were in a cab that was shot at? How come you found Angela? And what do you mean you followed the getaway car? Are you crazy?"

"Dan, shut up. You've got to turn yourself in. This is dangerous. Somebody's not afraid to kill people who get in the way."

"I can't, Rachel. If I turn myself in before I've got the evidence I need, the cops will stop looking for the real killer. But I need you and Sam out of it right this second. Tell Sam to let me handle everything."

"Too late for that," she snapped. "I'm scared, Dan. Really scared for you and the kids. Ray's even hired a private detective to find you."

"Ray hired… I'm not too worried about anybody that–"

"Don't be stupid. The guy he's hired is an ex-cop and he's the same guy the insurance company hired to find the missing money." She tucked her hair behind her ears, then undid the effect when she ran her hand through her curls nervously.

"How can Ray afford a…"

"Don't get hung up on the details," Rachel interrupted. Her heartbeat had returned to normal and for the moment she found herself more mad than worried.

"Listen, I can't talk for long. Maybe you should go away for a few days until all this gets straightened out."

"Just where would you like me to go? Paris might be nice this time of year. Of course I'd lose my job. I wouldn't be able to pay Sam's tuition. But hey, maybe I'll just–"

"How about Grandpa's farm? It's vacant right now, isn't it?"

"Dan, you know I can't go anywhere. I believe you're innocent, but for God's sake, Daniel Edward Thayer, everything Mac and the police have shown me says you did it, that you stole the money, killed your boss, and then murdered that poor grandmother without so much as blinking an eye. Turn yourself in. I'll find you a lawyer, and we'll let the professionals do their job." She finished her rant, breathless.

"Rachel, I hear you. But I'm being set up. The police will close the case once they have me in custody. I've got to find evidence that will clear me."

"Well how about you start explaining some of what Mac told me."

"Who's Mac?"

"Mackenzie Sullivan, the private detective I told you about. He's had my house staked out for days. And as an ex-cop, he's buddies with the police who are investigating the case."

"What do they have on me?"

"Did you buy a new car? A jeep? You've never owned a new car in your life? What the hell…"

"It's for you, Rach. I was going to give it to you to replace the heap you've been driving."

"I never asked…" Rachel interjected indignantly. "I couldn't let you buy me a car. You shouldn't have spent your money on that gold bracelet either."

"I bought the bracelet for your birthday. And yes, you could let me buy you a car. I'm making..., or I was making good money, for the first time in my life. You and Sam are my only family. I wanted you to have it."

"We'll talk about that another time. I assume you weren't sending me to Aruba," Rachel pushed. "Did you really plan a Caribbean vacation?"

Her question was met with silence.

"Dan, are you there?"

"They know about the cruise?"

"Don't you get it?" Rachel snapped, her voice rising. "They know about everything. You can't hide any of this stuff. Who were you going away with? Maybe she can help you."

Dan ignored the question. "This guy Mac, what else did he tell you?"

"Not much. But I think he'd help us if you'd turn yourself in."

"I can't, Rachel. If I can find what I need, then I'll be able to prove my innocence. Don't worry; I've got some friends helping me. I've got to hang up now. I've been on this phone too long. Tell Sam to go back to school. And, Rach, be careful."

"Wait," she cried, but was left with a lonely dial tone and more questions than answers.

"Where have you been?" Rachel asked sharply as the three kids walked into her office.

Sam looked surprised at the tone, but shrugged his shoulders and lifted his soda can. "Carrie was showing us the staff lounge. We just wanted something to eat."

Ray offered his bag of Cheetos, but Rachel shook her head. He passed them along to Carrie who scooped out a handful.

Rachel directed a cool gaze at her son. "You plan on ever returning to school?"

Sam suddenly found his soda can fascinating, rubbing the beading moisture around the aluminum, then drying his hand on his jeans. Ray and Carrie became equally fascinated by the orange cheesy curls in their hands.

Finally, he said softly, "I'll head back tomorrow morning. But first I need to get hold of Uncle Dan."

"Too bad, you just missed him," Rachel said sharply.

Three heads snapped up.

"Dan called me."

"Called you here?" Sam croaked.

"Yes. So if they've tapped this phone, he should be in custody within the next ten minutes," Rachel answered harshly.

A familiar voice came from the doorway. "I don't think they've got a tap on this line…yet."

All attention turned to the private detective, ex-cop, sometime taxi driver, standing at the threshold. "Until yesterday I didn't know you worked here, I doubt the police have discovered that fact either."

"How did you–"

"Never mind. Quite a party you have going here."

"Hey," Carrie exclaimed. "I remember you. You wanted the dog casket."

"God! Did something happen to Whiskey?" Ray asked.

Mac held up a hand. "Whiskey is fine. Or rather she's normal. Or at least the same as ever."

Carrie smiled. "He was doing some pre-planning. It's smart."

"Pre-planning for a dog?" Sam laughed. "Right."

"He was just under cover," Ray chimed in. "Mac's a private detective."

"You don't have a dog?" Carrie looked from Ray to Mac.

The private eye sighed.

"He has a dog, but she's not dead," Ray explained.

"Pre-planning is done before someone dies. That's the whole point," Carrie argued.

Rachel continued to watch the lob and volley without understanding the game.

"I'll gladly buy a dog casket, if we can stop this conversation now," Mac said.

"Anybody want to let me buy a vowel so I know what the hell is going on?" Rachel demanded, her voice rising.

"Sorry." Mac nodded. "I met Carrie a couple of days ago when I was…"

"When you were following me around trying to find out if I was my brother's accomplice?" Rachel said indignantly.

"Sort of," Mac agreed. "Did you say that you just heard from your brother? What did he say?"

"Not much. He's worried about me and the kids."

Mac frowned. "Maybe the kids could go check out an embalming and we could talk privately."

"I get a commission on caskets. Is he really going to buy one?" Carrie asked, as Rachel shooed the teens out the door.

"Oh, geez, somebody give her a clue," Sam mumbled.

Mac sat down in one of the chairs facing Rachel's desk. "If your brother is worried about you, he'll turn himself in."

"He wants us to go away for a few days until things die down. But I can't. Not now. So I need your help. I want you to talk to Ray."

"Fine," Mac agreed. "But I'm not sure I can convince him to back off as long as your son is determined to keep digging."

"Sam's going back to school later today, even if I have to take him there myself."

"Okay. I'll talk to Ray; now tell me where your brother is."

"I honestly don't know. He didn't tell me and maybe that's just as well since I would probably tell you and then he'd be in jail." Rachel twirled a pen in her fingers, focusing on the spinning motion while she tried to figure out what to do next.

"The cops have an exact time for Lopez's death," Mac revealed. "She was on her cell phone talking to her daughter when she was killed. They also verified that she called you. In fact, she called you several times over the past few days. Less than a minute each time."

"I didn't talk to her. But I had some hang up calls. I thought…" Rachel gasped. "Oh my God–her daughter?"

"Yeah, she's pretty badly shook up. Judging from the caliber of the bullet, the police are pretty sure that it's from the same gun used to kill Malwick. Course they won't know for sure until they recover the gun."

"So if Dan has an alibi for that time…"

"Yeah." Mac rose from his chair. "If you hear from him again, let me know."

"I'll try to convince him to turn himself in. If not, I'll try to find out where he was last night around 11:00 p.m."

"Don't play detective! If he won't turn himself in, have him call me. Let me talk to him."

"I'll see," Rachel said, reaching for a file on her desk.

"I've noticed that gold bracelet you wear. Looks new. Did Dan buy that for you?"

Rachel's head shot up, a guilty blush coloring her face.

"I thought so." Mac nodded. "Believe me, Mrs. Brenner. This isn't amateur night at the Rialto. Somebody's playing hardball and there are too many bodies showing up."

Fourteen

"So you've got a desk and everything," Ray said, grinning at Carrie, as he and Sam looked around her small office in the basement. "Pretty soon you'll be talking about quitting college and doing dead people make-up fulltime."

"I'm not quitting school, but it's not just make-up," Carrie protested. "Rachel and I fitted Mr. Malwick with an ear this morning. How many times in life does a person get an opportunity like that?"

"An ear?"

"Yeah, of course ears aren't that hard. People don't really notice ears so they don't have to be a perfect match. People see a whole face; they don't really notice small differences."

"Like invoices," Sam mused. "You look at the company name and the amount. That's it."

Ray chuckled. "Big jump, man. What are you talking about?"

"Mailing addresses," Sam exclaimed, speaking to no one in particular. "That's the difference! The two invoices had different mailing addresses."

"The files from last night? So what?" Carrie asked. "Why is that important?"

Sam crossed the room to stand next to Ray in the doorway. "I'm not sure, but Uncle Dan understands it. He's convinced those files will get him out of trouble with the police."

"Speaking of trouble, we need to chat." Mac appeared behind the two teens, putting one hand on Ray's shoulder and the other on Sam's. Tightening his grip, he muttered, "Jim Carrey and Adam Sandler, I presume."

The shorter leg on the junk store chair had turned out to be an effective tool for keeping Ray both physically and mentally off balance. Too bad Sam's chair didn't have the same flaw. Mac made a mental note to see if he couldn't find a second one the next time he went shopping–or maybe he'd just bring a saw from home and make his own modifications.

"And then we copied Dan's file to a disk and got out of there." Ray, giving the other boy an apologetic look, reluctantly finished his recitation of their black ops activities at Concordia College. He shifted his weight abruptly as Mac glared at him and the chair tipped sideways.

As he'd had to do a couple of times in the past hour, just to prevent Ray from landing in his lap, Sam quickly stuck out a hand and pushed against Ray's shoulder, returning him to a vertical position. "You've got crap for furniture, old man!"

Mac shifted his attention to Sam Brenner, finding the teen's resemblance to his mother striking, everything from his curly dark hair right down to the stubborn set to his mouth. The detective had given the boys two choices after the incident in the funeral home–come back to his office with him or take a ride down to the police station. He had agreed to let Carrie finish her shift and then go to class. He'd have to double-check the boys' stories against her account.

"Must be that I'm not charging my clients enough." Mac smiled at the boy, a smile that didn't reach his eyes. "If you call me old man one more time, you're going to be spending some quality time with a dentist in the near future."

The teen scoffed but edged his chair backwards a few inches.

"Did either of you stop to think that you were interfering in a police investigation, stealing evidence, plus committing breaking and entering?"

Ray raised a hand.

"What?" Mac's tone was harsh, harsher than he'd intended.

An anxious Whiskey hurried in from the back room where she'd been taking a nap by the electric heater he'd plugged in to take the chill off the frigid office. She nudged her owner's knee with her nose, as if warning him to calm down.

"We did have a key so I don't think–"

"Neither of you thought about anything," Mac shouted, rising to his feet. He'd been half-sitting on the edge of the receptionist's desk while he questioned the boys, but now he paced the room.

"There is a killer running around out there shooting people on that campus–hell, two people are dead who worked in the very office you ransacked." Mac looked at a belligerent Sam. "If you truly believe your uncle isn't the one pulling the trigger, then by going in that office and digging around, you've made yourself, Ray, Carrie, and your mother a target for the real killer."

Whiskey put the period on his pronouncement with a sharp bark.

Ray surreptitiously dropped one hand down beside his chair and wiggled his fingers. The big dog lumbered over and allowed him to stroke her head.

Mac and Sam watched Ray with the dog, letting the emotions in the room settle down to lie with the dust on the ugly carpet.

"Am I getting through to you?" Mac stared at one boy, then the other. "Don't you two get it? This isn't a game. People are dying."

Ray nodded but kept his eyes on the dog. Sam crossed his arms and stared straight ahead at the cracks in the plaster wall beyond the front desk.

"Where's the disk now?" Mac asked, trying to watch both boys' expressions at the same time.

Ray gave Sam a quick sideways glance and began a close inspection of the tips of Whiskey's ears.

Sam turned his eyes in Mac's direction, raised his chin, and gave the detective a self-satisfied smile. "My uncle has it."

Mac would have believed him except for Ray's reaction. The teen jerked and this time the chair tossed him straight into his lying friend. The two boys went down in a tangled mess of mangled furniture and flailing limbs.

Whiskey cocked her head to one side and whined in confusion.

"You guys are lousy liars," Mac grumbled, kicking one of the chairs aside so that he could haul the two teens to their feet. Keeping a tight grip on one upper arm of each, he added, "You're going to keep stumbling around in this mess until both of you get hurt. Well, I'm through coddling. I'm really not the sensitive wimp you seem to take me for."

Sam snickered and even Ray had to hide a grin.

Mac saw red. "Don't screw with me! Where's the damn disk?"

Whiskey barked and danced around the group in agitation.

Sam knocked away the hand that was still absently holding his arm and joined Ray near the door. "We don't need anything from you. Stay out of our business and stay away from my family."

Sam yanked open the door and rushed out into the dark parking lot.

Ray gave the detective a quick look, his face hardening. "Sam is right. It's not gonna work out with you working for us and the insurance company. Send me a bill for what we owe you and I'll pay it."

Mac sighed as the boy slipped out the door. "Well, girl. We just got fired."

The Irish wolfhound barked once at him and then walked back into the other room.

"Okay. I just got fired." Mac pulled his cell phone out of his jacket and punched in a familiar number. "Lieutenant? Sullivan here. I think Thayer might make an appearance tomorrow."

Mac paused, listening. "The funeral is my guess. His nephew has something he wants."

Fifteen

"Too bad I can't charge by the head," Jeff whispered, coming up behind the private detective who stood lurking near the registry book. "I'd make a killing."

Mac chuckled. "I'm surprised you haven't figured out a way to do that."

"Give me time." Jeff waved at a dark suited man who nodded in his direction. "Even the mayor is here. Hey, when you get a chance take a look at the deceased. We had to make a fake ear. I think it worked out pretty well. Although I'm not sure the lobe is just right, but it was a rush job."

"Keep that bit about the ear quiet. I don't think Greeley wants everyone knowing that piece of information. He's holding it back to help weed out any confessions he might get from the regular crazies and weirdoes that show up at the station trying to take credit for everything from the stolen Concordia mascot to JFK's assassination."

Jeff sighed. "Figures. My best work and I can't brag about it."

"I thought it was Rachel's work?"

"Remind me of this conversation the next time you need a car."

"Sorry." Mac chuckled. "I'm sure your fake ears are good, too."

"Here we go." Jeff touched Mac's shoulder, directing his gaze in the direction of a tall blonde dressed in a tight black dress coming in the door. "You wanted me to point out the widow. The guy with her is supposed to be her brother, but I have a feeling they don't share DNA in the way relatives do."

"Is that normal funeral attire these days?"

"No." Jeff shook his head. "Have to admit though–the sequins around her–uh, the top part–kind of brightens things up."

"Sequins? Right. Don't let Kathleen catch you admiring those sequins."

"Mr. O'Herlihy?"

The funeral director turned toward the elderly man in a black chauffeur's uniform. "Yes, Joseph?"

The man whispered something in Jeff's ear, then hurried away.

Jeff sighed, then leaned close and whispered, "Joseph just drove Mrs. Malwick and her brother here. He wanted to know what to do with certain undergarments the 'lady' managed to leave in the limo."

Mac raised his eyebrows. "Grief does terrible things to people."

"Speaking of grief–Greeley give you any idea when I'm getting my cab back?"

"Soon. Listen, I've got to go talk with Tom Atwood. He's running the inside surveillance."

"Where's his partner, Fat Eddie?"

"In a converted florist van in the parking lot. Eddie and a couple of the department tech guys are monitoring the sound." Mac spotted the young, black detective passing out programs at the entrance to the chapel proper. "I'll see you later. I know it's bad timing, but if you get a chance, think you could find me something else to drive other than that bug truck? It makes Whiskey nervous to ride in it now."

"Give her a tranquilizer. We've all got problems." Jeff pasted a smile on his face as the first wife and grown children of the deceased approached. "Right now my main one is keeping control of this circus. Even if the ex-wives don't draw blood, the killer might show up and decide to increase his or her batting average. I don't really want my business to become known as that kind of a one-stop-shop."

"Anyone here you didn't expect?" Mac nodded at the mourners as they filed past Tom, their outstretched hands accepting the small white programs with the sanitized facts of Vincent Malwick's life.

Tom shrugged. "Yeah. At least a hundred people we didn't plan on. Seems the college wanted a good turnout–I think they must be giving bonuses to employees who put in an appearance. A lot of students here too. The lieutenant is going nuts. He's calling in officers from the second shift to cover all the action here. Heck, even Roseanne's finally getting her chance to go undercover." Tom chuckled at the furtive look Mac cast round the room. "Don't worry; the boss cast her in the role of Pete Fiori's wife."

"Pete Fiori from Narcotics?"

"Yeah, the lieutenant is borrowing guys from all divisions. Pete's pissed. He had to cut his hair and shave for this gig. It'll be weeks before he can get back on the street with the dealers."

"Poor guy. A delousing and Roseanne in the same day."

Tom laughed, then sobered his expression when one of the milling crowd gave him a disapproving look. "Go away. You're going to make me blow my cover."

"Sorry. Are the bugs all working?"

"So far. Eddie says he's picked up a couple of new chicken recipes, some juicy gossip about the Mayor, and he now knows how to get red wine out of his linen tablecloths."

The private detective jerked his head toward the chapel. "I've got a seat picked out in the back row. I'd better claim it."

* * *

"I can't believe how many people are here. I hope Sam didn't really want me to make a list," Carrie whispered to Rachel Brenner as they walked into the marble foyer of O'Herlihy's main chapel. The line to sign the book of condolences snaked around the entryway and down the hall. A black-suited attendant advised them that the family was receiving visitors in the reception room to the right, and that the service would be held in the main chapel straight ahead.

"I can't believe Sam is still directing an investigation from his dorm room," Rachel snapped. "This is absolutely the last time I want you involved in this mess."

"Sure. Let's go and get seats," Carrie murmured and started forward, but was stayed by Rachel's hand on her arm.

"Not yet. I want to see the family."

"Why?" Carrie asked. "You're not going to talk to them about their bill right now?"

"Of course not. But I want to see who does talk to the family. The killer might be here. That's the main reason I let you talk me into attending this funeral, instead of staying in my office and balancing the accounts," Rachel hissed.

The two women bypassed the line of visitors waiting to offer personal condolences to the family and slid into the wood-paneled receiving room. Once inside, Rachel observed that guests were dividing their time between two groups of mourners. In one corner, two boys–one in his late teens, one in his early twenties, stood on either side of a middle-aged brunette and an elderly man.

"I guess that's the family," Rachel murmured.

"Yep. At least that's Tommy Malwick. He's in my bio class. I bet he got free tuition since his Dad worked for the college," Carrie whispered. "You think he loses the tuition benefits now?"

"Don't know." Rachel's attention moved across the room and settled on a bleached blonde in a black silk dress, with rhinestones edging the deep vee-neckline. She also greeted guests and frequently dabbed her black mascara-rimmed eyes with a Kleenex, while leaning heavily on a muscle-bound man at her side. "Who's that?"

"My guess is that's the second Mrs. Malwick or maybe she's the third. And I think that guy with her is from the college. I've seen him before." Carrie sniffed. "Judging from the looks Tommy and his Mom are shooting across the room, I'm surprised there isn't another funeral scheduled."

The guests seemed to be primarily college employees and friends of Malwick's sons and first family. Rachel didn't recognize anyone, and besides some college friends, neither did Carrie.

Organ music filtered into the room. Jeff O'Herlihy appeared and quietly announced that the service would soon begin. The guests, even those who hadn't been able to speak personally to the mourners, headed into the main chapel.

Mac's seat gave him a comprehensive view of the crowd. He'd made eye contact with Audrey Fieldstone as she'd entered and sat a few rows in front of him. Lenore Adams and another woman with blonde hair joined her a few minutes later. Mac made a mental note to find out who the woman was. Pete Fiori and an unusually conservatively clothed Roseanne took the seats behind them–no coincidence Mac mused. Greeley had probably assigned the pair to shadow Lenore–the only other person at Concordia besides Dan Thayer that the lieutenant considered worthy of special attention.

Roseanne looked back and smiled at him. He tried to ignore her–hoping she'd get the hint and pretend not to know him. Instead, she must have assumed he was blind. She gave him a little wave, stopping only when Pete slid his arm along the seat back and jerked her arm down.

Feeling another pair of eyes on him, Mac looked to the doorway and met Rachel Brenner's accusing gaze. Her eyes darted from him to Roseanne. Hell, he knew what she was thinking. Her expression said it all–she thought he was flirting with another man's wife. An uneasy feeling settled in his stomach and he reached into his suit pocket for the ever-present roll of Tums.

"Hi," a voice whispered in his ear as a female body tried squeezing in between him and the end of the pew.

He was forced to move over or risk having the person sit on his lap. Blinking, he looked into the grinning face of Lenore's secretary–Julianna something–JJ.

"Hi," he gruffly responded, irritated with himself for letting Rachel distract him. He tore off the end of the roll of antacids.

"The college gave us the afternoon off to come see old Malwick get planted. How's the investigation coming? Any hot leads?"

Mac considered the young woman. She still sported the blue fingernails and the spiked black hair. Instead of the cargo pants and boots, she wore a snug fitting black sweater, a very short black skirt, and black tights. The black ankle boots made her feet look half the size the work boots had. "Nothing too warm at the moment. How's things at the computer lab?" He popped a Tums into his mouth.

JJ sighed, and tugged on the knit skirt that threatened to roll up around her pencil thin waist. "Everything still feels off-balance. I hate it when things are out of harmony. Know what I mean?"

He offered the roll of Tums to JJ, surprised when she actually took one. He guessed heartburn was ageless.

Rachel and Carrie surveyed the crowded chapel, searching for two seats together, but found none.

"You take the one over by the plant," Rachel said softly, pointing to an open seat in the third row. "I'm going to sit back here. We'll meet in the lobby when it's over."

As the minister opened the service with a prayer, Rachel scanned the audience. She wasn't sure what to look for, but clearly the police thought something might happen. She'd recognized the detective named Tom, despite the black suit and a black armband marked O'Herlihy's, when he'd handed her a program. Probably some of the other guests were really just undercover cops, she mused, shifting her gaze from the right side to the left.

"What in the world is he doing here," she muttered, spotting a tall teen in an oversized jacket, his hair tied neatly back in a ponytail.

She watched as Ray slouched a little lower in his seat and hid his grease-stained fingernails in his borrowed jacket. Rachel stood with the congregation as the minister began reciting the Lord's Prayer. She tacked on a prayer asking God to protect her brother and if he wasn't too busy, could he consider stopping Ray from doing whatever idiot thing was in the boy's head.

Rachel stayed in her place, but was startled when she saw Ray join the line moving slowly toward the casket. She followed his progress and then noticed a spot of red in the line ahead of him.

Rachel narrowed her eyes. She had a scarf like the one on the tall woman with dark glasses. Not that she'd ever wear it to a funeral.

When Ray finally reached the casket, the woman with the scarf walked over to the far right aisle and paused as though to regain her composure. Ray briefly stopped in front of the casket, made the sign of the cross, and then quickly moved to the aisle–lining up behind the tall woman who began walking briskly toward the exits.

"What does he think he's doing," Rachel whispered to herself, watching Ray as he tripped and bumped into the woman, her red scarf sliding from her neck. She saw Ray's hand dip into the woman's raincoat pocket. Then he slid into a nearby pew, sitting down next to a startled Carrie.

"That's my scarf!" It finally dawned on Rachel what she'd just seen. The scarf lying on the chapel floor *was* hers. The last time she'd seen it was the night Dan had taken her out to dinner to celebrate his job at the university. Tired of its continual slide off the shoulders of her rayon suit, she'd taken it off and left it on his car seat.

Rachel stood and hurriedly scrambled over the feet of the people sitting between her and the aisle–the aisle her brother had just walked down in size twelve pumps.

Sixteen

When the viewing started, Mac left his seat and moved to stand by the back wall. Suddenly he tensed. Rachel Brenner was moving quickly down the center aisle, not stopping at the coffin to pay even the most minimal of respects. Instead, she headed for the far right aisle. She bent down to pick up the red scarf. When she looked up, she locked eyes with... Ray? Then, still clutching the red scarf, she headed for the exit.

"Shit!" He moved to intercept Rachel.

The line was packed with people filling the narrow aisle. He spotted Rachel's curly hair about three yards in front of him, almost at the door.

Rachel couldn't see her, him... Couldn't see Dan. With the funeral still technically in service, the entry hall was virtually empty. She stepped toward the coatroom. "Have you..." She stopped herself. She hadn't met all the employees yet. Maybe the coatroom attendant was an undercover cop. Just as she'd decided to head outdoors, Rachel felt someone grip her arm and spin her around.

"Where is he?" Mac hissed.

She struggled to slow her racing heart. "Who?"

"Your brother, dammit. Where did he go?"

"I don't know what you're talking about," Rachel sputtered.

"Mac, what did you see?" Tom Atwood raced up to join them. "Mrs. Brenner?"

"He's here or he was," Mac snapped. "Look for a woman, five-ten, 160 pounds, brown hair, wearing a tan raincoat."

Rachel glared at the private detective, but kept her silence.

Tom yanked out his walkie-talkie and quickly alerted all units. The hall became a beehive of activity, while the organ music swelled in the background. Suddenly the door to the main chapel opened, and the funeral home attendants pushed the casket out. Throngs of mourners followed the family. Rachel started to move away, but was held in place by the vise-like grip of Mac Sullivan.

"We're going to talk," he insisted.

"I've got nothing to say," Rachel retorted. "And if you don't let go of my arm this instant, I'm pressing charges."

"We can talk or you can accompany Ray Kozlowski down to headquarters when they take him in for questioning," a red-faced Mac warned.

Rachel froze, then nodded. Mac loosened his grip, and moved over to consult with Tom. The casket was being loaded into the hearse. The grieving widow and her "brother" were climbing into the first limo, with the Malwick family moving to ride in a second limo that Jeff O'Herlihy had thoughtfully provided. Throngs of mourners were crowding the front steps, but Rachel could see cops moving carefully through the crowd.

"Are you okay, Mrs. Brenner?" Carrie stood behind her, with Ray next in line.

"No." She glared at the two teens. "I've had it with people lying to me. Both of you were in on this–weren't you?"

"Carrie had nothing to do with anything," Ray hissed. "Go back to work, Carrie. I'll get Mrs. Brenner out of this."

"Not a chance," Carrie insisted. "I'm not going to leave–"

"Help us find him, Rachel. Someone is going to get hurt, if this keeps up." Mac Sullivan was suddenly at her side.

"I honestly have no idea where he is," Rachel said, thankful that for once she was telling the truth.

"Ray," the detective glared at the teen. "What did you give him? Was it that damn computer disk? And where is he now?"

The lanky mechanic shrugged his shoulders in reply.

"I'm not playing games here, kid."

"I don't know what you're talking about," Ray mumbled.

"Then what the hell are you doing at the funeral?"

"He came to swap cars with me. Mine's been stalling out constantly," Carrie offered.

"Oh, please," Mac snapped.

"It's true. Ask Mrs. Brenner. I called Ray this morning when it stalled again on the way to work and he offered to meet me and swap cars. He's gonna take my car to the garage and I'm driving Ray's truck home after work."

"Do you even know how to drive a truck?" Mac pushed.

"Of course. Girls know how to drive a shift," Carrie said impatiently. "Ray's gonna fix my car and bring it to me when we go to the movies tonight. We're gonna see a retrospective of the Terminator movies at the college."

Ray, who'd had his eyes glued to the floor, suddenly snapped his head up and grinned at the young woman.

"We found a brown wig and a pair of very large women's shoes in the Ladies Room, but no sign of Thayer," Greeley said, looking from Mac to the group waiting for him by the doorway. "Tell Mrs. Brenner and her kiddies they can go. But, Mac, you'd better find out what they know and quick. I've got more than enough right now to take them in for questioning."

Mac nodded and moved over to the wall where Rachel, Carrie, and Ray were huddled.

"Let's go to your office to talk," Mac murmured. "The lieutenant expects me to get back to him with some answers about what just happened here." Mac gave Carrie and Ray a warning look. "I'll catch up with you later."

Mac opened Rachel's door and waited while she and Whiskey made their way into the neat office. The dog settled down comfortably by the radiator, Mac moved to stand in front of her desk, waiting. A tense silence permeated the room. "Now, Rachel, now. We need to talk."

"You assume that we have something to say that the other wants to hear," Rachel snapped. She sat down behind her desk, and looked Mac square in the eyes. "Let me make this easy for you…for both of us."

Ticking off the points on her fingers, she said, "I didn't know my brother was going to the funeral. I don't know why he went to the funeral. I don't know where he is now. I don't know if I would tell you if I did, but in this case, it's not a problem because I honestly don't know."

"Okay. Tell me this. Why did you go to the funeral if not to meet him?" Mac countered, loosening the knot on his tie that seemed to have tightened on its own.

"It was in the same building? I thought Jeff might need my help?" Rachel shrugged. "Okay. I was there for the same reason you and the police were there. I wanted to see all the players in this nightmare."

"What about Carrie?" Mac asked, sitting down across from her.

Rachel leafed through some papers on her desk. "Carrie's very serious about her work. She wanted to see how Mr. Malwick's makeup held up under the lighting in the chapel."

"Right, don't play games with me. Why was she there? What does she know?"

"I don't know anything more than Mrs. Brenner." Carrie marched into the office carrying a vase of pink sweetheart roses. "These just came. They're for you," she said, putting the bouquet in front of her boss.

Rachel looked dubious. "Are you sure?"

"Absolutely, unless there's another Rachel Brenner who works at the O'Herlihy Funeral Home." Carrie grinned. "Aren't you going to see who they're from?"

Rachel hesitated then plucked the white envelope off the front of the vase. She scanned the enclosed gift card.

"Well?" Carrie asked, excitement dancing in her voice. "Who sent you roses?"

"No one you would know," Rachel said quickly. "Where's Ray?"

"His boss called and tore him a new one. He told me to tell you," she turned to face Mac, "that he had to go back to work before he lost his job. If you need him, call him after nine tonight."

Rachel stood. "Mr. Sullivan, is there anything else?"

"Sure there is. I've got a lot of questions and so far, no answers." Mac rubbed his shoulder; he still felt the effects of his tree-climbing stunt on Monday night.

"I told you what I know–which isn't much," Rachel insisted, fingering the card nervously.

"Do you know why Ray went to the funeral of a man he didn't know, and please don't start with the car repair story again." He shot a glare at the blonde teen who blushed and seemed to have a sudden urge to examine the state of her manicure.

"I was as surprised as you when I saw him," Rachel answered. She turned toward the Carrie. "Do you know why Ray was there?"

"Nope," Carrie said firmly. "I didn't even see him until he was suddenly sitting next to me."

"So you have no idea of what he passed to your brother," Mac pushed, keeping his gaze trained on the Rachel.

"I really don't," Rachel said. "And I don't want the kids involved anymore than you do. I sent Sam back to school today, so I'm hoping this is the end of it."

She narrowed her eyes, shifting her attention back to Carrie. "Carrie, if you know anything, I want you to tell Mr. Sullivan right now. I want all of you out of this mess."

"Tell me what Ray gave Dan Thayer," Mac ordered the young woman. "You were with him Tuesday night, weren't you? Does this have something to do with a computer disk?"

Carrie shifted uneasily under the detective's close scrutiny.

Rachel shook her head in annoyance. "Carrie! Whatever it is, tell him."

The teen took a deep breath, and said in a rush, "We downloaded one of Dan's files from the college computer system. I'm not sure why it was important, but Sam said Dan needed it. I think Ray gave Dan the disk with the file on it. Today. At the funeral." She glanced fearfully from Rachel to Mac. "Ray isn't in trouble, is he?"

"I don't know," Mac said, his face betraying nothing. If fear for Ray motivated the girl to tell him what was going on, he wasn't above using it.

His resolve lasted all of two seconds, the frantic protests of the two women and Whiskey's resulting whines causing him to gruffly admit, "Not yet."

The room got quiet.

"How did you get the files? Thayer's hard drive was impounded and his access to the college's network has been blocked," Mac asked, knowing the answer from his interrogation of the boys but wanting Rachel to hear it.

Carrie shrugged. "The files weren't stored in his computer. We used a backdoor into the college system."

"You did that in my house?" Rachel exclaimed, astonishment evident in her tone.

Carrie hesitated. "No. We kind of lied to you about going to the movies. Instead, we went to the Comptroller's office and used Mrs. Lopez's computer to access the files."

Rachel's face paled. "The woman who was killed? You were at the college? I thought Sam was joking about… You actually broke into…"

"No, no, we were there legitimately," the assistant said defensively.

Rachel looked doubtful, shifting her gaze from Mac to Carrie.

"It's a long story, but a friend of mine works in Mr. Malwick's office. We just volunteered to help her out with an accounting computer. Kind of a public service thing."

Rachel rolled her eyes and glanced at Mac who seemed lost in thought.

The detective broke his silence. "Did you see anyone near the office?"

"Besides the security guard when we entered the building, no. But lots of people had signed in the book," Carrie answered.

"No one at all?" he pushed, wondering how close they'd come to running into Angela Lopez's killer.

"No," Carrie said firmly, and then paused. "Not exactly. We didn't see anyone, but Ray heard the guard talking to some woman. They were on their way upstairs, so we left as fast as we could. We'd already hooked up the computer for Tia and copied the files. There was no need to hang around."

"What was in the files?" Mac demanded, wondering if she knew more than the boys.

"I honestly don't think there was much," Carrie admitted. "They were just orders for the Athletic Department–invoices for everything from soap and towels to office supplies."

Mac and Rachel both looked confused.

"Hey," the girl held both hands out, palms up, "I don't know what the big secret was either. Earlier, Sam had said something about his uncle proving he was being framed for some kind of computer scam, but I don't know what that has to do with purchases for the Athletic Department."

"When did Ray agree to meet Thayer?" Mac asked.

Carrie's eyes met his. "I don't know anything about that. Sam had the disk and planned to get it to his uncle at some point. Something must have happened after they left my place last night."

Mac was in the hallway and headed to the staircase when he heard Carrie ask, "Who sent the flowers, Mrs. Brenner?"

His feet seemed to stop of their own accord.

Whiskey looked up at him quizzically, but stood patiently waiting for him to continue.

Mac paused long enough to hear Rachel's soft answer, "Just an old friend named Roy."

Seventeen

It was dark, it was cold, and it was a gamble.

Mac sat in the 1996 Nissan that belonged to Sean O'Herlihy. After leaving the funeral home, he'd gone by Jeff's place to pick up a new set of wheels. He was sorry that Sean was in trouble again but glad to drive something decent for the night's stakeout. Whiskey laid stretched out, sound asleep, enjoying the back seat.

Mac had been parked at the end of the alley that exited on 29th Street for over an hour. He was hungry, cold, and the only one getting enough rest lately was his dog. And to top it all off, somehow he'd found himself in the middle of a double homicide, playing nursemaid to a bunch of kids and a prickly middle-aged woman.

At Mac's request Ray had returned to the funeral home for a little chat. Borrowing Rachel's office for the interrogation, he'd grilled the teen for half an hour about his funeral escapade. But most of what Ray told him wasn't anything he hadn't already figured out. Ray had reported that Sam had called him at six that morning and asked him to pick up the disk, telling him it would be hidden under a concrete garden troll in the neighbor's yard. Ray had gone on to explain that he'd had to borrow his boss' jacket for the funeral since he'd already been at work on an oil change when he got Sam's call. The teen had been apologetic that he hadn't been able to get all the grease out from under his nails before going to a funeral, explaining that he wasn't trying to "disrespect the dead guy."

Ray had revealed that he wouldn't have known Dan Thayer except that Sam had given him a heads up to look for the red scarf. The teen claimed he had no idea where Dan was now or how he got away.

The only useful thing Mac had gotten out of the whole interview was a glimpse at the photos arranged on Rachel Brenner's credenza, right next to the bouquet the woman had unexpectedly received earlier in the day. There were several photos of Sam, at different ages, and one with his Uncle Dan taken at an Orioles game at

Camden Yards. But what caught Mac's eye was a photograph in a Lucite frame of an elderly couple standing next to a young girl who had a head full of unruly brown curls. Next to them, a small boy astride a pony, clad in a cowboy hat and boots. Mac flipped over the frame: "Grandma, Grandpa, Rachel and Dan, Thayer Farms." The back of the photograph was stamped with the name of the store where the pictures had been developed: Rhodes Drug Store, Warrenton, Virginia.

So it was a hunch, and until he saw the headlights in the cold darkness, Mac had been wondering if he'd guessed wrong.

He watched the blue Dodge Caravan turn toward Connecticut Avenue. Not until the van was almost a block away did he turn on his own lights and pull out.

Mac dropped back further once they left the highway. There wasn't much traffic on Route 211 into Warrenton. He was counting on the dark night to hide his identity. Rachel had never seen him in this car. A black Nissan certainly blended in more easily than the bug-mobile, he thought.

Suddenly, he saw the blue van's blinking left turn signal. Rachel turned into the driveway of Napoleon's, a fancy restaurant that appeared to still be doing a brisk business despite the hour. Mac continued straight down the street, but quickly pulled over and doused his headlights. He watched Rachel get out of her car and head into the white Greek revival building.

He waited another minute before getting out, leaving a snoring Whiskey on the back seat. He clung to the shadows and peered in the restaurant's first floor window. More than half the tables in the softly lit room were filled, but he saw no sign of Dan Thayer or his sister. Mac moved down to a second window and glanced in. He considered his limited options and decided he didn't like any of them.

Walk into the restaurant and confront the siblings, if they were there. But suppose Thayer was armed and felt cornered?

Call for backup. But Mac didn't know the local police force and didn't have any standing in any case.

Wait outside for Rachel to come out, hopefully with her brother? But suppose Dan decided to exit out the back?

"Shit," he muttered. He ducked down under the window lintel and snuck around to the back of the building to check out the kitchen. Thayer had been a short-order cook. Maybe he'd found an old friend to hide him.

The backyard was dark except for the glow from the florescent fixtures in the kitchen. Deep shadows blanketed the lawn and a damp chill seeped into his bones. He inched along the back wall, moving closer to the kitchen window.

"Don't take another step." The voice was low, gravelly, and not ten feet away.

His heart skipped a beat, maybe three, before he dove behind the dumpster, fumbling for his gun.

"Shit," he muttered. His heart pounded hard and fast like a jackhammer on a city street; his breath coming heavy and ragged; his muscles ached as he plastered himself to the side of the metal garbage bin. He could hear footsteps moving closer. With both hands around his old service revolver, he leaped to a firing stance, his trigger finger twitching.

Rachel Brenner stepped out of the shadows and glared. Even in the dim light he could see her eyes flashing with unmitigated rage, quickly matched by his own.

"Are you an idiot? I almost shot you," Mac shouted. Realizing his hands were shaking, he lowered the gun and stuck it back into the shoulder holster under his jacket. "What the hell do you think you're doing? You could have gotten yourself killed. Stupid fool."

"What am I doing?" Rachel railed. "And who are you calling stupid?" She stepped closer, her face within inches of the detectives. "Why are you following me?"

"Don't be stupid."

"That's the second time you've called me stupid. Do it again and you'll be singing soprano in the church choir," she yelled.

Calming down, Mac prudently took a step back and put some distance between himself and Rachel's knees. "Where's your brother?"

"I don't know," she snapped.

"That's crap and you know it. What are you doing in Warrenton on a Thursday night if you're not meeting your brother?"

"None of your business. I can go anywhere I damn well please," she shouted. "But if you don't leave me alone, I'm going to get a restraining order against you." She glared at the private detective then spat out, "Do you think showing up in that death car is going to scare me into turning in my brother?"

"Death car? What the hell are you talking about woman? I didn't come within fifty feet of your precious van," Mac sputtered.

"You know exactly what I mean," Rachel insisted. "That's the car–or it's like the car we chased after that poor woman got…got killed."

Mac's jaw dropped and he was momentarily speechless. Then days of frustration finally boiled over. "Do you mean to tell me that you waited in the dark to confront whoever was driving the car or a car that looks like the one from the murder scene last night? You were going to what? Give the killer a piece of your mind? Lady, you *are* an idiot. Go ahead. Get yourself killed. Fat lot of good it will do your brother or son."

He turned and started to walk away, disgusted with the whole mess, but Rachel grabbed Mac's arm and spun him around. "Stay away from me and my family."

"You just don't get it," he growled. "I'm on your side. At least I have a more open mind about your brother's involvement than the cops do. If they find your brother before I do and he does something incredibly stupid, and given the way the rest of his family is acting I wouldn't be surprised…"

Rachel started to object, but kept silent when she saw the fierce look on Mac's face. His voice low, but firm, he added, "If your brother gives any hint of resistance, the cops will shoot him. They've got two murders on a big college campus to solve and they're not looking to make friends with the number one suspect on their list."

Rachel inhaled sharply and rubbed a hand over her face.

"Tell me where he is. Let me meet him and see if I can get him to turn himself in. I'll take him to Greeley myself," Mac urged.

Rachel stayed silent, weighing her options. Finally, taking a deep breath, she whispered, "I think he's holed up in the woods on our grandfather's farm. I'm meeting him in the barn."

"Take me there."

Rachel slowly nodded, then followed Mac as he led them back around the restaurant to her van.

"You have two flat tires," Rachel announced, dryly stating the obvious as the lights from her minivan illuminated the Nissan.

Mac turned his angry gaze from the Nissan's back tires to the woman in the driver's seat who was still staring in fascination at the disaster scene. "No kidding!"

"You have a lot of flat tires."

When he didn't respond, Rachel gave his darkening expression a quick glance.

Suddenly, he gasped. "Whiskey!"

Mac threw open the passenger door and, with a high school sprinter's speed, crossed the ten feet separating the van from the dark sedan.

She followed close on his heels.

The car was empty.

Eighteen

"Slow down!" Rachel stumbled as one foot caught the hidden edge of a grave marker. She stopped and leaned over, her hands on her knees, catching her breath. She was grateful that she'd chosen to wear her favorite purple Nikes for her meeting with Dan at the farm. If she'd worn the black pumps she'd started the day with, she'd be nursing a broken ankle at this point. She pulled up her jacket sleeve and pushed the button on the side of her watch, illuminating the dial– 12:05 a.m. She was already more than a half hour late. The irony of her attending a funeral at noon and running around a cemetery at midnight didn't escape her oxygen-starved mind as she worried about whether or not Dan would wait for her since Mac Sullivan certainly wasn't.

Straightening, Rachel glanced around her. The cemetery was a couple of blocks south and west of where their cars were parked. When the detective had discovered the broken passenger window and the unlocked door, he seemed to forget she was with him. She'd watched Mac take a flashlight out of the Nissan trunk and search the soft earth on the edge of the road. Then following some tracks that only he could see, he'd headed off into the night, all the while calling the dog's name. She'd debated for almost a minute whether to follow him or get back in her van and drive to the farm alone. It wasn't an easy decision, but worry over the dog won out. What if Whiskey were injured? How would Mac get the dog to a vet if she left him with a disabled vehicle? She might not care for the man, but she held no grudge against the dog.

"Mac?"

The wind was picking up and if he answered her, she didn't hear him.

"Mac? Where are you?"

A flash of lightening lit up the sky and she saw him for an instant. He was about 40 yards ahead of her, moving toward the back fence.

Hurrying, she reached the chain link fence just as the lightening flashed again. She was in time to see Mac bend down on one knee, his flashlight trained on a spot next to the roadway.

"Mac?"

She watched him turn toward her voice, then turn back round and pick something up off the ground. When he got to his feet, the light from his flashlight shone on a short piece of rope. She squinted, brushing the curls that were blowing around her face out of her eyes. No. Not a rope, she thought, her heart sinking. It was a leash–or rather part of one. A leather leash with a long grey hair clinging to the leather.

The detective walked stiffly toward her, his movements no longer belying his age, his expression one of grim exhaustion.

This time the thunder cracked the sky; torrents of rain followed the boom, drenching them both instantly.

Rachel didn't ask about the dog, just held out her hand to him as he neared. For a moment she didn't think he was going to take it, but then he ducked his head and the cold fingers of his right hand encased hers for the briefest moment.

With the pounding rain and his adrenaline seeming to slow, she didn't have any trouble staying close to him on the interminable trip back to the cars.

"Who do you think did this?" Rachel asked as they made their way through the graveyard. The raging storm had abruptly eased, leaving the rain a soft, but steady drizzle. The mud from the cemetery oozed in her sneakers and Rachel increasingly felt the cold from her rain-soaked clothes.

"I'm going to kill the bastard," Mac growled.

"Who?"

"If he so much as touches a hair on her…"

"Who?" She yelled again and yanked on his coat, trying to get him to stop.

Mac shook her off and picked up his pace.

Rachel reached for her cell phone. "Do you want me to call AAA?" She hustled to catch up with him.

Mac shook his head. "I don't belong to…"

"I do. We'll give my..."

He put up his hand to silence her.

"Look you can't leave the car on..."

"Shut up," Mac said sharply, stopping in his tracks.

"Excuse me?" Rachel snapped back.

He cocked his head, listening to the night sounds.

Rachel heard the rumble of a passing car on the highway about twenty-five feet ahead.

Suddenly, Mac began running.

"What's the matter now?" Rachel yelled, trying to keep up with him, but failing as he quickly outpaced her. She slipped on the wet grass but caught herself on the edge of a gravestone, banging her knee in the process. She struggled to right herself and half-limped, half-ran the last ten feet to the highway.

She saw Mac huddled on the ground next to her van. A keening sound filled the air.

"Are you okay?" she called as she neared his position. "Oh my God."

Ignoring her bruised knee, Rachel knelt down and brushed her hand lightly over the Irish wolfhound's body. Whiskey flinched when Rachel touched the dog's right hip, then struggled to stand.

"*Shh*, stay girl," Mac whispered, quickly removing the leather muzzle and the remains of the broken leash from the dog.

Whiskey settled back down, her muffled howls turning to whimpers.

"I've got a blanket and some bottled water in the car," Rachel said, getting to her feet. "How badly is she hurt?"

"No obvious wounds. Her hip seems tender," Mac said, feeling carefully along the dog's body. "I need to get her to a vet. But this time of night it–"

"We can take her to this emergency animal hospital in Rockville. It's open. We took our cat there when she got sick after eating my husband's wedding ring. I should have wondered then why it was on the nightstand instead of his finger," Rachel sniffed. "Anyway, there's a vet available all night."

Mac nodded and gingerly lifted Whiskey into the van, stretched her out on the bench seat in the back and tucked the blanket around her. He also tossed the muzzle onto the floorboard.

"Who did this?" Rachel had held off asking until they were well underway.

"Not sure," Mac said gruffly.

Rachel glanced in the rearview mirror. "Why?"

"Why what?"

"Why would someone take Whiskey? It's not like she just got out. That leash and muzzle means someone tried to kidnap her."

Mac didn't answer.

Rachel glanced again in the mirror, but the private detective was lost in thought, staring out into the darkness as his fingers tenderly trailed through the big dog's hair. She turned her attention back to the rain-slicked road.

"How's she doing?" she asked after another ten minutes had elapsed.

"Quieter," Mac said softly. "She's taken a little water…"

"Not too much," Rachel quickly interjected.

"She's breathing better," he added.

"Good." She paused and then said, "Who did you think did this?"

"I said I didn't know," Mac answered sharply.

"But you thought you did. In the cemetery. You said you'd kill the bastard," Rachel insisted. "Is this connected to the murders?"

"No. I think it's connected to a wannabe exterminator."

She glanced in the rear-view mirror. "Exterminator? A Hit Man?"

Mac shook his head, his expression grim. "No. A Bug Man."

Nineteen

"Hello? Is anyone here?"

Banging his head on the underside of the desk, Mac swallowed a curse and with all the grace of a crippled cow, pulled himself to a standing position. Two hours of sleep and too much coffee hadn't improved his disposition.

"Hi. Sorry if I..." Julianna Jarrett, dressed in her black funeral outfit minus the boots, used a rolled newspaper to point toward the desk and the computer boxes filled with packing foam scattered around it. "New computer?"

"Yeah." Mac blinked a couple of times, thinking maybe he'd hit his head harder than he'd thought. He couldn't think of any reason why Lenore Adams' secretary would be standing in his barely furnished office. He stared at her feet. Black high-top sneakers. Interesting choice with the black tights and short skirt.

"Mr. Sullivan?"

Mac raised his eyes from his contemplation of a time when shoes like that belonged only to teenage boys pounding up and down a basketball court. The young woman looked at him as though he'd missed part of the conversation. Maybe he had. Clearing his throat, he said, "This is a surprise. What can I do for you?"

JJ smiled. "I'm here for my job interview."

Mac's eyebrows moved upwards an inch. "What job?"

"The secretary job. The one you advertised in the newspaper," JJ added when Mac's blank expression didn't change.

He shrugged. "Must be a mistake. I didn't place an ad."

She unrolled the college newspaper and showed him the circled lines.

He couldn't see the print but noticed an angry red scratch on the palm of the girl's right hand.

"Hey, Mr. Sullivan? You still with me?"

"What?" He definitely needed to get some sleep–soon.

"The old guy at the funeral home told me to come over here at 5 p.m. I think I might have woken him up. Maybe he forgot to call you."

"Let me see that!" Mac squinted at the small print, self-consciously grabbing a pair of reading glasses off the desk. "Secretary/Assistant wanted for PI's office. Must like dogs and changing tires. Computer skills a plus. Salary based on commission. Inquire at O'Herlihy's Funeral Home for appointment."

JJ tugged on her skirt and walked around behind the desk, taking a look at the cords he'd been trying to attach to the back of the hard drive. "What's that mean? Salary based on commission?"

Mac turned to watch her. "How would I know? I didn't place the ad. Some crazy Irishman who decided to meddle in my business is behind this."

"Oh." JJ looked disappointed. "You don't need a secretary? 'Cause I think it would be pretty cool to work for a private detective. I know how to change tires. I mean, it's not like it's one of my favorite things to do, but it's not a problem if that's what you're worried about."

Mac chuckled. "Jeff was making a little joke with the tire thing. You wouldn't have to change any tires."

"What would I do?"

"You–no, wait!" He held up a hand in protest. "There is no job. I can't afford a secretary and I sincerely doubt my good friend Jeff is planning on picking up your salary. Sorry."

JJ disconnected a couple of power cords and reconnected them in different places. Then she sat down behind the desk and powered up the unit, waking up the monitor he'd been trying to turn on for the past two hours.

"I could set this up for you. Take about twenty minutes." She smiled. "Bet you have something else you'd rather be doing."

Mac grunted. He needed to make a dinner meeting with the Widow Malwick and he should check in with Rachel–see if she'd admit to any more contact with her brother–maybe apologize for his manners the night before. He also needed to pick Whiskey up from the vet's before the night was over. When he and Jeff had dropped by the clinic earlier the doc had insisted Whiskey stay until he got some blood test results back. Mac looked around at the computer and the half-unpacked boxes littering the room and considered that maybe he could use a secretary–just on a trial basis. See how it went.

Mac cleared a spot and sat down on the edge of the desk. "Are you still working at the college?"

JJ shook her head. "I quit yesterday. Lenore missed an important meeting and I got chewed out for not reminding her. Hey, it was on her desk calendar and is it my fault she hadn't listened to her voice mail in over a week? If she'd come into work once in awhile I'd have told her in person. Anyway, I'd had enough–more than enough."

"Lenore hasn't been into work lately?" He wondered how closely Greeley was keeping track of the Computer Lab Director's comings and goings. Maybe he'd better give him a call, plus with JJ's job vacant the lieutenant might want to slip a cop in undercover.

The young woman's fingers danced over the keyboard and a menu of preloaded programs appeared. "No. The last few days, I've talked to her housemate more than I've talked to her. Lenore's hardly been in at all since Malwick's murder. I think she's either got a new boyfriend or is having a nervous breakdown." JJ looked up and smiled. "With some people it's hard to tell the difference."

"I know I've asked you this before, but maybe now that you don't work for the lady, your memory might have improved. Did Lenore and Dan Thayer have a personal relationship?"

JJ shifted her eyes back to the screen, leaving Mac to stare at the shaved spot over her ear.

"JJ? This is important."

She sighed. "Yeah. Well. Maybe. I mean it's not like I ever saw them going at it or anything but there were vibes. And he was always calling her."

Mac nodded, thinking he'd get Ray to translate for him later. "Okay. Thanks."

He got to his feet and walked over to a file cabinet pushed against the far wall, removing an overstuffed file folder. "If you can collect payment on these jobs I finished last month, you're hired. I can't pay you much yet, but I'll give you $400 a week plus five percent of what you collect for me every month. If you want health insurance, research some options and if you're still here in six months, we'll renegotiate. In the meanwhile, you set up an accounting system that will keep me out of IRS hot water, take phone messages, and schedule appointments. No guarantees. We'll try it for a month or two and see how we get along."

"Six percent."

He frowned, but nodded.

JJ grinned. "Do I get to carry a gun?"

Mac grabbed his jacket off a nearby chair. "First, let's see how much money you can collect without it. I'll be back later. When you leave, lock the door behind you. There's a spare set of keys in the desk."

She nodded–her smile firmly in place.

"How's your steak?" Gina Malwick asked, eyeing the half-eaten slab of beef still covering most of the surface area of his plate.

Mac put down his fork. "Fine. But there's too much of it; seems like they made a mistake with my order and gave me the whole steer. I can feel my arteries clogging as we sit here."

Gina gave him a slight smile and took another bite of her salmon. Swallowing, she commented, "Vince loved their steaks. This was his favorite restaurant."

Mac had been waiting for the right moment to broach the subject of her dead husband. This appeared to be it. "When was the last time you and Vince were here?"

"Last week–Wednesday night. He had the prime rib and pie for dessert." She paused for a moment, then added, "Apple."

Wondering if she really thought he was interested in the menu, Mac reviewed what he knew about Vince's second wife, Gina Woodward Malwick: twenty-seven years old; former model and spokesperson for a local car dealership; and Concordia College alumna.

"How did you meet Vince?" Mac sipped at his beer, watching her face for clues as to her true feelings about her deceased husband. He knew the answer to his question–Gina had met Vince when she'd starting working in the Accounting Department while she was still a student. His research indicated that Gina wasn't the first or the last student to get some extra attention from old Vince during his tenure at the college. What Mac didn't know was if Vince's philandering had concerned his young wife?

Gina laughed and flipped her blonde hair over her shoulder. "At the college. He was the worst boss I ever had. A stickler for time–he docked me for every minute I was late getting to work and then wouldn't trust me to do anything but filing."

"Doesn't sound like love at first sight." Mac prompted.

"Hardly." Gina dabbed at her lips with her napkin leaving angry red slashes of lipstick on the linen cloth. "I couldn't stand him or the old bat that worked for him."

Mac's eyes were drawn to the stain, the red reminding him of the blood covering Angela Lopez's face. "You're referring to Mrs. Lopez?"

"Yeah. She was a real bitch." Gina's face flushed with emotion. "She was always watching me. Criticizing what I did and how I dressed. And anytime I'd go into Vince's office, she'd be two steps behind. I think she was jealous of my relationship with him."

"Doesn't sound like you had much of a relationship. When did," Mac's voice trailed off as he tried to decide how best to ask when sex with her boss was added to her job description.

"Oh, go ahead and say it. You're not the first to think I slept with Vince before I graduated–and before he was divorced," Gina bitterly exclaimed. "His ex-wife has certainly told anyone and everyone that I'm a slut. But it didn't happen. Vince and I got together a couple of years later when he came into the car dealership while I was there shooting a commercial." She picked up her wine glass and took a healthy swallow. "To celebrate his divorce, he bought the latest model BMW and asked me to dinner. We were married a month later."

"Why?"

"Why what?" Gina switched glasses. She sipped her Perrier, then plucked out the lemon slice and popped it in her mouth. Mac winced at the tartness he could almost taste.

"Wasn't it sort of a whirlwind romance considering you thought he was…that he had been…that Vince wasn't exactly…"

"Why did I marry a son of a bitch like Vince?" She smiled demurely.

"Well, yeah."

"Okay. Maybe I didn't exactly love him when I married him. But we had a good life together."

"Perhaps you shared a love of opera? Or drag racing?" Mac finished his beer and waited, hoping she'd continue. He also hoped his skepticism at her Cinderella story wasn't etched on his face.

Gina laughed. "Hardly, but we did share a love of fine wine."

He watched as she switched glasses again and sipped some Chateau St. Jean Merlot.

"We both adored five-star hotels in the Caribbean with room service at midnight, and to be honest..." She stared into Mac's eyes, "Vince ranked in the top twelve of the best lays I ever had."

Mac dropped the roll he'd started to butter, then struggled to recover. "Didn't crack the top ten?"

"No, but that one time in Aruba..."

Mac held up his hand. "Thanks for sharing. So Vince was a loving husband who will be sorely missed and..."

"Absolutely not," Gina interrupted. "The son of a bitch stole my money."

Mac's head snapped up. "Your money?"

"Damn right," Gina said sharply. "In the five years I'd been modeling, I'd managed to save close to a hundred thousand dollars. My money, in my name. Vince understood that from the get-go. Anyway, last February Vince tells me about a real estate deal he thinks is going to pay off big. Suggested I put my money to work instead of just hanging around in Treasury Bonds. The deal sounded good. Basically it was picking up on the cheap some crummy condos in this building out on Sixteenth Street. But Vince knew that Jack Starling was planning on buying the whole building and turning it into a luxury apartment house. It was going to be a fast flip on money and Vince promised...son of a bitch convinced me to put my money into the deal and..."

"Starling is a trustee of the college, right?" Mac asked, wondering if Starling was the man Lenore mentioned that Gina had her sights set on. He also made a mental note to round up a photo of Starling. Greeley might be satisfied with the guy's alibi but it wouldn't hurt for him to double-check a few things.

"Yeah. He and Vince had chatted at a trustee meeting and it

seemed like a sure thing."

"But…."

"But the son of a bitch put his name and his name only on the deeds. I'd found them when I went through his desk last Thursday. I couldn't figure why I hadn't heard from Starling's company since they had started buying out the current owners, so I decided to look around a little. Didn't take me that long to pry open that bottom drawer and discover that Vince was about to make a fortune with my money."

"And you?"

"And I was going to earn zero. Me who'd stood on a freezing soundstage in a yellow polka dot bikini hawking time shares in Kissimmee, I was going to end up with zip. Hell no." Gina said, bitterness oozing from every pore. "I confronted him that night. He claimed it was all a clerical mistake. He was going to take care of it. Like I was going to believe him. I learned a long time ago, the only one who takes care of Gina is Gina."

"Did he change the title on the apartments on Friday before he was killed?"

Gina reached for a roll and a butter pat. "I have no idea, but of course, it doesn't really matter now." She slathered the butter on the bread, took a bite, and smiled. "His will specifies that I inherit all property."

Ray hesitated. "I'm not sure we should just show up."

"You're paying him. Shouldn't he be giving you some kind of report every day?"

"I'm not sure you get that kind of service when you've only put down a dollar. Besides I think I fired him." Ray picked at the scab on his thumb, staring resolutely at the worn rubber treads on the steps. He hated arguing with Carrie, but he wasn't sure about this. In fact, that was wrong. He was absolutely sure that they shouldn't just show up at Mr. Sullivan's office, which was exactly what they were doing.

The two teens had been walking up the long flight of steps to the private detective's office when Ray stalled on the fourth step from the landing and voiced his objections one more time.

"You didn't give him written notice. You can't fire him without it," Carrie pressed, but Ray just gnawed on his lower lip and refused to move.

Carrie tried a different tack. "With Mrs. Brenner out sick today, we need to know what's going on before we call Sam. He's worried sick about his uncle and might end up dropping out of school if we don't take care of things down here."

She left the thought hanging in the air. Then without a word, Ray marched past Carrie and knocked on the office door with the hand-drawn sign, Sullivan Investigations.

"Come in."

Carrie and Ray exchanged confused glances at the feminine voice that invited them to enter, then walked in.

They stopped just inside the doorway.

"We're looking for Mr. Sullivan," Carrie declared.

"He's not here," the girl at the computer said without looking up.

"When will he be back?" Carrie asked.

"Don't know."

"Where is he?" Carrie pushed.

"None of your business."

"Let's go," Ray whispered, his hand on Carrie's arm, pulling her out the door.

The blonde shook off the restraint and marched across the room.

"Don't you go to Concordia?"

JJ slowly looked up and faced her questioner. She remained silent.

"Don't I know you from–from…Maguire's lit class?" Carrie insisted.

JJ stared at her for a moment, then let her eyes drift over to the doorway where Ray stood, one foot out in the hallway.

"Can I help you?" she asked, a small smile hovering at her lips.

"I was–we were–I need to see Mr. Sullivan," Ray sputtered.

"He's out of the office. Would you like to leave a message?"

"I'm not sure," Ray said hesitantly.

Carrie interrupted, "Tell him that Carrie Taylor and Ray Kozlowski want to talk to him."

JJ never took her eyes off the shy mechanic. "How do you spell your last name and where did you get the ankh?"

Ray's eyes widened and he moved his fingers to the heavy metal pendant that hung around his neck from a silver chain. With a small smile he said, "It's K-O-Z-L-O-W-S-K-I, and my mother gave it to my father when they got married."

"Do you know what it means?" JJ asked.

"Yeah, it's supposed to symbolize health and happiness, something like that," Ray answered, still rubbing the heavy pendant between his fingers.

"It was found in ancient Egyptian tombs. Kind of like the key to life. I have one too." JJ reached under her black T-shirt and pulled out a similar necklace.

"I never knew anyone else who had one," Ray said, moving closer to the desk.

"If you could just have Mr. Sullivan call me," Carrie said sharply. "He can reach me at the funeral home. He has the number."

"Does he have your number?" JJ asked, looking at Ray and continuing to ignore Carrie.

"Um, I'm not sure. I'll give it to you. It's 555-8706. That's my work number."

"It won't be your work number for long if you start getting calls there," Carrie interrupted. "Have Mr. Sullivan call me. Mrs. Brenner won't mind." She grabbed Ray by the arm and pulled him toward the door.

"I'll have Mr. Sullivan get in touch," JJ said, looking directly at Ray. "Or I'll follow up myself."

Carrie closed the office door with a flourish.

Sitting inside Sean's recently repaired car, parked in the lot outside the Nissan service department, Mac flipped his cell phone shut and replaced it in his jacket pocket. He turned to the occupant of the passenger seat. "Well, girl. The lieutenant is going to talk with Ms. Fieldstone tomorrow morning about getting a detective into Lenore Adams' office. Do you remember Bobbie? Greeley is going to pass her off as a student aide."

Whiskey tried scratching behind one ear, but Mac could see that her injuries made the movement painful. The vet had told him that there was nothing broken, just deep bruising. Whiskey would be walking gingerly for a few days. The blood tests hadn't shown any drugs in the dog's system but the vet suspected something had been used to subdue the dog. Mac agreed. Otherwise, Whiskey would never have let a stranger, or a friend for that matter, put a muzzle on her.

Whiskey whined and Mac reached over and scratched for her. She closed both eyes and made a deep sound indicating her satisfaction with his solution.

"Wish you'd give me a clue as to who took you out of this car last night." Mac stroked the top of her head, and then behind her ear again. "But hey, back to Bobbie. I'm thinking that as Lenore's new secretary, she might be able to pick up a lead on Dan Thayer. If JJ's vibe meter is any good, Dan and Lenore must be staying in touch somehow."

Whiskey growled, turning her head so he could reach her other ear.

"Yeah, I know. Could be the other way around–Lenore's the killer and Dan's just a patsy for her. She certainly has knowledge about the computer contracts and the ability to hack into the college accounting records."

Whiskey whined.

"Okay, but even if Dan didn't shoot Malwick and Lopez, he's gonna take the rap for it if he stays on the run. It's past time to bring him in."

The dog opened her eyes and gave a short bark.

"You're right. It's late, but I bet she's still up. Let's go see how Rachel's doing."

Twenty

Deciding to indulge herself, Rachel poured another capful of bubble bath into the steaming water before stepping into the old claw-footed tub. There had been no money to remodel the bathroom when she'd inherited the house. Now, she realized with an ironic smile, the old fashioned tub had come back into vogue. Maybe she'd get it re-glazed when she saved up some money.

Sinking up to her chin in the lilac-scented water, she double-checked that her cordless phone and cell phone were within reach. She'd waited all day for Dan's call; she wasn't going to miss it now.

Snickers watched from her perch on the vanity, the sounds of contented purring echoing off the bathroom tiles.

Rachel squeezed a blob of lilac bath gel onto a loofah and soaped up her arms and legs, noticing the large bruise on her knee from her close encounter with the gravestone.

"You're lucky I didn't break my neck–running around in the dark, trying to keep up with that man. Not that he even gave me a thank-you for hauling him and his dog over to the vets."

The cat spread her paws and licked each talon, ignoring the ruminations of her housemate.

"I don't care how worried he was. A simple thank you..." Moving the sponge to her feet, Rachel noticed her toenails needed polishing, badly. And her fingernails. "A hair cut too," she mused, an imaginary 'to do' list taking shape.

"Snickers remind me to tell Sam that I used some of the bath gel he got me for Mother's Day."

The cat looked up and stared, her expression reproachful.

"Hey." Rachel flicked a bubble at her.

Snickers hissed indignantly and then turned around to face the mirror.

Well, maybe not, Rachel considered, closing her eyes and mentally counting back the number of months since he'd presented her with it–two Mother's Days ago. Reclining backwards in the water, she rested her head against the porcelain and wondered where the days were going.

Even before this mess with Dan, time had been slipping away from her. She seemed to always be too busy to do all the things she intended to do, all the things she needed to do. All the things that cost money that she didn't have. She refused to ask Aunt Ella for help. Her finances were her own problem. Still it was a struggle to find the money for Sam's tuition and maintenance on the house.

Bored, Snickers stood and arched her back, stretching, before curling up in the sink basin.

Rachel sank deeper into the fragrant water. Her van needed a tune-up, probably more. She was going to break her neck if she didn't change the light bulb in the fixture above the stairs. She might break her neck changing it. Then there were the little things–renewing her TV Guide subscription, buying a new fern… There was never a minute she could call her own. There was no time for leisurely bubble baths. Now with Dan's situation and…

She sat up and leaned forward. Squeezing the loofah over one shoulder, she let the hot water and suds slide down her tense back. Repeating the action, she tried to shut off her mind and concentrate on the feel of the water flowing over her aching muscles. Charlie used to wash her back for… No! No, no, no, she wasn't going to take that route down memory lane. Not now. Not ever.

Okay. She straightened. Maybe she really wasn't the leisurely bath type. A five-minute shower in the morning left no time for this kind of depressing introspection. The commercials had it all wrong. Who could relax and drift away with all… The sound of the doorbell interrupted her analysis.

The cat's head popped up above the sink rim.

"Snickers, we have company. Thank, God."

Mac realized immediately that he'd gotten her out of the bath. The smell of flowers rushed out the open door, enveloping him and Whiskey. He took a deep breath. Whiskey sneezed.

"Hello. This is a surprise. Don't you guys ever sleep?"

He shrugged, a grin growing on his craggy face as he looked at her. Rachel's hair was pinned up–mostly. Several long curls had escaped and threatened to topple the rest. Her face was damp; the lack of makeup exposing a smattering of freckles, and the long baseball jersey and sweat pants looked as though she'd hurriedly thrown them on. The faded T-shirt was turned wrong-side out.

When he didn't say anything, Rachel blushed, a hand going toward her haphazard topknot. "What?"

"Blame Whiskey," Mac quickly asserted, realizing he'd been caught staring. "I told her it was too late to visit but she wanted to thank you for taking care of her last night."

Rachel smiled and held out a hand to the dog. "How are you, girl? Have you recovered from your adventure?"

The dog stepped forward and licked her hand.

"How is she?" Rachel asked, kneeling down and carefully stroking the dog's head.

"Bruised, but otherwise okay. The vet thinks she was drugged but couldn't find any hard evidence for me. The blood tests were negative."

"Shouldn't she be home resting? Shouldn't you? You look terrible."

Rachel gazed up at him in concern and Mac realized that his lack of sleep in the past forty-eight hours was showing. Or maybe the fact that he hadn't seen his razor since the day before was the problem.

"We were on our way home. I just wanted to check on you."

"Would you like to come in?" Rachel gave Whiskey one last pat and stood.

"No. We should..." Mac paused as Whiskey disappeared into the interior of the house. "Where's your cat?"

A yowl and a short yelp from the direction of the kitchen answered his question.

Rachel shook her head and motioned him inside. "Don't worry, Snickers can take care of herself."

Mac frowned and strode past her. "It's not Snickers that I'm worried about."

* * *

Whiskey nudged his knee and whined, the angry scratch on her nose a testament to her failure to make friends with the cat.

"You've had a rough week all right. Maybe you should stick

around the office until I get through with this case. Did I tell you I hired a secretary?"

"Are you talking to me or to your dog?" Rachel asked carrying in a tray loaded with a coffee carafe, cups, and a plate of cookies.

Rising, Mac took the tray and set it on the low table in front of the sofa. "Sorry. I have a habit of talking to Whiskey; it's my way of thinking out loud."

Rachel chuckled, sitting down on the sofa and indicating he should do the same. "Talking to a dog looks saner than talking to yourself. Carrie catches me at it quite often at the funeral home."

"Is your cat–"

"Snickers is on top of the refrigerator, feeling victorious. She's not a big fan of dogs."

Mac broke off a piece of oatmeal cookie and offered it to the dog. "I think Whiskey understands that now."

Rachel poured him a cup of coffee. "Do you use cream or–"

"No. Black is fine."

"You mentioned something about a secretary? It occurs to me that I know less about you than Whiskey knows about Snickers."

"Jeff O'Herlihy decided that it was past time I had some office help. He ran an ad and sent someone over this afternoon. Since I knew the girl, I hired her on a temporary basis. Actually, you might have noticed her at Malwick's funeral. She sat beside me."

Rachel grinned. "The girl with the shaved head?"

"Only part of it is shaved–a strip over one ear," Mac protested. He unthinkingly reached out and touched the relevant spot on Rachel's head.

He froze, staring at his finger as a brown curl seemed to wrap itself around it.

Rachel cleared her throat, effectively breaking the spell, and he dropped his hand back to the sofa cushion.

"How do you know her?" she asked, her voice cracking.

Mac faced forward and picked up his coffee cup. He took a swallow of coffee, feeling a little lightheaded. He knew he needed to get some sleep; he was definitely losing it.

"Mac?"

"Huh?"

"How do you know her? Your new secretary?"

"She worked at the college in the Computer Department." Mac considered his next words carefully. He trained his gaze on Rachel's face, watching for a reaction. "She worked for your brother's girlfriend–Lenore Adams."

Rachel opened her mouth and then closed it.

A thump from the kitchen attracted both their attentions.

Whiskey gave a short bark, rising to her feet.

"Snickers." Rachel stood and picked up the tray. "Let me feed her and then you can explain that last statement."

"Can I help you with that?" He pointed to the tray.

"Just stay here and keep Whiskey occupied. I don't think she's in any condition to go another round with my cat."

Mac and the dog watched her push through the swinging kitchen door. Both flinched a second later at the sound of breaking glass.

"Rachel?" Mac got to his feet, his fingers curling around Whiskey's collar to keep her by his side.

Her voice came through the door. "Everything is fine. I just dropped a cup. Stay where you are, I'll be right out."

Mac sat back down, glancing at Whiskey. "I think the mention of Lenore's name made her nervous. What do you think?"

Whiskey barked again, her eyes trained on the door.

Rubbing the knot that was forming at the base of his neck, Mac grimaced at the dog's bark. "Oh, come on. Get your mind off that damn cat."

"Hey, Sis. Any more of those oatmeal cookies? Or did you feed them all to your boyfriend?" A scruffy-looking Dan Thayer stuffed a cookie between his teeth and opened the refrigerator door, pulling out a half-empty carton of milk.

"Are you *crazy*? Lower your voice. He's not my boyfriend." Rachel quickly bent over and picked up the broken coffee cup that had slid off the tray when she'd come to an abrupt stop after catching sight of him sitting on her kitchen counter.

"I don't know. You two looked pretty cozy in there. Did you know your shirt is on inside out? How did that happen?" Dan raised his eyebrows and then laughed at her disgruntled expression.

Rachel looked down at her T-shirt and sighed. No wonder Mac had looked at her funny. "Mac is a detective hired by the college's insurance company. He's working with the police to find you. How did you get here? Is your car–"

He looked to the left and mumbled, "A friend dropped me off."

Rachel snapped to attention. "Who dropped you–"

"Don't worry about it. Nobody saw me. Tell me about your detective." He finished the last of the cookies he'd found in a jar on the counter. "It's after 10:00 p.m. The insurance company must be paying him really well."

She frowned at her brother, then took a glass from the cabinet and deftly grabbed the milk carton seconds before his lips touched the spout. She filled his glass and quickly replaced the carton in the refrigerator. "Here, drink this in the pantry. You need to hide until I get rid of him. Then I have a few things to say to you and you're going to explain to me how the hell you got into this mess."

Dan grinned. "It's nice to see you again, too. How come you never showed the other night?"

"I decided to take a moonlight stroll through a cemetery instead." She grabbed a cookie tin from the top of the refrigerator and handed it to him. "Here, knock yourself out. But do it quietly."

"Is the cat okay?" The detective watched Rachel's return with some concern. She seemed...agitated was the word that came to his mind.

"What?" She perched on the arm of an overstuffed chair, located at right angles to the sofa.

"Is the cat okay?" He repeated, a frown appearing on his face.

Rachel glanced over her shoulder toward the kitchen and gave him a quick smile. "She's fine. It was just a cup."

"The cat broke a cup too?"

"What?" She stared in confusion at him. "Oh the noise–before?"

Mac nodded, his attention diverted for a moment as Whiskey tensed and stared at the kitchen door.

Rachel shifted uneasily, her eyes on the dog.

"The noise?" he prompted, stroking Whiskey's head and urging the dog to lie down.

"No, I broke a cup. Snickers…she just…" Rachel stopped, her face flushing red.

He gave Rachel an encouraging look. "She just what?"

"Just knocked a can onto the floor," she said in a rush.

"Tuna, I'm guessing," Mac joked, wondering if her mind was dissolving or if the news of her brother's relationship with Lenore Adams was the cause of her obvious distress.

"Huh?"

"The can?"

"What can?"

Mac shook his head, deciding to cut to the chase before the woman broke out in hives. "Why don't you tell me what you know about Lenore Adams? Was she the woman who was going on vacation with your brother? And besides the affair–is Dan involved in some kind of fake invoice scheme with that woman?"

"No." Rachel bounced to her feet and began pacing the living room. "No to all your questions. Why do you insist on believing the worst of Dan? He's not a criminal; he's not a murderer. Why aren't you out there investigating? Out there finding the truth?"

Whiskey whined and strained against the fingers Mac had wrapped around her collar to keep her at his side.

"Tell me what you know about Lenore," Mac demanded. "How long has Dan been involved with her? Is he still in contact with her?"

Rachel made a dismissive gesture with her hand. "I don't know Lenore Adams. I don't know that Dan knows Lenore Adams. Why don't you ask her these questions? In fact why don't you go ask her right now and leave me in peace?"

Mac narrowed his eyes in consternation, but held his tongue. He didn't know what he'd said to set her off and at the moment he didn't really care. He did know she was giving him a headache and he was operating on far too little sleep to deal with her temper.

Rachel continued her rant, her words picking up speed at the same time as her feet. She marched over to the front door and flung it open. She turned to face him, her voice strident. "I'm sick and tired of looking up and finding you on my doorstep, or worse yet, following me around. I've got my own problems without you trying to make me responsible for finding my brother. You want my brother–get out there and find him yourself."

The detective gladly got to his feet, but before he could make his escape, the open doorway next to Rachel filled with people.

"Hi, Mrs. Brenner. Hi, Mr. Sullivan," Carrie said with a grin, walking into the house. "Are you two having a fight? We could hear the shouting from the street." Ray followed her, his hands stuffed in his back pockets, embarrassment etched across his face.

Whiskey continued to sit next to the sofa, her brown eyes following the action, but returning time and again to stare at the kitchen door, a soft growl marking her discontent.

Rachel swallowed hard and avoided everyone's eyes. "This isn't a good time for me. Maybe everyone could go home now and I'll set aside an hour tomorrow at the funeral home for an interrogation. You can all show up and question me to your heart's content."

Ray's expression changed from embarrassment to mortification. "See, Carrie! I told you we should have called first. You said yourself she took a sick day." Ray tugged on Carrie's elbow. "Sorry, Mrs. Brenner. We're out of here."

Carrie shrugged off his hand. "Don't tell me what to do Raymond Kozlowski. I have something important to discuss with Mrs. Brenner. And I need to talk to Mr. Sullivan about the case. Sam was counting on at least one of us to come through for him." She pulled her cell phone out of her purse and tossed it to him. "Maybe you should go wait in the truck. Here's my cell phone, since you misplaced yours at the kennel. Go call your new girlfriend, while I take care of business."

"She's not my girlfriend. Geez, Carrie. I don't even know her."

"But you want to know her. Guess maybe you'd pay me more attention if I shaved my head."

Mac, who'd been working his way around the arguing kids in his quest for the door and freedom, paused. "Are you talking about JJ? Have you been to my office tonight?"

Ray nodded. "A girl was working on your computer. We didn't get her name."

"Not because Ray wasn't interested," Carrie mumbled, walking farther into the room and plopping down on the sofa next to Whiskey.

"He thinks she–"

Pointedly ignoring Carrie's comment, Ray interrupted with," We wanted to know if you'd found any leads. Sam was already worried and then when Mrs. Brenner didn't go to work today, he about lost it. We promised to check on his mom and ask you what was going on."

"A status report," Carrie added, absently patting Whiskey's head when the dog laid her head in the teen's lap. "You write up status reports for your clients, don't you?"

Mac bit back a grin. "JJ is going to be doing that for me. I'll send her by the garage tomorrow with one."

Ray smiled at the detective, then looked down at the carpet, bracing for the explosion.

Carrie glared at both males. "We'll take a verbal one now. After all Ray isn't paying you enough for paper."

"Hey!" Rachel shouted from her position by the still open door. "Remember me? Last time I checked, this was my house. It's late and I want to go to bed. I don't know about anyone else, but I'm planning on going to work tomorrow. I don't want to be a bad hostess but everyone get out. Now."

"What about Sam?" Carrie pouted, slowly getting to her feet. "What should we tell him?"

Rachel sighed. "Tell him to call his mother. Tomorrow. After class."

"Tomorrow is Saturday," Carrie reminded her. "He doesn't have any Saturday classes."

Mac read Rachel's expression correctly and prudently motioned to Ray and Carrie to precede him out the door. He had to stick his head back inside to whistle for Whiskey.

"Keep up, will you," he grumbled to the dog as she finally appeared in the doorway. "I told you it was too late to visit."

Whiskey whined in response, turning her head back for one last look at the kitchen.

Between the street light and Dewey Wilson's new security lights, Rachel's front yard had the appearance of early dusk even though the sun had been down for more than six hours.

Mac and Ray watched Carrie angrily stalk past them without a word and get into Ray's truck.

Ray made no move to join her, instead reaching down to stroke Whiskey's head. "You're still driving Sean's car?"

"Yeah." Mac waited with his hands in his pockets, his eyes still trained on Ray's truck and the angry teen slouched down in the passenger seat.

"Sean called me. Told me what happened in Warrenton."

Mac nodded. "I figured. You hanging out with him now?"

"Not really. He's just bored, being stuck at home. His real friends are busy at school."

Ray kneeled down and took a close look at the dog. "Who would hurt Whiskey? I know it wasn't Uncle Dan."

"Yeah. Well, 'Uncle Dan' is going to get blamed for a lot of things, if he doesn't turn himself in–get this mess straightened out."

Ray looked up at the detective, appearing to consider and discard a response. He returned his attention to Whiskey. "Too bad Whiskey can't talk. She could tell you who the real killer is."

The dog whined and licked the boy's cheek.

Mac chuckled. "I'm sure if Whiskey gets within sight or smell of her abductor, she'll find a way to tell me."

"Ray, come on," Carrie yelled from the truck. "I'm supposed to work tomorrow morning, too. The dead can't wait."

Ray sighed, remaining where he was.

Whiskey gave him another lick.

"Animals are a lot easier to deal with than people," Ray mumbled.

"True." Mac looked back at Rachel's house, noticing that the lights were still on. A curtain moved in one of the living room windows and he wondered why she was watching them. "You better get going before Carrie wakes up the neighborhood."

Dan looked up as the door opened. "About time! Sitting in a pantry has to be the most boring thing I've–"

"Shut up and get out of there. Try hiding in a closet for hours while burglars or worse pillage and plunder though your house, then I'll listen to you whine."

"Pillage and plunder? Are you talking about last Sunday night?

I thought you said you just lost a smoked ham? It was probably just kids." Dan scrambled up from the floor and followed her from the kitchen to the living room.

"A half of a ham." Rachel blushed and then sheepishly added, "Someone put $20 in the funeral home mailbox the next day."

Dan grinned. "So the pillagers just robbed you of some pork. Scary dudes, all right. I'm surprised you're able to sleep at night."

She grabbed a pillow off the sofa and threw it at him. "Hey, having your house broken into is a big deal to normal people. I don't care what they took; they shattered a window and invaded my home."

"Sorry," he walked over and gave her a hug, "I'm a miserable excuse for a brother, and I've been nothing but trouble to you from the day I was born."

Rachel rested her head on his shoulder. She took a deep breath, tightening her arms around him, glad to have him where she could take care of him. "That's not entirely true. You were a cute baby. Much better than my dolls."

"And then I got big enough to pull the heads off your dolls."

She jerked back and glared at him. "Mom told me Buster did that!"

Dan grinned. "She knew you liked the dog more than me. Figured you'd forgive him."

Rachel leaned back and punched his shoulder. "I really do hate you."

"I know." He gave her another hug. "Got anything else to eat? All this talk of ham has me hungry again."

Twenty-one

"Your problem is that you don't understand women," Jeff announced as he signed for a UPS delivery. He pointed the guy in brown toward an empty table in the corner of his office. "Put the copy machine over there."

"What was wrong with the old copy machine?" Mac asked from his spot on Jeff's sofa. He was more than ready to change the subject. It wasn't as if either of them were experts on women, even if his friend claimed a certain expertise based on surviving thirty years of marriage and raising three daughters.

Jeff crossed his arms and leaned against the edge of his desk. "Sean and some of his friends were goofing off–well, let's just say that Myrna found one of the copies they made and refused to touch the old machine again. A man of my station can't be seen making his own damn copies, so it was fire Myrna or get a virgin machine."

"What is she, a hundred and five? Didn't Myrna work for your father?"

"Yeah. And she's been here since she was eighteen. I'm not sure she'd go even if I did get up the courage to fire her. The only way she's leaving here is in..." He pointed to the casket showcase room down the hall.

"What are you doing with the old machine?"

"You want it?"

"Well, the secretary you picked out for me gave me a list of vital equipment that I'm to acquire immediately. A copier is at the top." Mac grinned. "I don't think JJ will be freaked by the machine's spotty past."

"Very funny. I grounded Sean an extra week for that escapade."

"Consecutively or to run concurrently with his four-day school suspension?"

"Consecutively."

"Ouch. Where is he anyway? Have you banned him from your work place?"

"Hell, no. He'll be back here on Monday, minding the store while I'm in Baltimore buying caskets. Today, he's at home anxiously waiting for his sisters to arrive."

Mac raised his eyebrows. "Misses them, does he?"

Jeff laughed. "I should have said he's waiting for the presents they bring him. The girls spoil him rotten when they come for a visit."

"How are my favorite women?" Mac smiled, his eyes lighting up.

"According to their mother, they're doing well. I'll make up my own mind after I take a look at them."

"Has Mary Kathleen decided on what she's going to do after graduation? She told me that she'll mow lawns before she teaches, but…"

"Yeah, beats me what else a history major is going to do to earn a living. I really might have to look into making a trade for one of those John Deere riding mowers by summer."

"I saw Bridget's latest article. Doubt that she's on the Boston Police Department's Christmas list any more," the ex-cop chuckled.

"She'd never have been able to pierce the blue wall of silence if you hadn't given her that name…"

"Good cops hate bad cops as much as everyone else does," Mac said soberly.

"She could be a good writer here in D.C. I don't understand what she sees in that city."

The detective chuckled. "Yeah, you do. I hear she's sporting a diamond engagement ring."

Jeff glared at his friend. "Bridget's claims of being engaged are a mite premature. I've not even met the potential groom, much less given them my blessing on any engagement."

Mac held his tongue. Last time he'd spoken to Jeff's independent middle child, she'd hinted at an elopement. It might have been her intention that he tell her father, but that was one job Mac wasn't taking on.

Moving to a safer subject, Mac asked, "And how's my goddaughter?" His face beamed as he spoke of Jeff's eldest. "I think I woke her when I called last week."

Jeff's grin matched his oldest friend's. "They work the interns as many hours as they can. Maura claims she hasn't slept more than six hours in four months."

"What's her rotation this month?"

"Proctology," Jeff guffawed. "I heard Kathleen on the phone with her a couple of days ago. For a woman raised by the Good Sisters of Charity, the fart jokes were flying fast and furious."

Mac fell back against the couch laughing. At last, he wiped his eyes and asked, "Has Maura decided on a specialty?"

"Right now she's talking about being an Emergency Room doctor." Jeff grinned.

Mac got to his feet. "An undertaker and a doctor–don't let them bring you up on charges of collusion. Hey, you should get Mary Kathleen to go to law school. Cover all the bases."

"I'll suggest it to her. Or you can." Jeff stepped aside as the UPS man wheeled the large box into the room. "Kathleen is requiring your presence at her Sunday dinner table. Tomorrow at 1 p.m. sharp. I'm not supposed to take no for an answer. She said to bring Whiskey and she'd fill her up with roast beef."

The dog raised her head when she heard her name. She gave Jeff a short bark.

"Well, the dog's accepted. How about her master?"

Mac smiled. "I'm smart enough not to turn down one of Kathleen's home-cooked meals. Set a plate for both of us."

"You shouldn't be using my phone." Rachel nervously watched her office door, wishing she'd had a chance to lock it. When she'd picked up her phone, she'd never dreamed her brother would be on the line. He'd been sound asleep when she'd left the house, no doubt exhausted from his week on the run.

"I needed to talk to you," Dan argued. "I didn't think walking down the street to a pay phone was a good idea. Or maybe you'd rather I asked one of the neighbors to use their phone. I saw Elinor out sweeping the walk in front of her house earlier. Maybe–"

"Stay away from the windows too. Are you crazy?"

"No. I'm bored. When are you coming home? How come you don't have cable?"

"I told you I work Saturday mornings. And I can't afford cable. I'll be home around 12:30, which is what I said in the note I left tacked on the refrigerator door. Can't believe you didn't see it there!"

"Sorry. I wasn't interested in the stuff on the outside of the refrigerator. Do you know you're out of milk?"

"Yes!" She sighed and tried to calm down. There was no reason for anyone to suspect her brother was at her house–not with all the people who'd been going in and out. She really doubted that her phone line was tapped. And if it was, it was too late now to worry about it. "Hear any sirens approaching?"

"No." He chuckled. "Sis, are you okay? You need to lighten up. If me being here is freaking you out too–"

"I'm fine. No, actually, I'm not fine. I'm not going to be fine until you're no longer on the FBI's most wanted list. But I'd rather have you hiding out in my house than worry about where you are and if you're about to be shot by some gung-ho cop." She took another calming breath. "Okay. What was so important that you had to call me here at work?"

There was silence on the other end of the line.

"Dan?"

"I told you already. Do you really think I'm on the FBI–"

"Tell me again," she ordered, clenching her teeth in anticipation of his answer.

"Uh. You're out of milk."

Rachel slammed the phone down, hanging up before she said something she'd regret.

"Idiot!"

A knock sounded on her door and Carrie stuck her head in. "Did you find the mail I put in your in-basket? I took care of some of it for you, but I left the personal stuff. Some of it was forwarded from Franklin's."

Rachel nervously ran her hand through her hair. "Okay. I'll put it on my 'to do' list."

* * *

The smell was the first thing Mac noticed when he opened his office door. Paint. Fresh paint. Good thing he'd left Whiskey with Jeff. The dog had enough trouble breathing with her sore ribs; she didn't need to be sniffing paint fumes.

The second thing that caught his attention was the little bell that chimed as the door closed behind him. It hadn't been there the last time he'd come through the door.

The third was the absence of all his junk furniture.

"Hey." JJ stuck her head out of the back room, her black hair now sporting white streaks. "Hope you like white walls. I thought we'd go for a black and white look–kind of like those detective movies from the 1940s. A friend of mine who works in a body shop is painting all your old metal furniture black. Then, I've got a floor guy coming on Monday to remove the shag carpet. Did you know you've got wooden floors underneath? A lot of sanding, some stain, a little polishing–it'll look great."

When she paused to take a breath, Mac managed to ask the most important question on his mind. "How much is this going to cost me? Maybe I didn't make myself clear. When I said I couldn't afford a secretary, I also meant that I couldn't afford to redecorate."

JJ walked into the main room and Mac got a look at her outfit: baggy black jeans that were losing their battle with gravity, a purple tube top, no shoes, and a lot of paint.

"Won't cost you anything–well, not real money anyway."

Mac raised his eyebrows. "What kind of money?"

"I bartered your services and mine. I didn't actually spend a dime."

"And what are 'we' doing? Exactly."

"Snake, the guy from the body shop, needs you to find his sister. They got separated when their parents divorced. I already did a computer search and tracked her down. Thought I'd wait to tell Snake until next week, make him feel like he got a good deal."

"And the floor guy?"

"Philip? He's gay and wanted a date with you. You'll need to buy a leather outfit."

Mac blanched. "What the–"

"I was joking, geez. You need to chill out a little. The floor guy needs a computer for his kid and some tutoring on how to use it. I told him I'd find him a deal on a used one and meanwhile, he could come here a couple of hours a week and I'll have him surfing like a pro before the month is out."

Before he could ask, she added, "You have to evaluate the paint store's security system needs and supervise the installation of a new one. Two days work, tops."

"I don't have–"

"I told him it would be next month before you could do it."

Mac sighed and then reluctantly grinned. "No wonder Jeff liked you when you answered his newspaper ad. He probably sensed a kindred spirit."

JJ shrugged and shifted her bare feet, using one to rub at the dried paint that was splattered on top of the other. "I'm not sure he was sensing anything when I called. He sounded pretty out of it."

Mac stared at her feet. They were smaller than he'd thought considering the size of the work boots she usually clomped around in.

"I didn't want to get paint on my boots," she explained, noticing the direction of his gaze. "Don't worry I won't sue you if I step on something."

"Huh?"

JJ grinned. "Never mind. You know how to use a paintbrush? It's lots of fun. If you help we can finish in a couple of hours."

"Do I look like Huck Finn to you?"

"It was worth a try; worked for Tom Sawyer and his fence."

"I'd love to, but I have to track down a murderer and get a hair cut. I'm just here now to pick up some notes and to let you know about a delivery." He smiled proudly. She wasn't the only one who could find a good deal. "I acquired a copy machine for us this morning–top of the line model, color, only a couple of years old."

"Wow. I thought you were broke? How did you manage one of those?"

He looked around. She'd managed to paint most of the main room, except for the ceiling. "Good timing. I was in the right place at the right time. It's used but works fine."

"Great. It will make billing a lot easier. I'll cancel your Kinko's account."

He turned and glared at her. "Where are my files? And what Kinko's account?"

JJ pointed him toward the back room. "Let me worry about the details, why don't you. What you don't know won't bother you."

"Fine," he mumbled, exiting the room and wondering what other surprises she had in store for him. The back room was just as empty; except for some file boxes and a ladder.

"JJ?" he called out, kneeling down and sorting through a cardboard file box that had items from his desk drawers.

"Yeah?" She walked into the room and started up the ladder she was using to paint trim at the top of the wall.

"When the copier gets here, you might want to use some disinfectant on it." He grinned, staring down into the file box so she couldn't see his expression.

"Sure." She dipped her brush into a paint can balanced on the top rung. "Why?"

He chuckled and pocketed his notes. "What you don't know won't bother you. I'll be back by later this afternoon. If you're still here I'll bring you some takeout. Do you eat pizza?"

Her eyes lit up. "I like Chinese better."

"Chinese it is." Mac nodded. "I'll stop by the Golden Dragon on my way back."

Twenty-two

"Dan?" Rachel struggled through the doorway, her arms filled with grocery bags, purse, and a tote bag filled with the office mail. She was hoping that she'd get a chance to review it later in the day. She kicked the door closed behind her.

"In here."

"I could use some help," she called, leaning against the door while she tried to shrug off her coat without putting down the cumbersome bags. With a heavy sigh, she moved through the living room and stopped in the kitchen to stow the milk and yogurt in the refrigerator. The rest she left on the counter.

"Hope you got some food. I'm starved."

Rachel walked into the den to find her brother moving the computer's mouse as he rapidly surfed from one website to another.

"You really should get DSL, Rach," he said without bothering to look up. "This dial-up service is a dinosaur. Actually this whole computer must have been built in the stone ages. I can't believe you haven't upgraded…"

"It all costs money and that doesn't grow on trees," Rachel muttered. She could feel her stomach starting to roil as she saw the dirty plates and glasses strewn over the desk and on the floor.

"I finished off the ice cream. I'm not crazy about Swiss Chocolate. You know I've always preferred pistachio."

She took a deep breath, struggling for control.

"Hey, did you pick up any mustard? You're out and I sure hope you got some…"

"Shut up Dan. Shut up this minute before I pick you up and throw your pistachio-loving, mustard-eating ass out the door to the wolves or the D.C. police or anybody else who'll have you," Rachel exploded, her hands flailing in frustration.

She could see his hand freeze momentarily and then slowly move the mouse again, skimming through a document onscreen.

"And if you don't turn around and talk to me, I'll throw that dinosaur of a computer out the door with you," she spat.

Dan pushed the chair back and turned to face his sister. "You really have to calm down, Rach. You spazzing isn't–"

She crossed the room in two strides, grabbed Dan's shirt, and hauled him to his feet. "I've had it. You understand? I've had all I'm going to take from you. How dare you involve me and my son in your screwed-up life. Sam's cutting classes to save his precious uncle, who for all I know has killed two people in cold blood, stolen a half million dollars, and God knows what else. Damn it, Dan, I've had it with you. I want you out of here. Get out! Get out and leave me and Sam in peace."

The rant left her breathless. Suddenly Rachel didn't think her legs were going to support her. The room began closing in. As she started to slip to the floor, she felt a pair of strong arms envelop her and set her on the sofa.

"Don't move." She could barely hear him, his voice sounded so far away.

"Drink this." A chilled tumbler was pressed into her hands.

She gulped it down and then pressed the cool glass to her forehead.

Dan sank down next to her and they sat in silence for several moments.

"I'm sorry." Dan began to speak, his tone soft and hesitant. "This is a mess. I never wanted you and Sam to get hurt or involved. I've screwed up royally, but I swear Rachel, I haven't killed anyone. I haven't taken any money, and if you don't believe me, I don't know what I'll do."

She opened her eyes and stared into her brother's blue eyes. Eyes so much like their grandfather's. Eyes clear of deception–void of any trace of the violence it would have taken to kill not just one but two people.

"Hush." Rachel grabbed her brother's hand. "I'm sorry. I know you didn't kill anybody and that you didn't steal the money from the college. I was just scared and tired and frustrated. It doesn't help that you've been acting like this is some kind of game."

"I'm sorry. I-I guess I figured if I pretended it wasn't so serious it wouldn't be real," Dan said, his eyes now glued to the floor. "I don't know what the hell to do."

"Turn yourself in," Rachel implored, squeezing his hand. "Turn yourself in. It's all that's left."

"I can't. If I'm locked up, they'll stop looking for the real killer," Dan insisted. "I've just got to buy some time to figure out what really happened; to figure out who's behind all this."

Rachel silently considered his reasoning. "I'll give you until Tuesday. If we can't find out who the killer is by then–or at least come up with another suspect–promise me you'll turn yourself in. I'll talk to Aunt Ella and we'll get you the best lawyer in D.C." She reached out a hand and ruffled his hair, smiling as he grimaced. "You always were her favorite. I know she'll mortgage the farm if that's the only way to pay the legal fees."

Dan drew in a sharp breath and then nodded. "I guess I don't have a choice."

"Tell me what you know," Rachel said, sitting up and reaching for the yellow pad and pen on the coffee table. "Start at the beginning."

Ray opened the door and wondered for a moment if he'd stepped inside a giant marshmallow. Paint particles seemed to hang in the air, giving the room a surreal feel. The sight of the ugly orange carpet beneath his feet was actually reassuring.

Ding, ding, din… The bell hit a high note and hung there. The teen winced at the clamor. His arrival at Sullivan Investigations had been announced.

"Back here!"

Ray stepped around a pile of empty paint cans and made his way carefully into the back room, finding the girl he'd met the night before standing on the top of a ladder wielding a dripping paint roller.

"Hi. I was hoping…" He hesitated until JJ gave a nod for him to continue. "I was hoping to talk to Mr. Sullivan about some work he's doing for me. But mainly I wanted to make sure Whiskey is okay." Ray held up a cellophane bag. "I brought some of her favorite treats."

He watched as JJ pushed the roller as far as she could reach without falling–a three foot strip of the ceiling–a shower of texture and paint descending with each stroke.

When she didn't respond, he ventured a little further into the room. "Is Mr. Sullivan around?"

JJ dipped the paint roller in the bucket balanced on the top of the ladder. "Do you see him anywhere?"

Ray blushed then stepped to the middle of the room and laughed. "Not unless you painted him too. Where's Whiskey?"

"They are both smart enough to be elsewhere. God, I hate painting ceilings."

"Aren't the fumes getting to you? Do the windows open?"

"Only with a brick," she responded, leaning out and pushing the roller over another dingy strip of ceiling.

Ray walked over to the large window facing the street. Banging strategically on the corners, he managed to loosen the decades old paint enough to open the window. Cool air flooded the room.

As he finished his story, Dan ran his hand through his hair, leaving the ends sticking up in different directions.

"Anyway, I was a little surprised that I got the job since my degree in American Lit doesn't exactly qualify me to be an assistant comptroller, but my interviews seemed to go okay, and I figured that Jack Starling had given me a good recommendation. I told myself that it was just some good karma finally coming my way. And once I got the job, frankly, the work wasn't that hard. It was boring and repetitive, but not particularly challenging."

"What did you think of Vince Malwick?" Rachel asked.

"A real son-of-a-bitch. From day one, I didn't like the guy. I mean I wouldn't have killed him," Dan interjected hurriedly.

Rachel waved him along.

"Anyway, he had a mean streak, but he seemed to know the business and was more than willing to let me do the grunt work. He was also perfectly happy to take the credit for anything good I did. I didn't mind until I developed some software to keep better track of the accounts payable. He presented it as his own to the President. I'd never have known except…" Dan stopped.

"How'd you find out?" Rachel pressed.

"It doesn't matter," he hedged.

"Did someone tell you? Was it your girlfriend? The one you were going on a cruise with?" Rachel demanded.

"How exactly did the cops find out about the cruise?" he asked defensively.

"The paperwork in your desk. When the cops were building an embezzlement case against you, it sure didn't look good that you were buying a new car and going to Aruba." Rachel sighed.

"And they told you?"

"How else do you think I found out about it? Every time I turn around I've got a cop or a private detective one step behind me with your name on their lips."

"That was my money. I earned every dime," he protested. "I didn't steal anything."

"I know that. And you know that." She raised her chin and stared into his eyes. "But think about how it looked."

"I didn't know when I was buying the car and booking the vacation that I had to worry about how it would look to the police," Dan insisted. "I didn't know some psycho was going to start shooting and stealing money the minute I signed on the dotted line."

"Who is she? The woman you were going away with?"

Dan shook his head. "It's not important. She didn't do anything wrong either."

"Listen, little brother, you don't know what's important and what's not. And you don't know if your girlfriend's involved or not."

"She's not," he said flatly. "And I'm not giving you her name so you can offer her up to your detective friend. I care about her and I'm not bringing her into this anymore than she already is."

"Well, okay. I mean, Dan Thayer says that the mystery woman is innocent so that clears that right up. For God's sakes, Dan, who the hell is this woman? What is she to you?"

"It's just somebody I met at the college. It didn't start out as a serious relationship, but now after... Anyway, I sure as hell don't think she deserves to be dragged into this mess."

"Is it somebody named Lenore?"

"Who told you that?"

"Her name keeps coming up. Is she your girlfriend?"

"Leave her out of it. None of that has anything to do with the missing money or the murders."

"That's just fine, Sir Galahad, but if your girlfriend is the one who told you that Malwick was grabbing credit for your software, then I've got to assume that she's pretty high up in the administration. She may know more than you think." Rachel glared at her brother who matched her steely gaze.

"I didn't say–"

Suddenly the doorbell rang, followed by the sound of someone trying to open the front door.

"It's not locked," Rachel whispered, her eyes widening in realization. "Oh, God. Dan, you've got to–"

The two siblings started to rise, eyes scurrying around the room looking for a hiding place.

Rachel pointed to the kitchen a half second before they heard a thump and a wheezing male voice. "Miz Brenner? It's Edgar Freed. You left your van door open. Is everything all right? I've got my cell phone with me and the police on speed-dial. Miz Brenner?"

Twenty-three

"How do you know Mac?" JJ asked fifteen minutes later as she knelt down and used a screwdriver to pry open another can of paint.

"I work part-time at a kennel where he sometimes leaves his dog. Have you met Whiskey yet?"

JJ shook her head, her eyes focused on the can. "Not yet." She got the top off and set it aside.

"Whiskey is a great dog. Irish wolfhound."

"Yeah, well I'm not really that good with pets." JJ glanced up. "Kennel? I thought that blonde girl said you worked at a garage." She stood, holding up a paintbrush and a roller. "Do you have a preference?"

The teen glanced at his boots and grabbed the roller. "I'd rather be on top."

"In your dreams," JJ dryly responded, handing him the open can. "You're too young for me."

Ray blushed and climbed the ladder. "I work full-time at Mickey's Motors. And you're not that old. Carrie said you were taking classes at Concordia."

"Yeah. I was. Or rather I am. Two classes this term." JJ knelt down again and started painting the baseboards. "Since I don't work at the college anymore, I probably won't be able to afford to enroll in any classes next semester."

"Why did you quit?" Ray smoothed the paint on the ceiling, his long arms allowing the roller to cover twice the distance JJ had managed.

"Well, it sure wasn't for the money or the working conditions here," she joked, moving down the wall a few feet and beginning on another section. "How come you're not spending the day with your girlfriend? What's her name? Carrie?"

"She's not…" Ray reloaded the roller with paint and made another long stroke across the ceiling. "Carrie is just a friend. From High School."

"Right," JJ scoffed. "We don't have to talk about her if you don't want to." She gave him a quick glance as he climbed down and moved the ladder over several feet. "What did you want to see Mac about?"

"I'm a client," he responded as he climbed back up and resumed painting.

JJ grabbed a rag out of her back pocket and wiped some of the freshest paint off her hands. "Yeah. I got that much from the last time you were here."

"It's confidential."

"So? I'm Mac's assistant." She scrubbed her cuticles, frowning at the white paint coating her blue fingernails.

Ray grinned and kept painting. "Yeah. I got that much from the last time I was here."

"So," JJ glared up at him, "that means you can tell me. I'm going to be typing up all his case notes anyway."

"Then you can wait and read all about it later." He glanced down at her, laughing when he noticed her disgruntled expression.

Irritated, she drew back her arm to throw the cleaning rag at him, but the sudden ringing of the bell on the outer office door startled her, affecting her follow through.

The rag fell short, landing on the top of one of Ray's shiny black boots.

JJ blanched and in her scramble to her feet, tripped over the paint can she'd been using. She screeched as she landed hard on her bottom, the overturned can creating a puddle around her.

On the ladder, Ray barely noticed her pratfall, although he did take note of some of the creative combinations of expletives that followed. With the paint roller in one hand and a half-full can of paint in the other, he carefully balanced on one foot and raised the other. Shaking his foot, he tried to dislodge the rag.

The ladder creaked ominously.

"I've got food out here. Come and get it." Mac's voiced filtered into the room.

The ladder's creak was an ominous warning. Ray stopped, freezing in place.

"Don't move," JJ advised, unnecessarily. She regained her

footing and hurried over to the ladder, plucking the rag from his foot.

They both looked at his boot.

"Hey," she grinned up at him, "you got lucky. No paint on the leather."

The teen gingerly lowered his foot. The ladder groaned, but held.

"No," Ray grumbled, "you got lucky." His words were threatening, but amusement was beginning to etch its way across his face.

JJ shrugged and reached up to take the paint can from him. "Really? That's a first for me. My luck has always been bad or non-existent."

"I was afraid that the murderer had shown up and was holding you hostage," Edgar repeated, sipping his second cup of coffee and declining a third chocolate cupcake or a second Twinkie.

Rachel gave the nosy old man a quick smile, fully aware that he must have been watching her house with the binoculars she could see sticking out of a pouch on the side of his walker. He'd explained his concern to her at least a half-dozen times since he'd thumped his way uninvited into her living room. "No murderer, just a ringing phone, and a cat that demanded to be fed. I completely forgot I had another bag to bring in from the van."

"Good thing I happened by then. Another five minutes and your ice cream would have melted." The man glanced around the living room. "You sure bought a lot of groceries just for you. Six or seven bags. Eat a lot of Twinkies do you?"

"Sam loves them. He's coming for a visit soon." She glanced pointedly at the plate balanced on the man's bony knees. "And of course I like to have something to offer people who drop in unexpectedly."

Edgar Tweed laughed, instigating a coughing fit. He fumbled for his oxygen mask and motioned for her to turn the valve on the small tank mounted on the backpack he was wearing.

"Do you need anything else?" Rachel asked, becoming concerned at the purple tinge of his complexion. "Should I call Elinor again? See what's keeping her?"

He shook his head. "I can walk myself back home. I've been trying to get into shape."

She hid a smile, wondering what the old man was getting in shape to do.

He coughed. "Might have a part-time job lined up. I need to get around without that damn scooter chair."

"Maybe you should start slowly. Build up your strength gradually." She had real doubts about his ability to cross the room, much less cross the street.

He took another hit of oxygen and then laughed. "When you're my age you don't want to spend a lot of time getting ready to do something."

JJ stuffed the empty cartons into a plastic trash bag. "I'm going down the street for more soda. Anyone else want something?"

Ray and Mac, sitting across from each other on the floor in the main office, exchanged glances. Mac jerked his head in the teen's direction. Ray shook his head and quickly filled his mouth with the last egg roll.

Mac frowned at him. Clearing his throat, the detective said, "JJ, Ray thinks you might want to change clothes first."

Ray started coughing and in response Mac slapped him firmly between the shoulder blades.

JJ tied a knot in the trash bag and then glanced at her paint-soaked jeans. "You don't think this is a good look for me?"

The ringing of the office phone–normally sitting on his desk but currently located along with everything else on the orange carpet–prevented Mac from having to respond.

"I'll get it," the detective offered, trying to untangle his legs and stand.

JJ waved him down and walked over to answer the phone. Picking up the cordless phone, she turned toward the guys. "Sullivan and Jarrett Investigations," she chirped, watching astonishment flash over Mac's face.

Surprised, Ray whipped his head around and stared at the detective, laughing when he realized JJ had rendered Mac speechless.

"Yeah, that's my last name. You'll have to ask Mac about that."

Mac and Ray listened attentively to JJ's side of the conversation.

"No, Ray's here. Been here most of the afternoon. No problem, we just finished dinner, I'll put him on."

JJ lowered the phone receiver, not bothering to cover the mouthpiece. "Ray, Carrie wants to talk to you. She sounds angry. I thought you said you weren't dating?"

"I hope you haven't ordered new letterhead yet," Mac warned JJ as she walked back into the front office, her painting clothes exchanged for black leggings and a red T-shirt.

Mac was sitting with his back against the wall, his long legs stretched out in front of him. He had several college yearbooks stacked beside him and one open on his lap.

"It was a joke." JJ grinned. "Odd–Ray's girlfriend didn't think it was funny either."

"You've got a talent for stirring up trouble," Mac grumbled. "Ray made a run to the convenience store." He pointed to a paper bag on the floor near the door. "There's sodas and bottled water in the sack over there if you're still thirsty."

JJ walked over and opened the sack, pulling out a can of diet soda. "Did Ray take off to make nice to Carrie?"

Mac chuckled and turned the page of the yearbook. Squinting at a page of photographs, he mumbled, "The kid said something about giving someone a ride."

She popped the top on the can and took a sip. "Want some help with what you're doing?"

"It's getting late. Am I going to have to pay you overtime?"

JJ crossed the room and sat down beside him on the worn shag carpet. "No overtime, but I might need to take care of some personal stuff during office hours. Is that going to be a problem?"

Mac shook his head. "Just as long as you take care of my stuff too." He handed her a yearbook. "I stopped by the college earlier and picked these up. Look for a student named Gina Woodward. I want to know what she was into and who her friends were."

JJ glanced at the date on the cover. "These are six years old. What does Gina Woodward have to do with…"

He waited, watching the thoughts flicker across her face as she flipped the pages in the yearbook to the back, found the name listed in the index, and then located the correct page.

"Okay, so Gina Woodward is Gina Malwick," JJ mused, staring at a photograph of a group of cheerleaders. "Her hair is still the same, although I think she's had some body work since she graduated."

"Let me see," Mac held the book up closer to his face, the overhead fluorescent lights creating a glare on the page. "Now that's interesting."

JJ frowned and self-consciously tugged on her T-shirt, fluffing it out. "Surprised you care about a boob job."

He laughed and held the book out so she could see. "I wasn't looking at her chest. I was looking at where the photo was taken."

JJ leaned over and stared at the photo again. "Creepy. They were standing in the clock tower."

Twenty-four

"Rachel, I'm starving. Did you let the old guy eat all the good stuff?" Dan rubbed a towel over his wet hair as he bounced down the staircase into the living room where Rachel was running a vacuum cleaner.

When she didn't answer, he pulled the plug out of the wall outlet.

"Dan!" She stood the powerless vacuum upright and glared at him.

"You're going to wear out your carpet if you clean it any more," he joked, snapping the damp towel at her jean-clad bottom.

"It's already worn out," she grumbled, gathering up the cord and securing it around the plastic holders built on the back of the appliance. "But it doesn't have potato chip crumbs on it anymore."

Dan gave her a guilty grin. "Speaking of which–I'm hungry again. Got anymore of those Twinkies that the old guy was scarfing down?"

"Yes, but you can't eat them now. Dinner will be ready in about a half hour. I've got a chicken baking."

"Are you going to make mashed potatoes too?"

"Only if you agree to stay upstairs. You were lucky Edgar didn't see you earlier. I've caught him over here before doing something in my flowerbed. He might have been trying to get close enough to the house to look in the windows."

Dan gulped. "Uh...which flowerbed? The one with the rose bushes?"

Rachel nodded. "What aren't you telling me?"

"He might have seen me burying a gun there."

Rachel sank down on the sofa, a dozen painful questions stabbing into her mind like darts hurled at a corkboard. She wouldn't ask the most important one; instead she asked an obvious one. "What gun?"

"Probably the one that killed Malwick."

"How did–" Rachel took a deep breath and started over. "Why did you have it?"

He sat down next to her, his elbows on his knees, his gaze directed at the spot between his feet. "Someone put it in my car. They made sure I'd touch it by stowing it under the driver's seat and positioning the seat so I'd have to move it backwards in order to get behind the wheel. I panicked when I saw it."

"And your first impulse was to hide it under my rose bushes? Thanks a lot."

He didn't look up.

"Dan!"

"Say it. I'm stupid, inconsiderate, and childish–running to you; expecting you to fix everything for me."

She got to her feet. "Yeah. Stupid. Trust me I'll come back to the rest. At the moment I'm more concerned about what's planted in my yard. We need to dig… Wait a minute!"

He raised his head. "What?"

"Mac Sullivan said the police had determined that same gun that killed Malwick was used to kill Angela Lopez. She was shot on Tuesday night. When did–"

"I found the gun on Saturday night when I left… When I got in the car to drive over to see you. I was planning to tell you about the new car I was buying you."

"When were you planning to tell me that you'd gotten fired?"

Dan looked sheepish. "Probably not until I found another one. Anyway, when I got here…"

"But you didn't visit that night. I was–"

"You weren't home."

"I was meeting with Jeff O'Herlihy about the new job. It took longer than I planned." Rachel covered her face with her hands and laughed. "So instead of leaving me a note, you left a murder weapon?"

"That was probably a bad idea," he agreed. "Someone must have followed me here and taken–"

"Not someone, Dan. The killer. The same person who killed Malwick and planted the gun in your car. And they probably retrieved the gun on Sunday night. Remember my late night visitors?"

"But..." He lurched to his feet and walked back and forth between the sofa and the stairs. "You said 'they'. They broke into your house. More than one person."

"Yeah. I think I heard at least two people."

He grabbed the banister post for support. "So it's more than just one person doing all this. Oh, God, Rachel, I screwed up. I should never have come here, not Saturday night, and certainly not yesterday. I've put you in danger."

"It's a little late for that realization," Rachel said wryly.

"I have to leave. Maybe get a flight out of Baltimore or I could drive down to–"

"You have to calm down and let me figure this out," she interrupted, abruptly getting to her feet and crossing the room toward him. He always reacted like this–maddening indifference, painful realization, then blind panic. "Maybe there were two different intruders or two different break-ins. That could explain the–"

"Rachel, I am so sorry. I need to get out of here–"

"Shut up. We need to call the police or Mac. He can–"

"No, please. You know I couldn't stand being in jail, being locked up, even for a little while."

Dan looked up at her and she saw in his eyes the six-year-old who'd managed to lock himself inside an old steamer trunk. Their mother was at work and Rachel had been in charge. It had taken her almost a half hour and a phone call to her grandfather in order to free him.

"Don't tell anyone, Rachel. Please."

She knelt down and ruffled his hair. The past had scarred them both. He couldn't tolerate small spaces or locked rooms and she couldn't refuse his pleas for help. "Okay. But you have to stay out of sight until–"

The ringing of the phone interrupted her.

Five minutes later, Rachel hung up the phone with a sigh. "That was the D.C. police. Someone broke into the funeral home and I'm on call. They don't think there's been any damage, but I've got to go down there and check things out. Besides Jeff, I'm the only one with the security codes."

"Did they say whether they think it's–"

Rachel shook her head and then gave him a hug. "They didn't mention you or the murders. I'll be gone a couple of hours. Please, please stay off the phone and away from the windows."

The bell over the door chimed as Sean entered the office. "Mac? I've got–"

Mac appeared in the doorway from the back room and Whiskey rushed over to greet him.

"How are you feeling, girl?" He knelt down and gave her a hug. Looking up at the teen, he smiled. "Thanks for taking care of her today. I thought things would be calmer at your place. She's still healing."

"Things are always calmer at a funeral home. Dad made me keep the office open this afternoon, so he could pick up Bridget at the airport. I was bored and decided to cut out early. Whiskey and I went to the park and just walked around." Sean looked around. "I like the paint job. When are you getting rid of the carpet?"

"Soon. And the paint job is courtesy of my new secretary."

"Ray mentioned her. Where is she?" Sean peaked into the other room.

"It's Saturday night. I think JJ had a date." Mac gave Whiskey another pat and stood up. "Don't worry you'll meet her soon. Heck, JJ hasn't even met Whiskey yet."

Sean smiled. "I talked to Ray this afternoon. Hope JJ makes a better impression on Whiskey than she did on Carrie."

Mac raised his eyebrows. "Yeah. Although in a fight, I think Whiskey's bite is probably less painful than either of the other two's."

"Yeah. And lucky Ray's the one with the tooth marks. Listen, I've gotta go. Mom's waiting outside. She drove us over in her new car–said to remind you about dinner tomorrow."

"We'll be there," Mac promised as he walked to the office door and held it open for Sean and the dog. "Whiskey, let's go home, too. It's been a long couple of days."

"Nothing obvious seems to be missing or damaged but I'll need to verify that with the owner." Rachel pulled an inventory list from a file folder and handed it to the middle-aged, female detective who, along with a male counterpart, had met her in the parking lot and escorted her inside. "After your call I was afraid someone had gotten into the basement; the preparation rooms. But they're still locked."

Detective Joanna Giles took a quick look at the multi-page list. "Have you noticed any strange characters hanging around here lately?"

Rachel laughed. "Living or dead? No, sorry. I haven't seen anyone stranger than usual. But I've only been working here about a week. I was surprised that you knew to call me."

Detective Giles smiled. "You'd be surprised what we know about you. How about your brother? Seen him lately?"

Sobering, Rachel realized that under normal conditions the funeral home break-in wouldn't have merited one detective, much less two. She looked over at the detective using her office telephone. She'd bet a month's salary that the detectives weren't concerned with any missing caskets.

"Thanks for the heads up, Tom. You think the funeral home break-in and the murders are connected?" Mac held his cell phone with one hand and pulled a clean shirt out of his closet with the other.

Whiskey whined but made no move to get up from bed where she was stretched out.

Mac finished his conversation and flipped the phone closed. "Come on girl, get up. I know I told you that we could have an early night, but something is happening at the funeral home. We need to dig into it."

Whiskey growled and stuck her head under a pillow.

"Okay. Bad pun." Mac lifted up the corner of the pillow. "Give me a break. This time I need you for more than just a pretty face. We're going to put your sensitive nose to the test. If Dan Thayer is hiding out in the funeral home, you're just the dog to find him."

* * *

Detective Giles closed her notebook and perched on the edge of Rachel's desk. "Anything else you want to confess while the uniforms are searching the building?"

"Confess?"

"Sorry. Occupational hazard." Detective Giles smiled. "Any other information you can give me about this break-in, or the one at your house, or what the heck, as long as I'm here–want to tell me what you know about the Malwick or Lopez murders?"

Rachel shrugged. "Sorry. I don't know anything more than I've already told the police."

Detective Giles stood. "I doubt that."

"I think maybe the killer doubts it, too."

Both women turned to see sweating Detective Fiori standing in the doorway.

"What is it, Pete?" the policewoman asked.

"You'd better take a look. Someone left something in one of the hearses."

Twenty-five

"Is that what I think it is?" Mac asked as he crouched next to the crime scene technician. He held the flashlight steady as he watched the young man carefully lift the substance lying on the seat of one of Jeff's oldest hearses.

"Just what the hell do you think it is?" Lieutenant Greeley asked, his gravelly voice coming from directly behind the private detective.

The technician jumped at the sound, dropping the blood-smeared object with a splat onto the leather.

Mac barely flinched. "Afterbirth."

"Feel free to elaborate."

Mac set the flashlight down and stood. He took a few steps back, drawing the lieutenant away from the hearse, and earning a grateful look from the nervous technician. "Pete Fiori found what he suspected was blood on the outside of the hearse door. Out of a sense of excessive caution, and because both detectives were afraid something more sinister was going on, Detective Giles called in the crime lab. The technician examined the hearse and found a dead kitten and...well, what you saw him scraping up."

"I hope to God that kitten was murdered or Detectives Giles and Fiori are going to be footing the lab bill."

Mac chuckled. "Sorry. You could order a necropsy, but it looked stillborn to me. I think someone left the window open and a cat–"

"Yeah, right. I get the picture." Greeley glanced around the parking lot and the back of the funeral home building. "That the door the beat cop found open?"

"Yeah."

"Why's the hearse way out here? Someone try to steal it too?"

"According to Mrs. Brenner, the hearse won't start. It was pushed out here where the employees park so it would be out of the way and the tow truck could back up to it easily. She said, quote, "It's been beached out by the dumpster for the last two days. End quote."

"So the only crime here is a jimmied door and the waste of the taxpayers' money?"

Mac grinned. "Well there's the problem of the missing cat and an unknown number of kittens. I've got my partner checking into that."

Rachel sighed as Mac and Whiskey walked into her office. It was late and she really wasn't in the mood for more questions. "Let me guess. You listen to a police scanner in your spare time. I wish I could have had this kind of attention for the break-in at my house. Maybe the burglars would have been caught by now."

Mac grinned. "Whiskey and I were just in the neighborhood and saw the lights."

"Right." Rachel pulled out a file from the drawer she'd been thumbing through. "Shouldn't your dog be home recuperating?"

Whiskey whined and looked up at the detective.

"I tried to tell her that, but she wasn't having any of it."

Rachel looked at the dog whose sleepy attitude belied the detective's words. "Well, even if Whiskey hasn't, I've had more than I want from this day. As soon as the police clear out, I'm headed home. So whatever you're here for, get to it. And before you ask, Dan isn't here."

"Then you won't mind if Whiskey and I take a walk through the building, see what might have wandered in through the back door."

Rachel shrugged and slammed the file drawer shut. "Knock yourself out. Watch out for ghosts."

"Don't get too close," Mac whispered, tugging an excited Whiskey back from the wiggling fur ball of kittens. The newborns were hidden in a half-filled box of copy paper on the bottom shelf of a storage room. "I think we've already scared off mama."

Whiskey whined, voicing her displeasure with his decision.

"Did you find something," Detective Giles asked, appearing in the doorway.

"Whiskey found the dead kitten's siblings. No sign of the mother cat."

"No sign of Dan Thayer either," the policewoman added.

"Crime scene techs just left. Since they were already here, they pulled a few prints from the back door and took some swabs of the blood drops Pete found on the outside of the hearse."

"Greeley still here?"

Detective Giles flinched. "Yeah."

"He'll get over it."

"Maybe." She sighed. "And maybe I'll be on parking meter patrol next week. Leave the cats for Mrs. Brenner to deal with tomorrow. Greeley wants us to wrap this up pronto."

Mac grinned. "Bet my next retainer those weren't his exact words."

"Try it now," Pete Fiori suggested, his voice muffled by the open hood of Rachel's minivan.

"What did he say?" Rachel asked Mac. The police had finally finished checking out the funeral home and declared it burglar-free although not feline-free. Hoping to make a quick getaway, she'd hopped in the Blue Dog and prayed it would start. God's direct line must have been busy. So instead of being at home dealing with her fugitive brother, she was sitting in the driver's seat with a police detective banging on something under the van's hood and a private detective hovering at her elbow.

Whiskey let loose several short barks.

She amended her thought–a private detective and his unusually agitated dog. "In English please."

Mac chuckled. "Pete wants you to try to start it again."

Rachel turned the key and the van started up with a pop and a bang.

Whiskey barked again and strained at her leash.

"Easy girl, Rachel doesn't need us to tell her that she has vehicle issues."

Rachel smirked. "At least I own my own vehicle." The van coughed and she pressed on the gas petal. "Such as it is."

Pete slammed the hood down and jogged toward the squad car where his partner was waiting.

"Charming guy," Rachel remarked, watching the detectives speed out of the parking lot. "I would have thanked him, if he'd stuck around."

Mac grinned. "His undercover jobs haven't improved his social skills. I'll pass on your thanks the next time I see him."

Whiskey barked again, straining at her leash.

Rachel leaned out the van's window and took a look at the dog. "What's wrong with her?"

"She wants to check out that hearse. Probably still smells the dead kitten."

Rachel sighed and buckled her seat beat. "I put out some water for the mother cat. Hopefully, she's made her way back to the storeroom with her kittens now that things have quieted down. I'll come in tomorrow and deal with them. Don't suppose you–"

"Don't even go there," Mac said with a chuckle. "Whiskey's interest in cats doesn't extend to sharing her turf with them."

"Yeah, I figured." Rachel put the van in gear.

Mac tugged on Whiskey leash, turning her head back toward him. "Stubborn mutt! Give it up. That cat is long gone."

The dog barked and pulled at the leash, leaning her body toward the hearse and the far corner of the parking lot.

Rachel frowned. "I don't think she believes you."

"I have that problem with all females. You want us to follow you home?"

"No." His question reminded her of who was waiting for her. She absolutely did not want him to follow her home. She shook her head in case he missed her answer. "You go ahead. Maybe you could entice Whiskey to forget the kitten with some food. The hamburger place a couple of blocks over is open all night."

Whiskey's head turned at the word 'hamburger' and she licked Mac's hand.

Rachel laughed. "Does she know…"

Mac frowned. "You bet. And now that you've brought up the possibility, the only question will be if she wants cheese on it or not."

Whiskey sat up and placed one paw on Mac's elbow.

Twenty-six

"Thank God you're here, Uncle Mac. Will you please remind my father that I'm an adult and can live with a man before I marry him."

All eyes at the big mahogany table flashed to the dining room door.

Mac held up his hands to deflect the pleading glances of Jeff's middle daughter. "Bridget, darlin', I'm not getting in the middle of this argument. I'm just here for your mother's Sunday dinner. Besides which I'm not about to tell a father that his baby girl can date, let alone share a bed, without taking some vows before God and her parents."

"I thought you were on my side," Bridget O'Herlihy pouted.

"I am. I always am." He grinned, leaning over to kiss the fiery redhead. "But you'd have an easier time trying to get this big mutt to agree to homemade funeral pyres than your cohabiting with a man without the benefit of clergy. Why don't you do what kids have done since the start of time?"

"What's that?" Jeff's middle child growled.

"Sneak around," Mac answered in a perfect stage whisper.

"Thanks, Mac, I don't need your help," Jeff muttered, rising from his chair at the head of the table to offer his friend a warm hug and pat the Irish wolfhound as she headed for the kitchen.

"Sorry, I'm late. That new assistant you hired for me insisted I had to review the overdue invoices before I could head over here. What's the point of having your own business if you can't take off when you want?" Mac said, sitting in the chair next to Jeff.

"Sounds like she's going to make your agency profitable whether you want to or not."

Kathleen's voice sounded from the kitchen. "Whiskey, stop eating the cat's food. Mac, get your hairy hound out of my kitchen."

"Come here girl," Mac whistled. The dog appeared in the doorway with crumbs of kibble on her lips. After a moment's hesitation, she ambled over to Sean, who immediately broke apart a dinner roll and put it down on the floor for her.

"Uncle Mac, what's in the bag?" the eldest O'Herlihy offspring asked with a twinkle in her eyes. "Anything that combines chocolate and caramel?"

"Maura, would I dare come into your presence without a box of turtles?" Mac grinned reaching into his bag and extracting a pink box of chocolate treats.

Maura immediately ripped open the cellophane wrapping and popped one in her mouth.

"And for me?" Bridget giggled.

"Jelly beans, of course. And yes, I got extra very cherry, green apple, peanut butter, and caramel apple."

"Yes!" Bridget pumped her fist in the air, and scarfed down a handful of the tiny confections.

"And for you, Ms. Mary Kathleen."

"*Moi*?" Mary Kathleen batted her eyelashes at her favorite "uncle."

"Strawberries dipped in dark chocolate," he presented with a flourish.

"I've died and gone straight to hell and I don't care," the youngest O'Herlihy daughter mumbled, her lips betraying the delicious morsel she had just consumed.

"Mackenzie Sullivan, are you plying my kids with sweets before I get this meal on the table," Kathleen accused as she walked into the dining room, carrying a large platter piled high with roast beef and potatoes.

"I confess I did," Mac said solemnly.

"What did you bring me?" Kathleen demanded with a grin.

"Godiva Chocolates deluxe edition," the detective said pulling out a gold box from his bag.

"Then you're forgiven," Kathleen said, smiling and sitting down at the table.

Sean put a huge salad bowl before his "uncle," as well as a green bean casserole.

"*Psst*, Sean, move the healthy stuff to the other end," Mac nudged the lanky teen. Reaching back into his sack, he offered the sole O'Herlihy male offspring, a bag filled with gummy worms, bears, and sharks.

"Thanks."

"And how about me?" Jeff demanded with a stern look on his face. "Did you forget the guy who works 24/7 to provide you with an ever-ready source of wheels?"

"Ah, the head of transportation for the O'Herlihy clan speaks," Mac answered. "I brought something that might wet the whistle and delight the taste buds as well." He drew out two six packs of Guinness Irish stout.

"For later," Kathleen warned.

"Oh, for heavens sake…" Rachel made her stand near the sofa, crossed her arms and gave her son the same glare she'd given him when he and Ray had arrived home after cutting school to attend a Jerry Garcia-less Grateful Dead concert.

"Surprise." Sam gave his mother a weak smile and moved to hug her.

Rachel allowed the hug but didn't respond. She'd barely managed to hide Dan and his half-eaten lunch in the pantry after hearing the front door open. With any luck, she'd be able to get rid of the kids before they discovered she wasn't alone in the house.

Undeterred, Sam leaned in and gave her a quick kiss on the cheek. "Did you miss me?"

"When you called me yesterday what part of, 'Sam, stay at school. Don't come home,' didn't you understand?"

"Yeah. I figured this was coming." He plopped down on the sofa and looked toward the front door where Ray and Carrie were standing.

Rachel turned her gaze on his accomplices. "Sam and I need to have a serious discussion before I drive him down to the train station. I'd appreciate it if you two would visit another time. Oh, and next weekend's trip is off. Sam will be celebrating his birthday in the Penn library."

Ray tugged on Carrie's elbow. "Let's go. Sorry, Mrs. Brenner."

Carrie glared at Ray, but reluctantly turned to leave.

"Wait," Rachel suddenly ordered. "Get back in here and sit

down." Rachel pointed to the sofa and waited while the two teens obeyed her.

"It's got to stop." Rachel said forcefully, her eyes trained on the three friends who refused to meet her look. "You're not the Hardy Boys or Nancy Drew. This isn't some police show on television where you're going to solve the mystery in the last five minutes. Two people are dead. Do you understand that?"

"Mom, you're over-reacting," Sam angrily shouted. "Just like you always do."

"*I'm* over-reacting? I saw a woman with her brains splattered all over the parking lot and I'm over-reacting? What, are you *crazy*?" Rachel gestured wildly, knocking a picture frame off the mantel. The glass splintered on the floor and the three teens momentarily froze in stunned silence.

Carrie started to rise.

Rachel's head whipped around and she glared at the girl. "I told you to sit down!"

The young woman instantly shrank back, scooting a little closer to Ray.

Rachel took a deep breath and tried to clear the memory of blood and death from her mind. Her hands were trembling as she picked up the fractured frame, and the largest shards of glass.

"This is my decision to make, not yours. I'm not going back to school until I know Uncle Dan is safe," Sam angrily declared. "I owe him."

"Sam, you don't understand–"

"Mom!" His voice grew quieter as he added, "I can stay here with you or I'll bunk with Carrie. Your choice."

Rachel hesitated. She heard a creak in the kitchen.

She gripped the glass too tightly and felt the blood coating her fingers. She opened her hand and let the glass fall to her feet. "Come with me to the funeral home."

"You're going to work now? On a Sunday?" Sam shook his head in disbelief. "What about Uncle–"

"There was a break-in last night at the funeral home. I need to start an inventory today and relocate a cat. I could use your help."

"Mom–"

"Sam, no matter what's going on with your uncle, I need to keep my job. We'll talk about Dan at the funeral home."

Over on the sofa Carrie frowned and whispered to Ray. "Cat? Did she say cat? As in cat burglar?"

"So am I allowed to ask what you're planning to do after graduation?" Jeff speared another slice of roast beef from the platter and plunked it down on his plate. He looked expectantly at his youngest daughter.

"No, you may not," Mary Kathleen responded. "I've got lots of options none of which I'm ready to discuss. And no, I don't want you to buy me a riding lawn mower."

"I gather I can't talk about this Romeo who's planning on moving into my daughter's apartment," Jeff growled, viciously cutting up his meat into small pieces and turning his attention to his middle daughter.

"Nope." Bridget smiled, reaching for another roll. "And just to be clear, I'm moving into his apartment because it's four times the size of mine."

"I don't think you should give up…"

"I know Dad, I know what you think." Bridget sighed, carefully slathering butter on the steaming bread and avoiding eye contact with her irate father.

"Well, I assume I can ask about your work, Maura," Jeff grumbled. "Or is that off-limits too?"

"No, no, let me tell you about the compound fracture that came into the ER yesterday." Maura grinned devilishly. "The bone was almost at right angles to the thigh and the blood was shooting out of the femoral artery like…"

"Mom," Sean pleaded, as he pushed aside the remains of his rare roast beef.

"Maura, give your brother a break," Kathleen said patiently. "You know he has a weak stomach."

"Big baby." Maura winked.

"I know an interesting topic," Kathleen said with a sly grin. "Why doesn't Mac tell us about the new woman in his life?"

All eyes moved as one to the face of the private detective who was mopping up the gravy on his plate with a roll.

Mac looked up guiltily, popping the last remnant of bread into his mouth. He swallowed, reminded of a horror movie where a staked-out goat was surrounded by a herd of raptors. He suddenly knew how the goat felt and decided to stall.

"You mean JJ? Ask your husband, he hired her."

"I'm talking about Rachel Brenner, the woman you've been spending most of your time with." Kathleen stared pointedly at the blushing Mac. "I figure Rachel must be the reason you're at the funeral home all hours of the day and night. Or maybe you're having an affair with Myrna Bird?"

"And Dan just gave you the disk?" Sam asked his mother as she filled a bowl with dry cat food and set it to one side to take downstairs. "I can't believe that–especially after all the trouble Ray went through to get it to him in the first place."

"Believe it." She glanced at the trio sitting at the table in the employee lounge. Hamburger wrappers and stray French-fries littered the surface.

Ray shifted uneasily in his chair. "It's okay, Sam. I mean it's not like I was arrested or anything. And Mr. O'Herlihy is still bringing in his cars to the garage for me to work on, so I don't think he was too mad about me disrupting the Malwick funeral. Of course Mac Sullivan wasn't too–"

Sam interrupted the teen. "Like anyone cares what that detective wannabe thinks."

"Sam!" Rachel shushed him. "Dan wanted me to put it in a safe place. And I did."

"What a minute!" Carrie awoke from a semi-doze. "He gave you the disk!"

Sam glared at her. "Try and keep up."

"I didn't get much sleep last night." Carrie paused and frowned at Sam. "My point is that your mother must have seen him in person. He didn't mail it to her and she didn't just talk to him on the phone. She saw him."

Sam rose and stood near his mother. "When did Uncle Dan give you the disk and where did you put it?"

Rachel shook her head and handed him the cat bowl. "When isn't important and I won't tell you where I hid it. No one but me is ever going to find it until I decide the time is right to give it to the police."

Sam stared into his mother's face. "Mom, where is Uncle Dan right now?"

Rachel walked toward the hallway leading to the front offices. "I can honestly say that I don't know exactly where he is at this moment."

"Damn it!" Sam slapped the bowl down on the table, spilling kibble everywhere. "He was there–at the house. Wasn't he? That's why you didn't want me coming home this weekend. I can't believe–"

Rachel kept walking. "You're repeating yourself, honey. Let's go to my office and I'll run a printout of the office equipment and chemical supplies. We can check to see if any of those are missing. I'll save the caskets and urns for next week."

"Mom! I'm going back to the house. He's probably still…"

"Don't bother. He left last night," Rachel said quickly. "Bring the cat food with you, Sam, and I'll tell you what else he said. Carrie, you and Ray can look for the mother cat and her kittens. Start in that storeroom by the stairs."

"Uncle Mac's got a girlfriend?" Bridget snickered and then yelped when one of her sisters' feet found her shin.

"The girlfriend is kind of old," Sean volunteered. "But he's got a really hot college girl working for him."

"You think that JJ's hot?" Mac inquired, surprised that Sean had noticed, and astonished that he wasn't too timid to mention it in front of his sisters.

"Well, not exactly hot, but…." Sean stumbled as the herd's eyes focused on him.

Mac relaxed, only feeling a little guilty for sacrificing the boy.

"So where are they?" Carrie asked as she helped Rachel stuff plastic garbage bags with the soiled Xerox paper that the cat had appropriated for a litter box the night before.

"Probably curled up in a casket with someone," Ray joked as he and Sam shifted the boxes of paper to one corner of the storeroom. "The next funeral should be fun."

"I moved the bowl of cat food into my office. Maybe the mother cat will come to us."

"What now?" Sam asked, dusting off his hands on his jeans. "Haven't you kept us here long enough?"

"Sam, I love you, but I don't like you very much right now," Rachel warned. "Your uncle wants you out of this as much as I do."

"Let him tell me that himself."

Rachel ignored him. "Carrie and I will take out the trash and meet you by the backdoor."

"I'm stuffed," Jeff said leaning back in his chair with a groan. "You outdid yourself, Mrs. O'Herlihy. You shouldn't have forced that second piece of cake on me."

Kathleen's eyes flashed. "Forced is it? Perhaps we should all try that diet that's so popular. The one with no sugar and no bread."

Mac watched as the family members surreptitiously pulled their cake-filled plates a little closer. All eyes turned toward the head of the clan.

Jeff coughed and gave Mac a sideways glance.

"Getting back to Mrs. Brenner, she seemed really concerned about Whiskey the other night at the vet's. How's she doing, Mac?"

Mac frowned and silently vowed to replay his friend's kindness at the first opportunity. He took another bite of cake.

Kathleen took the bait. "Yes, Mac. How are you and Mrs. Brenner getting along? It was very kind of her to drive you to the vet's. But your next date should be someplace without dog hair and the smell of cat urine."

* * *

"The lid is down." Carrie announced, halting her toss of the garbage bag in mid-swing. "Why's the lid down? The lid's not supposed to be down."

"You're right." Rachel thought the girl had a special talent for stating the obvious. "The police probably did that last night. I think we can lift up the lid, if not we'll have to go get Ray or Sam."

"I vote we get Ray," Carrie mumbled, setting the bag down. "I don't know how you've lived with Sam all these years. Have you noticed that he's really a moody person?"

Rachel gripped a corner of the metal lid, the action opening up the cut on her hand, blood seeping through the band-aid she'd hastily applied and dripping onto the metal. "Damn, damn, and damn," she repeated.

"Sorry, I thought you probably knew." Carrie said, grabbing the other corner.

"What?" Rachel gave the lid a push. It didn't budge.

"About Sam and his…" Carrie's eyes focused on Rachel's hand. "Your hand is bleeding."

Rachel laughed. "Carrie, I don't know what I would do without you."

"My parents say the same thing all the time. Old people love me." Carrie grinned. "Want me to try to lift the lid? I'm stronger than you think."

"Sure. My old bones appreciate it. Just be careful. Push the lid straight up. I'll stuff the bags inside."

"Do you smell something?" Carrie asked as she managed to lift the lid.

Rachel nodded. "Probably more dead kittens. The police took the dead kitten they found for some reason–probably to justify the expense of calling out the crime lab. But I guess they might have missed another."

With visible effort, Carrie pushed up the dumpster lid open about six inches.

"A little higher," Rachel said, holding one bag near the small opening Carrie had created.

* * *

"You should ask her out for dinner at that new Italian restaurant. Jeff knows someone who can get you reservations."

"Don't be playing matchmaker, Kathleen O'Herlihy. Rachel and I–"

"So it's Rachel now," Maura interjected. "On a first name basis."

Bridget smiled. "Uncle Mac would need some new clothes if he's going to date anyone."

"Is it too heavy for you?" Rachel asked as Carrie struggled to raise the lid higher. "Let me call Sam and Ray."

"No, I've got it." The teen extended her arms and shoved.

The lid flipped backwards with a loud clang.

Carrie screamed loud enough to wake the dead.

Mac's head snapped to face his goddaughter. "What's wrong with my clothes? Whose side are you on? Give me back my damn jelly beans." He glanced around. "In fact I want every box and bag of candy I generously distributed back in my hand before I leave here!"

The table erupted in laughter at the red-faced detective.

In a stage whisper to Sean, Jeff said, "At least he forgot about my beer."

The laughter got so loud that Mac could barely hear the ringing in his pocket. He glanced at the caller ID and then quickly motioned to the group for quiet.

"Sullivan," he barked. He listened intently. "I'm on my way. Call the police too. Don't touch a thing. I'll be there as soon as I can."

Twenty-seven

Mac made good time considering Sean's car lacked flashing lights and sirens. He pulled into the funeral home parking lot right behind an unmarked D.C. police car.

"Mac." Joanne Giles greeted him as she exited the driver's door.

"Detective." Mac smiled at the dark-haired policewoman. "We meet again. I see you got stuck partnering with Pete. My sympathies."

The scruffy narcotics detective grinned as he got out of the police car. "I'm the one you should be giving condolences to. Joanne must have been a cab driver in another life. It's going to take awhile for my stomach to retreat back down my throat."

"Go ahead and whine, you wimp. I've got seniority and if I want to drive, I'll drive." Joanne turned her attention back to Mac. "What do you know?"

Mac shrugged. "Probably not more than you. Rachel Brenner called me about twenty minutes ago. She reported finding a body in the funeral home dumpster. Female, maybe a college student at Concordia. Her assistant thinks she knows the deceased."

Pete took a toothpick from his pocket and slowly unwrapped the cellophane covering. He nodded at the group of a dozen police cars between them and the front door of the funeral home. "It looks like a full house in there. Maybe I'll nose around out here first. That's Mrs. Brenner's van, isn't it?"

"Yeah." Mac watched the man stick the toothpick in his mouth and walk toward the vehicle in question.

Joanne sighed and tapped Mac's shoulder. "Here comes trouble."

Mac trained his eyes on the overweight cop glaring at him from the funeral home entrance. "I guess it was too much to hope that on a Sunday afternoon Eddie would have been passed out in front of the TV too drunk to answer the phone."

"Well, I've personally never been that lucky. Sorry to leave you to him, but I've gotta check in with Greeley. See what he wants Pete and me doing," she nodded her head toward her partner who was walking slowly around the van, "other than parking lot duty."

"Pete's got a problem with crowds," Mac warned. "But he's a good cop to have covering your back."

"Yeah, I know." Joanne frowned. "You think that body was here last night and we missed it?"

Mac glanced toward the dumpster surrounded with yellow police tape. "I didn't look in–"

"Mac Sullivan. Looks like your girlfriend's brother racked up another kill," Eddie Gorden yelled as he approached the two.

"Later," Mac whispered to Joanne before she stepped away.

"Hey, Sullivan, I'm talking to you. You know where Dan Thayer is, you better cough him up," Eddie declared, passing Joanne with a smirk. "There's some real cops here today."

Mac hoped the stain on the man's dress shirt was spaghetti sauce and not an indication he'd been screwing up evidence. "Did you decide to wear your lunch?"

Eddie flushed and then grinned as he appeared to remember his mission. "Greeley wants your ass inside. Says he needs you to get the funeral lady's attention. I tried warming her up for you, but I guess I'm not her type."

When Mac didn't immediately respond, Eddie jabbed him again. "Where's your mutt? You look kind of lopsided without that flea-bitten horse leaning on your leg."

At that moment Whiskey emerged from the bushes where she'd gone to do her business.

Eddie grinned. "Have you been letting that dog take a leak in the crime scene? The lieutenant isn't going to like that."

Mac gritted his teeth and cut a wide circle around the cop as he headed for the funeral home. He was afraid of getting within arm's reach; afraid he might just do Greeley a favor and have a gun malfunction.

"I'm not talking to you any more without an attorney," Rachel declared, exhaustion and fear slowing her speech dramatically. It seemed like they'd been questioning her for hours instead of only a few minutes. The first police cars had arrived less than five minutes after her 911 call. Ten minutes after she'd removed Dan's keychain from where it was draped over the girl's cold fingers.

"There's a phone. Call one," Lieutenant Greeley responded, crossing his arms and leaning back in Jeff O'Herlihy's chair. "I'll wait. In fact we'll all wait, right here. No matter that a killer is getting away and every minute counts. Take your time and let me know when you feel comfortable answering a few simple questions about what you are doing here on a Sunday." He paused and took a cigar out of his pocket.

Mac walked into the room. "Talk to him Rachel. He may not look like it, but he's one of the good guys."

Greeley frowned and glanced down at his black suit. He tugged downward on his grey vest. "What do you mean? I look real good today. Hell, I look good every day."

She raised her eyes and stared at Mac, wondering why he'd been her first call and why she was relived that he was here. It didn't make sense. He was one of them. He'd blame the death of that young girl… Carrie had said her name was Tia Hu. Rachel blinked, but she could still see the long black hair and mixed with the darkened blood on the girl's head. The smell had been terrible. Somehow it was different when they were inside on a prep table.

"No white hat." Mac pulled out a chair and sat down.

The motion of the chair moving caught her attention and drew her away from the nightmare scene playing over and over in her head.

"What?" Rachel's eyes wearily moved back and forth between the men, her mind hadn't registered their conversation.

Mac strummed his fingers the tabletop. "Rachel, why are you here?"

"What?" She looked accusingly at Greeley and then back to Mac. "He said I couldn't leave. And he's got the kids locked up somewhere too. Can he question them without me being there to–"

Mac held up a hand. "Yeah, they're all over eighteen. The police can question them."

"They don't know anything," she protested. "As soon as I saw the body, I sent them to the van to wait." She had sent them to the van and then had reached over into the dumpster.

Mac paused and then tried again. "What I meant was why are you here–in the funeral home–today? Isn't it closed on Sundays?"

"After the break-in I needed to come back today to do an inventory and deal with the cat. Someone must have been here last night, hiding until we left." She left the rest of her thoughts unspoken. The killer had been hiding and waiting for a chance to dispose of the body and frame Dan.

"Hiding along with a body in tow?" Greeley asked. "The coroner says the body was moved. Miss Hu wasn't killed here. Why do you suppose someone would dump a body at this funeral home?"

"I don't know." But she did know, or had her suspicions. Only a chance ray of direct sunlight had spoiled the killer's plans. The gold horse-shaped fob on the keychain that she'd given Dan last Christmas had glinted brightly inside the dumpster.

Greeley raised his eyebrows but refrained from comment.

Mac stared at her. "The police checked the building. Plus, Whiskey and I did a walk through. Nobody was here when we left."

Rachel turned to glare at him. "Did you check the dumpster? Did the other two detectives who questioned me actually look in there?"

The detective sighed.

"Maybe the dumpster wasn't the only place you didn't check out." Rachel looked from a silent Mac toward Greeley.

"Hey, tell your story and your theories to Mac. I'm just going to sit here awhile and listen."

Rachel was finding it harder to draw a deep breath. "I need to get some air. The smell is... Is it hot in here?"

Mac looked toward Greeley.

Greeley shrugged. "I don't smell anything but Bryant's aftershave. What did you do swim in the stuff?"

The young cop blushed.

"I can still smell...when Carrie opened the dumpster..." Rachel looked from one man to the other, feeling her stomach churning. "There was an odor... Can't you smell it?"

"Was anything missing?" Mac asked softly. He could tell she was confused. Probably in shock. He wasn't even sure she was hearing him.

Rachel pushed her hair back from her face. "I beg your pardon?"

"You said you needed to do an inventory. Was anything missing? What did you find when you got here?"

"When we arrived? I already told them. I don't think I can... You don't smell anything?"

"Don't think about the body. Think about when you got here this morning. Was everything still locked up?" Mac watched her face carefully, noticing that she seemed paler by the second.

"I didn't notice anything." She paused. "I used my keys to get in."

"Why were the others with you?"

"Sam and I were having an argument. I wanted to keep them out of trouble; keep them busy." She stopped and Mac waited. "I don't feel well."

Mac looked over at the lieutenant. He could tell from Greeley's expression that if he didn't continue the questioning, Greeley would have someone else do it. "Did you have lunch? Do you want something–"

"God, no," Rachel answered, raising her hand to her mouth.

Mac pressed again. "Was anything missing?"

"We couldn't find the mother.... I brought some food, but we couldn't find her."

"Mother?" Greeley asked, breaking his silence.

"She's talking about the cat," Mac explained. "It was missing last night, so we left the kittens here."

"No one has said anything today about finding a cat." Greeley motioned to a patrolman standing nearby. "Officer Bryant, go check that out."

The young officer nodded, making a note in his book.

Greeley sighed. "No APB, son. Just look for a cat."

"That's cats, plural, big and small," Mac offered, ignoring the expression on Greeley's face and hoping that the moment of levity would ease the tension in the room.

Rachel looked blankly from Mac to Greeley and then glanced at the patrolman. "I know you. You're the basketball player."

Mac and Greeley looked at each other and then Joe Bryant.

The young cop blushed and put his notebook back in his pocket. "I used to have a pretty good 3-point shot."

The nausea was worse. Rachel was having trouble hearing them over the noise of the blood pounding in her head. "I think she may have gotten outside again. But I brought some food just in case…"

Greeley shifted in his chair, attracting Mac's attention.

"What?" Rachel asked, looking at Greeley. She flinched as her voice seemed to echo inside her skull. Taking a deep breath, she held very still in hopes that the clamor in her head would quiet. This was ridiculous. She'd seen dead bodies before. Lots of them.

Greeley removed the cigar from his mouth. "Let's try to move away from the cat topic. According to the girl, what's her name, Carrie, the victim worked with your brother and reported to Mrs. Lopez, the woman who was killed a few nights ago. Four people worked in that office. Three are now dead. The way I see it the one who's left is either the killer or the next victim."

Killer. Victim. Killer. Victim. Dan. A roaring sound slowly replaced the echo in her head. She returned her hands to the table, gripping the edge to steady herself, as the waves rushed in.

"Rachel, do you know who killed that girl?" Mac's blue eyes found hers and latched on.

"No." The roaring was deafening. She tried not to think about what she'd wrapped in a tissue and hidden inside her bra.

"Rachel?"

Mac's concerned face swam in front of her as the waves engulfed her.

Twenty-eight

"Mrs. Brenner's okay," Joanne said as she emerged from the Ladies' Room. "Just throwing some cold water on her face. She'll be out in a second."

Mac nodded at her. "Where are the kids?"

"In the employee break room. So far they're not talking much."

"Don't let Eddie near them," Mac warned.

"I'll try but I think they all know more than they are saying. Somebody needs to tell them it's time to come to Jesus." Joanne fixed Mac with a hard look.

He shook his head in disgust. "I'm no good at sermons, but I'll see what I can manage. Do me a favor. You stay with the kids and make sure they don't get into trouble. I need to talk to the lieutenant and then I'll talk to them. Where is he?"

"Out front, arguing with a reporter."

Mac raised his eyebrows.

"The story is already out. The brass is having a fit. Calling in the crime lab last night, even if it was for the wrong reason, is the only thing saving my gold shield. They took some swabs of the blood on the hearse. It was human."

Mac put his hand on her shoulder. "Don't worry about it. Everyone thought–"

"Yeah, but cat or no cat, I should have checked that dumpster myself. The lieutenant isn't happy."

"You're not the only one who screwed up. I'm going to see if I can steal a look at the scene before they move the body."

"Mackenzie Sullivan! I thought you retired to a fishing boat in Florida." A tall woman with a long gray braid smiled at him.

"That lasted about a week. Then I'd had all the fish I could enjoy." He held out a hand to Greeley's favorite medical examiner, a fifty-something woman with an addiction to Camel cigarettes and country music. "How are you, Georgia? Still smoking a pack a day?"

"I'm cutting back. Most days I'm down to one cigarette per autopsy." She waved off shaking his hand, instead holding up her blood smeared, latex-covered ones for his view. "What's your business here?"

"Long story. Can I take a look?"

"If it's okay with Greeley, it's fine with me. You know the procedure. Gloves and shoe covers are over there." She pointed to a black case positioned against the brick funeral home wall. "You'll need to stand on the ladder to see inside. Try not to touch anything inside the dumpster or all you'll smell for the next few days is decaying flesh."

"Cause of death?"

She chuckled. "Unofficially–.38 caliber gun shot to the back of the head. Officially–the same thing but typed up tomorrow along with the results of a bunch of lab tests."

"Time of death?"

"Body is still in full rigor so with these temps, not more than forty-eight hours, maybe a few hours less. I'll need to check the stomach contents to narrow it down more."

"Best guess?"

"Early Friday night."

Mac ticked off the days in his head. The night after Whiskey was abducted. The night Rachel Brenner practically threw him and Whiskey out of her house.

"Mrs. Brenner is lying. She knows where her brother is and I'm ready to let her enjoy the comforts of the D.C. jail until she tells me what she knows," Greeley announced when Mac came back inside the funeral home.

"On what charges?"

"Accessory to murder, make that murders, plural. Aiding and abetting a fugitive. Material witness. I'm sure I can come up with enough to hold Mrs. Brenner until she coughs up her brother."

"I'm not sure she knows where he is," Mac offered weakly.

"He's getting help from someone. He's been playing us for fools, practically parading down Constitution Avenue then disappearing into thin air. He's got help, damn it, and I think the lady is in up to her skinny armpits."

"She's cooperated..." Mac began. "Did you ever check out the girlfriend angle? What about Lenore–"

"We've been looking into Ms. Adams. I've got someone watching her house and office. You concentrate on Mrs. Brenner." Greeley narrowed his eyes. "Unless you've gotten so personally involved that–"

"You know me better than that." Mac tried a different tack. "I think maybe it's slipped your mind that you haven't charged Dan Thayer with anything yet. She's not aiding a fugitive."

"Whose side are you on?"

Mac shrugged. "Whichever side the truth is on. Rachel Brenner believes her brother is being framed. From what she can see, he's already been tried and convicted by the D.C. police. And I'm not at all sure she's wrong."

The lieutenant slammed his hand against the brick wall. "That's bullshit and you know it. I think you may be a little too close to the suspects in this particular case."

"Let me talk to her and the kids. If I can't get Rach–Mrs. Brenner to tell me what she knows, then you can bring in the rack and thumb screws."

Greeley stared wordlessly at the private detective and then nodded. "You've got ten minutes. Talk fast."

"Give us a few minutes," Mac said to the narcotics detective sitting with Rachel in her office.

"Sure, I'll check with Joanne, see what she wants me to do." Pete cocked his head toward Rachel who had her head down on her arms which were resting on the desk. Her eyes were closed. "She's been pretty quiet."

Mac sat down in the chair across from her. "Rachel."

When she didn't stir, he cleared his throat. "We need to talk."

"All I know is that a young girl was murdered and dumped in a garbage bin." Rachel sat up slowly. Her eyes were hollow and a spasm passed through her body. "Someone killed a kid, no older than Sam, and for what? They killed her and tossed her in that dumpster like–"

"Listen to me," Mac reached over and touched Rachel's hand to force her to focus on him. "I don't know who is responsible for this. But I do know the killer is running scared and killing anyone who gets in his way. You're in danger. Sam and his friends are in danger."

"It's not Dan," Rachel said, her voice hollow and thin.

"He, she–I don't know who the hell it is, but that person will just as soon kill you, as sneeze. Greeley has got three murders on his plate and he's looking–"

"For Dan, whether he's the killer or not," Rachel interrupted.

"Yes, he wants Dan Thayer for questioning. But right now the lieutenant thinks you're harboring a fugitive. You've got to tell him everything you know, and frankly, you know a lot more than you've said."

"I–"

Mac held up his hand to stop her. "It's a lie, Rachel Brenner. You know more than you've told me. You went to Warrenton last Thursday night specifically to meet your brother. I know you're in contact with him. Was the plan that he'd be here this afternoon?"

"No," Rachel asserted, then closed her lips and looked away.

Mac stood up. "Whether you believe it or not, I've been trying to help you."

"Then find the real killer," Rachel implored. "Dan didn't do it. He just couldn't have killed somebody and thrown her in the trash. He just couldn't."

Mac laughed. "Disposing of a body in the garbage isn't his style? That's the best defense you can come up with for him?"

Rachel stood toe-to-toe with the private detective. "Stop it. I've got nothing more to tell you. I'm taking the kids and we're going home."

Mac grabbed her arm as she started for the door. He spun her to face him. "You don't have to talk to me, Mrs. Brenner. But Lieutenant Greeley wants to have another word with you. If you lie to him again, he'll throw you in jail."

"I didn't–I don't believe you." She searched his face. "You're just trying to scare me."

"Hell, you don't have the good sense to be scared."

Rachel stuck out her chin. "I don't have to talk without a lawyer. I know my rights."

"No you don't have to talk. You can sit in a six by eight foot cell and remain as silent as you want." Mac shook his head in disbelief. "Why are you protecting a grown man who doesn't have the balls to stand up for himself? Someone who hides behind his big sister's skirt?"

"Stop shouting at me! Dan's not hiding."

"Really?" Mac swept his arm outwards. "Where is he? Where is he when you and the kids are in danger? He seems to be perfectly happy to let you take the fall for his disappearing act."

"Leave me alone. I'm going home."

"Not yet," Mac said, opening the door and motioning for Officer Bryant to step forward "Just remember I gave you a chance to do it the easy way."

Twenty-nine

"Mrs. Brenner, I'd like to ask you some questions." Greeley began as she approached the table where Sam, Ray, and Carrie were seated. Carrie was sniffing loudly and dabbing at the corners of her reddened eyes. Ray was next to her, one arm tight around the young woman's shoulders.

A movement against the far wall drew her attention. The four detectives who'd been hunting Dan stood at attention, apparently waiting for something. Joe Bryant joined them.

Rachel felt like laughing, wondering if they were waiting for her to make a run for it. They didn't know she wasn't the running type. At least not any more.

"Mom, you okay?" Sam started to rise, but Rachel motioned for him to stay in place.

"Lieutenant, I'm not answering anything unless I have a lawyer present. I'll be glad to come to the station tomorrow–"

"Mrs. Brenner, we can do this easy or we can do this hard." Greeley motioned for Rachel to take an empty seat at the table.

"Don't threaten me," Rachel snapped. "I've had just about enough of your harassment. I've committed no crimes and broken no laws that I'm aware of." The thought crossed her mind that tampering with a body might qualify as something but she was the only one who knew about that.

The lieutenant held up his hand in self-defense. "I'm not threatening you. And it's not my intent to harass you. I'm asking for your cooperation."

"And if I don't choose to give it?" In her peripheral vision, she saw Mac and his dog quietly enter the room and the dog immediately take up a position next to Ray. Mac stood near the window. He was waiting too, probably for her to beg for his help. She wasn't the begging type either. Never had been.

Greeley locked gazes with her. "Then I'll be forced to find other ways to get to the truth. And that's a promise, Mrs. Brenner, not a threat."

Mac knew what Greeley was going to do. His former boss was very good at getting suspects to cooperate. He just hoped Greeley remembered that Rachel and the kids weren't criminals; the worst they'd done was try to help a man they believed to be innocent.

"Giles." Greeley's sharp tone brooked no nonsense. The female detective immediately moved to the center of the room.

"Yes, sir."

"Take Sam Brenner into one of the viewing rooms and get his movements for the past week. Have him account for every day and get the names of people on campus who can verify whether he was in class when he claims he was. I also want to know where he's been for every minute of the last twenty-four hours."

Startled, Sam looked toward his mother.

"Leave him alone," Rachel insisted.

Mac saw her glance in his direction, but he couldn't help her now. He'd tried to gain her trust, but she'd made her decision to go it alone.

"Giles, I gave you an order," Greeley commanded.

The female detective tugged at Sam's arm. "Come on, kid. Let's go."

The teen stood. "It's okay, Mom. I can handle this."

"Sam." Rachel stepped in front of her son. "Don't say a word. We're not going to discuss anything without a lawyer present."

"I'll be fine." Sam touched his mother's hand. "Don't let them bully you."

"Giles, now."

Mac watched the detective push the teen ahead of her out of the room. He had no doubt that the worst Joanne would do to Sam would be to offer him a soda and, if he didn't smart off to her, a candy bar. Greeley just wanted Sam out of his mother's sight.

"You so much as touch a hair on his head…" Rachel warned, her voice shaking in fury.

Greeley's expression was stone cold. "There are rules for interrogating suspects."

"How is he a suspect?" Rachel demanded. "Sam was in

Philadelphia when this whole mess began. You can check–"

"I can't eliminate anyone for the murder of the girl," Greeley pointed out. "I don't have a time of death. She was discarded in a dumpster to which he had access. She's a–or was–a pretty college co-ed. Your son spend any time on the Concordia campus?"

Rachel stormed across the room. "This is crap and you know it."

"Three people are dead and I want to talk to your brother about what he had to do with the murders."

"Dan didn't have anything to do with these deaths," Rachel insisted, glancing toward Mac again.

"Then he should turn himself in and–"

"And you'd stop looking for the real killer," Rachel finished.

Rachel and the head of detectives glared at one another. Finally, Greeley took a deep breath and whirled around to face Mac.

"Sullivan," Greeley barked.

Mac stepped forward. He'd been expecting this too. Greeley didn't want Rachel to have any support in the room.

"Get out."

"Sir?"

"You heard me the first time. Get out. This is official police business."

"Lieutenant, I'd like to stay–"

"I don't give a damn what you'd like. Get out."

Mac stiffened, then gave a mock salute. "Yes, sir."

He clicked his fingers for Whiskey. The dog whined and settled closer to Ray, rubbing her nose against the young man's jeans. Maybe leaving Whiskey in the room was a good idea. Mac looked from the hound to the teen and then to the lieutenant.

"Seems like my dance card is coming up empty. I'll be just outside. Call me if Whiskey confesses to the crime. I'll post bail." Mac sauntered out.

The lieutenant cocked his head toward the table. "Mrs. Brenner, please take a seat. Now!"

Rachel hesitated, then walked slowly to a chair opposite the young couple. She gave them a quick glance, trying to evaluate how much more of this they could take. Carrie nodded and moved even closer to Ray, practically sitting in his lap. Her eyes, swollen from all the tears, darted between the two adults in the standoff.

Ray gave her a tight smile, one arm still around Carrie's shoulders, his other hand nervously combing through the wiry hair of the Irish wolfhound.

The lieutenant leaned back against the bookshelf. "When did you last see your brother?"

"I've got nothing to say." Rachel stared wearily at Greeley and waited.

"I can bring you in as a material witness to a crime."

Rachel's hands were shaking so much that she clasped them together to still their movements. She forced herself to hold the lieutenant's fierce glare. "I'm not talking without my lawyer."

"Okay, we can play hardball if you want." The lieutenant pointed to the two detectives across the room.

"Fiori, Gorden." The two officers stood at attention. "Read Kozlowski his rights. He's under arrest as an accessory to murder."

Ray's head snapped up, his eyes moving between the lieutenant and the overweight detective who was pulling a set of handcuffs from his back pocket. Whiskey growled and bared her teeth.

"Down girl," Ray soothed. Whiskey ignored the command and started to pace, moving to the window and whining.

"You have the right to remain silent..." Fiori intoned the litany.

"No," Carrie screamed, clutching frantically at Ray's arm.

Whiskey began barking.

"Tell me where Dan Thayer is," the lieutenant ordered.

"I..." Rachel hesitated.

"Put Kozlowski in a squad car and take him to central booking," the lieutenant snapped.

"Mrs. Brenner, you can't let them do this to Ray," Carrie cried.

Greeley stalked out of the break room and Rachel followed on his heels. Behind them they could hear Pete Fiori continue to intone the Miranda warning.

"...and refuse to answer questions."

"This is outrageous." Rachel grabbed Greeley's wrist.

The lieutenant shot a look at the woman who quickly withdrew her hand.

"Leave Ray alone," she implored. "He doesn't know anything."

"He's a material witness, withheld evidence, tampered with a crime scene. I'm sure I have enough to hold him. He'll be arraigned tomorrow and released…if he can make bail." A small smile tugged at the corners of Greeley's mouth.

"You are a sorry son of a bitch. Ray doesn't know anything about these murders and you know it."

"But you know something about them, Mrs. Brenner. I'm tired of your games. Three people are already dead. How many more are going to have to die before you decide to come clean?"

"Get off him you big baboon." Carrie voice carried into the hallway.

"Okay bitch, now you're under arrest too, for assaulting an officer."

Carrie screamed.

Rachel pivoted on her heel and raced back to the break room, gasping when she saw that Eddie Gorden had twisted Carrie's arm behind her back. The situation was out of control.

"Give me another set of cuffs," Eddie yelled to Pete Fiori. "I'm under attack."

"Get your hands off her," Ray warned, using his shoulder to shove the cop against the table and away from Carrie.

Eddie roared like a wounded bull and charged at Ray. He slammed his fist into the boy's stomach, and immediately followed it up with a second blow to the solar plexus. Winded, the tall, gangly young man doubled over, sucking desperately for air. At that moment, the cop delivered a stunning blow to the back of the teen's neck. Ray sank to his knees.

Carrie lunged to the teen's side and threw her arms around him. Whiskey's barking reached a frenzy. Mac suddenly appeared. Breathing heavily, Eddie pushed Carrie aside and jerked Ray to his feet. He grabbed the boy's arm, twisting it. "Now you can add assault and resisting arrest to the list of charges."

"Anything you do say may be used against you in a court of law," Fiori continued without pause. "You have the right to consult an attorney before speaking to the police…"

"Stop!" Rachel screamed. She had no choices left. Dan would

have to take care of himself. "I'll tell you whatever you want to know."

Whiskey's barking had gotten him back inside the funeral home; Rachel's scream had propelled him across the room. "Let the kid go," he yelled at Eddie above the din. "It's over."

Eddie ignored the private detective and twisted Ray's arm in a tighter hold, forcing the teen to cry out in pain.

"Let him go you jackass," Mac demanded. "I won't tell you again."

"Like hell I will."

"Now." Mac grabbed Eddie's arm and yanked it away from Ray. Enraged, the cop swung wildly at Mac, who easily deflected the blows.

"You're under arrest Sullivan for assault, battery, and interfering in a police matter," Eddie screamed, his face beet red.

Whiskey raced across the floor, teeth bared. Ray grabbed the dog's collar. Whiskey barked wildly, frantically tugging to get free.

"You're running out of handcuffs, Gorden."

"Call off that mutt of yours or I'll shoot her."

Mac turned and Eddie landed a solid punch on his jaw.

"And never draw another breath, you fat bastard." His mouth bleeding, Mac threw an uppercut, the force of the blow lifting Eddie up and dropping him to the floor.

"Break it up, NOW!" Greeley shouted from the doorway.

Eddie scrambled to his feet, his leather shoes sliding on the floor. He charged toward Mac, but Pete Fiori reached out and grabbed him by the back of his belt, holding him back.

The lieutenant stormed over to Mac. "I thought I told you to get out."

"Keep your trained apes under control and I wouldn't have to be here." Panting for breath, Mac glared at the lieutenant, then walked over to Ray and Whiskey.

"You okay?" Mac asked, resting his hand on the young man's shoulder.

The teen nodded, still too winded to speak, but managing to hold steadfast to Whiskey's collar. The dog's frantic barking had quieted to dangerous growls.

Mac took a leash from his back pocket and clipped it to Whiskey's collar, then moved to the far side of the room, away from Eddie who was still gasping for air and straining to escape Fiori's hold.

"Detective Gorden," the lieutenant called to the overweight cop. "Check with the medical examiner to determine when the body can be released."

Fiori suddenly let go and Eddie almost ended up on the floor again.

The cop's face turned from red to an ugly shade of purple. "What? No way. Send Fiori. This is my case and I want–"

"I gave you an order. Get outside now."

"What about Sullivan?" Eddie said, hunched over as he tried to catch his breath. "I want him in cuffs. Attacked me. I'm pressing charges." He sucked in another breath.

"We'll discuss what charges will be filed later. Are you disobeying a direct order?"

"I'm calling the union," the cop wheezed as he barreled past the lieutenant.

"You do that," Greeley answered, then turned his attention to Rachel who was huddled on the floor holding Carrie in her arms. The young woman was sobbing incoherently.

"Sit down at the table, Mrs. Brenner. You've got thirty seconds to tell me where your brother is. Otherwise I'm locking all of you up, including that damn dog."

Thirty

"She must have fell out of the ugly tree and hit every branch on the way down."

Rachel glanced up from her perch on her front steps. She half-listened to Edgar Freed, who'd declared himself almost a partner in the Sullivan Detective Agency, wheeze his way through another rendition of how he had spotted the 'butt-ugly serial killer' who'd been holed up in "Miz Brenner's house." How he told Elinor, when this "ugly tall drink of water in an ugly Pepto-Bismol pink blouse–"

"A blouse I was donating to charity," Elinor Freed interjected. "And it wasn't ugly. I paid more than $20.00 for it at–"

"Let me finish the story, old woman. They don't care where you shop," Edgar snapped. "Anyway, as soon as I saw that 'sissy-man' slink out of Miz Brenner's house, I said, 'Elinor give me the phone. There's trouble across the street'. And Elinor said–"

Rachel tuned out the chatter, the two-way radios, and the flashing lights of the police cars and crime scene vans blocking Rittenhouse Street. Dan was gone, long gone, if Edgar Freed's timetable was correct. Dan had bolted from the house, clad in some of the charity clothes she'd collected for the women's shelter, in a D.C. cab about fifteen minutes after she and the kids had left for the funeral home.

Now six hours later, she was sitting on her steps, her house being torn apart by the D.C. police looking for a gun. She pulled her sweater tighter around her and closed her eyes.

Someone nudged her knee.

She opened her eyes and drowned in the dark, warm eyes that promised unconditional affection.

"Looks like you could use a friend." Mac pushed Whiskey to the side, but first the dog offered her a long, sloppy kiss.

Mac chuckled as she wiped off her face with the sleeve of her sweater. "Sorry about that." He sat down on the steps next to her.

"Sam get off?"

"Yep. I dropped him off at the station in time to make the 6:00 o'clock train. Gets into Philly at 7:36."

"Thank you," she murmured.

"No problem. Your son isn't talking to me so it was a long ride down to the station."

"Yeah, Sam is royally pissed at everyone, except for Dan." Rachel chuckled without humor. "But there was no point in him staying. I'm not letting Sam ruin his life…"

"Yeah. The kid needs to be in school. What about Carrie and Ray? Do I need to–"

"No. Greeley let them go home about forty minutes ago." Rachel looked up in alarm. "You don't think that animal, what's his name, Eddie, will go after Ray again?"

Mac gingerly rubbed his cheek and felt his own swollen lip. "Nah. Greeley will keep him on a short leash after that fiasco."

She looked closely at the private detective's face. "How are you feeling?"

He gingerly touched his mouth again and then shook his head. "Like an idiot. I can't believe I let that fool get the drop on me."

She glanced back at her house, still full of shadows moving between the rooms. An officer emerged from the front door carrying her hard drive, as well as the file box with all the data disks. Two others followed, hauling the area rug that laid in front of her mantle, as well as several plastic evidence bags. "What are they doing?"

"A department computer geek is going to analyze your hard drive." Mac leaned forward and whispered, "Hope Sam hasn't been visiting any porn websites because it's all going to come out."

"Why my rug?"

"Blood evidence."

Rachel inhaled sharply. "They don't think…" she stammered, holding out her bandaged hand. "I cut myself on a piece of glass. It's my blood not-not–"

"They've got to check everything."

"Tell me that again." Mac moved a little farther away from the activity on the Brenner front porch and cupped one hand over the ear not pressed to his cell phone.

"Did you hear the part about the homecoming queens?" JJ impatiently asked.

Mac frowned. "No. Start over–from the beginning. Where are you?"

"I'm over at the college newspaper office. I–"

"It's open on Sunday?"

"No, but I know a guy who knows the guy who edits the paper."

"Of course you do." Mac smiled. His new secretary seemed to know lots of guys who knew guys who could get her what she wanted.

"Are you being sarcastic?"

"No. That was admiration in my voice not sarcasm."

"It sounded like sarcasm."

"JJ, I only have 1000 minutes a month on this cell phone. Get to the point."

"I could probably get you a better deal. Do you have roll over–"

"JJ!"

"If you hadn't interrupted me, I'd be done by now."

Mac noticed Greeley coming out of Rachel's house. "Talk fast JJ or hang up."

"Remember that photo in the Clarion–the one the guy shot of the clock tower while lying on his back?"

"Yeah." He watched Fitz, his arms full of plastic evidence bags, walk off the porch and head for the crime lab van.

"I figured he probably shot lots of photos that weekend. More than what showed up in the newspaper. So I called up–"

"Skip ahead to the good part."

"I found a group shot of Concordia's past homecoming queens–or at least the ones that showed up for homecoming–and some of the Administration elites. The photo was taken in front of the clock tower on Saturday–before the game."

"Keep going. I'll let you know when you say something interesting."

"That's sarcasm."

"Sorry. It's been a tough afternoon. There was another murder."

"Where?"

"Rachel Brenner's funeral home." Mac saw Joanne and Pete join

Greeley on the porch. "JJ, I don't have much time. Tell me about the photo, please."

"Gina Malwick was front and center."

"Okay."

"Lenore Adams was standing next to her."

"You've got my attention. Who else was in the photo?"

"Couple of old women I didn't recognize. Must have been former homecoming queens. A younger woman with blonde hair. I've seen her around campus a few times. Some guy who's on the board of trustees. I think his name is Starling. President Krenek, Coach Morgan. Ms. Fieldstone. She's a–"

"I know who she is. Who else?"

"Well, Tia Hu of course and–"

"Wait. Tia Hu was in the photo."

"Well. Duh. She's this year's homecoming queen; of course she'd be in the shot."

Mac sighed. "Tia is the third murder victim."

"Bummer."

"JJ!"

"Sorry. It's just that Tia was so… Wonder who will get the crown?"

"I don't have time for this. Can you get copies for me?"

"Sure, but there's something else."

"What?" Mac saw Rachel stand and go into the house along with Greeley and Joanne.

"I haven't been through all the photos but I think Dan Thayer is in the background of a couple of them."

A cloud of white dust hung in the air. Fingerprint powder littered every surface. Rachel glanced around the upturned living room, then followed Greeley into the kitchen. Every cabinet door hung ajar–evidence of the police's thorough search for the weapon.

The lieutenant motioned for Rachel to take a seat at the cluttered table. "I'll need you to sign these ." He gestured to a pile of forms. "They are releases for the computer, disks, rug, and other evidence we've taken. I appreciate that you didn't wait for a search warrant and that you and the kids let us take your fingerprints for comparison to those we found in the dumpster and here. We may also want a blood sample. There was blood on the edge of the dumpster."

Rachel looked down at the fresh bandage on her hand. "I've got nothing to hide,"

"The issue is whether your brother hid something here," Greeley said.

Rachel winced, remembering that Dan had originally stashed a gun under the rose bush in her flowerbed. But someone, presumably the killer, had conveniently removed the incriminating evidence. Of course, now she was concealing incriminating evidence. The police had searched her house, but not her. The keychain was still safe.

She scribbled her name on the forms.

"I'm going to ask you again. You have no idea where your brother went?"

Rachel shook her head. She was so tired that she could barely hear the cop's questions anymore.

"Mrs. Brenner?"

The sharp tone startled her.

"I don't know. I honestly don't know where he is. He was supposed to stay here until I got back from the funeral home. I don't know where he went or why."

The grandfather clock in the living room chimed eight times. Rachel almost smiled. The old timepiece had carefully guarded Thayer family hours for more than a century. The deep, hourly ringing never ceased to comfort her, a constant memory of an era that had once been peaceful. She shivered. Those days had passed.

It was just after eight o'clock but felt like midnight. The last of the crime lab technicians had finally left. Rachel found the pillow cushions that had been discarded on the floor during the search and tossed them back on the sofa. She sank down wearily, unable to fathom straightening and cleaning up the mess.

There was a quick knock at the front door and then Mac and Whiskey came in. They'd gone out to talk to Greeley before he returned to headquarters.

"The lieutenant says you don't have to come into headquarters tomorrow, but not to think about leaving town." Mac sat down at the opposite end of the couch.

Whiskey hopped up next to Rachel and put her head in the woman's lap.

Mac snapped his fingers. "Down girl. You know better."

"Leave her alone." Rachel gently scratched behind the hound's ears and was rewarded with a gentle rumble.

"Where's your cat?"

Whiskey's ears pricked up.

"At Althea's. The lieutenant let me take her over there before they started the search. I'll get her in the morning…if she even wants to return. Althea waits on her hand and foot–or should I say, paw." Rachel started to laugh, and then just as suddenly, burst into tears.

Mac fumbled in his pocket for a handkerchief. He handed the wrinkled cotton cloth to her. "It's clean."

"Thanks," she mumbled, wiping her eyes and drawing shaky breaths.

"I can't believe this nightmare. My brother's accused of multiple murders, my son is practically flunking out of college, and-and strangers…" Rachel dissolved into a fresh set of heart-wrenching sobs that made the rest of the sentence almost unfathomable.

Mac smiled softly when he finally deciphered her mumbled, "Strangers pawed through my underwear looking for a gun."

Mac let her cry for a few minutes.

At last, Rachel's cries quieted to unevenly spaced sniffles. She sat up, wiped her eyes, then blew her nose into the handkerchief.

She glanced across the sofa and found concerned eyes. "Sorry."

Mac locked eyes with Rachel. "You really have no idea who his girlfriend is? Nothing that he ever said over the last few months to give you a clue. I picked up a rumor about him and Lenore Adams."

"I don't know. Her name keeps coming up. So maybe." Rachel ran a hand through her curls, tucking the errant locks behind her ears. "Frankly, I haven't spent any real time with Dan in months."

Mac shifted in his seat and turned to face Rachel. "Whoever killed Tia is getting more dangerous."

"What do you mean?"

"Think about it. The first murder was in the clock tower. Nobody found the body for 24 hours. There was plenty of time for the killer to get away, cover his tracks. The second murder, I'm convinced, was done out of desperation. Angela Lopez knew something important and was going to tell you. The killer took big chances that night, but I think because he got away with it, he got more fearless."

Rachel nodded. "Whoever killed Tia wanted me to find the body or at least tie the murder to my brother by dumping the body in the funeral home dumpster. But why?"

"I don't know, but whoever it is, knows who you are and thinks you're a threat. You know something and don't know that you know it."

Rachel eyes grew wide. "But I don't know anything."

"I think you do. It's something you saw. Something that…"

Mac stopped. He studied Rachel's face. "What did you see at the funeral home?"

Rachel flushed again. Despite the private detective's admission that he believed in Dan's innocence, she worried that he'd change his mind if he saw what she'd hidden in her bra.

"You saw what I saw," she insisted. "The body in the dumpster was horrifying and I'll never forget it, but there was nothing there that told me anything about the killer."

Mac continued to stare at her.

Rachel looked downward and began stroking Whiskey's head with trembling fingers. She waited for Mac to call her a liar; waited for him to demand to see what she'd removed from the murder scene.

He waited too.

Only the ticking of the clock broke the silence.

Rachel flinched as the sound of the clock seemed to get louder and louder.

Finally, Mac shrugged. "Well too bad the killer doesn't believe that."

"Do you…do you think the killer will come back here? I mean there's nothing left. The police have strip-searched my house." Rachel winced at her own words.

"Maybe you're right. No point in breaking in again."

Rachel exhaled loudly and slumped back against the cushions.

"Unless…"

She tensed. "Unless what?"

"Unless you've hidden something so well–"

"I haven't…," she protested.

"Or you don't know you have it. But if the police have missed it and it's that important to the killer, then…"

Rachel's heart raced. "He's not going to stop until he finds it."

The clock chimed the half hour.

Mac rose from the couch. "You should get some rest."

Rachel looked up, eyes wide, sleep an impossible concept.

"Look, how about if I leave Whiskey here. She'll be on guard duty while you get some sleep."

A gentle snore rumbled from the hairy hound.

Mac grinned and was rewarded by a matching grin from Rachel.

"You don't mind? I'm thinking maybe I should get one of those alarm systems like Althea has, but until–"

"No problem. Whiskey will keep you company. If you need me, you can reach me at my office…"

"At this hour?"

"Yeah. JJ called. She's got some stuff I need to look at. I'll swing by there on my way home."

"You like your new secretary?"

"Yeah. She's really good with computers and she's slowly getting my business records into shape during lulls in her office remodeling work." He grinned. "I never know quite what to expect when I walk in the door, but so far so good. Yesterday I managed to convince her that a Taser gun wasn't one of the top ten things a private detective's secretary needed to do her job. We're still arguing over spy cameras and some kind of laser eavesdropping equipment."

"I'd laugh, but after just having my privacy shredded none of that seems very funny." Rachel moved Whiskey over a little and stood. "What do you really know about this woman? Where's she from?"

He considered her question for a second. "I don't have a clue. I turned around one day and there she was. She's a mystery."

Thirty-one

"You don't have any food in here." Sam slammed the refrigerator door shut. "I'm starving."

"Do I look like your mother? If you're hungry go to the store or a restaurant or better yet–go home." Carrie was standing in front of the bathroom mirror, applying makeup, and trying to ignore the uninvited guest who was rummaging through her kitchen. "Your mother is going to go ballistic when she finds out you didn't go back to Philly. I don't want her mad at me for helping you."

"Don't worry. By the time Mom finds out, we'll have found Uncle Dan and gotten him to some place safe. Maybe Canada." Sam searched through the cabinets next to the refrigerator.

"I'm not going to Canada. I don't have any vacation days."

"You don't have to go to Canada. Ray and I can handle it." He shook his head in disbelief at the bare shelves. "You don't even have cereal. Who doesn't have cereal?"

"Hey, I have some Ramen noodles. And I think there's a pizza in the freezer."

He pulled out the frozen pizza and started reading the instructions on the back. "We should leave to pick up Ray soon. I don't think we have time to cook the pizza. It says eighteen minutes, minimum."

Carrie stuck her head out of the bathroom door, a towel covering her freshly-washed hair. "If you keep talking to me, it's going to take me another eighteen minutes–minimum–to get ready. If you don't want pizza, we can pick something up on the way to Concordia."

"Okay, but I need to get some cash before we do anything." He tossed the pizza box back into the freezer and slammed the door. "Why aren't you ready yet?"

"Someone keeps interrupting me." She disappeared back into the bathroom, calling out, "You're messing up my routine. Sit down and relax. Ray said we were absolutely not to show up before 10:30 a.m."

"Any chance you could look at Sean's car next?"

Ray recognized the voice if not the dark shoes, the only part of the man he could see. God, he hoped Sam and Carrie didn't show up early. He figured Mac would be almost as mad as Mrs. Brenner if he knew Sam had boarded the train to Philly and then immediately hopped off as soon as Mac was out of sight.

Ray rolled out from under the Mustang and looked up at the detective. "What's wrong with it?"

Mac shrugged. "It's been coughing a little and there's some hesitation when I accelerate. It's getting worse. I was hoping not to have to call Jeff. He's starting to get an attitude about the condition of his vehicles when I bring them back."

Ray grinned, his swollen bottom lip, a match for the detective's. "I can take a quick look but I'm swamped today. Have to get this Mustang ready to go in less than an hour."

Mac reached out a hand and helped Ray to his feet. "How come you don't have the Mustang up on the rack?"

"Broken." Ray sighed. He walked out the open garage doors and over to Sean's car. "My boss put it on my list of things to fix today. You wanna pop the hood?"

Mac opened the driver's door, leaned in, and found the hood release button. He groaned as he stood upright again. "I think I pulled a muscle yesterday. You feeling okay?"

Ray's face flushed as he remembered the cop's blows while he was handcuffed and helpless, but he waved off Mac's concern. "I'm fine."

Mac chuckled, moving his hand from the small of his back to his bruised jaw. "It's a good thing you wore him out some before I had to tangle with him or I'd be in some real pain. It's been a long time since I took a punch."

"I appreciate what you did." The car hood muffled Ray's voice. "Turn it over, will you?"

Sputtering turned into a backfire, before the car shuddered and died.

Ray leaned to the side, looking around the hood at Mac. The teen's face reflected his amazement that the older man could be such a great detective and know absolutely nothing about cars.

"It wasn't that bad before. Really." Mac's face reddened. "Maybe I should have–"

Ray slammed the hood shut. "I'll need to blow out the fuel lines. New fuel filter. Maybe a new fuel pump. Check the timing." Ray looked at his watch. "Do you need a ride back to your office?"

Mac shook his head. "Nah. JJ said she'd pick me up. Should be here any minute."

Ray smiled as a figure dressed in black leather, riding on a motorcycle, roared into the garage parking lot. "She's got a nice Harley. Try to remember to lean into the turns."

"Oh, shit."

"So have you talked to the cops yet?"

"Yeah, but they didn't buy me food." Tia's rail-thin roommate licked her fingers before choosing another donut from the box on the table in front of them. "These are great."

Sam and Ray watched in fascination as the girl ate her third pastry.

"What did they ask you?" Carrie pushed the box a little closer to the girl.

"Just when was the last time I saw Tia and did she have any enemies."

"Did she, Vicky?"

"Huh?" Powdered sugar had drifted down the front of the girl's navy sweater and she was busy brushing it off.

"Did she have any enemies?"

"I don't know. I mean it's not like I really knew her or anything. I just met her six weeks ago when school started. Think I'll get another roommate or they'll let me have a single?"

"I can tell you two were close. Hope this conversation isn't too painful," Sam said, ignoring Carrie's frown and grabbing one of the few remaining donuts.

Vicky nodded, wiping her mouth. "I was too sad to go to my first class but I'm better now. I think she might have been wearing my new top. It's missing from my closet. You didn't happen to notice–I mean since you saw the body–it was blue with a thin green…"

"No." Carrie's eyes filled with sudden tears.

"We didn't notice her outfit," Ray interrupted, putting his hand over Carrie's trembling one. "But if she was wearing your sweater, you can kiss it good-bye."

"Did she ever mention Malwick's murder?" Sam asked, taking over the interview.

"Huh?"

"The guy that got shot in the clock tower? Remember?"

"Yeah." Vicky glanced at Ray and picked up the last donut, placing it on a napkin in front of her. "She was bummed out that she had to keep working in that office afterward. Then when the old lady bought it, she said the place gave her the creeps. She'd filled out some paperwork to transfer to another work/study job a long time ago, but nothing ever happened."

"Did she ever mention Dan Thayer?"

Vicky took a bite of the donut and nodded.

Sam waited, tapping his fingers on the table. When she didn't elaborate, he pushed. "Well, what did she say about him?"

"That he was kinda hot."

Sam started coughing and Ray thumped him on the back.

Carrie reached across the table and stilled Vicky's hand as she lifted the donut to her mouth. "Tia thought Dan Thayer was hot?"

"Well, in a nerdy, old guy kind of way. But it didn't matter." She popped the last morsel in her mouth. "He had a girlfriend. Tia once almost caught them hooking up."

Three sets of eyes riveted on the now-full roommate. Finally Sam squeaked out, "Do you know who she is."

"Tia didn't tell me her name. But the rumor is that he and…" Vicky glanced around the Student Union, her eyes lighting on two women seated in the corner, sipping coffee.

"That's her," she pointed. "That's Dan Thayer's girlfriend."

"Lenore Adams," Carrie said, staring at the familiar face. "She runs the computer center."

Sam nodded. "She looks like Uncle Dan's type. Let's go, maybe she'll lead us to him."

Balancing two cups of coffee and carrying a newspaper under his arm, Mac shouldered open the office door and immediately spotted JJ sitting on the bare floor reading the back of a can of stain.

"Is it too late to get the carpet back?" He chuckled at the expression on the young woman's grime-smeared face. "Just kidding. The place is looking good. Are we going to get the furniture back soon?"

"I asked Snake to keep your stuff another couple of days. It's taking longer to get the floor finished than I expected. Phil can't sand it until tomorrow. So I can't put the stain on until the day after that."

She set down the can and took the cup he was holding out to her. "Wanta help me clean?"

"Can't." He grinned. "I've got a lunch meeting at the college. But if you need an assistant, I know someone who'd probably enjoy spending the day with you."

"I thought Ray had a full-time job at a garage."

"I was thinking of someone a little younger and with more time on his hands. Sean's got another day of suspension, so he's stuck at O'Herlihy's unless he's gainfully employed elsewhere. And since you've got to drop me by there to pick up a car…"

JJ's eyes narrowed. "The undertaker's son? Please. I'm not interested in any high school kid."

"Hey, Sean's not a bad kid. You could do a lot worse, besides Jeff's loaded." Mac laughed, thinking that Jeff and Kathleen would learn not to meddle in his love life. "Where's the phone? I'll give him a call."

"Back room, but don't plug it in. We've been getting crank calls."

"Get used to it. My best customers are cranks."

"Are you sure there's nothing else?"

"Like I told you on the phone. This is it."

"How about that ice cream truck?"

"Dad rented it out. Sorry."

Mac didn't think Sean looked all that sorry as he tried to hand him the keys to the bug truck. The kid was probably angry about Mac messing up the Nissan. "And to think that this very morning, I was putting in a good word for you with JJ."

"Really?"

Mac and Sean both winced as the teen's voice cracked, ending the word with a high-pitched squeal.

Before Mac could dash Sean's hopes with the news that JJ wasn't too receptive, his cell phone rang.

"Sullivan."

"Hi, Mac. It's Bobbie."

"Are we still on for lunch? I'm running a little late. Car trouble." Mac glared at the teen.

Sean jingled the keys in front of him and Mac frowned, grabbed them, and put them in his jacket pocket.

"They what?" He listened to the undercover detective with growing anger. "When?"

Bobbie told him she'd seen Rachel's son and two other teens about a half-hour before. She'd been too busy to call him until just now.

"Damn it. I put that boy on a train last night myself. And I just saw…" Mac realized that Ray had been waiting for the other two to arrive.

The undercover cop laughed, suggesting that he might want to invest in some electronic tracking devices.

"Or shock collars," Mac joked. "I'll be right there. No, I know you can't leave Lenore's office."

"Are you sure it was Ray Kozlowski? Lots of kids his age here on campus. They all dress alike." Mac felt like he was using that phrase, 'are you sure' a lot for one morning. He was having a hard time believing some of the stuff he was encountering was really happening–it wasn't even noon yet and his day had already gone to hell in a hand-basket.

Bobbie shook her head. "I remembered him from the funeral, the tall kid that Pete was chasing. I saw the girl there too, the one with Mrs. Brenner."

Mac sighed. "They must have heard the rumors about Lenore and Thayer. Have you been able to confirm the relationship? I'm assuming Greeley's got all her phones tapped, in addition to planting you outside her door."

"No phone taps since there's nothing concrete. But we're watching her house and Thayer hasn't shown up–as least as far as we've been able to determine."

"Thayer was last seen dressed as a woman. Have you seen any tall women in Lenore's vicinity?"

"Nah. Well, her housemate's tall, but I've met her. She came by the office the other day to pick up Lenore. Long blonde hair. Blue eyes. Looks like a model. Believe me, that woman was not Dan Thayer in drag."

"What's Lenore's schedule for today?"

"She cancelled her appointments for this afternoon. Said she wasn't feeling well, claimed that something she ate in the Student Union wasn't agreeing with her." Bobbie shrugged. "I've been eating over there and I don't doubt for a minute that the food could make her sick."

Mac rubbed his shoulder. "You think the kids followed her home?"

"That would be my guess. Last time I saw her," Bobbie pointed to the window overlooking the open area between the Student Union, the clock tower, and the computer science building, "the kids were trailing her."

"Okay. I've got Lenore's address in my notes. I'll head over there and see if I can round them up before they get themselves arrested."

Bobbie grinned. "So what are you driving these days?"

He grimaced. "You know exactly what I'm driving. I'm sure the frost-bitten cop I saw throwing the Frisbee radioed you two seconds after he saw me get out of that exterminator truck."

"Joe Bryant is doing a great job pretending to be a student. He's been camped outside for the last few days playing with that thing," Bobbie said with a laugh. "He's trying to impress Greeley so he can get permanently assigned to the detective squad. He really wants out of that patrol car. He's been on the edges of this case since the first call. Were we ever that damn young and eager?"

Mac started for the door, but then turned around. "Speaking of cars–you said Lenore's roommate came by to pick her up the other day?"

"Housemate. Yeah."

"What was wrong with Lenore's car? Why did she need a ride?"

"She didn't say." Bobbie stared at him. "You think that's important?"

He shrugged, thinking Lenore might have loaned her car to her boyfriend. "Maybe, especially if her boyfriend is Dan Thayer."

"Where did you get the binoculars, Sam?"

"My Dad gave them to me a couple of years ago–before Tina-the-'ho arrived on the scene–when he still remembered birthdays." Bitterness oozed from the teen's pores. "I grabbed them from the house the other day and stuck them in my bag. Thought they might come in handy."

Ray shifted his position so he could see the doorway to Lenore Adams' house. "Do you see anything?"

"No. Least not since that tall woman with the hat arrived."

"You sure that wasn't your uncle?"

"I'm sure." Sam chuckled. "That woman was centerfold material."

Carrie frowned and pulled her jacket closed. She knelt down next to the two boys behind the hedge. "Are you looking for your uncle or what? Cause I've got other things I could be doing–"

"You all have other things you should be doing." Mac's voice was loud enough that all three jumped and Carrie gave a little scream.

"Quiet," Sam said, glaring at Carrie and then the detective. "Do you want everyone to know we're out here?"

"Everyone knows already. I'm here to give you one chance to leave voluntarily before the police arrest you."

Sam scrambled to his feet. "Bullshit. It's a free country. We're not on private property. We're not bothering anyone."

"You're screwing up a police investigation. Obstructing justice. If that's not enough they can tack on a charge of being annoying as hell." Mac put a hand on Sam's shoulder. "I want all of you to–"

"Keep your hands off me, old man." Sam took a step back, shrugging off the detective's hand. "We're not going anywhere."

Ray touched Sam's arm. "I don't think we're doing any good

here anyway. Dan doesn't seem to be around."

"Guys, is that–"

"We haven't been here long enough to find out anything for sure. Lenore hasn't been home more than twenty minutes. We only–"

"Centerfold? I don't think so."

"Mac, I'm sorry about earlier," Ray said, his expression contrite. "I couldn't tell you what we were planning–"

"Guys," Carrie grabbed Ray's arm to get his attention just as a car's security system beeped, signaling its disengagement.

"What?" Ray asked. All three males stared at her.

She sighed and pointed toward Lenore's house.

Mac and the boys parted the branches in the hedge so they could see.

Lenore and her housemate were standing at her car, a third figure hovering in the house's doorway.

Mac thought Carrie had a point. The woman definitely wasn't centerfold material.

"That's Uncle Dan getting into the car," Sam whispered, punching Ray's shoulder. "I told you we could find him."

"You and everyone else," Mac said as a half-dozen police cars screeched onto the scene and the couple dashed back into the house.

Thirty-two

Rachel pushed open the funeral home doors and steeled herself for getting through another day of chaos.

"Mrs. Brenner? Do you still work here?" Myrna Bird asked, glaring at her over her bifocals. "It's practically the middle of the afternoon."

"Sorry. Mr. O'Herlihy is aware of my situation."

"Why do you have Mr. Sullivan's dog in here?"

"There's a possibility of cats roaming the viewing rooms. Whiskey is here as a consultant to help us deal with the situation."

Whiskey made a sound that Rachel took as agreement.

Mrs. Bird made a sound that Rachel took as disbelief, before she hurried off to answer a ringing phone.

"Rachel, dear, how are you today?" Althea Martin appeared behind her carrying a foil-covered plate. "I knew you wouldn't have eaten anything substantial after that terrible experience you went through yesterday, so I fixed you some lunch. I stopped by your house first, but I must have just missed you. Did you walk again–I noticed your van was still at your house."

Whiskey raised her nose, seeking the source of the food smell.

"My van wouldn't start–again. I'm fine, even if everything else is falling apart. I spent the morning cleaning the house and trying to…well, you understand." Rachel unlocked her office door. "I'm so sorry that I haven't picked up Snickers yet."

"No rush at all, dear. I love the company. In fact I'm considering getting a pet." Althea set the plate on Rachel's desk and gave Whiskey a pat. "I see you've acquired another companion."

Rachel smiled. "She's just on loan. I'll be returning her to Mr. Sullivan today."

"Well, I have to get to my women's club. Kathleen O'Herlihy is presenting her research on pharmaceutical stocks." Althea gave a pained laugh. "With the number of prescriptions I buy each month, I already feel like I own stock in the drug companies."

"Thank you so much for the food." Rachel smiled at the woman and then glanced down at Whiskey, whose twitching nose was resting on the desk only inches from the foil-covered plate. "I'm sure *we'll* enjoy every bite."

The phone rang and Althea waved her goodbyes.

Rachel moved the plate to the safety of the center of her desk and answered the phone. "Rachel Brenner, how can I help you?" She lifted up a corner of the foil and peeked inside. Roast beef, mashed potatoes and gravy, hot rolls. Comfort food.

Whiskey whined her interest.

"Hi. I'm Julianna Jarrett, Mac Sullivan's assistant."

"Yes. Mr. Sullivan has mentioned you." Rachel balanced the phone between her head and shoulder, while breaking off a piece of roll for the dog.

"Mr. Sullivan wanted me to pass on a message, he's having cell phone problems."

"What's the message?"

"Let me read it to you. Sam didn't go back to Philly–"

"He *what*?" She absentmindedly held the roll aloft, concentrating on the caller's words.

"Your son didn't go back to college. Mr. Sullivan said that Sam and his friends were playing detective and stumbled into the middle of a police stakeout."

Whiskey gracefully rose up on her back legs and delicately relieved Rachel of the burden of holding the roll.

"No. That's just not possible. Sam went back to Philadelphia last night. Mac took him to the train himself."

"Well, I don't know about any train. Mr. Sullivan said that he talked the police into releasing them into his custody a few minutes ago and that he wants you to meet him at his office as soon as possible so he can hand them over. He's not a babysitter, you know."

"Okay. I'm sorry. I know you're just passing on the message." Rachel took a deep breath. "Can you give me the address to his office?"

She grabbed a notepad and wrote down the street and building number, thinking Mac hadn't chosen a great part of town to locate his business.

"Okay. I've got it. I'm leaving now. Thanks."

"No problem."

Rachel disconnected the call and then dialed her son's dorm room number and listened to the phone's ring go unheeded long enough to wake the dead–or a college freshman.

She slammed the phone down. Her son was not where he was supposed to be. Mac Sullivan was right. She only hoped the detective was able to keep him out of trouble long enough for her to get to his office and pick up Sam and his partners in crime.

Whiskey whined and nudged her hand.

Rachel pulled the foil off the plate and set it down on the floor. The news of her son's antics had eliminated her appetite, but someone should enjoy Althea's food.

Her office door suddenly opened and Ms. Bird stuck her head inside. "The local stations are airing it live. Your brother is in a shootout with the police."

"The house is surrounded. Come out with your hands up."

Crouched behind a police car, its lights still flashing, the head of the SWAT team relayed his demands through a bullhorn.

Ray watched dumbstruck as uniformed officers traveled to nearby houses, moving neighbors out of danger. He shook his head trying to clear his thoughts. He felt detached–as if he'd been plopped down in the middle of an action movie and didn't know his lines.

"Let me talk to him," Sam pleaded to the lieutenant who roamed the scene. "He'll listen to me. You don't have to hurt him."

"I want all three of these kids taken into custody," Greeley ordered. He shifted his steely gaze to the private detective standing with them.

Mac stepped up. "I'll be responsible for them."

"We don't need your help." Sam snapped. He started forward, fists clenched, but was stopped in his tracks when Ray grabbed his arm.

"Yes we do." Carrie turned tearfully to the lieutenant. "We'll stick with Mr. Sullivan."

"I'm thinking of having him arrested too," Greeley growled, but then moved over to the group of sharpshooters who had their rifle sights trained on the front door.

"Thayer!" The cop with the bullhorn called out to the silent house. "Pick up the phone, Thayer. Don't make this hard on yourself."

A police negotiator stood with a cell phone against his ear. He shook his head. "He's not answering."

"How long do we wait," one of the cops asked Greeley.

A loud bang shook the air startling everyone.

A white-faced Sam ran toward the house, breaking through the police line. Two patrol men tackled him before he crossed the street.

"Hold your fire," Greeley ordered, waving a hand at the other officers. "Cuff the kid and put him in a patrol car. I don't want to see," he paused as Sam began screaming his uncle's name, "or hear him again today."

Ray's eyes met the lieutenant's. He read Greeley's expression and he prudently moved over next to Mac, pulling a frightened Carrie with him.

Greeley grabbed the bullhorn from the patrolman standing next to him and faced the house. "Thayer, the boy is fine, but this has to stop before someone gets hurt."

"What's happened?" Ray asked.

"Car backfire," Mac answered. "Sam thought someone was shooting so he ran right into the middle of it. I think that trait is one he inherited from his mother."

"Thayer, answer the damn phone. Now!" Greeley said, his voice booming through the bullhorn once more.

After a moment, the police negotiator handed a cell phone to Greeley. The lieutenant listened for a moment, then answered Thayer. "The boy's unharmed, in police custody. But if you don't give it up now, I can guarantee you someone is going to get hurt. I've got some tear gas canisters that I need to use before the expiration date expires."

Ray looked from Greeley back to Mac. "He's not really going to…"

Mac shook his head. "Only if he has to."

The door to the house opened.

"Hold your fire," Greeley ordered the officers. "He's agreed to come out."

Dan Thayer, Lenore Adams, and a tall woman with long blonde hair gingerly stepped out onto the house's front porch with their hands held high above their heads.

Rachel's hands shook as she grabbed her purse, briefcase, and Whiskey's leash. "Okay, I've got to go."

"Do you want me to call someone for you? Maybe a lawyer?"

"Thanks. I-I don't know yet. First, I've got to get my kid away from this mess. Then, I'll do what I can for my brother."

The dog, apparently sensing a leisurely lunch wasn't going to happen, scarfed down the rest of the food, before the leather strap tightened and she had to abandon the plate.

Rachel turned in the doorway and surveyed the room and the paper-filled desktop. "I haven't had a chance to go through today's mail. I've got the rest in my bag, but I haven't had a chance to review–"

"Don't worry about this place," Myrna said. "I can keep things going. I've been doing it for more than sixty years. Go take care of your family."

She nodded gratefully. For once she was going to follow Mac's advice to the letter. She was going to meet him at his office and drive Sam back to Philadelphia herself.

Reaching the lobby, she paused as it occurred to her that she wasn't driving anywhere–her van was at her house–sitting dead in her garage. Digging her cell phone out of her purse, she speed-dialed the local cab company. Having a car that was always broken down had necessitated her programming in their number.

The line was busy.

"Rachel? Are you okay? Everyone is talking about the–"

Rachel waved her hand in a dismissive manner at Kathleen O'Herlihy.

"The police are trying to arrest your brother," Kathleen explained.

Rachel set her cell phone on reception desk and searched for a phone book. "I know. I know. But right now I need–"

Myrna joined them. "What do you need, Rachel?" She had to

leave to deal with another ringing phone before hearing her answer.

Rachel found the phone book. "I need a cab. My van's not–"

"I'll drive you wherever you need to go," Kathleen offered, giving Whiskey a pat on the head. "The ladies can do without my stock tips for another day or two."

"Kathleen, thanks. Can we leave right now?"

"Sure. Where are we going?"

Rachel frowned. "I think I left the address in my office. Mac Sullivan's detective agency?"

"I know where it is." Kathleen nodded, taking Whiskey's leash. "Let's go."

Mac looked through the one-way glass into the interrogation room. He sipped a lukewarm cup of coffee and tried to make sense of what the suspect was saying. Dan Thayer had waived his right to an attorney and was being grilled by Detective Giles.

Tom Atwood joined him at the window. "Lieutenant Greeley thought Joanne might be the best choice to get Thayer to open up–might remind him of his sister."

Mac raised his eyebrows and took another sip of coffee.

"Yeah, I know." Tom sighed. "Bobbie is trying to take a statement from Sam Brenner, but the kid's clammed up. Says he not talking without his mother present. Bobbie tried to tell him he could invoke his right to an attorney, but there wasn't a right to his mother–not at his age."

Mac handed his cup to the young detective and pulled out his cell phone. "I tried calling her house, no answer. Tried her cell phone and just got her voice mail. I'll try again."

Another invitation to leave a message at the beep, and Mac snapped shut his cell. "She's not answering." He frowned. "She's going to go ballistic when…"

Atwood nodded. "Maybe you should call the funeral home."

Mac punched in some numbers, stepping into the nearby hallway.

"O'Herlihy Funeral Home."

"Rachel Brenner, please."

"Mrs. Brenner has left for the day. Can I help you?"

"Myrna, this is Mac Sullivan. Do you have a number where I can reach her? It's important."

There was a momentary silence. "I'm sorry, no. Mrs. Brenner was called away on–on family business."

"So she knows about her brother?" Mac asked.

"Yes. She heard it on the news and is on her way."

"Thanks." Mac snapped shut his cell phone and walked back to the interrogation room. "She's coming in."

Atwood nodded and focused his attention on the agitated suspect and the deceptively calm cop.

"Anything we didn't know?" Mac asked.

"Nah. Joanne's waiting for Greeley. Right now she's just taking him through his contacts in the college administration. Says he'd never met Malwick until he started in the Comptroller's office. Got the job through a college trustee who was on the board of the shelter where he'd previously worked."

Mac nodded. It all fit with the background information he'd gathered on Dan Thayer.

"Said that somebody named Fieldstone put in a good word for him. And that Malwick was a son of a bitch from day one."

Mac's cell phone vibrated. He glanced at the number and walked back into the hallway.

"Hey, what's up?"

"Have you seen Kathleen?" Jeff began without preamble. "She's not answering her cell. She's not at home. She's not at her women's club meeting. Sean has no idea…"

Mac laughed. "You need to put a tracking device on that woman." He glanced up as the door to the interrogation room opened and Joanne Giles walked out. "Can I call you back? I'm sort of in the middle…"

"You haven't heard from Kathleen?"

Mac snorted. "She doesn't tell you where she goes, why on earth would she tell me?"

"I just thought maybe. You sure she didn't call. Maybe she needed the car…"

"Don't you remember? I've got the bug-mobile," Mac said, lowering his voice when a couple of uniformed cops started to stare.

"Right. I forgot."

Mac frowned; it wasn't like Jeff to track his wife's every move. "What the hell is the matter with you?"

"Nothing." Jeff's voice was barely a whisper.

"Hey buddy, you okay?" Mac asked. He was momentarily distracted as he watched Joanne start for the stairs. He waved to grab her attention. She mouthed "Ladies Room," and he nodded.

"Sure. Just... I need to find Kathleen," Jeff answered.

"Sorry, I haven't heard from her. When I'm finished here, I'll..."

"Where are you?" Jeff demanded.

"Now? I'm at police headquarters."

"Good. I'll meet you there in fifteen minutes."

Mac dug deep for patience. "I don't think you need to put out a missing persons report because you can't get your wife on the phone."

Jeff ignored the jibe. "Fifteen minutes."

"Why don't you..." Mac stopped when he heard a dial tone. "Damn. Everyone's going nuts."

Thirty-three

Kathleen found a single parking place for her Sebring right in front of the building housing Mac's office. She carefully maneuvered the car in front of a black van and behind a white BMW. She'd barely shut off the motor before Rachel had the car door open.

"Thanks for the ride," Rachel said, clipping the leash on Whiskey and gathering up her things.

"I'll come in with you."

Rachel tried to keep from frowning. At the moment, she didn't have the time or energy to deal with Kathleen's good intentions. "That's not necessary."

Kathleen exited the car and locked the doors. "I'm not going to leave you here without transportation until I know Mac's here. I'd call him but my cell phone battery is dead. As soon as I see him, I promise to go away and leave you to it."

Rachel blushed, maybe she hadn't been as subtle as she'd intended. "I'm sorry. I just–"

The other woman brushed off her apologies and took Whiskey's leash. "Don't worry about it. We hardly know each other. Jeff always says I'm too pushy. Let's find Mac so you can figure out what you need to do next."

"Thanks." Rachel noticed the dog licking at Kathleen's hand. "Looks like you and Whiskey are old friends."

"We go way back." Kathleen gave the dog a pat and then held open the building's main door for Rachel. "It's upstairs. I'm not sure which office."

Rachel stepped inside the dark, drafty foyer and frowned. "Not exactly prime office space."

Kathleen started up the stairs. "I haven't been inside Mac's office yet, just heard horror stories from Sean. Apparently the office does need some work."

"The whole building could use some work." Rachel smiled as Whiskey strained at the leash. "I think Whiskey can find it."

The two women and the dog clattered up the old wooden steps.

"A lot of empty space in this building," Kathleen remarked as they proceeded down the hallway, past two empty offices–the doors open and the interiors in shadow.

Whiskey whined, and then barked, pulling at the leash.

"Good dog," Kathleen said, leaning over and giving the dog a hug. "You know where you are, don't you. Did you miss Mac?"

Rachel saw the hand-drawn sign on the door–"Sullivan Investigations." She turned the knob and pushed, looking up as a string of bells chimed. "This is it."

"Come on girl," Kathleen said, tugging on the leash.

Whiskey whined again, refusing to budge and Rachel looked back to see what the holdup was.

Kathleen shrugged. "Strange. She doesn't seem that interested in going inside. Guess you've been feeding her better than Mac."

"Not me, my neighbor. She makes great roast beef." Rachel held the door open and Kathleen finally coaxed Whiskey inside. "Whiskey had both our shares earlier."

"Can I help you?" A young woman appeared in the open doorway between the back office and the front one, a broom in hand.

"Are you JJ?" Rachel asked, stepping into the empty room. "We spoke on the phone earlier."

"Yeah." JJ leaned the broom against the pristine white wall. "Who are you?"

"Sorry. I'm Rachel Brenner and this is Kathleen O'Herlihy. I'm sure you know Whiskey."

JJ shook her head and smiled. "Whiskey and I have never crossed paths." She bent down and held out her hand to the dog.

Kathleen unclipped the leash and the dog padded over to the girl.

Whiskey sniffed the proffered hand, then stared at the girl for a few seconds before giving her an approving lick.

"Where're Mac and Sam?" Rachel asked, looking at her watch. She also wondered what was happening with her brother. She could only hope Dan would give himself up without making things worse .

JJ gave the large dog a final pat and stood. "Last I heard he was going over to the campus. He had a lunch meeting. Can I take a message?"

Rachel frowned. "What do you mean he's not here? You told me on the phone that–"

"Hang on," JJ interrupted. "I didn't talk to you."

Rachel shook her head. "You called me less than an hour ago and relayed a message from Mac. He wanted me to meet him here."

"Nope."

"What do you mean 'nope'? You–"

"I've never spoken to you before in my life."

Whiskey suddenly stood, growling. She lunged toward the door just as it opened.

Startled, Kathleen dropped her purse and the leash, instinctively reaching out and managing to grab the dog's collar and hold her back.

The bells continued to clang nosily, but no one noticed. Everyone's attention remained focused on the pointed gun.

Mac walked back to the interrogation room. Greeley was talking to Tom Atwood and Joanne Giles, but stopped when he saw the private detective approaching. Mac hesitated, but joined the group when the lieutenant cocked his head in invitation.

"Thayer asked for you. Something about his sister."

Mac's arched eyebrow asked the question.

"You can sit in, but not a word out of you, got it?" Greeley answered.

Mac nodded and followed Greeley back into the small room. Dan Thayer was pacing, his face flushed as he stared at them from behind the bars. Joanne Giles unlocked the door to the holding cell and nodded toward the steel table and chairs in the outer area.

Thayer rushed from the cell and took a deep breath before sticking out his hand to the detective.

"Mr. Sullivan? You've been good to my sister. Thanks."

Mac hesitated, then shook the suspect's hand. "How are you doing?"

Thayer shrugged and sat down in the chair Joanne indicated.

"Okay," Greeley started. "You've got Sullivan in the room. We can't locate your sister. And you've waived the right to an attorney."

"Yes. I'm-I'm ready to talk, but could I..." Thayer had abandoned his feminine disguise at Lenore Adams' house and was now dressed in worn jeans and a plaid flannel shirt. He ran his hands through his mop of curly dark hair and Mac was struck by the familial resemblance to his sister.

"No more deals, Thayer." Greeley cut him off.

"I wasn't–I'm not–Just…tell me that Sam and the kids are okay."

"They're fine. We're not holding the tall kid and the girl, and your nephew refuses to talk unless his mother is present. We're taking that to mean that he is insisting on counsel."

Dan's shoulders slumped. "And what about Lily and Lenore?"

"We may be releasing the house-mate. But Lenore's got reason to worry," Greeley stated. "Of course if you tell your story first…" He left Thayer to draw his own conclusions.

"Lenore's got nothing to do with this mess," Thayer protested. "And Lily, well Lily was just–"

Greeley slammed his hand down on the table. "Look, either start talking or get back in the cage."

Startled, Thayer pushed back in his chair. "I will. I'm just a little nervous. And I…don't do well in locked places."

"Then I suggest you start explaining yourself, unless you are planning on spending the rest of your life in a smaller room than this," Greeley warned.

"We understand," Joanne Giles interjected. "We want to be on your side. Tell us what you know. Start with the missing half million dollars."

"I'm pretty sure, in fact, I'm positive that Malwick has some off-shore accounts. Find them, you find the money," Thayer answered.

"Back up a little." Greeley held up his hand. "Tell us how you got to be assistant comptroller if you majored in American Studies."

Thayer took a deep breath and began.

"I don't have a degree in accounting," Thayer shrugged, "but this wasn't rocket science. I'd handled the books for the shelter and I like to read, so when I got the job at the college, I took out a stack of books on accounting and figured out what I needed to know."

"You didn't think it was strange that you had so much responsibility without the necessary training?" Giles pushed.

"Malwick told me that I had 'potential'." Thayer made air quotes with his fingers. "But the week before Malwick was killed, I had finally realized that my real potential was to be the fall-guy for an embezzlement scheme."

Greeley leaned forward. "Okay, I'll bite. How did the plan work?"

Several seconds passed before Rachel was able to lift her eyes from the steel-blue barrel to the face of the fiftyish woman she'd last seen at Malwick's funeral, the woman who'd sat with Lenore Adams.

"Julianna is correct," the woman said. "I believe you spoke with me earlier."

"Who are you?" Rachel asked, her expression a mixture of anger and fear.

The woman waved the gun at JJ. "Don't be rude, dear. Introduce us."

JJ swallowed hard, glancing from one woman to the other, then at the snarling dog. "Vice President Fieldstone, this is Mrs. Brenner and Mrs. O'Herlihy. And I believe you may already know Whiskey."

"That incessant barking is giving me a headache." Audrey Fieldstone aimed the gun at Kathleen. "Shut the dog up in the other room or I'll shoot you and the mutt."

Rachel looked over at Kathleen, worried that the woman wasn't strong enough to control the frenzied dog alone. "Maybe I should–"

Fieldstone shifted the gun toward Rachel. "You should be quiet until I ask you a question. It would have been much easier if you'd just arrived on your own, without involving Mrs. O'Herlihy or Sullivan's dog. Now things are going to get complicated and I absolutely abhor complications."

Rachel wisely refrained from saying anything else, but did lean over and pick up the leash. She held it out, a question in her eyes.

"Well, give it to her then," Fieldstone ordered. "Afterwards, move over against that wall and sit down."

Rachel clipped the leash on the frantic dog's collar and then sat down as instructed.

"Come on, girl," Kathleen urged, dragging the angry dog toward the back room. Whiskey's nails scraped across the bare wood, the sound further irritating the older woman.

"Help her." Fieldstone waved the gun at JJ, who then rushed

over to assist Kathleen in forcing the large dog into the other room.

As they half-lifted, half-dragged the barking dog, Kathleen whispered to JJ. "Phone?"

"On the floor, back room, unplugged."

Fieldstone smiled. "No talking, ladies. Keep moving."

JJ nodded her agreement. Kathleen glared.

Rachel hoped that Kathleen's expression wasn't an indication of her intentions. She sensed that Fieldstone wanted an excuse, any excuse, to use the gun. She caught Kathleen's gaze and shook her head, trying to discourage her from resisting the woman who was holding all the cards.

"Hurry up." Fieldstone followed JJ and Kathleen, stopping in the doorway between the two rooms. "Put her in the bathroom and shut the door."

Whiskey's barks turned to howls as the door closed and she was left alone in the small restroom.

"It was simple." Thayer flattened his palms on the table and looked directly at the lieutenant. "He just got into the vendor file, changed a mailing address, and then processed an invoice that he created. The check was mailed to an apartment he was renting."

Greeley shook his head. "Wouldn't the real vendor complain when they didn't get paid? Wouldn't the college notice the extra costs on these contracts?"

"I think in the past Malwick limited the scam to small amounts and remembered to change the mailing address back when real invoices from that vendor came into the office." Dan sighed. "If I were advising the college, I'd have them check every contract for the past five years–see what was paid versus the amounts the vendors actually received."

"Well, since I don't think you're going to be working at the college again unless you're cleared of murder," Greeley snapped, "you should concentrate on convincing me that you know what you're talking about. How did you discover the scam and when?"

Thayer flushed. "Sorry. It began about six weeks ago. I'd developed some software that simplified our billing system." He paused, then added, "Malwick, by the way, took complete credit for the system, but that's another story."

"And..." Greeley drummed his fingers on the table.

"But in transferring the data from the old system to the new one, I was literally comparing invoices to entries just to make sure that there weren't any glitches. I then compared the totals to the contract specifications. I found several accounts over the last few years where the actual payments continually exceeded the estimates in the contracts. Then when I started entering some of the more recent transactions, I found a half dozen very large invoices from two vendors–DMG and Computer Doctors. I had been involved with the bid specs for DMG and I knew that the amount invoiced was six times what it should have been."

"The missing $500,000?" Greeley asked.

"Yeah, it was about that much–adding the Computer Doctor invoices and the DMG ones. I got into the Computer Doctor account and saw one of the altered mailing addresses before Malwick had time to change it back. I hid copies of what I found in another unrelated file."

"What did you do then," Mac interjected.

Greeley glared at the private detective, but motioned Thayer to answer.

"I asked Angela Lopez if she'd seen any recent invoices from DMG and Computer Doctors. She showed me her books. The ones I saw weren't in there. Malwick had to be the one ripping off the college and then covering his tracks."

"So you confronted him?" Mac guessed. "Instead of calling the police, you tipped him off that you knew what he was doing."

Dan flushed. "I didn't think things were going to get out of control. I'd heard about the anonymous e-mail to Jack Starling and I thought Malwick's embezzlement was going to be exposed. So yeah, at that point I decided to tell him what I knew."

"So that was Friday," Greeley said.

Mac leaned forward. "Ganseco hasn't found the money in any of Malwick's bank accounts. Where do–"

"Hey. This is my interview." Greeley shot a fierce look at Mac, then turned back to Thayer,

Thayer nodded. "I confronted him on Friday. You've got to

understand. Malwick was a son of a bitch under the best of circumstances, and we'd already had several run-ins that week about him stealing credit for my software."

"So you were pissed," Greeley said.

"Yes."

Greeley followed up quickly. "Pissed enough that you might have lost your temper? Maybe threatened him?"

"No. I..." Thayer twisted his hands together. "I don't know what you mean."

"We've got a witness who swears that less than week before Malwick was offed, you threatened Malwick." Greeley moved in for the kill. "Did you? Did you scream out, 'I'll make you wish you'd never met me'?"

"Out here," Fieldstone ordered, herding the two women back into the main office and closing the door to the back room, muffling the dog's howls. "Sit next to Mrs. Brenner."

When everyone was arranged to Fieldstone's satisfaction, she stood in front of the group, pointing her gun at Rachel. "I feel that it's only fair to explain that I'm not a very patient person. I've spent years working on that flaw, but what can I say? I failed."

Fieldstone smiled again, and Rachel was reminded of those nature shows on public television stations–the ones where the alligator placidly lies on the riverbank, waiting for prey to get close.

"I will not tolerate lies. If you lie to me, someone will get hurt. If you lie to me twice, someone is going to get killed." Fieldstone took a step closer to the group. "Now, who doesn't understand? Raise your hands."

Rachel felt Kathleen's growing anger begin to override the fear that they'd all been feeling.

JJ must have felt it too, Rachel decided, because the girl shifted her body, so that she was sitting on the balls on her feet, ready to escape if the worst happened.

Fieldstone's eyes darted toward the girl.

"We understand," Rachel said, trying to distract the woman's attention from the other two. It worked, too well, Rachel realized as the Fieldstone's expression darkened.

"Didn't I say 'no talking'?" Fieldstone reached into her jacket pocket and brought out a metal cylinder. "I really thought I'd mentioned that rule earlier."

The three women stared in horror at Fieldstone as she proceeded to screw the cylinder onto the end of the gun barrel.

She pointed the gun at Rachel. "Hold up your hand, dear."

Rachel slowly held up her right hand.

"Spread your fingers. I don't want to blow off more than one or two for such a tiny mistake."

"You crazy bitch," JJ screamed. Springing forward, she knocked the woman backwards.

A single pop echoed though the empty room.

Whiskey's howls increased. Everyone could hear the dog gnawing and scratching at the bathroom door, as though trying to eat her way through the wood.

Before Kathleen and Rachel could get to her, Fieldstone had regained control of the situation. She fired once at the women's feet, the bullet striking the wood with a dull thud. "Stay back."

Rachel calculated the odds if she and Kathleen…no. They wouldn't be able to move fast enough, not without the element of surprise. Maybe not even then. It didn't take long to pull a trigger.

Fieldstone brushed a hand over her hair, smoothing it . She then tugged on her jacket, saying, "Rule number 3–no vulgar language."

"Oh, my god." Kathleen's gasp drew Rachel and Fieldstone's gaze to JJ's unmoving body and the spreading red stain.

Silence blanketed the interrogation room.

Mac noted that Greeley had ensnared Thayer with his own words. The assistant comptroller had publicly threatened to kill his boss, and less than a week later Malwick was dead.

Thayer started to stand, but the fierce look on Greeley's face settled him back down. "Yes, I said that–but only because of the software thing."

Greeley lowered his voice. "So let me get this straight. Malwick grabbed the credit for something you'd been working on for several months. He publicly humiliated you and then, in front of everyone, fired you–and twenty-four hours later, he's dead. But you know nothing about his death?"

Thayer sat speechless.

Greeley continued, relentless in his accusations. "In fact, on that Friday you were afraid that he was setting you up to take the rap for the missing money. You knew no one would believe your word over his. That you'd be sent to prison for stealing a half million–"

Thayer suddenly found his voice. "But I couldn't have stolen the money. It's been going on for years."

"Maybe you and Malwick were working this scam together," Greeley accused. "Maybe you got greedy and wanted a big chunk of money up front in order to remain quiet. You tampered with the accounts and withdrew too much–"

"No. I'm telling you that I never took a dime," Thayer cried out.

"Then how did you afford the cruise with your lover and the jeep for your sister?" Giles interjected.

Thayer threw up his hands in frustration. "I was making a decent salary for the first time in my life. That was my money."

Greeley abruptly switched gears. "Where were you on Friday night from nine to midnight?"

"At home."

"Can anyone verify that?"

Thayer looked down at the table. "No."

"No phone calls, no pizza deliveries? No girlfriend?" Mac suggested, ignoring Greeley's sound of irritation.

"No."

"What about last Tuesday night? Where were you?" Mac asked.

Thayer looked a little sick. "I was staying in the barn at the farm near Warrenton."

"Alone?" Greeley questioned.

"Yeah. Barns aren't popular for entertaining," Thayer joked.

"So you don't have an alibi for Malwick's murder nor for Lopez's." Giles folded her arms across her chest. "You're a real unlucky guy. Or a cold blooded murderer telling conspiracy stories."

"Someone is setting me up," Thayer exclaimed. "That's why they put the gun in my car. They wanted me to look…"

Greeley smiled. "Gun? A .38 caliber, I presume."

Thayer looked at Mac, desperation clouding his eyes. "Make

them understand. Please."

Mac took a deep breath. "A witness saw you bury a gun in your sister's flowerbed the Saturday after Malwick was killed. Did you go back and retrieve it before you shot Lopez?"

Mac felt Greeley's eyes on him. He knew he was going to catch hell for not passing on Edgar's information. Of course if the police department hadn't put the old man on hold… Nah, that wasn't going to get him off the hook.

"So messy," Fieldstone mused, staring at the still body of the young girl. "Now Mr. Sullivan will have to have the floor bleached. Blood is very difficult to clean up."

"You shot her!" Rachel exclaimed. She peered into hard blue eyes and suddenly comprehended that it really didn't matter at all to the woman if they lived or died.

"Yes," Fieldstone replied, pointing the gun at Rachel. "I've shot lots of people. And I don't mind adding you and your friend to my list, if you don't do exactly what I tell you to do."

"Go ahead and shoot me," Kathleen said, walking deliberately across the few feet separating them and kneeling down beside JJ. She tugged off her sweater and unbuttoned her white cotton blouse.

Fieldstone trained the gun on Kathleen's pale back as the woman tried to staunch JJ's bleeding with her blouse.

Rachel saw the woman's finger caressing the trigger. "Please," she begged, again trying to divert the Fieldstone's attention. "I'll do whatever you want. Just let Kathleen help her."

Fieldstone smiled. "Fine. I'm a reasonable person. Give me the key and I'll be on my way. I'll leave all of you tied up and I'll even call 911 once I'm out of state."

"Key?" The only key Rachel could think of was the keychain of Dan's that she'd found beside Tia's body. "You want the key that Dan–"

"Yes, of course. Give it to me."

Rachel shook her head. "It's at my house. I hid it there after the police search."

Fieldstone stroked the barrel of the gun against her left forearm as she seemed to consider her options.

"Get dressed, Mrs. O'Herlihy. We're going to take a road trip."

The sound of Whiskey's barking followed the women down the hallway toward the staircase. Kathleen and Rachel carried a semi-conscious JJ; their clothes spotted with the girl's blood. Audrey Fieldstone walked behind them, her gun trained on Rachel.

"Stop."

Rachel turned her head so she could see the older woman.

Fieldstone waved her gun toward the abandoned office on the left. "Take her in there."

"We're not going to leave her," Kathleen protested. "She might bleed–"

"Shut up," Fieldstone snapped. "I'm not going to have her bleeding in my car. As the kids say, 'been there, done that'."

"We can take my car," Kathleen countered. "Please, she's just a kid."

Rachel knew the answer without waiting for Fieldstone. She'd seen the 'kid' that Fieldstone had already killed.

"In there, now. Unless you want me to put another bullet in her." Fieldstone walked closer, the gun aimed at JJ's head.

Rachel began shuffling backwards into the empty office, her feet stirring up dust that hadn't been disturbed in years. Kathleen, supporting JJ's head, was forced to follow.

Fieldstone surveyed the dimly lit room, the windows smeared gray with dirt and grime. "Put her on the floor."

Rachel knelt down and looked at JJ's wound. Most of the bleeding had stopped except for some oozing over a rib. She noted that Kathleen's shirt had been lost at some point during the move.

"How is she?" Kathleen asked, Fieldstone standing close behind her.

Rachel shook her head and took off her jacket. She spread it over the girl's torso. "I think she's in shock. She's bleeding badly."

Rachel kept her eyes trained on Kathleen willing her to understand the truth.

Kathleen nodded. "So there's nothing more we can do for her?"

Rachel lowered her head and leaned over the body. "I'm afraid not." She adjusted the jacket over the girl's shoulder, the cloth hiding the motion of her fingers as she slipped off her bracelet.

They left the room, Fieldstone taking the time to pull the door closed behind them.

Thirty-four

"Well, that's that." Greeley turned off the speaker. "Any reason why I shouldn't throw you into jail for interfering in a police investigation?"

Mac had been expecting the question since he'd disclosed the information about the buried gun. "Can I get back to you on that? Maybe next week after I pick up some of those cigars you like?"

Greeley grunted. "Think Ms. Adams was part of the frame?"

"So you believe Thayer too?" Mac was unsuccessful at hiding a smile.

"If Roseanne ever manages to get me a background check on Thayer's alibi witness and if they're willing to support Thayer's claims about where he was when Tia Hu was killed–then, I believe him."

"I'll bet my retainer that Thayer didn't make up Sophia Fernandez and her family. He's got a pretty good recall of the woman, where she lives, where she works, and the grade point averages of all her exceptionally bright grandchildren."

Greeley nodded. "Hopefully Mrs. Fernandez spent some of the bus ride paying attention to what her seatmate looked like. If she can identify him, he's in the clear for the murders, since the same gun was used in all three. Hell, he's probably innocent of embezzlement too."

"It always comes back to the money," Mac mused. "Thayer was probably hired to... He was hired by Malwick to..." He tried to replay the interrogation in his mind. There was something that Thayer had said about how he was hired that didn't match.

Greeley watched the detective closely. "I've seen that expression before–just before you solved the Ruttan murder. What are you thinking?"

"I need to talk to Thayer. Confirm something he said earlier."

Greeley shook his head. "Right now he's being processed."

"What charge?"

"1st degree stupidity." Greeley bit off the end of the cigar he'd been holding. "I want him locked up until we catch the killer–for his own good."

"Mac?"

Mac turned as Jeff called his name again.

Detective Bobbie Everette was escorting Jeff down the hallway.

"I can't find Kathleen anywhere. No one here has seen either her or Mrs. Brenner."

Mac pulled out his cell phone and hit the redial button. "What's the big emergency? Can't find your favorite shirt?"

"Bridget's eloping. Moira spilled the beans to Mary Kathleen who told Sean."

"Sean told you?"

"Damn right he told me."

Mac raised a hand to hush his friend. "Are you sure that…" He paused as he heard someone answer the funeral home phone.

"O'Herlihy Funeral Home."

"Myrna, this is Mac Sullivan again. Rachel hasn't shown up at the police station. Do you know where else she might be?"

"Mr. Sullivan, I'm really busy right now. I've got cats running all over the place. The Tuckman service is about to start and Mr. O'Herlihy isn't here."

"This is important. Rachel's son is in a jail cell waiting for her."

"Okay, let me check. Here's her cell phone. She must have laid it down… Oh, there's another cat. I need–"

Mac groaned, realizing that the damn stray cat was complicating his life again. "Tell me again where Rachel said she was going? Exactly."

Jeff tugged on Mac's jacket. "Ask her about Kathleen."

"I will if she ever comes back on the–"

"Hold on, Mr. Sullivan, I'll check her office. She mentioned something to Mrs. O'Herlihy about leaving the address on her desk."

Mac covered the receiver with his hand. "She's checking for an address Rachel wrote down. I don't think she was headed here."

"Where else would she go?" Greeley asked. "The news of her brother's arrest is all over the television."

"I don't know." Mac turned his attention back to the phone. "Yes, Myrna. I'm here."

"There was a note on her desk. Says 60… I can't read the next number...then 5 New York Avenue."

"Thanks." Mac disconnected the phone and dialed a number he was very familiar with. "Rachel was headed for my office." He listened to the phone ring about a dozen times, then disconnected the call. "JJ might have knocked the phone off the hook. She's in her Martha Stewart phase in my office."

Jeff turned to leave. "I'm going over there."

Mac faced Greeley. "Let me know when I can see Thayer, I'm going to check that everything is okay at my place."

"Why don't you tell me what you think you know," Greeley suggested as he strode after Mac. "I can talk to Thayer."

"I'm not sure yet what I know," Mac replied, weaving his way though the crowded lobby.

"Just tell me what you're thinking!"

Mac pushed open the lobby door and saw Jeff staring with disgust at four flat tires on his limo.

"Uncle Dan?" Sam gingerly pushed open the door to the interrogation room. His uncle was seated on the wooden bench in the cage, but the steel-barred door was open.

Thayer slowly opened his eyes, and then smiled. "Hey kiddo, you okay? They didn't charge you with anything?"

"I'm fine. No charges," Sam whispered, standing uneasily outside the door of the holding cell. "Should I come in there?" he gestured with his hand, "Or are you allowed out?"

Thayer shrugged. "Not sure."

"So they haven't actually charged you with..."

Thayer shook his head. "I think they believe me, but they won't let me go and they did take fingerprints. I'm waiting for your mother." He stopped rambling and looked up into the confused eyes of his nephew. "Come here," Thayer motioned, and then patted the space next to him on the bench.

Sam took a seat next to his uncle. "This is an unholy mess."

Thayer tousled his nephew's curls and smiled. "Yeah, it sure is."

Embarrassed, Sam shook off his uncle's affectionate gesture. "What's going to happen?"

"Well, first you're going to get on the next train to Philadelphia and get your ass back to school."

Sam stiffened. "No way. I'm not leaving you."

"Yeah, you are. This unholy mess might take weeks to sort out and you've already missed too much time."

"I'll make up the work," Sam insisted.

"Hell, I'm not worried about classes, that's your mom's job," Thayer said with a grin. "You've missed too many parties, too many football games, too many women who are hot for your body."

Sam blushed furiously.

"Now listen to me," Thayer said, his voice dropping its playful tone. "I screwed up by getting you involved in this mess to begin with. I put you, your friends, and your mom in danger because I was too proud and smug to get help when I needed it. It stops now."

"But I want to…" Sam interrupted.

Thayer sighed and put his arm around his nephew's thin shoulders. "Yeah, I know what you want, Sam, my man. But for a change, you going to listen to your old uncle and do what he asks."

Sam locked eyes with his uncle, then after several moments nodded in agreement. "Okay, but I want to stay until Mom gets here. Once I've passed the baton to her…" He smiled.

Dan snorted. "Your Mom is going to beat me black and blue with *that* baton. You'd better take off before it's your turn."

Sam joined his uncle in laughter. "Yeah, hell hath no fury like Rachel Brenner on the warpath."

"What happened?" Mac asked as he and Greeley joined Jeff.

Jeff glared at him. "Somehow this is your fault. I've changed more tires since you opened your damn detective business than I've done in my entire life."

"Hey, Mac," Bobbie Everette yelled across the parking lot.

Mac turned and located her.

"Isn't that your ride?" She pointed to the bug-mobile and the maniacal little man, wearing a hat with a cockroach on top, who was revving the motor.

"Frank Flynn," Jeff shouted, his face turning beet red. "Shoot him, Greeley. Shoot him or loan me your gun and I'll do it myself."

Greeley laughed and called to the policeman exiting the building along with Tom Atwood, "Officer Bryant, we've got a stolen vehicle and destruction of private property. Go haul in that bug-mobile and the big bug in the driver's seat." Greeley pointed to the vehicle that seemed to be stuck in first gear as it moved down the street.

Officer Bryant beamed and took off running down the street, easily catching the truck before the end of the block.

"Hell," Greeley chuckled, watching the young officer hop up on the running board and convince Flynn to stop the truck. "He could have taken a squad car. That boy is way too eager to please."

"Yeah, once he realizes detectives have worse hours than patrol officers and pay just as lousy, he'll get over that gung-ho attitude," Mac mumbled before turning back to his old friend. He clapped a hand on Jeff's shoulder. "Why don't you let Flynn have the truck? It's not worth the aggravation. Let's go find Kathleen and Rachel."

"And how might we be getting there?" Jeff asked, watching as Joe Bryant handcuffed Flynn and started marching him back to the police station. "That little bug flattened my tires."

Tom Atwood joined their group and volunteered to drive. "I need to ask you some questions about Lenore Adams, anyway. How she met Thayer doesn't match with what he's saying. Just a minor point but you have to wonder why someone would lie about–"

"Wait." Mac held up a hand to quiet the police detective. "There was something..." He turned to Jeff and Greeley. "I need to run and ask Thayer a quick question. Won't take but a few minutes."

Jeff glanced at his watch. "Hurry up, or I'll go without you."

"Tom, walk Mac up. Thayer's probably meeting with his nephew now."

Mac looked at his old boss in astonishment.

Greeley coughed. "Okay, maybe I'm getting soft. I thought it would settle the kid down if he saw his uncle all in one piece."

"Works for me." Mac turned from Greeley to Tom. "Let's go."

"Hey," Greeley laid a hand on Mac's arm. "After you see Thayer and check out your office, I want you back here. No more lone ranger stuff. You tell me everything."

Mac nodded. "Will you make sure Ray and Carrie have a ride?"

"Sure," Greeley grumbled. "I run an all purpose travel agency."

"I should kill you right now." Fieldstone pushed the barrel of her gun against the back of Kathleen's head. "Then shoot a few dozen of those protesters out there."

"Do you have that many bullets?" Kathleen flinched as Fieldstone jabbed the barrel forward against her scalp.

"You said turn on Massachusetts Avenue," Rachel said. "She just did what you told her to do."

"I don't like her attitude," Fieldstone responded, glancing over at Rachel who was in the front passenger seat. She turned back to Kathleen, who was driving, and poked her again. "Did you hear me? I don't like your attitude."

"Ouch." Kathleen took one hand off the steering wheel and rubbed the back of her head. "And I don't like your–"

"I'm sure the police will clear a lane soon," Rachel interrupted. "It's some kind of protest–they're marching to the Brazilian embassy."

Fieldstone lowered the gun and looked out the window at the marchers, most with hand printed placards. "Ethanol? They're protesting imports from Brazil? These people need to get a life."

"They're corn farmers from Minnesota," Kathleen offered, looking at Fieldstone in the rearview mirror.

Fieldstone glared at her. "My point exactly. A farmer's life is no life at all. Everyday is exactly the same. Your life revolves around tending to crops or animals–to their needs–instead of your own. Feeding, shoveling, feeding some more, shoveling some more. You wake up the next day and start all over again. That's not living."

"And being a murderer and a thief are better career choices?" Rachel asked, her tone sarcastic.

Fieldstone laughed but her eyes turned icy.

"They pay better. You know what? You're funny." Fieldstone nodded at Rachel but raised the gun to the back of Kathleen's head again. "You..." She glared at Rachel and lightly tapped the back of Kathleen's head with the end of the gun barrel.

"Are..." She tapped Kathleen's head again. "A funny..." Another tap. "Funny lady."

"Hey," Kathleen yelped, as she threaded the car though the crowds. "Why are you hitting me? I didn't say anything."

"You're within easy reach and I don't like you."

"The feeling is mutual. But if you keep doing that I'm going to run over someone."

"Then run over them. Just get this car moving. Go back and head north on 16th Street."

Kathleen grimaced. "I don't know if–"

"Shut up." Fieldstone turned to Rachel. "Check the glove box. There should be a map in there. Find us a quicker way to your house or not all of us will arrive breathing. Plus, remember poor Julianna bleeding all over that abandoned office floor."

Rachel found the map and unfolded it. "Is this…the stain…It looks like dried blood?"

Fieldstone shrugged. "Sorry about that. My last passenger was terrible at reading maps. When I dumped her, I should have trashed the map too."

Rachel swallowed. "We'll have to use Dupont Circle again."

"The physical embodiment of one of Dante's circles of hell," Kathleen mumbled.

Fieldstone laughed. "Maybe you're not as stupid as I thought."

"Call 9-1-1 for JJ," Kathleen suggested. "We're far enough away that you're safe."

"When Rachel gives me what I want, I'll consider letting you call." Fieldstone chuckled. "So if you're worried about JJ, drive faster."

"Tell me why you did it?" Rachel asked, refolding the map. "Why did you kill Vince Malwick?"

"Vince became a liability and his usefulness ended. Stupid man. Of course he was always stupid, but his new wife made him greedy too. Not a combination that I found suited my purposes any more."

Fieldstone sighed, her voice regretful. "When I came to Concordia I quickly discovered what he was up to and improved on his little scam. For a couple of years we had a nice little bonus income. Last spring Vince decided he wanted a bigger cut. I told him no. Then a few months ago he tried to set up a separate deal on the side–expand the operation. The fool was going to bring us both down. Like I said–the man was stupid and greedy. I needed him gone and some extra money for a new start somewhere else. If everything had worked the way I planned, the missing money would have been discovered and tied to Vince's murder–and your brother would have been blamed for all of it."

Rachel frowned. "What about Mrs. Lopez and Tia?"

Fieldstone didn't answer; instead she glanced out the window and noticed their location.

"Don't miss your turn," she warned Kathleen, nudging her with the gun. "Get over in the other lane."

"Watch your blind spot," Rachel added, tensing as Kathleen jerked the car back at the last moment.

Incensed, Fieldstone grabbed a handful of Kathleen's hair, pulling hard. "You stupid–"

"Dammit," Kathleen exclaimed, "I can't concentrate with that gun against my head. If you're going to shoot me do it, otherwise back off and let me drive."

"So your girlfriend," Sam raised an eyebrow at his uncle. "What's up with that?"

Thayer smiled. "I think I finally found someone who'll put up with me and all my baggage."

"She's hot. I got a glimpse of her when she stalked through the hall."

Dan furrowed his brow. "Was she upset? Crying?"

Sam snorted. "Hell no. I think she had the cops on the ropes. She looks like she could take the skin off a rhino with a single look. Those kinds are man-eaters." He shuddered, then grinned.

"That's Lenore. You described her perfectly. But…" Dan shrugged. "Never mind. This isn't the time or place."

Just then the door opened. Mac walked in, surprise evident on his face when he caught a glimpse of Dan Thayer and his nephew in the cage.

"You know you could sit at the table." Mac gestured to the only other furniture in the room.

"That's okay. We'd like to think of this as a home away from home," Dan said, standing up and stretching. He glanced over at his nephew who stared straight ahead stonily. "But Sam was just leaving."

The young man glanced between the two adults, shrugged and headed out the door.

Looking at Mac, Thayer asked, "Any news from my sister?"

"I think she's over at my office. I'm headed there now to bring her back. Maybe we can get this mess straightened out, or at least your part of it. But I've got a quick question…"

Thayer looked hopeful. "Shoot."

"How did you hear about the job at Concordia?"

Thayer looked confused. "You mean, who told me there was a job opening?"

Mac nodded.

"I ran into Dre′ last spring at a fundraiser for the homeless. I said I was soon going to be out of a job, and she told me that there was an open slot in the comptroller's office. I didn't think I had the qualifications, but she insisted that I shouldn't let the lack of paper degrees stop me. Told me to get Jack Starling–the guy's on the shelter's board and Concordia's–to write me a recommendation. Dre′ told me that I couldn't tell anyone that she was involved in getting me the job. She'd have gotten into trouble for favoritism since the job was supposed to have been ad–"

Mac cut him off. "Dre′ is Audrey Fieldstone?"

Thayer nodded. "Sorry. I've known Dre′ for years. Her dad owned a farm up in Vermont. Mean son of a bitch, at least that's what his daughter used to tell me when we'd be doing tequila shots in this hole in the wall bar in Manchester, comparing notes about our different impressions of farm life in Vermont and Virginia. She hated it. I loved it. That last year her dad was dying, she'd have to come up a couple of times a month. It was damn nice of Dre′ to see that I'd turned my life around and…"

Mac held up his hand to stop the trip down memory lane. "Don't go nominating Ms. Fieldstone for the Mother Teresa award just yet."

Thirty-five

"Sam told me where the spare key is. We can go inside if you want."

Carrie shook her head. "No. I think Mrs. Brenner has had enough uninvited guests. Let's just sit here on the porch and wait."

"Okay." Ray sat down on the concrete step beside her. "What did Mrs. Bird say when you called the funeral home?"

"She wanted me to come into work. Apparently the mother cat and kittens are still in the funeral home. Animal Control is there. A funeral is going on. It's a mess." Carrie reached down and scratched her ankle. "I told her I wasn't licensed for animals."

"I hope you don't lose your job over this."

Carrie shrugged. She scratched at her wrist, a red swelling appearing. "Are there mosquitoes out this time of day?"

Ray shrugged. "Not normally but with all the rain…"

They sat in silence for a few minutes. Carrie dug around in her purse and pulled out a pack of gum. She offered him a stick. "How's your Dad?"

"Okay." He folded the gum into his mouth and then slapped at a mosquito as it came in for a landing. "Dad's thinking about getting a second job, delivering milk. It's another $400 a week for a few hours work in the morning."

"But you hardly see him now."

Ray shifted on the step, leaning forward with his elbows on his knees, his fingers folding and refolding the foil from the gum.

Carrie put a hand on his arm. "I'm sorry."

"It's okay." He looked down at the ground. "He's just doing what he has to do."

"Remember that tree-house your dad built? The one with the pirate's plank?"

"Sure. It's still in my backyard." Ray turned his head and grinned at her. "Don't start with that again. Sam and I *never* made you walk it."

"You said I couldn't be a member of your club if I didn't." She sighed and set her purse down beside her feet. "It wasn't so bad. Breaking my arm got me out of piano lessons for that whole summer."

He chuckled. "And since you didn't fall until you'd walked more than half the length of it, you qualified for the club."

"Ray?"

"Yeah?"

"Do you like JJ?"

"Sure."

She frowned. "No. I mean really *like* her?"

Ray grinned and punched her shoulder. "Not enough to ask her to walk the plank."

"There's Kathleen's Sebring," Jeff pointed out. "Pull in behind it and I'll check it out."

Tom parked the squad car in front of Mac's office building and both of his passengers hopped out.

"Well, hell. There's her cell phone." Jeff used his key to unlock the car. He reached in and pulled the phone out of the console between the front seats. "Dead battery."

"Maybe they're all upstairs–helping JJ stain the floor," Mac said with a tight laugh. "JJ is very persuasive."

"Right. You don't believe that for a minute," Jeff said. "Rachel Brenner would have been at the police station demanding to see her brother and son if she was able. Something is wrong."

"Let's don't jump to conclusions." Mac opened the door to the building and the three men entered.

Mac had only put one foot on the staircase, before he heard Whiskey's howls.

"Oh, God." Jeff ran up the stairs behind Mac, both men leaving Tom to follow well behind in their wake.

The sounds of Whiskey's barking were much louder on the second floor. Mac pulled his gun from his shoulder holster and motioned for Jeff to stay behind him.

Mac tried the office door and found it unlocked. Remembering JJ's bells, he opened the door only a few inches and reached up with one hand and unhooked the string. He carefully handed them back to Jeff who in turn placed them on the hallway floor.

Mac nodded at Tom, who'd caught up with them at that point. He pointed to the other side of the door and Tom took up a position there, his gun at the ready.

"There are three rooms counting the bathroom. Bathroom opens off the back office. There's an old door in the bathroom that leads outside to a fire escape. Don't think it's been opened in the last fifty years. No other exits."

Tom nodded again, both hands on his weapon, as he prepared to enter behind Mac.

"I'll go left," Mac whispered, pushing open the door

Ray opened the kitchen door with the key, he'd found under the back step. "Come on Carrie, I'm sure Mrs. Brenner isn't going to care if you use her bathroom."

"Okay. That old guy with the binoculars was giving me the creeps anyway. Think he's a pervert?" Carrie walked inside and was immediately greeted by a hungry cat.

"That's Mr. Freed." Ray laughed. "Mrs. Brenner's complained about him before. But even if he is a pervert, I don't think he's in any shape to do the deed."

"Maybe." Carrie set down her purse on the kitchen table and picked up Snickers. "Are you hungry, baby?"

"You bet," Ray answered, smiling as Carrie looked up and blushed. "I know. You were talking to the cat."

She set down the cat and grabbed her purse. "Make yourself useful. Find some cat food for Snickers, while I visit the bathroom."

"Okay."

Ray looked down at the cat that was staring at him as if willing him to act. "I said okay. I'll look and see what I can find."

He walked over to the pantry and opened it. "Want to split a peanut butter sandwich?"

Mac hugged the wall, until he reached the doorway to the back office. Tom joined him on the other side. The door between the two offices was closed, something he and JJ had never done.

Mac pulled a handkerchief from his pocket and used it to turn the knob, preserving any fingerprints that might be there. He didn't let himself think too much about why he was worried about fingerprints. He had to concentrate on making sure the office was clear before he thought about what he'd seen on the floor as he'd entered the main room.

As Mac turned the knob, Tom indicated he was going first.

Mac opened the door and made sure to push it open all the way against the wall, leaving no room for anyone to hide. The small room was obviously empty.

Mac holstered his gun and indicated that Tom should do the same. He knew from the sounds of Whiskey's barks that anyone that might be in the bathroom with her would be no threat.

Mac opened the bathroom door.

Whiskey leaped out and knocked him to the floor. She licked at his face and then rushed into the other room.

Tom let out an audible breath of relief. "Glad your dog seems to be okay."

"She's not overly concerned about my health." Mac gingerly picked himself up off the floor, noticing that the phone was unplugged. "There's one reason we never reached anyone."

Tom holstered his gun, then leaned over and plugged the phone into the wall. "I don't think that's the only reason. I'd better call this in. Greeley is gonna want to send Fitz's team over here."

"Yeah," Mac grimaced, and rubbed his shoulder. It felt like someone had stuck a knife in it. "Was that blood out there?"

Tom nodded and the two men walked back into the main room to find Whiskey, standing at the main office door whining and walking in circles, and Jeff kneeling on the floor, a bloody cloth in his hand.

"Jeff?" Mac crossed the room and put a hand on his friend's shoulder.

"It's Kathleen's." Jeff looked up, his face stark white. "It's my Kathleen's blouse. She had it on this morning. It's one of her favorites. I gave…"

Mac waited for Jeff to stop rambling and ask the question that was on all their minds.

"Tell me the truth." Jeff looked back down at the bloodstained blouse in his hands and the large stain on the bare floor. He took a deep breath. "What do you think happened? Is Kathleen dead?"

* * *

She usually found a sense of peace when driving down Rittenhouse Street. But not today. Today, even the leaves on the trees seemed angry–a riot of reds and oranges.

Rachel sighed softly. Peace of mind was elusive when the cold metal of a gun was pressed against the back of your neck. In truth, home as a safe haven had vanished with the break-in a week earlier.

"Bout damn time," Fieldstone groused. "I could've driven to Vermont and back by the time Mrs. O'Herlihy got us up Connecticut

Avenue."

"If you hadn't been waving around that accessory of yours," Kathleen sniped, "I might not have gotten rattled and missed the turnoff on Dupont Circle."

"Well, if you hadn't braked for every damn yellow light," Fieldstone shot back.

"Well, if you hadn't insisted we skip Military Road," Kathleen responded.

"If you hadn't been playing cutesy with the traffic cop," Fieldstone growled, waving her gun, "I wouldn't have had to make you take a detour. Now, why are you stopping?"

"Stop sign." Rachel answered for Kathleen, pointing to the red sign on the corner. She glanced down her street and inhaled sharply when she saw Edgar Freed in his scooter chair on his front porch. She prayed that his binoculars were tucked under the blanket covering his spindly legs.

"You can park right here," Rachel pointed to the spot in front of the Freed house. "I'm right across the street."

Kathleen pulled into the vacant spot and cut the engine. Rachel hit the automatic door locks and was halfway out the door.

"Wait." A red-tipped, well-manicured hand grabbed Rachel's sleeve.

Rachel and Kathleen froze.

"Not here."

Rachel turned slightly in her seat. "Why not?"

Fieldstone glanced at the invalid on the porch, who shifted his gaze from the car a second too late. "I think we might want some privacy for our little tea party. Pull around to the back. You can park in the garage behind that heap of yours." The cold, flat tone of her voice brooked no nonsense.

Kathleen started the engine again.

* * *

Whiskey danced around the closed office door, whining her displeasure that no one was opening it for her.

"Lieutenant, it looks bad." Mac was using the office phone while Tom talked to Fritz on his radio. "My secretary is missing, along with Jeff's wife, and Rachel Brenner. You need to put out an APB on Audrey Fieldstone now!"

"I told you–you haven't given me enough to do that," Greeley said. "The woman has no police record. No witness has put her at any of the crime scenes. Thayer doesn't even finger her for the missing money. Fieldstone is a university vice president, member of several charity boards. Hell, she's a Red Cross volunteer. The mayor gave her a damn plaque last year."

"Did you at least have Roseanne get me a vehicle description and a tag number so I know what I'm looking for? And we need to get some officers over to Rachel Brenner's house. Even if you don't believe me about Fieldstone, you have to acknowledge that Rachel's kid might be in danger."

"I believe you, Mac. But I can't put out an APB." Greeley sighed. "I'll send Joanne over to sit on the house as soon as she gets back from lunch. And I'll send Pete Fiori over to the college and to Ms. Fieldstone's home. See if he can locate her. And in case we're both wrong–I've got Eddie calling hospitals and clinics just in case one of the missing women had an accident and the other two are hanging around a hospital waiting room, filling out forms."

"Thanks, you're a real pal." Mac hung up the phone, cutting off Greeley's elegantly phrased string of profanity.

Whiskey barked at him, demanding his attention.

Mac frowned. "Not now, girl. Just settle down. I'll take you out in a minute."

"Well?" Jeff ceased his pacing long enough to ask, "Has Greeley got people searching for that woman from the college? The one you think has Kathleen and the others?"

Mac nodded. He wasn't really lying to his friend. Greeley did have some people looking–they were just doing it quietly.

Jeff's cell phone rang and he walked into the other room.

Tom finished his conversation with the crime lab and motioned Mac over to him.

"Listen, Mac. I'm gonna get written up if the lab guys get here and find Whiskey and Mr. O'Herlihy still wandering around the crime scene." Tom sighed. "I know the guy is freaked about his wife, but…"

"I'll get him to take Whiskey out–she's still wound up from the whole incident anyway. A walk would help both of them."

"Thanks. Too bad Whiskey can't talk."

Mac nodded and walked into the back room to convince Jeff of the merits of his plan.

"Sean, please just stay at home and call me if you hear from your mother." Jeff looked up and saw Mac. "I've got to go."

Jeff flipped his cell phone closed. "Any news?"

Mac shook his head. "Nothing yet. But I need to wait for Fitz and the crime lab technicians to get here. Can you take Whiskey outside? Maybe give her a quick walk around the block? She's driving Tom nuts."

"Okay." Jeff stuck the phone in his jacket pocket. "I could use some air myself. You'll call me if–"

"Of course." Mac watched him pick up Whiskey's leash and open the main door.

The dog didn't wait to be invited; she was out the open door in a flash, yanking the leash loose from Jeff's fingers.

Jeff spun around and followed the dog down the hallway. "What the hell? Whiskey?"

"Damn. What's wrong with her?" Mac ran after the two. "Whiskey! Get back here."

The dog stood in front of the abandoned office next to the top of the stairs, waiting for them. When they neared, she began howling.

Jeff put out his hand, but before his fingers could touch the doorknob, Mac stopped him.

"What are you trying to tell us, girl?" Mac drew his gun and motioned for Jeff to grab Whiskey's leash.

The door wasn't completely shut, so he was able to push it open with his foot.

A body on the floor wasn't what he was expecting to find.

"Oh, my God." Mac rushed into the room and bent down. JJ's face was waxy pale, her breathing raspy. "Hey, kid. Can you hear me? Open your eyes."

"Jeff, call–"

"I am." Jeff put his hand over the cell phone microphone, "I'll get the paramedics on the way and then go get Tom."

"Thanks. Tell him we need the whole building searched. Now!"

Whiskey padded into the room and lay down next to JJ. For the first time since Mac had released the dog from the bathroom, she was quiet.

"Sorry I wasn't listening, girl. You did the best you could. I'm the one who screwed up."

Mac lifted the jacket covering JJ, trying to see where she was hurt. Her blouse was soaked with blood, but none of it looked fresh. He decided not to risk moving the cloth and restarting the bleeding.

As he laid the jacket back over her, he saw it.

A glint of gold on the dusty floor.

A bracelet.

He picked it up and squinted in order to read the inscription. *Rachel.*

"Get it."

The three women had barely walked in the back door when Fieldstone prodded Rachel in the back with her gun.

"It's–it's upstairs. I'll just go…"

The raised eyebrow of the woman holding the gun stopped Rachel in her tracks.

"Duct tape." Fieldstone gestured for Rachel and Kathleen to move into the kitchen.

"What-what do you want?" Rachel turned.

"I want duct tape and I want it now." The voice echoed in the narrow back hallway.

"I keep some in…" Rachel pointed a shaky finger at the wooden hutch that was on the far wall of the kitchen.

"Get it." Fieldstone shoved Kathleen down on one of the oak chairs that surrounded the round, claw-footed table.

Rachel jerked open the drawer, grabbed the all-purpose tape, and wordlessly proffered it to her captor. Fieldstone cocked her head toward Kathleen.

"Tie her to the chair."

Rachel taped Kathleen's arms and legs securely.

"That's good enough." Fieldstone prodded Rachel with the gun. "Now let's go get my key."

Suddenly the pipes rattled from the flush of a toilet in the front of the house.

Both women froze.

"Who's here?" Fieldstone whispered angrily, pressing the gun next to Kathleen's head, as she glared at Rachel.

Rachel paled, frantic that Sam had come home. "I-I don't know. Maybe my son. Let me try and get rid of him."

Fieldstone nodded.

Rachel sped toward the dining room, but Carrie entered the kitchen from the second doorway that led to the den.

"Did you get something to eat?" she called, then stopped short when she spotted Rachel.

"Oh, Mrs. Brenner, I hope you don't mind. I had to use the bathroom. I couldn't hold it another..."

Suddenly, the teen realized that they weren't alone. Her eyes widened as she finally comprehended that Mrs. O'Herlihy was sitting at the kitchen table with a gun pressed against her temple.

"What-what's happening? Ms. Fieldstone, what are you doing here?" Carrie looked from Rachel to the Vice President, then back again. Confusion, then finally understanding, played across her face.

"It was you." The words came out as a statement rather than a question, as the young woman started to sway uncertainly.

Rachel grabbed Carrie before she slid to the floor.

"Drink this." Rachel handed Carrie a glass of water.

The teen sipped the liquid slowly, then cautiously dipped her fingers into the water and rubbed the back of her neck. The purple streaks in her hair stood in vivid contrast to her stark white cheeks. With shaky hands, she slid the glass back on the table, and looked wide-eyed from her boss to the Vice President of her school who was, at that moment, pointing a gun directly at her heart.

"Who else is here?" Fieldstone demanded.

Carrie was silent for a moment, then looked around the room. "You, Mrs. Brenner, Mrs...."

"Not them, idiot. Who were you talking to when you came in here? Something about food." Fieldstone waved the gun dangerously in the air. "Who else is in the house?"

"No one," Carrie said forcefully. She sat up a little taller. "I was talking to Snickers–Mrs. Brenner's cat. I knew she wanted to be fed. See..." Carrie pointed to the empty dish on the floor.

Fieldstone considered the explanation, then inched over to the den and peeked in. Satisfied that they were alone, she lowered the gun. "Okay, enough with the Dr. Doolittle stuff." The Vice President shifted her attention to Rachel. "Tie this one to the chair and let's get that damn key."

"I'm out of tape." Rachel held up the empty spool. "I have some more in the pantry."

"I'll get it." Carrie started to stand.

"Sit down," Fieldstone snapped. "I give the orders and I want Brenner to get the damn tape."

Rachel patted Carrie on the shoulder, then moved past her to the pantry doors. "I'm pretty sure I have more duct tape, but if not, how do you feel about scotch tape?" She walked into the dark recesses of the storage closet. "Or forget the tape, how about just some scotch," she added under her breath.

Rachel had inherited her Great Aunt Rose's house. One of its best features was the oversized pantry. And although she didn't keep the pantry as fully stocked as the former owner of the house, she was every bit as organized. Like her great aunt, Rachel believed that everything had a place and there was a place for everything. Not bothering to flick on the light, she reached toward the household supplies shelf.

Silently, a hand slipped across her mouth and stifled her scream. She started to struggle, bumping against the wall. A can crashed to the floor.

"What's going on?" an angry voice shouted from the kitchen.

"It's me," Ray breathed in her ear.

Rachel slumped against him in relief.

"What are you doing in there?" The sharp tone of the voice brooked no nonsense.

Ray withdrew his hand and her eyes, now accustomed to the darkness, could make out his pale features.

"Nothing." Rachel winced, her voice, at least two octaves higher than normal, sounded suspicious even to her. "I just knocked over a can of corn."

Ray handed her a full roll of tape and nodded for her to go.

Rachel emerged shakily from the closet and held up the roll. "I've found some more."

Carrie stared at the closet door. Rachel locked gazes with the teen, willing her to lower her eyes away from the pantry. ESP seemed to work because Carrie suddenly switched her focus to her lap.

"Tie her up fast. I don't have all day." Fieldstone grabbed two dishtowels from the rack over the sink. "And gag them both. I don't want any chatting."

"Tell me again–why did you kill Angela Lopez and Tia? What could they have possibly done to you?" Rachel tore off a piece of duct tape and wrapped it around Carrie's wrists.

Fieldstone shrugged. "They knew too much about my dealings with Vince. Lopez found some vendor check stubs and a foreign bank account number taped to the bottom of Vince's desk drawer. She would have turned it all over to the police after showing you.

Luckily, I was in the hallway in the Administration building and overheard her cell phone call. It was a perfect time to tie up that loose end and acquire Vince's secret stash. His trampy wife doesn't deserve the money. Can you believe she's having an affair with Jack Starling? Some people are beneath contempt. Her husband's only been dead a little more than a week."

"You're a fine one to question anyone else's morals," Kathleen pointed out.

Fieldstone walked over and raised her gun, the barrel pointed directly at the redhead. "You really don't have the proper demeanor for a hostage."

Kathleen raised her chin and glared at the woman.

"What about Tia?" Rachel asked, trying to distract Fieldstone before she decided that Kathleen was expendable.

Fieldstone lowered the gun several inches. "What about the twit? The reigning homecoming queen was well on her way to following in Gina's footsteps. I probably saved some young man a world of pain–and alimony."

Rachel knelt and taped each of Carrie's ankles to the wooden chair legs. "But why bother to kill her?"

"She saw me arguing with Vince late one night in his office. I wasn't sure how much of our conversation she'd managed to overhear. When I needed to turn up the heat on your brother, it occurred to me that killing her and leaving her someplace you'd be sure to find her would solve two problems with one bullet." Fieldstone laughed. "I didn't even have to go find her. She came to me–wanted to get her work-study job changed to another office. I was happy to take care of that problem for her."

"Are you the one that hurt Mac Sullivan's dog?" Carrie asked, her voice shaking.

"Mr. Sullivan needed to be refocused. I thought if he believed Thayer took his dog, he'd go after him a little harder. I ordered Tia to move the dog, but she was worse than useless. Young people today have very few skills and even less imagination. She couldn't get the muzzle on the mutt to save her life, even after the dog had gobbled down two hamburgers laced with sleeping pills." Fieldstone laughed. "Not that it would have saved her life, but Tia didn't know that."

Fieldstone checked the tape around Carrie's wrists. "Tie them tighter. Too bad the leash broke that night, Rachel. I was planning on you finding a dead dog along with Tia."

"You're sick," Kathleen exclaimed, finally earning another rap on the head with the gun barrel.

"Shut up."

"I hope you rot in jail, you crazy old–"

Fieldstone pointed her gun at Rachel. "I told you before to gag her. Gag both of them now. I don't want to waste another bullet."

Rachel complied, making sure to do it properly, knowing that Fieldstone would check her work.

Fieldstone tugged on the knots, then smiled in satisfaction. "My dear, you may not care for me, but I'm a product of my environment, no more and no less. I just do what I have to do to get what I need. And what I do, I do very well. My dead father could attest to that. He was taking way too long to die naturally. I had to help him along. No one ever suspected anything and I was able to make a small fortune selling the farm to a developer."

"But you've made mistakes," Rachel argued, wondering just how many people the woman had killed during her life? "You made a mistake hiring Dan. He was smarter than you expected and he'd stopped drinking. He figured out what you and Malwick were doing before you were ready, didn't he?"

"No. I was the one who made the call to start the outside investigation." Fieldstone shook her head. "My only mistake was in not realizing that Vince had a better developed sense of self-protection than I'd ever imagined. When that pompous fool demanded to meet me in the clock tower–like some scene from a b-grade thriller–I knew he was going to demand a bigger cut of the money. I just didn't expect him to try to blackmail me. That was the final straw. Our partnership was over."

Fieldstone laughed. "After I shot off his ear, Vince gave me the details about his little insurance package and where to find the key to a safe deposit box. But I'd had enough of him. When the clock struck midnight–his time was up. Too bad Dan had already given you the key. Otherwise none of this would have been necessary."

"What kind of insurance?" Rachel made sure that her expression didn't change while her mind was scrambling to understand what Fieldstone had just said. Dan hadn't given her any safe deposit key. The only key she had of Dan's was the one she'd found near Tia's body. It was the key to the Warrenton house. She'd thought that was what Fieldstone wanted.

"Taped phone conversations about the fake invoices and the

checks. Poor Vince. He spent the last few minutes believing that his hidden evidence would keep him safe."

"But you killed him anyway?" Rachel wondered if Malwick had ever known how dangerous his boss was.

"Of course I killed him. I just hadn't expected that getting that safe deposit key would take so much effort. Vince said he hid the key behind the photo. Then I figured out that Dan had taken the photo with him after his argument with Vince. Why he took that from his desk, but not his other things… Ironic isn't it?" Fieldstone walked over and made sure the door was securely bolted. "Since I'd prepared ahead of time and copied all of Dan's keys, I was able to check out his apartment and his car. It wasn't there. That's when I realized he must have given it to you."

"Yeah. So that's what you were looking for when you broke into my house."

Fieldstone waved Rachel ahead of her. "I think calling digging in your postage-sized garden a break-in a bit pretentious, don't you? Enough chitchat. Let's go get my key." Just as they started out of the room, Carrie's cell phone went off in her pocketbook.

Fieldstone reached into the cavernous bag, grabbed the shrieking instrument, and slammed it against the counter. The phone shattered.

"Guess it will go to voice mail," Fieldstone said with a grim smile. With a nudge from the gun barrel, Rachel headed for the stairs.

Thirty-six

Mac winced as Tom carefully lifted JJ's blouse, exposing the bloody gash running diagonally across the girl's left rib cage–a rib cage that was a mosaic of blue and purple, covered with smears of clotted blood.

Tom took a large piece of gauze from his first aid kit and laid it gently over the gash.

"Well?" Mac remembered that the young detective had originally trained as a paramedic before joining the police department.

"The bullet grazed her. Caused a lot of bleeding and cracked some ribs. That's why she's having some trouble breathing."

Mac knelt down beside Tom. "Why is she unconscious?"

"Shock, most likely. Maybe blood loss. She'll probably be okay once the EMTs get an I.V. going."

"Tom, I've got to leave. Will you stay with her?" Every minute counted now. Mac figured that Fieldstone must be looking for something–something she thought Rachel had. She'd probably been the one who had broken into Rachel's house a few nights after Malwick was killed. If Rachel had what Fieldstone wanted, she'd give it to her. And once she did, she and Kathleen were dead.

"Mac, let Greeley handle it. You don't know where to look."

Glancing at the clue Rachel had left, Mac knew where to start. He got to his feet. "If I get close, I'll call it in. I promise."

Tom shrugged, as he taped down the bandage. "Okay. But be careful." He looked up. "What are you using for transportation?"

Mac smiled and showed him a set of keys–keys that Tom had loaned Jeff earlier when he'd sent him to fetch the first aid bag from the trunk of the patrol car.

"No way." Tom huffed. "I'll lose my job. You don't have a badge anymore."

"Tell them I stole the car. You'll be in the clear–you were busy saving JJ's life."

"Stealing a police car?" Tom shook his head. "Man, you don't wanta do that. You'll lose your P.I. license for sure even if Greeley doesn't throw your ass in jail."

"You're right. Thanks." Mac clapped a hand on the detective's shoulder and smiled. "Tell them Jeff stole it."

He counted the footsteps as they marched up the stairs. At ten, he slowly pushed open the pantry door and caught Carrie's eyes, wide with fear, staring in his direction. A raised eyebrow asked if it was safe to come out.

Carrie nodded, silently urging him forward.

Ray crossed quickly to the bound women, flicking open the blade of his Swiss Army knife. He could hear Rachel and Fieldstone's movements down the second floor hallway to the master bedroom.

"It's somewhere in my bureau, I just have to…" Rachel's voice carried down the stairs.

Carrie wriggled anxiously in her seat and Kathleen inched her chair forward.

"She did a good job with this tape. Give me a sec," Ray whispered to the squirming teen, then froze at the sound of a creak from the back porch. "Shit."

"*Mmmmph*?" Carrie mumbled, straining against her bonds to see who was there.

"I don't know," Ray hissed. He abandoned the women and crawled quickly to the backdoor, peeking through the gauzy curtains.

"Thank God."

Lightning-fast, he snapped the deadbolt and held open the door for Mac and Jeff.

"Sweet Jesus." Jeff cried, as he saw his wife, bound, gagged, bruised, and covered in JJ's blood.

"Quiet," Mac ordered, his voice low, but firm. "Where's Rachel?"

Ray pointed toward the ceiling. "Upstairs getting some key for the crazy woman with the gun. I don't know who she is but–"

"Okay, you and Jeff get Kathleen and Carrie out of here. Call the cops and wait next door until they arrive, then fill them in on what's going on." Mac moved toward the hall, gun drawn.

Jeff knelt beside Kathleen and pulled down her gag. "It's okay Katie, my girl. I'll have you out of here..." He froze as he heard voices on the steps.

"Okay, my departure date has been pushed up a little by your idiot brother's interference..."

"Dan doesn't even know..." Rachel's voice projected into the kitchen.

Jeff immediately pushed the gag back over his wife's protesting mouth, kissed the top of her head, and scrambled into the pantry with Ray. Mac ducked into the den.

"You have the key; let me call 911 for JJ." Rachel stopped on the landing. The barrel of the gun pressed against her back.

"Keep moving."

"You said that once you had the key, you'd let me call..."

"And you believed me?"

The laugh sounded demonic to Rachel.

"You are a naïve little person."

Rachel struggled to keep her voice calm. "She'll bleed to death."

"And I'm soooo worried about that possibility," Fieldstone moved the gun to Rachel's temple. "You know I'd hate to add murder to my list of sins. Oh wait, I already did." She laughed again.

Rachel gulped and stepped back slightly from the gun barrel. She turned to face her captor. "What happens now?" She spoke loudly, hoping her voice carried to the kitchen.

"Don't shout," Fieldstone snapped.

"Sorry." Rachel said more softly. "I'm...I'm just nervous."

"Understandable." Fieldstone nodded agreeably. "But get moving."

"What are you going to do?" Rachel stayed in place.

"We're going to take a little ride to the bank." Fieldstone again moved the gun to Rachel's head and this time the younger woman began to walk down the steps.

"You don't need me at the bank. I'd just be in the way."

"You're not going into the bank." Fieldstone explained patiently.

"Then why…"

Fieldstone smacked Rachel on the back of the head. "I'm not stupid, you know."

"I don't understand."

"I know that somebody is going to start looking for those two in the kitchen. I'm leaving them behind to make it clear that I have you and will kill you if anyone so much as makes me wait too long at a stoplight. Now get moving."

"Mom." Sam flung open the front door. "You home?"

Rachel froze on the bottom step. Fieldstone bumped into her, surprised by the sudden stop.

"There you are. I've been trying to get you on the phone. Did you leave your cell at the funeral home or did it run out of juice again?" Sam prattled on, oblivious to their company.

"Sam," Rachel croaked. She cleared her throat. "What are you doing here?"

"I know you're pissed at me." He held up his hands in defense. "But first, can I have some money to pay the cabdriver and then I'll– Who's she?"

"Get out," Rachel pleaded. "Turn around and leave now. If you won't stay in school, you'll have to go live with your father."

Time slowed as she saw her son glance from his mother to the woman behind and she could literally see the lightbulb moment.

He opened his mouth and nothing came out. Then with a whoosh, "Holy shit. What the hell is going on?"

"Let's test your cognitive skills. Do you know what I have in my hand?" Fieldstone pointed the gun at Sam.

He frowned, his eyes darting from the gun to the woman holding it. "Who are you?"

"That's one miss." Fieldstone shoved Rachel down the last step. "I expected more from you, Samuel. I thought Penn had higher entrance standards than Concordia. But then you've been spending most of your time playing boy detective. Let's try an easier one. How many bullets do you think it would take to kill you at this distance?"

Sam paled. "Are you–"

"Answer her," Rachel warned, remembering JJ's fate.

"One." His voice broke as his eyes flitted from his mother to the bizarre woman with the gun.

"Very good, young man. You bought yourself a little more breathing time. Or should that be breathing room?" Fieldstone smiled. "Never mind. Your mother and I have somewhere to be. I'm afraid you're going to have to join the others in the kitchen."

"You're not going to get away with it," Sam blurted out.

Fieldstone gestured toward the kitchen. "Rachel, we need more duct tape."

The taxi horn sounded, the sudden noise filling the room.

Fieldstone jerked in alarm, convulsively pulling the trigger. The glass door on the nearby Grandfather clock shattered, setting off the pendulum, causing the clock to chime repeatedly.

Rachel screamed as Sam dove for the floor.

"You okay, Mom? It's just the cab. I told you I needed to pay..." Sam looked up and took a deep breath, his stunned expression mistaken by Rachel for pain.

"You *bitch*!" Rachel roared as she pulled from Fieldstone's grasp. She threw herself toward her son, lying flat on the hardwood floor. "You shot him!"

"Get back here," Fieldstone demanded, grabbing fruitlessly at the back of Rachel's shirt, trying to restrain her.

"Go to hell." Rachel scrambled to her feet, turned, and swung wildly at the woman. She didn't care where she landed a punch. Fieldstone planned to kill them all; it was just a matter of when.

"Mom, don't!" Sam tried to get up, but slipped on the broken glass.

Fieldstone easily dodged the blows by taking a step back, but Rachel charged ahead. The woman brandished her gun in Rachel's face. "Do I really need to kill someone else to make you understand that I'm in charge here? Get the tape."

Rachel ignored her, kneeling down beside her son. "Sam, where are you hurt?" She couldn't see any blood but then again he was lying on his stomach. She needed to think, but the noise from the clock was making it impossible.

"Mom, please." His voice shook as he watched the woman waving the gun.

Fieldstone yelled for both of them to shut up, nervously glancing around, her finger trembling on the trigger.

The Grandfather clock continued to bang out its noisy death rattle.

"I'm warning both of you for the last time. Get into the kitchen or else."

Sam glanced up and caught a glimpse of someone moving from the den along the side of the staircase. "Mom?"

"Are you all right?" Rachel urgently ran her fingers over every inch of his head, then his back and shoulders. "Baby, tell me where it hurts."

"Mom," he protested, shaking off her hands and stumbling to his feet. "I'm…" Sam saw Mac Sullivan appear behind Fieldstone.

The detective shook his head and mimicked grabbing his stomach.

Sam immediately wrapped both arms around his middle and let out a gasp much like a balloon with a puncture. "Mom, help me. She shot me."

"Oh, my God," Rachel got to her feet and tried to move his arms so she could see.

Sam jerked away, his thin frame hunched over, as he stumbled around the area near the front door.

Rachel followed, still frantically trying to get a look at her son's wound. "Sam. Stop. You're probably bleeding internally."

Fieldstone waved her gun at the two, yelling, "You're both crazy. I didn't shoot him yet, I shot the clock."

Moving up on her from behind, Mac grabbed the woman's hand with both of his, crushing her fingers around the metal gun. "Drop it, Fieldstone. Your time's up."

Fieldstone shrieked and managed to squeeze the trigger again, putting the clock out of its misery.

* * *

The sound of a gunshot and breaking glass drove Jeff and Ray out of the pantry.

"Ray, cut Carrie loose and get her out of here. Now!" Jeff pointed the teen toward the young woman.

Ray set to work on Carrie's bindings. She mumbled something

behind her gag.

"What?" Ray asked, covering her body with his own as he sliced through the tape.

Carrie ripped off the gag with her free hands, while Ray worked on her bound ankles. "We should go out some time."

"Yeah, sure," Ray answered, yanking the freed young woman from the chair and hauling her toward the back door.

Jeff grabbed a butcher knife from the wooden block on the counter. With the sharp blade, he was able to slice quickly through the tape binding Kathleen's arms. Kneeling on the floor, he could hear the grandfather clock clanging from somewhere in the front of the house as he sawed through the bunched tape holding her ankles to the chair legs. He needed to hurry.

With her hands free, Kathleen managed to tug off her gag just as he freed her legs. "Oh, God. Jeff!"

She fell into his arms. "Did you find JJ? She was–"

Jeff stood, bringing Kathleen to her feet also. He gave her a quick kiss and brushed the red curls out of her eyes. "We got her." He looked at Ray who was dragging Carrie out the door. "Go with them."

"Not without you." Kathleen dug her nails into Jeff's arm.

"I'll be fine." He spun her around and shoved her toward the back door. "Ray," he yelled, "Call the cops."

The young man looked back, grabbed the older woman, and tugged her down the stoop.

* * *

The woman was stronger than she looked, Mac thought as he tried to pry the gun from her hand. "Let go, damn it. Before I have to hurt you."

"Go ahead and try. I'll enjoy killing you." Fieldstone kicked at his leg and connected, her shoe whacking his shin with the force of a baseball bat.

His leg went out from under him, but he managed to maintain his two-handed hold on the gun and Fieldstone's hand. Off balance, both of them fell to the floor and rolled.

Fieldstone got another shot off, exploding a lamp in the living room.

"Rachel, get out. Take Sam and…" He struggled to gain control of the woman who'd just bitten his right hand. "Shit. I hate that."

Mac jerked his injured hand free and punched the woman hard enough that she was going to need extensive dental work before biting anyone else.

The back of her head bounced against the floor but she didn't let go of the gun. "I'm going to put a bullet right between your eyes, old man," she hissed, even as blood dripped from her mouth.

He prepared himself to hit her again, then sensed rather than saw that Rachel was behind him–directly in the path of Fieldstone's next wild shot.

"Mac?"

He rolled over causing Fieldstone to be on top and the gun to point toward him and the floor. "Get out, Rachel."

In a blur Mac saw Rachel swing something large and gold. Glass shattered, raining over his head and face. He closed his eyes, only to pop them open after Fieldstone's forehead cracked against his chin.

When the stars cleared from his eyes, he pulled the gun from Fieldstone's limp hand and shoved her unconscious body off him. He sat up and looked at Rachel. "What the hell was that?"

She smiled and held out a hand to him, helping him to his feet. "The matching lamp to the one she shot. I never liked them much anyway."

They both turned as Whiskey rushed into the room, barking and running in a circle around the woman on the floor.

Jeff ran into the room only a few seconds behind the dog. "Need any help?"

Thirty-seven

It seemed like days, but it had been just over an hour since the last of the police had left. For a while her house had been overflowing with detectives, patrol officers, and, of course, the ambulance crew that had whisked a handcuffed Fieldstone off to the emergency room to check out the damage caused by Mac's fist and a twenty-year-old lamp.

Rachel listened to the conversation around her and smiled. So much had changed since Fieldstone had marched her and Kathleen into the house at gunpoint. She'd been worried about dying and protecting the others held hostage with her. Now her biggest worry was about whether she'd ordered enough pizza.

"Jeff, you're going to be up all night. You know pepperoni doesn't..."

"Katie, my girl," Jeff reached over and brushed the back of his hand across his wife's cheek, "Irish Regimental Bagpipers marching through my bedroom won't wake me tonight."

"There goes my plans to reward you for rescuing me," Kathleen said with a laugh as she pushed the pizza box closer to her husband.

"Hey, you two, save the mushy stuff until you get home," Mac said, as he walked into the dining room. "I see everyone waited on me to start eating. Thanks."

"We knew you wouldn't want us eating cold pizza," Jeff answered, picking up another slice. "How's the kid?"

"JJ is going to be fine. No surgery. She's got two cracked ribs. They're keeping her overnight just to be safe. She said she's got someone with her, but I'll check on her in the morning."

Rachel heaved a sigh of relief. "Thank God. There was just so much blood. You're sure..."

Mac reached over and patted Rachel's hand. "I'm sure. She's already complaining about the bullet holes in her freshly painted office and giving me instructions for the guys coming to sand the floor tomorrow."

"And before I forget–we got a reprieve. We don't have to go down to the station tonight. Greeley changed his mind, said for us to come in tomorrow and sign our statements."

Rachel let out the breath she hadn't realized she was holding, and then looked up, a new worry line on her forehead. "Are you in much trouble with the lieutenant? Will you lose your license?"

Mac chuckled as he sat down in the chair next to her. "Yes, and probably not. Greeley will chew me out for at least an hour and he's entitled. Then I'm betting he'll let me buy him some lasagna and Chianti at Luigi's and we'll call it even."

Whiskey appeared at Mac's elbow, an empty paper plate in her mouth.

Mac put a slice of pizza on the plate and set it on the floor beside his chair.

The hairy hound offered a gentle woof, then turned her attention to eating. Snickers, who had taken a strategic retreat to the top of the mahogany buffet, shot death ray glares at the intruder, who studiously ignored her.

Mac reached for a beer. "So…are we going to put a hit out on Bridget's beau?"

"Nah, just make his life miserable for the next fifty or so years," Jeff mumbled, before biting into another slice.

Kathleen lightly smacked the side of Jeff's head. "No need for that. I spoke to my darling daughter and we came to an agreement."

Mac raised an eyebrow.

"Let's just say that Miss Bridget won't be marrying anyone this weekend. She's bringing the young man home so he can ask her father properly for her hand."

"Any pizza left?" All eyes snapped to the doorway.

"Uncle Dan." Sam jumped to his feet and ran to hug the former fugitive.

Rachel waited for her son to finish, then wrapped her arms around her brother. "We've been waiting. They said they'd released you hours ago."

Dan shrugged. "Some idiot named Eddie was doing the paperwork and…"

Mac snorted.

"Sit down. You must be starved." Rachel pushed her brother into the empty seat next to Mac and filled a plate with pizza. "You want coffee, tea, some soda?"

"Rach, stop fussing and sit down." Dan smiled.

After a moment, she grinned back. "Okay. You're on your own again."

Once she was seated, Dan cleared his throat and looked around the table. "I know I've been a jackass about this whole mess."

"No argument there," Rachel interrupted.

"But, if I may continue…" He cocked his head at his smirking sister, who nodded her assent.

"First, I'm so grateful to Sam, Ray, and Carrie for believing in me when there was absolutely no reason on earth to do so."

"No big deal," Sam said quickly, waving his uncle off.

"It was a big deal, Sam, and I won't ever forget it."

"And," Dan grinned, "you need to get your sorry ass back to Philadelphia."

Sam held up his hands in defense. "I'm going, I'm going. I already promised Mom that I would be on the 6 a.m. train back to school."

"And you two…" Dan faced Carrie and Ray. "Do you need me to square things with your bosses? I mean I think I have an "in" with at least one of them." He glanced over to his sister.

"Nah." Carrie winked. "My boss is a pussycat. If she ever knew what I really did during my coffee breaks…"

"Enough." Rachel laughed.

"How about you, Ray?" Dan asked.

"I'm good. As long as Mr. Sullivan keeps screwing up Mr. O'Herlihy's vehicles and bringing them to my boss's garage, I'll be in good shape," the lanky teen said with a straight face, but a twinkle in his eyes. "My boss says that Mr. O'Herlihy's business alone more than pays my salary."

The group exploded with laughter.

"You're determined not to let me express my heartfelt thanks," Dan groaned. "I'm trying to–"

"It's okay," Mac clapped a hand on Dan's shoulder. "You can express all your emotions when you write out a check for my bill.

Let's see, Ray gave me a retainer of $1, so I figure you owe me–"

Dan threw up his hands in defeat, then grabbed his pizza and took a big bite.

"Wait a minute." Carrie raised one hand as though in a classroom. "I've got some questions."

The group looked at the young blonde, who colored at all the attention.

"First, where's the computer disk with the files we copied using the computer in the Accounting Office?"

Rachel smiled. "It's in my office at the funeral home. No elaborate hiding place. I just added it to a box of blank disks."

"Okay. I guess that was as good a place as any." Carrie frowned. "But I still don't understand, Mrs. Brenner, about the key. What key did you have that Ms. Fieldstone was ready to-to kill for?" Carrie shivered involuntarily and Ray slid an arm around her.

The young woman smiled and rested her head on his shoulder. Then it was Ray's turn to blush.

Rachel shrugged. "Well, the key I gave her would have given her access to my will and divorce papers."

"What key did she want?" Dan asked.

Rachel looked at her brother. "A safety deposit key that she insisted you'd given me. Apparently Malwick kept evidence of Fieldstone's involvement in the embezzlement in a safety deposit box. I didn't have a clue as to what key she was talking about, so I gave her mine. I was just trying to buy some time."

"I don't understand," Dan said, shaking his head.

"Fieldstone bragged that she'd frightened Vince into telling her that he'd hidden the key behind a photograph–one that was on your desk."

"Frightened?" Jeff mumbled, "She shot the poor man's ear off."

"Jeff," Mac warned, "that's privileged information."

"And a poor choice of table conversation," Kathleen added, pushing her plate away.

"What photograph?" Dan looked confused. "I did send you a photo of us at the farm. I just wanted you to know where I was going to be hiding. I thought it would keep you from worrying."

"Why would you ever think sending me that photo would tell me where you were? Why couldn't you have just said, 'Rachel, I'm going to the farm'?"

Dan took a bite of pizza and swallowed while everyone waited for his answer. He grinned, tomato sauce dotting his bottom lip. "Well, I guess that would have worked too."

Rachel shook her head in amazement. "When did you…"

"I mailed it last week. I told you to watch for it."

"No, you didn't."

"Yes, I did. When we spoke on the phone–"

"No, you didn't."

Mac cleared his throat. "Rachel did you get something in the mail from Dan?"

"I haven't had time to go through my mail," she confessed. "I threw it all in my briefcase."

"Where's the bag?" Mac asked.

Rachel stood and grabbed it off the buffet, opened it and tossed the contents on the table.

Dan picked out a large manila envelope. "Here it is."

Rachel opened the envelope and pulled out a silver picture frame that held a photo of Dan, Sam, and Rachel sitting on a porch swing, grinning for the camera. She flipped it over, looked at the frame and the cardboard backing, and then laid it on the table. She picked up the envelope again and turned it upside down, shaking it. "No key."

Mac reached across the table and picked up the frame. He examined it carefully before sliding open the back panel. Taped to the inside was a thin safety deposit key.

"The key to my innocence. If only I'd…" Dan shuddered.

Mac left the key in place. He picked up the envelope and put the contents back inside. "I'll deliver this to Greeley in the morning. It might just broker me some peace with the lieutenant."

"Little brother, I have to admit that it was another key that had me wondering if your luck had finally run out."

"Huh?"

"I found your key to the farmhouse. Remember the keychain with the brass horse?"

"Trigger? You found Trigger?" Dan sputtered. "I lost that a few weeks ago. I thought maybe I'd misplaced it in the move. That's one reason I was camped out in the barn for three long miserable days. I didn't have a key to the house."

Rachel got up and crossed to the hutch. She slid open the silverware drawer, took out something, then walked back and stood in front of Dan. "Take a look."

She held out the keychain she'd found next to Tia's body.

Dan grabbed it. "How did you get it?"

"It was next to…" She inhaled sharply. "It was in the dumpster, next to…"

Dan nodded his understanding. "I guess…guess that Dre' must have stolen it and left it after-after…you know, to implicate me. She probably made copies of all my keys. I know she was in my car at least once."

The siblings stared at the keychain until Dan tightened his fingers around it and slipped it in his pocket.

"I've got another question," Jeff piped up, breaking the uncomfortable silence. Looking directly at his best friend, he said. "You'd already figured out that Fieldstone was the killer before we ever got to the house. What tipped you off?"

"A stupid little lie by Fieldstone," Mac answered. "It's always the little things that trip up criminals. When I'd interviewed the woman, she'd been adamant that she'd never met Dan before he came to Concordia. Then Dan told me at the jail that he'd known her in Vermont. It shouldn't have mattered that they knew each other before, so of course the question was, why?"

Kathleen glanced at her watch. "Well this has been lovely. Let's do it again real soon, Rachel." She pushed back her chair, eyes twinkling. "But next time it's my turn to bring the duct tape."

Rachel laughed and everyone began to gather their things.

Carrie and Ray started for the door.

"Just a sec," Rachel admonished. She looked solemnly at her young assistant, then pulled her in for a hug. "Thank you," she whispered.

Carrie threw her arms around Rachel and squeezed tightly, then stepped back. "I'll see you tomorrow morning at the funeral home…but not too early."

In response to Rachel's raised eyebrow, Carrie added with a

giggle, "I'll bring the coffee."

Rachel moved to stand in front of Ray. "You're quite a fine young man, Raymond Kozlowski."

The tall teenager grinned from ear-to-ear, then leaned down and kissed Rachel's cheek. "You should bring your van into the garage soon. Let me give it a tune-up before winter."

"No way," Dan interjected. "She's a got a new Jeep Cherokee coming. That old van is history."

Rachel shook her head. "You don't have a job. I'm not letting you buy me a car."

Dan grinned. "Did I forget to mention that Jack Starling called me? He said Concordia was very sorry for any 'inconvenience' that Fieldstone and Malwick might have caused me. I think he was trying to head off a lawsuit. Wanted me to know that my old job was waiting for me–with a raise. I told him I needed a couple of weeks off to recover from the trauma, but that I'd like to come back."

"Oh, Dan." Rachel smiled. "That's wonderful. You and your girlfriend can take that cruise."

"That's something else I need to clarify. People have gotten the impression that Lenore Adams and I are a couple. We aren't. I've been seeing her sister, Lily."

"The house-mate," Mac guessed. "I never had a chance to run a background check on her. But you were using Lenore's car."

"Sometimes. She'd do anything to help her sister–and by extension me." Dan gave the detective a knowing look. "Lenore also volunteered to pump you for information, but you kept giving her the brush-off. Really annoyed her that her flirting had no effect on you."

Rachel glanced from Dan to Mac. "What did she–"

Sam laughed. "I'm too young to hear this. I'm going with Carrie and Ray. We're thinking banana splits might be needed to calm our nerves. I'll be back in an hour or so."

Rachel nodded absently at her son, then returned her gaze to Mac.

"Lenore Adams tried to–"

"There's nothing to hear. Nothing happened," Mac protested. "I rebuffed her advances."

Everyone laughed and the teens headed out into the cool night air.

The O'Herlihys followed, after many hugs and promises to get together soon.

Dan yawned. "I need to go pick up a bag I left with Lily. But is it okay if I stay here tonight? I'll take Sam to the station in the morning."

"Of course," Rachel responded. "But when am I going to meet Lily?"

"Soon." Dan smiled and gave her a hug, whispering, "Don't say anything yet, but Lily and I might be using that cruise as a honeymoon trip."

Rachel grinned and gave him another hug before releasing him.

Dan turned toward Mac and stuck out his hand. "Thanks doesn't seem quite enough," he said quietly.

"Glad I could help." Mac grasped the younger man's hand firmly.

Finally it was just Mac and Rachel, and a snoozing Whiskey, left.

Rachel stacked the dirty plates and empty soda cans.

Mac scooped up the pizza boxes and followed her into the kitchen.

"Oh you don't have to do that," Rachel admonished.

"No problem. As my blessed mother always said 'you make the mess, you clean it up'."

"Seems like you've been doing that for over a week now," Rachel said softly. "Cleaning up I mean. I'm really sorry I was so stubborn and rude and…"

Mac put a finger to Rachel's lips to stop the torrent of apologies, and then withdrew it quickly as the woman blushed.

He bowed slightly. "Rachel Brenner it's been a pleasure to know you." He offered a crooked grin, which was soon matched by a smile on Rachel's face.

The two stood in awkward, yet comfortable silence for a moment–until a small crash broke the interlude.

Whiskey, who'd been digging through the trash, looked up guiltily, pizza crumbs on her lips.

"Well, I guess that's the signal that I should be going," Mac said, grabbing his dog's collar and tugging her away from the garbage. "Come on girl, time for you to start eating dog food again."

"It is late," Rachel agreed. "Well, um, thank you again for everything."

"No problem," Mac stuttered, and then moved toward the front door.

Rachel suddenly found her feet. "How are you getting home? Jeff and Kathleen left…"

Mac looked out the front window and chuckled. "Actually they're waiting for me outside in the car."

"Oh, in that case…" Rachel's voice trailed off.

"Well, good night," Mac said, and reluctantly walked onto the front porch with Whiskey at his side.

"Right, good night."

Rachel closed the front door, and then re-opened it immediately.

"Mr. Sullivan, Mac…"

"Yes." He turned around, a grin on his face.

"I was wondering…it's just that I thought I'd go visit JJ tomorrow and…"

"I was going to go too," Mac said quickly.

"So if your bug-mobile is out of commission and Jeff doesn't have a hearse to spare…" Rachel grinned.

"I'd need a ride." His smile matched hers. "Yes, thank you, Mrs. Brenner. I'll need a ride tomorrow if you'd be so kind."

"Well, okay then. I'll pick you up. What's your address?"

"Meet me at my office. JJ gave me instructions on stuff I need to bring her."

"After today, I certainly know where your office is located." Rachel shook her head refusing to think about Fieldstone and her craziness any more. "10 o'clock okay?"

"Dandy," he said, wincing at his choice of word. "See you then."

The two stared at each other until Jeff sounded the horn. Whiskey gave a bark and bounded for the car.

She nodded toward the car. "You better go. Kathleen's got a wedding to plan."

"Yeah." He grinned.

As Rachel was closing the door, she heard him call out.

"Rachel!"

She stepped outside.

"Here. I almost forgot." He reached into his jacket pocket and took out her bracelet. "You probably want this back."

"Thanks." She smiled and held out her hand.

His fingers brushed hers as he placed the gold bangle on her palm. "I'm sorry if–"

Whiskey barked as she ran past them, racing though the open door and back into the house.

"Whiskey!" Mac started to go after her. "She must have caught a glimpse of the cat."

Rachel stopped him, slipping on the bracelet. "Let them work it out. Snickers won't hurt her too badly. Just a swipe or two across Whiskey's nose–just enough to change her attitude about cats."

Mac glanced anxiously in the house, but stayed outside on the porch with Rachel. "You're pretty trusting. You think everyone can change? Even old dogs?"

"With enough time," she grinned, and looked down at his bandaged hand, "and pain."

Thirty-eight

Rachel watched the car carrying the O'Herlihys and Mac disappear down the street, before shutting and locking the front door. Almost immediately she felt Snickers rubbed up against her ankles. "So you decided to come out of hiding? I was afraid you'd decided to leave me, too."

The cat purred, but when Rachel reached down to pick her up, the feline scampered off, racing up the staircase.

"I know you're tired, but I'm not ready to go to bed. We have to wait up for Sam and Dan to come home."

Rachel sighed as she surveyed her living room. Kathleen had helped her pick up the worst of it while they waited on the pizza to be delivered, but Fieldstone's shooting spree hadn't done her furnishings any good. Rachel straightened a cushion on the sofa, noting the bullet hole. As she brushed her hand down the side, she felt something hard in the space between the cushion and the arm. Ray's missing cell phone. The one they thought he'd lost at the kennel. She stuck it in her pocket, realizing that her own cell phone was still at the funeral home on Myrna's desk.

The funeral home–she was going to have to miss another day of work. She needed to spend tomorrow visiting JJ in the hospital and finishing the endless paperwork the police department required of anyone held hostage by a serial killer. Too bad victims didn't have the luxury of refusing to make statements.

Victims also had to sweep. Rachel could see tiny pieces of glass on the floor in the entryway. They sparkled like diamonds... Diamonds. Maybe Dan would like their grandmother's diamond for Lily? She'd get it out of the 'treasure chest.' That's how second grader Sam had described her great grandmother's antique silver jewelry box. Most of the contents had more sentimental than monetary value, but to a little boy the brightly colored costume jewelry and the small velvet bag filled with a dozen silver dollars seemed like a pirate's fortune. Unbeknownst to her, he'd taken it to school and displayed its contents for show and tell. The teacher, seeing the expensive diamond ring among the baubles, and correctly guessing that the class was getting an unauthorized showing, had confiscated the 'treasure chest' and called Rachel.

She tossed the broom to the side. "To hell with the cleaning," Rachel announced to herself. "I'm going treasure hunting."

* * *

A thump came from her bedroom and Rachel shook her head as she opened the door. She flipped the wall switch, turning on the bedside lamp. "Snickers, what are you doing? I don't need any more messes to clean up."

The butterscotch cat was sitting on the floor next to her cordless phone. She hissed when Rachel walked into the room.

Rachel chuckled, picking the phone up on her way to the closet. "Now I remember why I started leaving this phone downstairs. You don't like having it on the nightstand, do you? Does it put off some kind of white noise that keeps you awake? Too bad. I don't ever intend to be stuck up here without it again."

She turned on the closet light and stepped inside, planning to get the 'treasure chest' out of the old hat box that was stored on the shelf above the clothes. She smiled, thinking that the jewelry box was safe now that Sam was more interested in dating than playing pirates.

The smell of aftershave intruded into her memories. Old Spice. There was no reason that odor should…

Light reflecting off shiny steel, caught her gaze. A steel knife, next to a pair of angry brown eyes.

Brown eyes staring back at her from behind the filled hangers.

Rachel screamed as she stumbled backward.

Hands followed.

Large male hands.

Basketball player hands.

* * *

Someone was screaming. It took her a several seconds to realize the sounds were coming from her. She knocked over the hockey stick and a stack of shoeboxes as she tried to back out of the closet.

"Bitch. You've been nothing but trouble. Where the hell is it?"

She finally found her voice. "What-what do you want?"

"Where is it, damn it? Where's the damn jewelry box?"

The knife flashed at her and she batted it away with the cordless phone in her hand.

The sound of the metal scrapping against the plastic made her stomach roll with nausea. In slow motion she watched the phone and the knife fall to the floor of the closet along with more shoeboxes, as the man gained his footing and she lost hers.

The hockey stick pressed into her back, as useless as it had been a week ago when she'd hidden from what she now knew was the same intruder. It wasn't Fieldstone who had broken into her house that Sunday night; it was Joe Bryant–friendly, puppy-dog-like, Old Spice-wearing Officer Bryant.

"This is your fault," he shouted, his large fingers pressing into her arms. "You should have gone down to the police station and signed your statement like you were supposed to."

Rachel took in a breath and managed to gasp out the words, "Stay away from me."

"It's too late for that. You know who I am."

She struggled to twist away from him, her frantic movements resulting in an avalanche of clothes and hangers burying both of them.

His fingers tangled in her hair, jerking her head toward him, as she tried to swim out of the cotton and rayon morass. "Stop it. You never do what you're supposed to do. You told the neighbors that you were going to a conference in New York. You weren't supposed to be home that Sunday night, just like you weren't supposed to be home now. This is all your fault."

No. She was responsible for most of the mess her life had become, but not this. She wasn't responsible for this. She swept her hands outward, searching for something to use as a weapon, her fingers finding only clothes and more clothes.

His hands found her throat.

She stared up at him as he robbed her of air. She wanted to tell him that he was blaming the wrong person. The neighbors got it wrong. Or he heard it wrong. The Wilsons were the ones out of town that night, not her. She was just starting a new job; there were no out–of-town conferences for her.

He squeezed tighter. "I didn't want to hurt you. Nobody ever got hurt in those other break-ins. Like I told you, smash and grab. I just wanted the jewelry; the stuff Sam showed my brother. You weren't supposed to be home."

Her fingers touched leather–a shoe. Blindly she struck out at him, flinching as she felt the narrow heel sink deep through tissue and then hit bone. $89 dollars on sale, never worn. Worth every cent.

"9-1-1, please state your emergency."

"This is Rachel Brenner at 2587 Rittenhouse Street." She glanced over at the closed closet door. She could hear him yelling and even with only one good eye, he'd managed to find his knife. She could see the door shaking as he stabbed at the wood.

The door was solid oak–warped but strong. He was no match for it.

Snickers jumped up on the bed beside her and she comforted the cat, even as she held Ray's cell phone closer in order to hear over the noise Officer Bryant was making.

"State your emergency," the operator repeated.

"This is Rachel Brenner. I have a burglar trapped in my bedroom closet. Could you send a patrol car?"

"Please stay on the line. Are you injured?"

"I'm fine." Rachel smiled and shook her head. She was like that door. A little warped, but strong.

"I'm just fine."

The End

Who is Evelyn David?

Evelyn David has a split personality and an incredible number of out-of-body experiences. Or maybe she's just able to teleport from the East Coast to the middle of the country in the blink of an instant message.

For the last twenty years Evelyn's used her biology degree to reclaim the coal mines of Oklahoma. Or for the last twenty years, Evelyn's used her political science degree to write nonfiction books on parenting and education topics...and quite frankly wouldn't know a coal mine if she fell down the shaft. But one thing is true about these dual personalities - they've both had the same dream: to write a mystery that's a roller coaster of a ride, filled with humor, danger, romance, and a nail-biting ending that will leave you breathless.

And by golly, Evelyn David has done just that.

As for that teleporting stuff? It may show up in a sequel, but in the meantime, please meet the two halves of Evelyn David.

Marian Edelman Borden is the Northern half of the mystery-writing duo. She lives in New York, has written eight nonfiction books, has four kids, and an imagination that turned deadly when she met Rhonda Dossett, the Southern half of Evelyn David. Rhonda lives in Oklahoma, is the coal administrator for the Oklahoma Department of Mines, and sees dead bodies - or at least can envision them in mysterious and often hilarious scenarios.

The Irish Wolfhound

Whiskey, the co-star of **Murder Off the Books**, is an Irish Wolfhound. To learn more about this magnificent breed, please visit the website of Hillary Rupp, www.irishwolfhounds.org. Ms. Rupp kindly shared photos of her dogs with us.

If you're interested in supporting the wonderful work of Irish Wolfhound rescue groups, please check out the links at: www.netpets.com/dogs/dogresc/breeds/dogiwlf_hnd.html, or contact your local Irish Wolfhound club.

Irish Wolfhound Association of New England, www.iwane.org

Irish Wolfhound Association of Delaware Valley, www.iwadv.org

Irish Wolfhound Association of the Greater Smokey Mountains, www.geocities.com/iwagsm

Irish Wolfhound Association of the Mid South, www.iwams.org

Potomac Valley Irish Wolfhound Club, www.pviwc.org

Rocky Mountain Irish Wolfhound Association, www.rmiwa.org

Irish Wolfhound Association of the West Coast, www.iwawc.com

Northern California Irish Wolfhound Club, www.nciwc.us

Irish Wolfhound Club of America, www.iwclubofamerica.org

Irish Wolfhound Club of Canada, www.iwcc.ca

Irish Wolfhound Clubs in Australia, www.irishwolfhound.org.au

List of Irish Wolfhound Rescue Groups, www.irishwolfhounds.org/links.htm#three

Konstanze Somerhausen's *Irish Wolfhounds of Our Valley*, www.irish-wolfhound.be